THE DROP-OFF

Patrick Quinlan

headline

First published in Great Britain in 2008
by HEADLINE PUBLISHING GROUP

1

Cataloguing in Publication Data is
available from the British Library

ISBN 978 0 7553 3549 7 (hardback)
ISBN 978 0 7553 3550 3 (trade paperback)

Typeset in Fournier MT by Palimpsest Book Production Limited,
Grangemouth, Stirlingshire
Printed and bound in Great Britain by Clays Ltd, St Ives plc

Headline's policy is to use papers that are natural, renewable and
recyclable products and made from wood grown in sustainable
forests. The logging and manufacturing processes are expected
to conform to the environmental regulations of the country of origin.

HEADLINE PUBLISHING GROUP
An Hachette Livre UK Company
338 Euston Road
London NW1 3BH

www.headline.co.uk
www.hachettelivre.co.uk

For Noah Lukeman

'A man cannot be too careful in the choice of his enemies.'

– Oscar Wilde

1

Amazing to feel so good when you're about to die.

As soon as the drug hit Denny Cruz's bloodstream, he started to relax. It happened even faster than he expected. He was not a big guy — five feet, nine inches tall, maybe a hundred and sixty-five pounds. He had a fast metabolism and, within a minute or two, he was more relaxed than he'd ever been in his life. More than relaxed — he was chilled right out.

The plastic surgeon: telling Cruz deadly lies, but smooth, calm, business as usual while he did it. Not the slightest hint of a shake in his hands. Nothing out of the ordinary happening here, we do this every day. The guy missed his calling — he could have been a spy, the way he played it.

He gave Cruz the shot after a half-hour session during which he described the surgery, carefully and in considerable detail. The surgery was called scar revision, and he was going to try a technique called dermabrasion. Of course, Cruz needed to understand that there were no guarantees here. The procedure might work or it might not, but either way, there would still be a scar on Cruz's face. It would just be much less noticeable than the one there now.

The funny thing — *the totally awesome thing* — Cruz thought with a mind now blown off its moorings, was the fact that there wasn't going to be any surgery. That was never in the good doctor's plans.

Cruz spared a moment to recall the doctor. Bill Williams his name was, and he was tall and slim, fit and friendly. The Florida sunshine agreed with him — he was deeply tanned, so tanned his skin was more gold than brown, and trending towards orange. He looked like some kind of rare tropical fruit. In fact, he was beautiful to look at. Big jaw, like a caveman. Through long experience, Cruz believed that men with strong jaws were more confident and assertive than other men. Blow-dried hair. Rolex watch. This was a guy who probably got outdoors a lot — golf and tennis at the club, maybe some sailing. No wedding band. There was good money in plastic surgery, and ol' Doc Williams was a good-looking guy. He probably didn't have much time for a wife.

'Valium', Williams said as he prepared the hypodermic needle, 'begins to work within one to five minutes after injection. It stimulates the action of GABA, or gamma-aminobutyric acid, which is the most abundant inhibitory neurotransmitter in the brain. It operates in a primitive part of the brain called the limbic system, and it's very effective in reducing over-excitation.'

Cruz stared at him, waiting for the translation.

'It makes you calm,' Williams said. 'Very, very calm.'

Williams had patted Cruz's arm before he went out, a move that very few people had ever made. The vast majority of people avoided touching Cruz if they could help it — most people could barely look into his eyes. Cruz had murderer's eyes. Residents of the straight world looked in there and saw more than a hundred fresh corpses staring back at them — it was too much for most people to handle.

But not Doc Williams — he was as blissfully unaware as a man could be. Nobody got murdered in his world. Probably, nobody was even impolite. Then again, Cruz wasn't a killer any more. He had turned a new page in his life, and maybe it was starting to show.

'Just lie back, take a deep breath, and take it easy,' Williams said. 'Let the Valium do its work. In a few minutes, you're going to be feeling pretty good.'

Three big goons – hired killers – had sauntered into the small, clean operating theatre a few moments after the plastic surgeon had stepped out. Cruz would never know much more about the good doctor – judging by the men who had just come in, Doc Williams was dead now. Tough break, but he had gone out a winner. His final piece of doctorly wisdom was right on target: Cruz was feeling pretty damn good.

'If you wanna die fast and easy,' one of the goons, a guy with a bushy moustache and sideburns, said in an offhand tone, 'then you'll tell us where the money is. If you wanna die slow and painful . . .' The guy shrugged and trailed off.

'What money's that?' Cruz said.

'Two and a half million dollars, asshole. You know what money.'

Cruz smiled. Things were really beautiful, you know? The operating theatre was positively gleaming. The chair Cruz lounged in, his head and neck perfectly nestled into the headrest . . . had he ever reclined in a more comfortable chair? He didn't think so. Through the window, the late afternoon sun cast a glow that caused Cruz to think of the wonder of creation. For the first time in his forty-eight years, Cruz considered the possibility of the existence of God. Maybe it wasn't the story they tried to sell you. Maybe God was everywhere – across the sky, deep in the earth, the life throb of eternity, beating in the hearts of every living thing.

Awesome. Totally fucking awesome.

If he lived through this day, perhaps Cruz could find a way to help people. He could spend the rest of his life doing just that – helping people. Certainly, he wasn't going to find a cure for cancer, not at this late stage, but maybe something . . . It was a lovely idea. He wished he had thought of it sooner.

The three men stood around Cruz in a rough triangle, well-dressed gorillas in custom suits, guns already drawn. Two of them trained their barrels directly on Cruz. The third, the biggest of the three and the man of most interest to Cruz, stepped into the centre of the circle. He was older than the others – fifty-five, maybe sixty – a balding ape with a thick brow and hairy knuckles. Cruz had known the guy in a previous life. It seemed like that life had ended a long time ago.

Mr Goodman, the guy always called himself, though that wasn't really his name. His name, Cruz knew, was Alphonse Guglielmo.

Cruz remembered how the name annoyed Goodman. It annoyed him for several reasons, but most of all because people of the all-American persuasion tended to pronounce it wrong. 'Goo-YEL-mo' was the correct way to say it.

'GOOG-lee-elmo' was the common mistake.

To have someone – a desk clerk at a hotel, someone paging him at an airport, whoever – suggest his name contained the syllable 'goog' would make the thick vein in the big man's forehead stand out in sharp relief, and his hands clench in fists of rage.

So he got rid of the name. He became Al Goodman instead. Mr Goodman to you, right before he sent you to see Jesus. MISTER. GOOD-MAN.

People who knew him called him Goodie.

Cruz smiled. He felt good. Really good. It was a wonderful fucking day and it was a wonderful fucking drug. 'Goodie,' he said. 'Nice to see you. Looking good. You been working out?'

Goodman cracked his hairy knuckles. He smiled and shrugged. 'I been on a programme. Diet, exercise, hormone optimisation. Been doing it about ten months. I work out with a trainer three days a week. Give myself a little shot of human growth hormone every day – it doesn't even hurt, like a pinprick. Get a couple bigger shots in the ass twice a week. Takes five minutes – the guy comes right to my office. I gotta tell you, I never felt better. It's the fountain of fucking youth. I've already gained three inches around on my arms, four inches around on my legs. I'm sixty-two years old, and I'm ready to screw at the drop of a hat. I got a twenty-eight-year-old girlfriend. She can't believe the difference in me. She loves it.'

'Well, it suits you.'

'Thanks, Cruz. I appreciate that.'

'Say, Goodie, where's the doctor?'

See, that was the thing to remember. Cruz had come here for cosmetic facial surgery, to get an old scar removed. It was a four-inch wound that came down the side of his face like a jagged stretch of highway. He'd had it since he was a child – a souvenir from one of his mother the drug addict's many boyfriends. Even now, if he closed his eyes, Cruz could see the guy – pockmarked face, greasy hair hanging down in front of dark flaming eyes yellowed with jaundice. A madman. They were sitting on counter stools in the dismal, battered kitchen of a tiny apartment, and the guy gripped Cruz's hair with one strong cruel hand, as the other hand moved to cut little Cruz's eyes out with a steak knife. At the last second, Cruz jerked his head, leaving a clump of hair in the man's hand as the knife plunged into Cruz's cheek and ripped a jagged canal down the side of his face. Then Cruz was out of the apartment, down the stairwell and on to the darkened streets, running and screaming, blood all over his shirt, blood all over his hands. He ran and ran, straight into the waiting arms of the Child Protective Services.

For years, Cruz had left the scar there, against all the best advice of well-meaning people. 'Hey, Cruz,' they used to say, 'you got plenty of money, why don't you get rid of that scar? One day a witness is gonna see that thing and you're gonna go down.'

'I don't leave witnesses,' Cruz would answer.

In truth, he had worn the scar like a trophy, like the men used to wear them in German duelling societies before World War Two. His scar was a badge of honour, but in recent days he had decided to finally get rid of it. His reasoning went like this: he didn't want to kill any more, but there were people out there who wanted to kill him, so it was better if they didn't recognise him. And that reasoning had led to this . . . situation.

Goodman, serious now, pressed the barrel of his silenced semi-automatic to Cruz's temple. 'The doctor?' Goodman said. 'He went the same place you're going. Only he got there a few minutes sooner.'

Goodman had gotten the call two days ago.

He was in the office over his video arcade and pool hall just off A1A – right in the thick of the Fort Lauderdale beach meat market. It was hot out, and through his window he could look at palm trees, and watch the young babes sauntering back and forth to the beach in their bikinis – hips swaying, boobs jiggling, and tongues darting out, licking ice cream cones. Jesus. Just a couple years ago, he was starting to feel like a grandfather to these girls – now, with the hormone treatments and the weightlifting, he felt like he could run out there and hop on any one of them.

Through the floor of his threadbare office, he could hear the re-assuring sounds of machinery pinging and clanging, the shouts of the kids playing air hockey, the explosion of the cue hitting the racked-up balls – even in the off season, these kids dropped money on Goodman all day and all night. Goodman owned this arcade and a couple of small motels nearby. That was his business, and that's what showed on his books. What was also his business was the silent stakes he held in three of the big hotels in town, two golf courses, and the call girls who serviced the guys who flew in to town to play golf at Goodman's courses and stay at Goodman's hotels.

Money, money, money – people in the know often asked Goodman how he could stand to have his office upstairs from that noisy arcade.

'You hear all that racket down there?' Goodman would say. 'That's the sound of me making money. I like that sound.'

Goodman had a majority stake in a real nice course up in Boca Raton. The guy who designed it was known all over the world. One day the manager up there called and told Goodman they had a special guest coming in tomorrow. The next afternoon, Goodman made sure he was at the bar in the clubhouse when pro golfer Ralph Benjamin – the legendary Maestro – came in from his round. They brought him over and Goodman shook his hand. The Maestro had a firm grip. White teeth. Sandy-brown hair swooped back over his head like a helmet. Plaid knickers and lime-green golf shirt with his signature logo on the breast – a cartoon image of a classical music conductor. He was smaller than Goodman imagined him, maybe an inch shorter than Goodman himself, so call it six feet even. He looked bigger on the TV. All the same, he seemed *real* – more real, somehow, more here, than Goodman himself.

'Hey, Maestro,' Goodman said. 'Whaddya think of the course?'

'She's a beauty,' the Maestro said. After the handshake, his hand had moved and was now gripping Goodman's arm high up near the shoulder. That lingering hand, and the way the Maestro looked into Goodman's eyes, almost made Goodman feel like they shared some secret together. It was an intimate moment. 'I'd like to have a go at her again sometime.'

'Anytime,' Goodman said. 'You call us. Everything's on the house.'

The fucking Maestro had played Goodman's golf course. OK? The money was pouring in. His steady and caring wife of thirty-seven years (Clara) and his spicy Cuban girlfriend of four years (Rita) had finally come to terms with each other and with their places in Goodman's life. Sometimes Goodman couldn't believe the way things were going. He couldn't believe that he used to work with his hands. He couldn't believe that he used to get paid by the job. He couldn't believe that he once spent eight years in prison just for trying to make a living. Couldn't believe it, that is, until the call came in. It only came once in a while, but when it did, it really did. For the record, it hadn't come for over three years.

The private line rang and Goodman had it on the first ring.

'Yeah?'

A man's voice came on. 'Goodie.' It was a deep, rough voice. It sounded like gravel being dumped from the back of a truck. The voice didn't introduce itself, but Goodman could imagine the voice's owner without even trying. Big, stone-faced, the dark caricature of a ruthless killer. Big Vito.

Goodman's heart sank at the thought of him. If Big Vito was calling, that meant Goodman was back in business. They let you go your own way sometimes, they let you think you were out of debt, but when the call came in, you knew what it was about: you owe us, buddy, and it's time for you to pay. A call from Big Vito was a call that dragged you back into the past, a call that fucked up your programme big-time.

'I got a problem,' Big Vito said.

'I know about your problem,' Goodman said. Who in this life didn't know about the problem Vito Calabrese had recently had? Even Goodman, enjoying something like semi-retirement, knew. In fact, his knowledge had invaded his sleep during the past several nights. Only now that the call had finally come, did he realise how much he had expected this moment, and how much he had dreaded it.

'How is this phone?' Vito said.

Goodman shrugged, then realised Vito couldn't see the shrug. 'It's clean.'

'How clean?'

The question was annoying. Did Vito think Goodman didn't know his own business? 'This whole office gets swept for bugs every week. If I say it's clean, it's clean.' He heard the edge in his own voice and didn't like it.

Goodman looked out his office window at the street heading down to the palm trees and the beach. A moment ago he had been enjoying his day, his week, his life. Now he wasn't quite sure. He spent twenty minutes on the phone with Vito. Afterwards, the thing that had just been a rumour was confirmed, and Goodman had all the details.

Denny Cruz had disappeared a few weeks ago all the way up in Maine, along with a mark he'd gone after named Smoke Dugan, and a big chunk of money Dugan had stolen from the organisation more than three years back. It was all a bit murky, but Dugan'd had a beef with a boss named Roselli — to this day nobody seemed to know for sure what it was all about. Rather than work it through, Dugan had whacked Roselli, taken about two and a half million in cash from Roselli's safe, and blown up Roselli's house for good measure.

Rather than bring Dugan in like he was supposed to, Cruz had met Dugan, met Dugan's money, and had gone over to the dark side. Now, Cruz had resurfaced, right in Goodman's backyard. Cruz was trying to get his tell-tale scar removed by a tony Fort Lauderdale plastic surgeon with an office just off Las Olas Boulevard — Jesus, not even a mile from here. The surgeon had dropped a dime on him. Goodman was supposed to grab a couple of his boys and go take care of Vito's problem.

'Can't you get somebody else?'

'Goodie, he's right up the fucking street from you. What's the problem?'

'Vito . . .'

Big Vito sighed. It sounded like a massive hydraulic lift. 'Not in this short time-frame. Nobody as good as you.'

'What about the people he has with him?' Goodman said. He glanced at the notes he had taken during the call, read them back to Vito. 'This guy, Smoke Dugan?'

'You know what to do with Dugan,' Vito said.

'OK, but what about the girlfriends? Lola Bell and Pamela Gray. What am I supposed to do with them?'

'After everything's finished, you drop them off,' Vito said. And here he hesitated, as if he didn't quite want to complete his own thought. 'In the ocean.'

Goodman looked at the sexy beach babes walking the strip outside his window. He tried to picture killing any one of them — couldn't see it. Goodman took a deep breath, then exhaled it slowly. Three years since the last call, three long years since he had killed anybody. He was feeling rusty.

'OK,' he said, 'consider it done.'

A few minutes ago, Goodman had done the doc himself, with a garrotte.

He had done it to get the feeling back in his hands. The doc was a manicured pretty boy by the name of Williams. Big Vito had gotten the idea that if Cruz surfaced, it would be while trying to get his scar removed. With the scar gone, maybe nobody in the life would recognise him. Vito had a sense about things like that, and he was right this time. He had a mailing made up with an old mug shot of Cruz, sent out to over two hundred plastic surgeons on the East Coast. The mailer showed Cruz, and described him as a fugitive wanted for questioning by the Department of Homeland Security. If he comes to you looking for an operation, call this toll-free number – bingo. Williams called the number, bringing doom on both himself and Cruz.

Williams gave Cruz the dose and came back into his private office. Goodman was there with Marty and Joey, a couple of young guys he kept around to do odd jobs and lay on the muscle when need be. The two of them were monsters – they could be linebackers. Probably were, back in high school. Between the combined bulk of Goodman, Marty and Joey, there was barely anywhere in the office left to stand. In fact, there was barely any air to breathe – it had all been displaced.

But Goodman was aware that these two guys of his were . . . what? He couldn't say, exactly. He just had a hunch that, a million years ago, when he was an underfed teenager back in Brooklyn, he could have eaten them both for lunch. Jesus, the bushy moustache and the mutton-chop sideburns Marty wore – the whole look was mortifying to Goodman. Somehow worse were the diamond studs that crew-cut Joey had in both ears, and the muscle-hugging silk shirt with the extra-wide collar he wore under his sports jacket.

What was this, the disco era?

Goodman was also painfully aware that none of them – neither he, nor his two boys – looked anything like feds. Marty and Joey looked more like pro wrestlers, or oversized rock stars, than cops. OK, that was OK. This would be quick. Williams had told his three staff members to stay home that day. The con job only needed to last another few seconds.

'In five minutes, he'll be totally docile,' Williams said with a sort of breathless triumph. Goodman nearly cringed in embarrassment – Williams the patriot, proud to do his duty. *What'd they ever do for you, you prick?*

'I gave him twice the normal dose. You fellas can go in there and slap the cuffs on him. He shouldn't give you any trouble at all.'

Williams stood in the centre of the three of them. He was tall, but they were bigger, wider. 'Doc, can I ask you a question?' Marty said. Williams turned to face him. Goodman slid in behind him, slipping the garrotte out of his jacket pocket as he did so. It was nothing more than a piece of chicken wire attached at either end to a block of wood. The blocks of wood were his grips. Goodman made sure the wire was thick – in the old days, he had once used a thin piece of filament wire and had just about chopped some poor fucker's head off.

He put the wire around Williams's neck, criss-crossed his arms, and squeezed hard. The veins in Goodman's forearms bulged from the effort. Williams made an initial gasp, a few glub, glub, glubs, and after that never made another sound. He hadn't even struggled very much. It wouldn't have mattered if he had – Goodman felt as strong as a fucking beast these days.

As Williams's lifeless body slid to the floor of the office, Goodman reflected that the doctor had been completely surprised – it had probably never even occurred to him that such a thing could happen.

Now, moments later, as Goodman held his gun to Cruz's temple in the bright operating theatre, he reflected how easy it would be to pull this trigger. *Bang*. Cruz's silly smile erased, Cruz's brains all over Williams's fancy surgical chair, and the job abruptly over. Call it an early night for Goodman and the boys.

Goodman could phone Big Vito: 'Cruz got uppity and pulled a gun. I had to ice him right there. I don't know where the money is. I don't know where the girls are. I don't know where Smoke Dugan is. But look at it this way – at least Cruz got what was coming to him.' He'd have to get Marty and Joey to stick to the script on this one, but it shouldn't be that hard. A couple extra grand in each of their pockets should keep them quiet, right? He could trust them.

Right?

Goodman glanced around at his two crew members, and didn't like what he saw. How well did he even know these guys? Come to think of it, not that well at all. A couple of young punks, they came down from New York a few years ago – just sort of appeared one day. Maybe Vito even sent them down. In any case, Goodman's hopes for an early evening died with the next words out of Cruz's mouth.

'I'll take you to the money,' Cruz said. 'It's in a boat out on the water. I don't remember the name of the marina, but I know how to get there. Hell, you can have the fucking money. It's been way too much trouble. I don't even want it any more.'

Goodman jabbed the gun against Cruz's forehead. 'If you're fucking around . . .'

'Hey, I'm Cruz, remember? *Cruz*. Would I fuck around?'

Goodman looked at Joey. He indicated Cruz with a slight nod of his head. 'Put the cuffs on him. I guess we're going for a ride.'

The beautiful people were loose on the streets.

Lola Bell, twenty-five, dark and lovely, was on hair-trigger alert. She was out walking with her friend Pamela Gray among the throngs in the fabulous shopper's paradise of Las Olas Boulevard, just as the sun began to set. They had just stopped in at a small boutique and bought two jaw-droppingly expensive bathing suits – a white bikini for Lola, and a Paisley boy shorts and top ensemble for Pam.

Lola had sea legs today – this was the first time she had set foot on dry land in weeks, and the sidewalk seemed to gently pitch and roll beneath her feet. It made her nauseated. Worse, a young man up ahead on the street had set Lola's teeth on edge. He had nothing to do with what was going on now – that much was clear. He had everything to do with bad memories.

Last night Lola had dreamed of a sturdy oak door. She was on one side of the door, trying to keep it shut. On the other side were a dozen men trying to push their way in. With a giant effort, Lola was able to slam the door closed, but then found out that the lock was broken.

To the west of Lola and Pamela the sky glowed, golden like a pharaoh's tomb, the light reflected in hundreds of windows on a steel and glass office tower. To the east, dark blue clouds lowered. The air itself seemed heavy with electricity – a storm was threatening to come in off the ocean.

Regardless of the weather, during the last thirty minutes the street had begun to fill with glittering, well-dressed specimens of humanity, almost as if a nearby dam had burst, and instead of water, these hip and lovely people had gushed forth. The restaurants and sidewalk cafés were filling up, as were the shops and galleries. Pedicabs moved alongside the tightening traffic on the street. Diamonds flashed and caught the light. Coach bags plunked down on café tables, and manicured hands carefully pawed through their contents. Cell phones rang – none of them, actually ringing like a telephone, but instead playing a medley of hits from the 'eighties, 'nineties and today.

The two women had shared a taxi from the marina to the plastic surgeon's office with Pamela's new boyfriend Denny Cruz a little less than an hour before. They'd left Smoke Dugan – Lola's boyfriend of more than a year – on the boat with his maps, and his wine and his cigar, not to mention all the money he'd stolen. Now Pam and Lola were checking out the town. Lola thought it was a place she might want to live if given another chance to live somewhere. That seemed out of the question now. The four of them were going to be moving around for a while, and maybe for ever. Although they might one day enjoy their lives again somewhere, probably in another country, there was a good chance they would never be able to let their guards down completely.

Up ahead, leaning against an ornate street lamp as the people swirled around him, was the young black man, little more than a kid. He had a white hat pulled low over his eyes, wore a wife-beater T-shirt that showed off the muscles of his upper arms and shoulders, and a pair of jeans that gave new meaning to the phrase 'loose-fitting'. They hung so low that Lola could see the little red hearts all over his boxer shorts. The kid had gold rings on every finger and a gold chain hanging from his neck. He looked almost comical, like he was in costume auditioning for a hip-hop video. All the same, he brought up unsettling memories for Lola – vague, half-formed thoughts about dangerous young men in the Chicago housing projects where she grew up, teenagers on the fast track to nowhere.

Drug dealers. Murderers. *Rapists*. Before she had gotten out of there, they had shaped her attitude towards men, towards people, even towards life itself. But Fort Lauderdale was an upscale city, and Lola had recently happened into a great deal of money – no matter what else might occur, she would never be forced back to the kind of place where she had lived during her early life. That was the theory, at least, and Lola hoped that events would prove it true.

'Hey, baby,' the kid said as she and Pamela passed. 'I'm liking that ass.'

Lola turned to him, heart beating. The kid was young. There wasn't a line on his smooth face. He looked like he had never even shaved. In fact, the mixture of cockiness and inexperience she saw in the kid's face allowed Lola to relax a little bit. The kid would go into a fight overconfident, and he'd probably be unmanned by confusion and frustration when any prey showed more than token resistance. Meanwhile, nearly ten years of martial arts training had made Lola's body into a weapon – in the recent past, she had taken down much rougher customers than this one.

The kid scowled and shook his head. 'Not you.' He gestured at Pamela. 'Her. The white girl.'

Lola glanced at her room-mate. That was the funny thing: being on the run agreed with Pamela. The Pamela Lola used to know had been a shy, awkward, retiring librarian. She wore baggy, loose-fitting clothes, her hair pulled back to her scalp. The new Pamela seemed to have thrown caution overboard. And as caution fell to earth like so much ballast, Pamela's balloon sailed towards the sky. Where to start? Take it from the top. Her hair flowed loose, cascading down to her shoulders, and Lola was sometimes astounded to see how much of it there really was.

Pamela wore wraparound aviator sunglasses, and ruby-red lipstick. At this moment, she was wearing a halter top and a miniskirt, the former showing off the toned muscles of her arms, the latter giving everybody a look at the legs she had honed from years of long-distance running, and the tight little ass that went with it. At the bottom, she wore big, clunky mules on her feet, and over her shoulder hung a bag that had in it, among other accessories, a nine-millimetre semi-automatic pistol with silencer attached – a gift from her new boyfriend, the former mob hitman, Denny Cruz. On the boat, when they were far from land and there were no other boats on the horizon, Cruz would pull out the guns and teach Pamela how to shoot.

'You like my ass?' Pamela said to the kid.

'Oh yeah.' The kid's smile showed gold fronts on his teeth.

'Then why don't you kiss it?'

'Anytime,' the kid said. 'Anytime at all.'

Lola and Pamela moved on.

Times had changed. In the old days, when the two of them walked together through the downtown streets of Portland, Maine, it was always clear who the people would turn around to gawk after – Lola. Today, on crowded Las Olas Boulevard, it was no longer clear. In fact, the intensity of the stares on them made Lola just a tad uncomfortable – they were under an electron microscope.

Lola knew what they were looking at – two sexy women, one black, one white, out for a stroll together and showing some skin. She knew men well enough to know what kind of fuel that was for the rich male fantasy life that began in adolescence, continued on through middle age and stretched towards the horizon. Out here, many of the men, and maybe a few women, were thinking how they'd like to be the meat and fixin's in a Pamela and Lola sandwich. Maybe that was all it was, maybe they were safe here, but being on the street made her uneasy nevertheless.

After all, the two women were marked for death.

Pamela felt perfectly at ease as they turned off the main boulevard and headed down the quiet, tree-lined street where the doctor's office was located. They were going to stop in at the office, find out how much longer Cruz was going to be, then go out to dinner while they waited.

At first glance, Pamela liked this town. She was looking forward to sitting down to a nice meal, maybe in one of those open-air cafés along the sidewalk. She planned to order whatever expensive seafood items she and Lola wanted from the menu, including a couple of drinks. Then she planned to stun the waiter by paying for it all with a stack of cash.

She smiled. Her little interaction with the black guy made her feel good. Then she thought of Denny Cruz and an image flashed in her mind: she and Cruz, together in their cabin on the boat, in the dark, the sea rolling and churning just beyond the walls. In the cabin, the two of them moving in rhythm, rolling like the sea themselves, then clashing like jungle cats, tearing and biting and ripping each other apart.

The hours would pass like minutes, the two of them up all night, night after night, their bodies soaked, and the bed saturated, in sweat and other bodily secretions. Honestly, she hadn't known there could be so much fluid involved.

When she first met him, she had thought Denny Cruz was going to kill her. Instead, he had opened her to a new world. In fact – and she didn't mind thinking of it this way – he had turned her out. Actually, she loved it. She wanted it all the time now, wanted him in a way she had never before experienced.

More than that – she was beginning to think that she loved him. Cruz was a good man. In their quiet conversations together, he'd revealed to her a dark and terrible childhood – in fact, it wasn't really a childhood in the way people normally used the term. He had been forced to live by his wits at an early age. As a result, he had done some very bad things. Yes, he had killed people, but he was putting that life behind him now. He could have killed them all – Pamela, Lola and Smoke – and chose not to. And he had a sense of fairness and integrity that few people in the so-called straight world seemed able to match. The truth was Cruz inspired her. When Pamela thought of the things she had so recently lost – her job at the library, her quiet life, the cute little apartment she had shared with Lola – she realised they were nothing compared to what she had gained. Life with Cruz was a revelation.

She cast her memory back to her childhood in sleepy Newmarket, New Hampshire. Quiet, tree-lined roads – the trees probably bare of their fall foliage by now. The white church with its steeple. Life flowing along in its seasons, relatives stopping in to say hello, going to the movies with friends, bake sales happening, school years passing. Bookish, studious Pamela pulled down straight A's. Silent, intense Pamela excelled at basketball and long-distance running. At home there was her mom. Her dad. Her little brother. They all played board games together on Friday nights. She loved them, of course, but she didn't love what their lives represented to her.

Boredom.

Railroad tracks passed right through the centre of town. The tracks were just on the other side of the chain-link fence from her family's backyard – they were fifty yards from the back door of the white, 1830s farmhouse they lived in. From her bedroom window, she would watch the freight trains pass, moving so slowly, maybe slow enough for an athletic girl like her to run alongside. On every train that passed, a few of the sliding doors on the freight cars were open – sometimes just a crack, sometimes gaping wide like a big mouth. Once in a while, she saw people riding in there. And she imagined herself running along the tracks next to an open car, reaching up towards it with one hand, a strong hand extending down, taking hers, pulling her up, whisking her away . . .

. . . to a life of adventure. This life.

Pamela snapped back into the present moment. Something funny was happening. Not funny ha-ha, but funny odd. Scary. Not good.

Just down the street from her and Lola, a large black sedan was double-parked. Pamela could tell it was a Cadillac from the emblem on its grill, currently winking in the last of the sun. As they strolled towards it, four men came out of the building – three big men and a smaller one. The men moved in formation. A big one fast-walked out in front, popped open the door to the back seat, then walked around to the front of the car and slid behind the wheel. The three men in the back – the small one book-ended between the mighty shoulders of the two bigger ones – moved as a unit towards the open back door. They moved with precision, like dancers.

Only one brief misstep soiled the beauty of the choreography. The small man slowed and dropped back half a step from his two minders. The bright sun winked off the iron bracelets around his wrists. His head turned right to face the girls. It was Cruz! Of course it was. Did he give them a wink? She couldn't be sure, but she was nearly ready to swear to it. The bastards had Cruz in cuffs, and he turned to give her and Lola a wink and a smile.

A second later, Lola was already running. She had dropped her bag and ran ahead towards the car, big strong legs in khaki shorts pumping, skippy sneakers slapping the blacktop.

'Hey!' Lola screamed. 'Hey you! Wait!'

'Cops?' Pamela shouted at Lola's rapidly dwindling back. 'Bad guys?'

'Not cops!' came the reply.

Pamela whipped the nine-mil out of her bag and chambered the first round, just as Cruz had taught her. Dimly, somewhere in the back of her mind, she realised she was making a split-second decision. That was good – she had read a recent pop psychology book about this and knew that people often made better decisions when they had no time to think about them. She had decided to trust Lola totally – she didn't even question it. It pleased Pamela to know that she was going on instinct. Just as she had suspected all those years ago, she was *good* at this. Action. Swashbuckling adventure. But she also realised that if Lola was right, then trouble had followed them here, and any feelings of safety she might have had a moment ago were utterly and dangerously misplaced.

These thoughts passed so fast she barely registered them. The major thought that stuck, plastered across her consciousness like the words on a highway billboard, was this:

Holy shit! Cruz!

Up ahead, Lola reached the car just as the back door slammed and locked. Pamela took the shooter's crouch, as Lola pounded on the passenger side windows. The car peeled out, coming straight at Pamela. It began to accelerate. The driver leaned on the horn. Pamela ignored the peal of the horn and sighted on the dark windshield.

Looming now, coming faster.

Ready for the recoil? Ready.

The grill seemed like a malevolent smile. Coming to eat her. Close now. Very close.

She pulled the trigger. And again.

Clack. Clack, clack, clack, clack. The gun barely made a sound.

The bullets skipped off the windshield like she was firing ping-pong balls. Pamela didn't move. The car veered to her right, scraped along the parked cars there – an awful sound, chrome ripping chrome – then kept going. Pamela spun around like a top and began firing again. Sparks skipped off the rear window, and then the car was too far away to keep firing. She saw its brake lights come on red as it reached the corner and prepared to turn into the heavier traffic.

She stared.

Then Lola was there next to her, breathing hard, like a pro athlete between plays. 'Are you crazy? You could've been killed!'

'I hit that car at least five times,' Pamela said. 'Nothing happened.'

'They probably have bulletproof windows. They are gangsters, after all.' Lola gave Pamela a hug, then picked up her own bag. 'Come on, honey. We gotta go.'

Then she was running again.

'Lola! I'm wearing a skirt and high heels!'

Lola barely turned around. 'Lose them!'

Pamela glanced down at her legs and feet. She shrugged. She kicked off her chunky mules – she loved those shoes; hated to leave them behind – and pulled her tight skirt all the way up around her stomach. Man, she'd been getting spicy with Cruz – she had switched from good-girl white cotton panties to thongs. Today's thong was bright orange.

Shoes gone, butt hanging out, gun in hand, she ran after Lola. It was time to get her man back.

Clark Westfield lounged behind the wheel of his top-down BMW Z3 convertible. He sat in early evening traffic on Las Olas. Weeknight traffic – bad, but not terrible. Lots of people out on foot – his eyes scanned the crowds for the sexiest women.

He'd been hitting a lot of red lights – he was stuck at one right now, the first car in line – but otherwise it was a good evening. Early

November, rain about to come in – pretty soon he should put the top back up, but not yet. The last of the sun was still in his rearview mirror, still reflecting off the storefronts and buildings in front of him. He had taken the Z3 today precisely because the weather was so nice. He had fired off nine holes of golf at the club this afternoon – thirty-eight, two above par, not bad – and then had knocked back a couple of early gin and tonics in the clubhouse.

Now he was cruising over to Amanda's apartment. Amanda had that Generation Z laziness – Westfield knew that she probably wouldn't even have changed out of her bedclothes today, which was exactly how he liked her. A beautiful young girl, blonde, with a wonderful body – Amanda wanted to be a fitness model or an actress when she grew up, but she didn't want to work for it. She was twenty-three now, time passing, and she was content to live in the apartment that Westfield paid for. She wore the clothes and jewellery that Westfield gave her, designer-made though they were, and spent her evenings eating out or dancing in clubs. It was all OK by him. He loved her just how, and where, she was.

Westfield was a local Master of the Universe. Oh, he had no pretensions of matching up with the big boys in New York or London or Chicago. No, he was a big fish in the local pond. He'd made his first million before thirty – during the merger mania of the late 1980s. He'd grown his stake over the years in real estate. In recent times, he'd done mortgage origination, but a few years ago, he'd smelled the end of the real estate boom and had gotten out. OK, he was a year and a half early, but at least no investment house was coming to him and demanding he take back the bad loans he'd written. Man, his instincts were like an animal's – he just sensed the change in the weather before it happened, and he acted on it.

As he waited at the lights, he ran the stats, which was something he often did. Fifty-one years old. A millionaire twenty times over. An ocean-front home just off A1A. A lifetime membership at the Lauderdale

Club. Two small businesses, both of which were largely run by his very competent business manager. Westfield spent, on average, about four hours a day in the office. Rebecca – a wonderful, caring wife who spent her time involved in the PTA, was a board member at the performing arts centre, and did various other charitable work besides. He had great love and respect for Becca even now, after twenty years of marriage. Three great kids, smart, athletic, wonderful kids.

And Amanda, only six years older than Westfield's eldest son, a hot young thing with a motor that was constantly running. There were others besides Amanda. Westfield was out of town on business at least once a month, and on those trips, wherever he was, he made sure to sample the local flavour. Nevada was the best – they left little catalogues of the girls right in your hotel room. You could order them up like room service.

The thing was, you *could* have your cake and eat it, too. Clark Westfield was living proof of that. Indeed, there was only one little item in his entire life he wasn't ecstatic about – he could stand to lose a few pounds. OK, more than a few. But he was thinking about hiring a personal trainer to help him get in shape. His ideal body was just one more thing he could make happen, once he set his mind to it.

The light was about to change. He could tell by the blinking 'Walk' sign facing the side of his car to his left. It had turned red. Soon it would stop and say 'Don't Walk'. Then his light would turn green and he'd be off to a hot, early evening tryst with a horny little hellcat less than half his age. He tapped his rings on the steering wheel.

Up ahead, he noticed a car moving away from him. The left side of the car had been stove in. Actually, it had just turned on to the boulevard, coming from his right. He had noticed it subconsciously, but hadn't quite registered it. He'd been too lost in thought.

Now a black girl was standing in front of his car. She put her hands forward, palms outward, a gesture that seemed to say, 'Don't go'. Hmmm. She was sexy, no doubt. Long curly hair. Great body, in one of those tennis skirt-shorts combo things, and a tight black T-shirt. What the hell was she up to? She was moving towards him slowly, hands still outstretched. He didn't really like it. It gave him a nervous feeling. He'd go around her, but now traffic was coming from the other direction.

'Hey, honey,' he shouted, 'what are you doing?'

'I need your car,' she said.

What the? 'Get out of my way, little girl,' he heard himself say. His voice didn't seem quite itself. It sounded . . .

Alarmed.

He pointed at her. 'In another three seconds, I'm gonna run you over.'

A woman walked towards him from his right. He caught sight of her in his peripheral vision, and turned to look. She came fast, and he barely had time to notice that she was barefoot and wearing only bright orange panties and a halter top. Normally, that might excite him, but most of his attention was dominated by the gun in her hand. She came to his passenger door and pointed the weapon into his face. He'd never looked down the barrel of a gun before.

The blood roared in his ears. His heart beat like the gallop of a race-horse. He lifted his gaze to the woman's face. He couldn't see her eyes because of the dark sunglasses she wore.

'Get out of the car, fat boy,' the woman said, her voice flat and metallic. 'Before I blow your fucking brains out.'

'I thought it was *Terminator III*,' he would tell the police later that night.

Absently, he reached for the ignition as he slid out the door.

'Leave the keys,' she said. 'You won't need them.'

2

'You know, I like this town,' Goodman said.

He sat in the back seat of the car, with little Cruz sandwiched between him and Marty. Joey was up front, doing the driving. 'Lauderdale has charm. Everybody knows that. I even used to like to come out for dinner here on Las Olas. But the last few years, it's like what the fuck happened? All this traffic. It's been getting so bad, I usually try to split town before the zombies leave work each day.'

Goodman gazed out at the action on the boulevard as they headed to the marina. Yuppies and young skate punks milled around. The night seemed electric, almost neon with excitement out there. Goodman looked at the sideview mirror again. The BMW convertible was there, the one with the two chicks in it. They were stuck in traffic about three cars back, but still in pursuit. He hated to see them there, and hated that they had at least one gun on them. Two young chicks were the last people he felt like killing tonight – he'd rather see them dancing in one of his clubs than catching bullets over a prick like Cruz. Cruz was a pro, his buddy Dugan was a pro, they had stolen money, and they had killed people into the bargain. These two little girls were dumb to get swept up in it.

Goodman sighed. They were stuck at another red light, about six cars from being able to make their left-hand turn. 'This is about the slowest fucking car chase in the history of the world, you know that?'

He turned to look at Cruz.

Cruz, zonked on happy juice, smiled at him. 'Slow motion ocean, baby.'

Goodman shook his head. He felt real disdain for Cruz right now. 'You know what, Cruz? You're gonna get those two girls killed. You know that, right? I mean, holy fucking shit, you piece of shit. Can't you call them off or something?'

Cruz shrugged. 'What can I do? They're back there. I'm in here with you.'

'Do they have a cell phone we could call?'

'I think they do, but I wouldn't know the number. I try not to talk on telephones. Cell phones are the worst. Cops can snatch those conversations right out of the air.'

'Fucking A. Marty, do me a favour and go back there and tell those girls not to make the next turn. All right? If they make the next turn, then it's out of my hands. If something bad happens, it's on them.'

Marty smirked. 'Wassamatter, Goodie? You getting soft in your old age? Didn't Vito say to do the girls too?'

'Who pays your salary, you hump? Me or Vito?'

Marty's smirk faded the tiniest bit. 'I'm liable to go back there and get shot.'

'You're gonna get shot if you stay in this car another three seconds, OK? So just do what I ask and don't give me no bullshit.'

Lola couldn't believe her eyes.

A big guy in a dark sports jacket and slacks, hair slicked back, cross hanging against the T-shirt under his jacket, was walking back through the stalled traffic towards their car. Already she thought of it as 'their' car, though she knew they had to dump this sporty little convertible fast. Sitting in all this traffic did them no good at all – if the cops spotted them, then they were in deep trouble.

The beefy guy was moving back quickly, probably trying to beat the next light change. He had a thick moustache and sideburns. He waved a white handkerchief, casually asking for a truce. It was a subtle move – so subtle, in fact, that no one on the street seemed to notice.

Pamela noticed. 'Oh my God. What does this clown want? What the hell is the story with that haircut?' She reached down by her side and came up with her gun. 'I think I'm gonna shoot him in the nuts.'

'I don't think you can do that,' Lola said. 'He's waving a white flag.'

'What if he's lying? What if it's a trick, and he comes back here and kills us?'

Lola looked at Pamela's gun and shrugged. 'That'll be some trick.'

'All right!' Pamela shouted. 'That's far enough! One more step and I shoot you right in the balls.' Her voice cracked on the word balls. People in nearby cars, windows closed to keep the air-conditioning in, were utterly oblivious.

'OK,' the man said, not shouting, though his voice was clear and calm. 'I'm just here to give you a message.'

'What's your message?' Lola said. 'And who sent it?'

'The message is from my boss. And it's just that you shouldn't follow us any more. We're going left at the next light, over to the marina where your boat is parked. You should just go straight and put all this behind you. Don't bother with these two guys. They're too old for you. They're gonna be dead soon. They're not gonna have the money any more, or the boat. You can have safe passage. You can have your old lives back. Nobody'll ever bother you again. All you need to do is keep driving.'

Pamela raised the gun into full view.

'Pamela,' Lola said, 'that's probably not a good idea.'

'I know what I'm doing.'

Jesus, Pamela really had changed, or some undiscovered part of her had erupted to the surface. Lola didn't like it. The girl was going to get them in deep shit, waving that cannon around.

'Here's my offer,' Pamela said. 'You have three seconds to get back to your car before I kill you.'

'Lady,' the man said, 'that's the second time today somebody's given me three seconds to live.'

'You know why he gave me this bullshit assignment, right?'

From the corner of his eye, Cruz watched as Goodman fretted. Goodman hadn't wanted this gig and he had no problem telling anybody about it. The whole time the goon named Marty was out of the car, Goodman sat with his gun poking into Cruz's ribs, assuring him that one move, one fucking twitch, and he was a dead man. Now Marty was back, and had relayed the message from the girls – no deal.

'Who's that?' Marty said.

'Who do you think? Vito. In New York. You know why he stuck me with this?'

'Enlighten us,' Cruz said. The drug was still humming along, maybe even better than before, and he was enjoying Goodman's distress. Despite everything – the steel of the handcuffs digging into his wrists; the uncomfortable sitting position he was forced into with his hands behind his back; the imminent threat of his own death and the deaths of Pam, Lola and Smoke Dugan; hell, even the loss of the money – he felt really good.

Goodman turned to him. 'Shut up, you. You're the only good thing about this whole fucking mess so far. I'm gonna enjoy killing you.'

Traffic started moving again and Goodman faced forward.

'Turn here,' he said to Joey. 'Here, you fuck. Here.'

'OK, Goodie. OK.'

'The reason he put me on this job,' Goodman continued, 'is he's jealous. I'm five years younger than he is. He knows I'm down here, soaking up the sun, making more money in hotels and golf courses than he's ever seen in his fucking life. Legit businesses, and I'm raking it in. I barely even do scams any more, just here and there, to keep my hand in and stay sharp. Meanwhile, the prick is up in Queens, with his office upstairs from the dentist's office, doing the same shit he's always done. He's getting old, and he don't like seeing me pull ahead of him. He's jealous, that's all. He's embarrassed by my wealth. So every now and then, he tugs on the leash, just to show me who's boss.'

'In for life,' Marty said.

'That's right.'

'Don't you mean envious?' Joey said.

'What?'

Joey drummed his fingers on the steering wheel. 'You said Vito's jealous of you. Don't you mean he's envious? Like, he envies your money and success. He wants something you have. That's what envious means. He'd be jealous if you were banging his girlfriend or something. A lot of people make that mistake. They say jealous when they really mean envious.'

'You know what, Joey? Shut the fuck up.'

The outlines of several sailing ships and powerboats loomed up ahead. They came to a gate with a guardhouse. The guard got a glimpse of the new Cadillac and waved them through.

'So much for security,' Cruz said.

'If this car was a Buick, the dumb fuck would have done a full body-cavity search,' Joey said from the driver's seat.

'Anyway,' Marty said, 'we're here.'

The driveway opened into a wide parking lot. Out beyond the incredible mega-yachts parked in the marina slips, a forest of masts and bridges bobbed in the mooring field. Cruz scanned all the vessels, looking for the boat, the *Saucy Jack*. There was so much to look at, he couldn't seem to focus. It all swirled together in an impressionistic blur of dark colour, punctuated with jabs of light. Beautiful.

'It looks like a painting out there,' Cruz said.

'Great,' Goodman said. 'That's fucking great, Cruz.' He reached to the floor and came up with a gun. Cruz recognised it as a Mac-10 submachine gun, huge speciality silencer already attached.

Goodman eyed both of his boys. 'Let's do this. No screwing around. With any luck, we can all be home for a late dinner and drinks.' He turned to Cruz, gun pointed in Cruz's face. Cruz felt like he could almost crawl up into the dark, round barrel. 'OK, Mr Giggles, you lead the way.'

'What do you need that big thing for?' Cruz said.

'To show you I mean business.'

It was a lovely night on the water.

Smoke Dugan sat on the aft deck of the *Saucy Jack*, moored about a hundred and fifty yards out from the marina, gazing at the skyline of Fort Lauderdale, and thinking he should put up the deck's canvas covering. He held a glass of red wine in one hand, a lit cigar in the other, and reflected that in another few moments, the rain was going to come down hard. The wine was Chilean. The cigar was Dominican. Things could be worse.

Dugan, sliding down a slippery slope towards sixty, still felt young. His hair was still mostly sandy-blonde, with shades of red, and just a touch of grey. Sure, his face was lined with care, but his hands were strong, and if Lola ever deigned to sleep with him again, he could still operate in the bedroom with no problem. If they did get together – and from the way things were going, that looked like a big goddamned if – he would have no need for the sex pills they advertised on TV to men his age. He sighed. He loved Lola – she had to know that. She was angry at him, and distant from him, because of the lies he had told her. But he had lied to her because he had no other choice. He had tried to tell her all this, but it was no use – she just wasn't hearing him these days.

He grunted. In any case, he still felt young. The only place where he did feel his age was in his leg. His right leg, fucked up and withered since childhood, had made him walk with a cane his entire life. His limp was the reason people often thought of him as old – the reason teenage girls offered him the senior-citizen discount when he took Lola out to movie theatres back in Portland. That leg also acted as the local weatherman. Right now, Smoke's leg ached something terrible – he had felt this rain coming all day.

Before him on the table he had a pile of ocean charts. At the moment, he was studying one of the nearby area – the Intracoastal waterway, the many canals of Fort Lauderdale, then down to Miami Beach, and Biscayne Bay. In a day or two, when Cruz had recovered from surgery, Smoke wouldn't mind cruising down from here to Key West. Things seemed quiet, there hadn't been any sign of pursuit, so he didn't see why they couldn't.

The *Saucy Jack* was his baby, the fruit of a bank job back in 1989 or 1990. Smoke figured he had put in a grand total of six hours on that job. Bunch of kids – they had called him in at the last minute. Before they hired Smoke, they wanted to know a few things: did he know how to blow up a safe? Of course he did. Did he have the explosives handy? Sure. Would he take a ride out to Jersey with them and set the charge? OK, if he liked the plan. Turned out the plan was solid – they were good kids. Smoke walked away with nearly two hundred grand for less than a day's work; sometimes things just went like that. Not often, but sometimes. A month later, he spent half his payday on the *Saucy Jack*.

The *Jack* was a forty-eight-foot double cabin powerboat, built in 1986, and very popular at that time among the motor yacht set. It was a relic now, twenty years old, but impeccably maintained and had been stored high and dry in a boatyard in New York for the past three and a half years. The place was all a working man could ask from a home on the sea – solid fibreglass hull; spacious interior with fore and aft staterooms, each stateroom with its own tiny bathroom; step-down galley with an electric stove and oven, a large stainless sink with hot and cold water, microwave, and apartment-size refrigerator and freezer; with an attractive light-oak finish throughout.

The boat was big enough that they could stack two dinghies – one fibreglass, one a small inflatable zodiac – down on the swimming deck. Up top, there was a canvas-covered flying bridge. Newer boats were more aerodynamic and therefore faster, but with the *Saucy Jack*'s twin 350-horsepower inboard engines, the boxy *Jack* would cruise at fifteen knots, and top out somewhere around twenty-one knots. Smoke would trade speed for the comfort the *Jack* offered.

In simpler times, when staying one step ahead of the cops was his major worry in life, he'd kept the *Jack* tied up on City Island in the Bronx. He would ride out from there, sometimes heading east into the Long Island Sound, but sometimes heading south and west into the city. He'd power under the stark-red Hell's Gate Bridge, and past the bleak fortress of Riker's Island prison. From there, if it was a summer evening, he might cruise north up the Harlem River, Yankee Stadium lit up to his right, the shouts of the crowd drifting to him on the night air.

Or he might cruise south down the East River, Manhattan like the wall of a canyon to his right, passing under the bridges – the 59th Street Bridge, the Williamsburg Bridge, the Brooklyn Bridge, the Manhattan Bridge – heading all the way down, past the Statue of Liberty, and into the wide open water of New York Harbor. Then he would turn around, and approach the Statue from the south, gazing at it the way he fancied his mother and grandmother must have in the early part of the century just passed, holding hands on the deck of an over-crowded passenger ship, coming to start a new life in America.

Something in the words engraved at the base of that statue spoke to him more than any flag ever could. *Give me your tired, your poor, your huddled masses yearning to breathe free* . . . The promise of America.

Smoke shook his head to clear out the poetry, and the memories. That stuff was all in the past. Better to deal with the here and now, with life on the run.

He glanced around him. It had been a bright south Florida day, and hot in the sun. He'd had exactly nothing to eat in the past three hours, and the wine had gone straight to his head. The girls were going to bring him a chicken sandwich from town, and he was looking forward to that. Ah, the simple pleasures. A cool breeze came in from the sea, ahead of the approaching cloud bank. The breeze was colder than the local air, displacing it. It sent a shiver down Smoke's spine. And Smoke had a dark thought: Cruz.

Life at sea with Cruz had almost been more than Smoke could bear. Cruz, who had crash-landed with two hired goons into the middle of Smoke's quiet life of hiding in Maine. Cruz, who'd been sent by the organisation to get Roselli's money back, and who instead seemed to have fallen in love with Pamela. Cruz, who had helped Pamela, Lola and Smoke escape – but not until after striking a deal with Smoke for half the money.

Cruz was wired wrong, like most killers Smoke had known. Cruz didn't like being around people. Smoke knew the type – he could see it in Cruz as he, Smoke, steered the *Saucy Jack* down the east coast, staying far away from land. Cruz would stand on the deck, staring straight ahead, as the boat took the waves, all that nothingness, deep water, in front of him, smoking cigarette after cigarette.

Even though the *Jack* was roomy as boats went, it was still a small thing, a boat, especially out at sea. Take five steps. Turn. Take five more steps. Say hello to your neighbour. Nowhere to run. Nowhere to put all that murderous energy and intensity. Nowhere to go when the anger had built up so much that normally you would lash out. And kill. Bet on it – one wrong word at the wrong time, and Cruz could be back in business. Sometimes Smoke thought the best course of action would be to do everybody a favour and kill Cruz himself. It wouldn't be easy, he'd have to do it while Cruz was asleep. In cold blood. Dispassionately. Like a surgeon.

Certainly, it would make life safer, but Smoke didn't know if he had that kind of killing in him. His hunch, from previous experience, was that he didn't.

Anyway, what to say to Pamela if he did manage to kill Cruz? 'Well, Pam, you know, it's just that I, uh . . . you know how these things go.' Pamela had decided that Cruz was a changed man. More than that, Pamela had decided that Cruz had never really been a killer at heart. No, Cruz was just a decent guy who was born poor and got caught up in circumstances beyond his control. Now he was sorry that he had ever killed anyone, and was determined never to do it again. In fact, he couldn't kill again – he had a mental block and now it was impossible for him to pull the trigger.

It made a nice story, but Smoke had his doubts.

The last of the light was fading from the sky. Just then, across the water from him at the marina, some kids sent off a burst of firecrackers. In the back of Smoke's mind, it occurred to him that the firecrackers had been going off for a little while now, and that they didn't sound exactly like firecrackers. They sounded more like . . . suddenly, a massive explosion ripped through the darkness in the parking lot of the marina. A fireball went up, casting eerie shadows on the giant yachts in the nearby slips. The sound of the explosion rolled across the water to him.

In an instant he knew what the explosion was – a pipe bomb that he himself had made. And the fireworks he had heard? Sure. Gunfire.

'OK, so no chicken sandwich tonight,' Smoke said. He stumbled down the steps. It was time to untie from the mooring and get out of here.

Pamela stood next to the convertible BMW they had only just hijacked. All she heard was the blood pounding in her ears.

It sounded like great bass drums being beaten fast and hard by monsters living deep under the earth. She couldn't hear anything else.

Boom-boom. Boom-boom. Boom-boom.

It registered with her that the last light of the day was fading.

It registered with her that a salty fish smell was coming in on a stiff ocean breeze – and that the breeze itself was turning cold. And it registered with her that the three men from the other car had all drawn their guns. They were big men, and one of them – the biggest of the bunch – had drawn what looked to Pamela like a machine gun.

Cruz was standing near this big guy. The two other men were fast-walking towards her and Lola. Then something else registered with Pamela – she had taken her gun out, the semi-auto Cruz had given her, and had started firing it. She didn't remember when that happened. It seemed like they had pulled up, she had jumped out of the car with the gun, and just started shooting. Could it have been that simple? Yes, she tended to think that it was.

Pamela turned to look at Lola across the car. Lola was moving towards the back of the car, shouting something at her.

'What?' Pamela said. 'What?'

Lola waved. *Come on*, the wave seemed to say. *Come on.*

Pamela pointed the gun at the approaching men. They both had their guns out, pointing at her. Jesus. Now something was grabbing, dragging her back. It all seemed to be moving in slow motion. She turned, and here was Lola, pulling at her. Wow, Lola's hands were strong.

Boom-boom. Boom-boom.

Pamela let herself be dragged back behind the car. Lola pulled her down to the asphalt of the parking lot. The tarmac was still hot – it had been baking in the sun all day. When was the last time she had laid down on blacktop? My God, it must have been close to twenty years ago. It was a good feeling – it brought a sort of nostalgia for kickball games and ten-year-old boys.

The car seemed to be rocking. No, it was definitely rocking. Why was it rocking? She looked at the back bumper, which was level with her eyes. The right rear tyre suddenly went flat. Tiny cubes of glass sprayed all over them – must have been from the windshield. Sure, the windshield had exploded. It was funny how little sound the gunshots made. What the . . . ? Sure, of course. They had silencers on their guns, just like she did.

Lola was screaming something. Her eyes had gone wide with fear.

'Shoot! Shoot the gun!'

Pamela looked down at the gun in her own hand. Of course. That's what was happening with the car – the men were shooting at them. Chunks of metal and plastic and glass were flying all over the place. The guy that she and Lola had car-jacked it from was sure to be pissed when he got a load of it.

Lola worked feverishly on something she had taken out of her handbag. It was a metal canister about eight inches long. It had a small digital read-out attached to one end. Her hands shaking, Lola punched in numbers on the buttons.

'Pamela! Shoot back at them!'

'Yeah, yeah. OK.'

Pamela reached up from her position lying prone on the ground. Her hand just cleared the trunk of the car. She pulled the trigger and the gun bucked in her hand. Suddenly the gun flew out of her hand and went whizzing backwards, landing about five feet behind her and a little to the right. It was just out of reach, and in the killing zone – no way she was going back there to retrieve it. She pulled her hand down – it had seemed to stay floating in the air of its own accord. A stream of bright red ran from the back of it.

'Shot,' she said. 'I think I got shot.'

The car disintegrated all around them.

Pamela looked out on the water, trying to spot the *Saucy Jack*. Boy, it would be nice to be on that boat right about now. Then Lola's panicked face appeared front and centre again, and Pamela stopped thinking about the boat. The boat blinked off like a neon sign.

A thought flashed, a big yellow smiley face attached to it:

Out of sight, out of mind!

Lola's shaking hands held up the metal canister for Pamela's inspection.

'Pam, this is a bomb. OK? Smoke gave it to me. It's going to blow in another minute. I don't know what it's going to do, but it looks like it's our only chance. When I throw it, you get down as low as you can go.'

'I'm as low as I can go now.'

'Get lower.'

Lola sprang into a deep squat, body low, knees as high as her chin. She fired the bomb with a Kareem Abdul-Jabbar hook shot. Pamela's left cheek hugged the asphalt, and she watched the metal canister fly through the air, silver glinting in the day's last stab of sunlight.

These guys were clowns.

For a moment, Cruz soaked it all in. Pamela and Lola pinned down behind the little blue sports car. Goodman's two goons crouched on either side of the Cadillac sedan, lighting up the sports car. Really ripping it. *What the fuck?* They weren't even behind decent cover.

They'd torn the cap off a sleepy early evening here at the marina.

A few feet in front of Cruz, Goodman was crouched, watching the action unfold. He had his Mac-10 out and he couldn't be happy with the performance of his boys. He was shouting something at them, but Cruz couldn't hear what it was.

Know what'll make him even unhappier? Watch this.

Cruz walked up behind the big man and gave him a kick in the back of the head. *Hey, why not? Might as well get in on the action.*

For a second, Goodman lost his balance. He went down on a knee and one hand. Then he turned and stood up. He moved to cover Cruz with the Mac, but Cruz kicked it right out of his hands. It clattered across the blacktop.

Hey, I'm pretty good at this. Look, Ma! No hands!

'Is that what you want, Cruz? A fight?'

'Well, now that you mention it.'

Goodman ignored the gun on the ground and waded in, his solid bulk moving on Cruz. Cruz was feeling so good, it only occurred to him now that with his hands cuffed behind his back, he had no way to block Goodman's punches. Goodman connected with a hard right, his big meaty hand nailing Cruz's jaw. Cruz stumbled back. He got ready to kick. Goodman feinted with a left, and brought the big heavy right around again. It slammed Cruz on the side of the head and Cruz sprawled out on the tarmac.

Jesus. That rung his bell. He worked himself up to his knees.

'You know what, Cruz? I'm having a bad day. I think I'll just beat you to death.' Goodman grabbed Cruz by the hair and lifted him to his feet.

Another punch and Cruz went down again. He felt his back scrape against the hard blacktop. They were moving away from the car and closer to the water. Goodman lifted him up again, this time by the shirt.

They were right at the edge of the dock.

The shooting seemed to have stopped for a moment. Maybe the boys were reloading. Goodman held Cruz inches from the edge. A slight push and Cruz would go into the drink. Cruz glanced backwards. It looked to be a good ten feet drop to the water from here. He wasn't sure if he'd rather it was deep or shallow. Too deep and he'd probably drown. Too shallow and he'd probably break his back when he hit.

Current events were sure taking the nice edge off his pharmacology high.

'You a good swimmer, Cruz? Good enough to swim with your hands behind your back?' Goodman slapped him across the face, first with his palm, then with a backhand. Then he did it again. There was a lot of force in those slaps.

Behind Goodman, back by the cars, Cruz noticed a silver tube fly up into the air. It seemed to hang there for a couple of seconds, catching the last second of sunlight, like the world's smallest alien spaceship, then it dropped out of sight again. It made that silvery metallic sound as it rolled somewhere on the asphalt.

Things were very quiet now, dead quiet.

'Hey, Goodie?' one of Goodman's guys said. Cruz couldn't remember if the guy was Marty or Joey. It was hard keeping the names straight.

Goodman stared straight into Cruz's eyes.

'Yeah?' Goodman called back.

'Uh, something just rolled under the car.'

'Yeah, what is it?'

'I don't know. It looks like a pipe. Or maybe a metal thermos, like people take to the football games. I used to do it myself. You know, put some hot coffee in there, with a couple of shots of Irish. Or maybe—'

Cruz saw Goodman's eyes go wide. Cruz glanced past Goodman's shoulder. In the next instant, the dark sedan erupted in a ball of flame, blowing outwards in all directions. A goon had been crouched on either side of it.

A blast of hot air, Sahara-hot, bikini-atoll hot, rolled over them.

Then Cruz was falling backwards, Goodman above him. They fell through the air, and one thing was clear. The big oaf was going to land on him.

Cruz had time for one thought:

Please let this water be very deep.

Wow.

Smoke's bomb had worked, all right.

Lola stood up from behind the BMW convertible. It was wrecked, for sure. The guns of the two goons had ripped it full of holes. The windshield was gone. Inside the car, the upholstery was ripped to shreds. All along both sides of the car, the fibreglass had been torn apart. All the tyres were flat. Steam poured from the front end.

The BMW was in good shape compared to the dark sedan. Basically, the sedan was gone. Where it had been just a minute ago there was now a crumpled heap of metal slag, burning hot and bright, with thick black smoke pouring into the sky. It seemed to be almost liquid at the centre, like the earth's core, and the redness there reminded Lola of a malevolent, all-seeing eye. The air smelled like, and tasted like, burning rubber. All around her, greyish-white flakes of ash drifted down like some kind of post-industrial snow.

The men were toast. One of them – a man who had taken up position on the right side of the car and opened fire on Lola and Pamela – had been melted down as surely as the car itself. He was a small, burning heap, a tiny mirror of the blazing centrepiece five or six feet away. There was nothing left to suggest that he'd been human only moments ago. Somewhere inside, Lola realised that she had killed him. He'd been trying to kill her and Pamela, and she had killed him instead. It didn't make her feel good. It didn't make her feel anything.

Another man was maybe twenty feet from the burning car, face down, just a few feet from the edge of the dock. She caught the smoke rising from the back of his body, the pulsating red of his flayed skin in the grim overhead light of the sodium arcs, and the way his body twitched as if an electrical current were running through it. She quickly looked away. If he wasn't dead, he'd probably be dead soon.

Beyond the dying man, maybe thirty yards away, the *Saucy Jack* was pulling in, backing up towards the dock. She could just make out Smoke in his jaunty captain's hat on the bridge, one hand on the wheel, his body twisted around to watch what he was doing.

There was no sign of Cruz and the other goon, the biggest one. From this point of view, they were just gone, but Lola suspected that if she walked around the back of the sedan, she'd find them there, looking much the same as these two. That would bring her total for the day up to four, including one friendly. Bad news. Bad, bad news.

There was no sound except the crackling of flames. 'Pamela, honey, we gotta go.'

Pamela scuttled across the blacktop like a crab, retrieving her gun. Then she stood and they both trotted across the lot to the floating dock, half of it under water now.

'What about Cruz?' she said.

'I don't know. I don't know what happened to him.'

'Ladies,' Smoke shouted from the bridge, 'it's a good idea to leave right this very minute.'

Pamela looked around, wide-eyed, as Lola tried to pull her off the dock.

Lola swept the area with her gaze. No sign of Cruz anywhere.

Joey was alive.

He was face down on concrete. He smelled the burned dead flesh of his skin, he felt the searing pain of his burns and of the shards of Detroit steel that had been blown through him. His body jittered and jived uncontrollably. He knew he was going to die, and soon, but for the moment he was alive. For a few seconds, the thought depressed him – just twenty-eight years old, and what was it all for? So fleeting. So empty. But he didn't want to focus on that. Right now, he was still kicking, and that was good. Even better, he hadn't lost his gun – it was still there, gripped in his right hand.

He flexed his fingers and watched them move. He couldn't feel them, but he could get them to work. He pulled the trigger of the gun. Click. Empty. He had fired all his rounds. OK, that was OK. He had more. With a titanic effort – the single greatest effort he had ever made for anything in his life – he pulled his left hand under his body and to his breast. It was an act of will. He was going to die, but if he could, he was going to take somebody with him. He reached inside his suit jacket – although it seemed to have burned and ripped away in back, some shreds of the front were still intact. He kept an extra magazine for his gun inside his inner pocket. He reached, he touched, he found it. He slid it out and watched as his hands ejected the spent mag and drove the new one home.

Twelve more shots. He chambered a round – now to look for his targets. There. The two girls were twenty, maybe thirty yards away, talking to a guy standing on the back deck of a largish power cruiser.

The guy wore a red-striped sailor's shirt and a stupid captain's hat – he looked like a cartoon character. He leaned on some kind of cane, gesturing with his free hand, shouting something to the girls. A happy little knot of three – it was anybody's guess, but maybe the guy on the boat was the other guy they had come here to kill.

Didn't matter. In Joey's reduced circumstances, a bystander was as good as a bad guy – if the guy didn't want to get shot, he shouldn't be talking to these girls.

Joey lifted the gun. He aimed. Well, sort of – the best he could do.

He fired, again and again.

Thirty yards away, the three figures jumped and scattered as the bullets whined all around them. The man disappeared down into the boat. The two girls dove away, rolling across the dock. Joey couldn't move his arm to follow them, he was stuck pointing straight ahead.

Shit, shit, shit.

He tried to draw a bead on one of them, but couldn't do it. He had lost sight of them entirely. He was going now, feeling weaker and weaker. A few more seconds, and he'd be too weak to even pull the trigger. Oh well, fuck it. He fired again and again, straight into the back of the boat. Maybe the bullets would go through and hit that fucker, cowering in there somewhere. Man, he was ripping it, really punching holes in the fibreglass. He hoped they were gonna need that boat – he hoped he could fuck it up for them somehow.

He tried counting his shots: Six. Seven. Eh, nine. Shit. Eleven?

A sneakered foot appeared and kicked his wrist. He hardly felt the kick, but watched helplessly as the gun slid away. He screamed in frustration – the gun was two feet from his hand. He realised that he hadn't heard his own scream – he had only experienced the effort it took to make the exhalation. He turned his head just slightly and saw the black girl standing over him. Her eyes were soft as she looked down at him. Boy, she was pretty. She said something to him then, and he realised he couldn't hear any more at all.

Going away now.

He remembered running as a child, running down the street, somehow running headfirst into a parking meter. The blood had poured down his face from a gash in his forehead. He went home crying, more from seeing all the blood than from the pain, and his mother looked at him just as this woman looked at him now. And he remembered thinking how everything was going to be all right.

It was dark under the water. For Cruz, it was like he had gone to a watery grave. It was nice down there, and it would be even nicer to come back to the surface for some oxygen. The problem was that Goodman weighed a ton.

For several seconds, Cruz thought Goodman had died in the explosion, and now his epic bulk was tangled up with something under the water. In short, Cruz thought he would drown, Goodman's body pinning him beneath the water.

They had hit the water hard when they fell. There were some rocks here – flat ones thankfully – and Cruz had landed right on them. The water was only about four feet deep. Cruz kicked and thrashed and was finally able to get loose from Goodman. He kicked his way to the surface, gobbling up great gasps of air.

Then he went under again.

He worked his way to his knees, then was able to press himself into a standing position. Oh yeah. His back was going to feel that crash landing tomorrow. Above him the sky was turning black and the smell in his nose was like the air around an oil refinery on an ozone alert day.

Goodman stirred – Cruz got an image of a whale about to breach the surface – and came up out of the water. The big man blinked and put a hand over his eye.

'Hey, Goodie, I thought you were dead.'

'I think I lost a contact lens.' Goodman blinked some more. 'Yep, I did. That seals it. This has been the most fucked-up day I've had in ten years. I'm just about blind in one eye now.'

He turned to Cruz and punched him in the face. Cruz took the shock and fell backwards into the water again. He took a deep breath as he fell, and went under into the murky depths. With a little luck, maybe Goodman would let him stay down there.

No dice. Goodman's strong hands reached down and grabbed Cruz by the hair again, pulling him up. When Cruz broke the surface, Goodman's heavy round face was there, the glint of murder in his eyes.

'Don't think for a minute I forgot about you, Cruz. I can kill you with one eye as easy as two.'

'You could also untie my hands,' Cruz said, 'and we could see how that goes.'

'This is for Marty,' Goodman said, and fired another hard right hand into Cruz's face. 'And this is for Joey . . .'

OK, so Goodman was going to kill him right here.

'That's enough!' somebody shouted. A female voice. Cruz turned to look over his right shoulder. Lola and Pamela were there, about ten yards away, above them on the dock. Nice to see they were still alive. Even nicer to see that Pamela was stationed at the edge, both hands pointing her gun right at Goodman's head – just like Cruz himself had taught her.

'Hit him one more time, and it'll be the last thing you do on this earth.'

Cruz heard Goodman sigh.

'Man, what a day.' Goodman's meaty fist was reared back, poised to strike. He looked at Cruz. 'Will she do it?'

'You mean, will she shoot you?'

Goodman nodded.

'Oh yeah. She's my girl, Goodie. She'll blow your brains out and then order a nice meal.'

Goodman's shoulders slumped. He let his fist drop slowly. His face softened. 'Honestly, Cruz. Let me ask you a question. Not for nothing, but you think I got a valid grievance with Vito? I mean, what kind of bullshit job is this?'

'You're a hotel guy now,' Cruz said. 'I see it.'

'Golf courses. You know what I mean? For Chrissakes, the fucking Maestro played my course one time.'

Cruz shrugged. 'I think you have a leg to stand on, Goodie. I think you really do. Who does Vito think you are? The help?'

'Thanks, Cruz. I appreciate that.'

'Hey! Meatball!' Pamela said. 'What did I say? Let him go. Now. We need to get rolling here.'

Goodman shook his head and gazed up at the thick black smoke staining the sky. 'All right, Cruz. See you around.'

Cruz nodded. 'Yeah.'

Goodman looked at Pamela with the gun, and behind her, the big power cruiser waiting to take them out to sea. Somewhere not too far away, sirens had started up. Soon they would close in. It was time for everybody to make tracks. Goodman sighed again. It sounded like all the air going out of a tyre. Suddenly the rain came, the stormfront finally reaching the shore.

A few heavy drops fell, then more, and then the rain came hard, like a cosmic water bucket had been overturned, like the start of monsoon season in the tropics.

Goodman, already soaked from going into the drink, frowned as the rain pelted his head and streams of rainwater ran down his face.

'Hell of a fucking day,' he said.

Cruz could be a corpse.

Hours later, Pamela watched him as he slept off the drugs. He lay on his back, eyes closed, face muscles slack and serene, his hands folded across his stomach. It was true: he could be a corpse, except he was breathing so deeply.

She lay next to him on the bed, holding an unlit cigarette. The bed was a double – not a great big king, certainly, but at least it wasn't a narrow twin or single. It was narrow enough that she lay with one hand resting on his chest.

The small state room was dark, except for a small night light plugged into the electrical outlet. The boat made sounds – creaks and groans that made Pamela's stomach turn. As she watched, the cabin lurched from side to side and up and down. Sometimes, the wall across the room from their feet seemed to fall well below them – so far down, such a vertical drop, that to Pamela it seemed they should slide off the bed and fall towards it. Sometimes the wall seemed above them, as though it were actually the ceiling and not the wall. They were moving through heavy seas. She wasn't sure if she'd rather be upstairs watching the action happen, or down here, blind, getting knocked around and nauseated by it. The hand holding the cigarette was trembling. They could go down, she realised. Now. Tonight. They could be at the bottom of the sea before the next sunrise.

She had taken up smoking just recently. She was not a good cigarette smoker. She held the cigarette in her hand, and every now and then she lifted it to her lips and took a tiny suck as if she were smoking it. Actually, she was practising.

She tended to smoke away from any prying eyes. Smoke and Cruz both had laughter in their eyes whenever she lit up. And health nut Lola would just sort of frown and be disappointed. 'You can go for a new image, but you don't have to kill yourself in the process,' Lola said one day.

But it was more than just an image, the smoking. It was Pamela's way of accepting the dangers of the life she was leading. Today was another confirmation that she, or Lola, or Smoke, or even Cruz, could die any time. And there was no going back – they were outlaws now, on the run from the mob, on the run from the cops. Even if Pamela went back home, and tried to settle back into her old life, it wouldn't last long.

Just recently, she had been mild-mannered Pamela, quietly fanta-sising about a swashbuckling life of adventure. Now she was on the high seas somewhere off the coast, on a boat with more than two million dollars in cash, with a hitman for a lover, and with more hired killers after her. It was too much. Just thinking about it got her heart racing like a grande-sized dark Venezuelan coffee used to do. It was exciting, it was terrifying, and try as she might, she couldn't see a way for it to end well.

Hence, the smoking. She had come to accept that she was going to die; probably soon, and probably in an ugly way. The cigarettes would probably kill her in thirty years, and there wasn't much chance she would live that long.

Bottom line: if she was going to die, she might as well look cool doing it.

Lola opened her eyes.

The ceiling was low above her, and the room was dark – it could have been a cave deep underground. It could have been a tomb, reserved for her because she had died, murdered as a teenager living in the world's largest housing project.

Then she realised the tomb was moving – more than just moving, surging and falling – and she remembered she was on a boat. The knowledge fell on her like a lead weight. They were at sea, on the run because Smoke had killed a man and stolen more than two million dollars in cash. They had nearly been killed again today, all because Cruz had tried to get his scar removed. They were doomed to this life of running – never far enough, the murderers always just one step behind.

The tiny stateroom rocked and rolled. They must be in a storm. It had taken her the entire first week to get used to the movement on the water. Even now, she was not entirely used to it. At times like this, in the first few weeks, she would wake up alone and realise that Smoke was at the helm. The liar was at the helm. The man who had nearly got them all killed was up there, at the helm. Then she would wonder: is he really up there? What if he had been swept off the deck by a wave? What if he isn't at the helm and the boat is just drifting by itself?

That was why she would get up out of bed at three in the morning, or some such time, and go upstairs on to the bridge to see him. To see him with one big hand on the wheel, a cigar in his mouth, a cold cup of coffee in his other big hand, peering out into the night. Usually, she could smell the sweet aroma of his cigar before she ever caught a glimpse of him. It was a familiar, comforting smell — it smelled like home, a home she'd never had.

She had that urge again tonight — to see him, and be reassured by his calm presence. She hated that he had lied, she didn't know what the future held for them, but one thing was clear: he was a rock, and a relaxed stare from him somehow made the dark ocean less threatening.

She crawled out from under the blankets and put on some clothes — leggings, jeans, one of Smoke's old sweaters over a T-shirt, and a yellow rain slicker to top it all off. When she climbed up from the hold, the deck was slick and she saw, for the first time, how the boat lurched up and down like a cowboy riding the bucking bronco. The waves were gigantic, marching in a line off into the distance. Each rise up the face of a giant wave brought the certainty of a harrowing plunge down the other side. Lola clutched the wet railings and pulled herself up, first to the aft deck, and then up to the covered bridge. The wind blew her hair back and she realised that in the few moments since she came above, she had become slick with water herself.

Smoke was there, standing at the helm, peering out into the night. Normally, he would be sitting. She saw there was no cigar tonight, and no cup of coffee. Smoke's back was rigid and both hands were on the wheel. She came up behind him and touched his blue wool sweater — it was soaked through. Although the bridge had a canvas cover on top, the harsh wind drove rain into his face.

'Hey,' he said, without even looking her way. 'You shouldn't be up here. It's not safe.'

'You're here,' she said.

Smoke shrugged at that.

'Anyway,' she said, 'it hasn't exactly been safe for a while now, has it?'

'Good point.'

Good point – the phrase reminded Lola of happy times when they were together back in Portland. That was when her lover was a really nice guy named Smoke Dugan, and not the fugitive bomb-maker, bank robber and murderer Walter O'Malley, who just happened to be calling himself Smoke Dugan. They would sit on the back deck of her apartment overlooking the water in the East End of town, drinking wine after a nice meal, Smoke with his ever-present cigar. And they would drift into some debate about the state of the world, current events, or even what Lola ought to be doing for a living. She was a low-paid teacher's assistant, working with handicapped children. That was how they'd met – Smoke was supposedly a retired engineer making toys and adaptive devices for the children in his spare time. All the ladies at the school were agog over Smoke – so handsome, so distinguished, so charming.

He was charming, for sure. 'Young lady,' he said upon seeing Lola, 'if we've met before and I don't recall the exact date and time, then I'm growing old indeed.'

Smoke loved the children, but he thought Lola should be making more money, making a bigger contribution, giving more of herself to the world. She had too much to offer to spend her life doing that job. It was a conversation they came back to again and again.

'What better contribution to make to this world than to help its most vulnerable children?' she had said one evening.

Smoke had puffed on his cigar, and hesitated for a moment. 'Good point,' he had said finally, blowing a smoke ring into the painted summer sky. 'You're a smart girl.' It was what he always said when she won a round. It made her feel good that a man like Smoke – smart, worldly and thirty years her senior – could respect her for her brains.

Now, on the boat, deep at sea on a dark night, and deep into unhappy times, she made yet another good point. 'But am I still a smart girl?' she said.

He didn't look at her. 'I think you know the answer to that by now.'

Lola stifled an urge to put her arms around him from behind and nestle close. His lies had put all of their lives in danger. She wasn't ready to overlook that – she wasn't ready to forgive him. Instead, she kept it all business. She stood at his side and gazed out to sea. 'What's going on?'

Smoke gestured ahead and to their right. Lola followed his gesture, and for the first time noticed the light show in the distance. Clouds, and just behind them, lightning, like the world's greatest laser rock 'n' roll show. The lightning was too far away from them for her to hear any thunder.

'The storm's over there,' Smoke said. 'It's a big one. I'm trying to run north of it, but we'll see some more of it before morning. It's throwing these big swells up, and things'll probably get worse before they get better. They tell you never try to run the Gulf Stream in a storm, and now you see why. There's a lot of fucking water out here.'

'Doesn't sound like the kind of thing that worried you before.'

'Yeah,' he said. 'But we got all shot up back at the docks. That guy must have hit something important – maybe more than one thing. I've been losing oil pressure all night. That might be normal in rough seas like these. But I've also got an engine running at 125 degrees. That's not normal. Eighty is normal. Over a hundred is way too hot. If we lose the engines, even one of them, in this sea, we'll be in trouble. We'll barely have the power to move forward. If we lose them both, we might have to ditch.'

Lola gazed out at the open black water, the massive waves all around them, surging like so many giant, hungry beasts. Smoke stared straight ahead. 'If we ditch out here,' he said, 'we'll probably die.'

'Can you fix the problem?'

'Sure, if we make it through the night. I can't exactly stop to fix it now.'

'Are we going anywhere in particular? The Bahamas?' Lola had a vague notion the Bahamas weren't far from the coast of Florida.

Smoke shook his head. 'Not the Bahamas. It's too dangerous right now. We don't know what the coastguard knows. We don't know what the cops know. We need to go someplace where the customs and immigration procedures are a little more liberal than in the Bahamas. Somewhere folks are a little more open to persuasion. I know a place – a small island – it's barely even on the map. Saint Mark's. It has a sister island called Saint Joseph. I've been there. It isn't ideal. But for now, it'll have to do. We can park this thing in an anchorage a little bit offshore, keep a low profile, and run to the island for parts. Get her fixed up, and then we're on our way again.'

'Will they find us there?'

Smoke shrugged. 'I doubt it. Saint Mark's is inside a radius I would draw on a map if I were them, but that might not mean anything. They probably won't look at a map. Anyway, it's a big ocean and we're a tiny speck on it. There's a lot of islands to choose from. I'd say a few days on Saint Mark's . . . eh, we shouldn't have a problem.'

The thought of it made Lola feel a little better. It would be nice to have some safe time off to recuperate after today's close call.

'Saint Mark's it is, then.'

3

Harsh light burned into his eyes.

They called him Sticks, and he was a maniac. He had killed many, many people in his time, in many places and in many ways. Some of them had died just because they had underestimated him. How could somebody so small and slim be a killer? Indeed, people just didn't seem to see Sticks the way he saw himself. To them, he was just some little guy with slicked-back hair. But they should have looked closer. Sticks reminded himself of one of those dancing skeletons people used as Halloween decorations. Sometimes, if he looked at his reflection in the mirror just right, it seemed there were even dark holes where his eyes should have been.

He lay on the bunk in his cell staring up at the recessed light fixture as the rays of morning erased the darkness outside the bars of his window. They'd kept the fucking lights on all night – they knew he was gonna walk, and they wanted to get some last licks in before he left. When he closed his eyes, little exploding strobes pulsed and danced in his mind.

Sticks smiled. He liked these modern cells, and these modern jails. Bright white light beamed against pale cinderblock. The door to his cell was exactly that – a door, rather than bars that slid open and closed. The door was locked and unlocked by a fat screw who sat at the central control station, but it was a door nevertheless. When the door opened, Sticks could step out on to the floor of 'the pod', a big, open space with metallic tables, high ceilings and more wonderful light. Every day was a sunshiny fucking day in this place. Sticks had done time in old-style prisons – they were like dungeons, dark, decrepit places where bad shit happened. A place like this was bright, antiseptic, like a doctor's office. Bad shit could happen here, hell yes, but it would feel clean, like a trip to the dentist.

Sticks was alone – no cellmate. He lay with his head cradled in his hands, staring at the ceiling, although he didn't see it at all. Even now, hours later, he was trying to look deep into the fog of his past. The Big Boys had come to see him last night.

Before the meeting, a couple of screws had brought Sticks out of the pod, down a series of hallways, and into an office. The office was bright and clean and new. They sat him at a table. They cuffed his hands behind him and through the iron slats of the chair. The position made him a little uncomfortable, forced him to slump.

A few minutes later the Big Boys walked in. Two men in suits, one guy slim and older, his back bent almost like a question mark. His face was lined and craggy with experience, and his eyes were bright with dark knowledge. The other one was big, like an enforcer – his suit was too small for his bulk. They both carried side arms in shoulder holsters.

The older one sat down. The big one stood, ramrod straight, flat-top haircut, thick arms folded – sure, ex-military. He stared at Sticks like he would stare at a bug, or a rodent about to undergo an experiment he'd seen conducted a thousand times before on a thousand previous rodents – his face was United States government-issue, impassive, made of stone. Sticks took a moment to imagine what the guy would look like without that face on – big eyes bulging, black hole where the nose had been, wet denuded bone glistening in the glow of the overhead fluorescent. Oh yeah. An hour alone with Sticks would do wonders for the big guy – it'd give him a miracle makeover.

'How are you, Jimmy?' the old one said.

Sticks stared at the table. He smiled, despite himself. 'Jimmy. Haven't heard that name in a while. Do I know you?'

'At one time, you did. Maybe not so well any more.' Sticks watched the old man take a pack of Lucky Strikes out of his suit jacket and light one. The old boy extended the cigarette across the table. Sticks took it in his mouth and inhaled deeply. Nice.

'Luckies separate the men from the boys,' Sticks said. 'But not the girls.'

'You like being handcuffed, Jimmy?'

'Fuck you.'

A small grunt of laughter escaped the man.

'Nobody's heard from you in quite a while. And it's been a while since you turned up anywhere. Some of our friends had come to believe that you'd decided to be a good boy. Of course, I never believed it. You were always too naughty for that. A few thought maybe you were dead – that I had no trouble believing. Do you know where you are right now?'

'Sure. I always know where I am. I'm in jail. Portland, Maine. Some kind of bogus weapons beef. The judge refused bail. So here I sit, waiting for a jury of my peers to decide my fate.'

'Yes, here you sit. But your fate has already been decided.'

'Is that a fact?'

'Listen, we know the story. A friend of yours turned up dead, buried in the sand on the beach near here. Roland Moss was his name. A hotel clerk says you visited his room the afternoon of the night you were arrested – the night he disappeared. This was two days after a man was found incinerated in a tool shed behind a house in South Portland, and one day after a hotel room and several cars were blown up, and another man was gunned down in broad daylight in another part of South Portland. It's funny how the bodies start piling up when you're in town, isn't it?'

The man paused and picked up a piece of paper off the table in front of him. 'None of that even takes into account the missing people: James

"Smoke" Dugan of South Portland, also known as Walter O'Malley of New York City, also known as Barry Fillmore and several other aliases, missing. Lola Bell and Pamela Gray, both of Portland, both missing.' He put the paper down.

'Listen, you don't happen to know about any of this, do you, Jimmy? Because I'll tell you, the police here seem to think you do.'

Sticks shrugged. He knew all about it, not that he'd ever talk. Cruz and Moss had come up here to retrieve Smoke Dugan and a couple of million missing dollars, things had gone horribly awry, and a bunch of people had died. Sticks himself had been sent up to put things right, but by then it was too late to fix anything. Now he was sitting in jail. 'I told the cops . . .' he began.

'Yeah, we know what you told the cops. And we told the judge, and the corrections officials, that you're telling the truth. So tomorrow morning, they're going to let you go, courtesy of your friends in high places.'

'Just like that, eh?'

'Just like that.'

Sticks smiled around the cigarette. For the first time, he looked the man straight in his dark eyes. Sure, maybe he knew the man. It was hard to know sometimes, what was real, and what wasn't. A long time ago – the man was much younger then, some kind of spook, or bodyguard. He'd be there sometimes, at the lavish parties in big mansions, on board the private jets. He was attached to somebody, watching out for some-body important – somebody in government.

The man's features were familiar to Sticks, but time hadn't been kind. The man was thinner than before, lined, and his skin colour was bad, almost grey, like boiled meat. Somewhere deep in Sticks's mind, a super-fast computer connected the dots, pulled all the variables together, and then drew a picture for him. Sticks liked what he saw.

'I must be a lucky man,' Sticks said.

Tiny red veins were visible against the whites of the old man's eyes.

'Well, it's a lucky thing to have friends who care about you. And it's a lucky thing for people like us to have a friend like you. You're moving up in the world, Jimmy, whether you realise it or not. Times are changing. Certain people are getting old. Other people are dying. Depending on how things shake loose, depending on how assertive he is, our little Jimmy could suddenly find himself in the driver's seat before too much longer. A man like that would be a very nice friend to have.'

Sticks spat the cigarette at him. It landed on the table and rolled about a foot, ember glowing and dropping ash on the stainless steel. And Sticks shared the data he'd got from the super-fast computer. 'You look like shit, you know that? You look like they drained all the fucking blood right out of you. It's cancer, right? You got the Big C, didn't you? Good for you. Send me a postcard from hell, you prick.'

The old man picked up the lit smoke. He put it in his own mouth and inhaled deeply. His face was dead serious now. 'Maybe I'll see you there.'

A moment later, the two men left. Soon after, the screws came and Sticks was deposited back in his cell. After that, he'd spent the night thinking about the man and where he'd met him before. Long ago, Sticks had been a kid in . . . he wanted to say Indiana. It rang a bell somehow. Indiana, outside of Indianapolis somewhere. He'd had a family – at least a mom. He lived with her in some kind of shitty trailer. He could see her clearly in his mind sometimes – stringy blond hair, angry blank eyes, not smart, drunk, passed out on the floor, entertaining various men. He'd never gone back there to verify the truth of any of this, or to find the place, but in his heart he knew it was right.

One morning they had come for him. Three men. He didn't get a good look at them – hell, he was just out walking early in the morning, along the side of a road. Why was he doing that? He couldn't remember. A dark car pulled up. Nondescript, maybe a Reliant K sedan. It wasn't even black, he did remember that much. It should have been black, but it wasn't. It was more like a dark green. He figured it was somebody asking for directions. Or maybe some old queer wanted to show him his whanger.

For a second, he had a weird feeling – you couldn't see through any of the windows. They were all smoked. That couldn't be a good thing. Two men jumped out, grabbed him and pulled him into the backseat. They tied a bag over his head. Everything went black.

He lived for a time in a basement. A big black guy came and . . . made him do things. Sometimes there were other kids there. A few girls, but mostly boys. Sometimes he was tied up. Sometimes he was free to move around. They had a TV set with a video player – nothing but porn on there. Something went on upstairs but Sticks had no idea what it was. There were no windows down here. No light came in from the outside.

Then, just like that, he was older. Not twelve now, maybe fifteen. There were parties. Sticks was at these parties. He knew not to speak. His job was to be seen and not heard. There were a lot of powerful men around. Sticks came to understand he was living in Washington DC – he didn't know how he knew that. He flew on airplanes sometimes – always private planes. Sometimes he stayed in nice hotels. One night, a skinny man in a suit took Sticks and another kid for a late-night tour of the White House. Or some big old house. They padded down echoing hallways, looking into bedrooms, and at paintings on the walls. When a guard stopped them, the man called the guard by name, and said, 'These are my sons.'

Now, Sticks opened his eyes and stared up at the recessed light in the ceiling of his cell. Who was that guy? Were these things even true? What seemed real, undeniable, was that from time to time, Sticks wound up in jail. And whenever he did, eventually someone would show up, some person who might have been from the Government, and would get Sticks sprung. They were watching him, following him, and had been his entire life. Or so it seemed. Why him? He didn't know. He shook his head. Fuck it – it was impossible to know the past. Sometimes, it was even hard to know what was past and what was present.

He glanced to his left. A big, balding screw stood in the doorway. He just stood there, hands on hips like he'd been watching Sticks for a while.

'Is it now?' Sticks said.

'When else would it be?' the screw said with a smirk. 'Yesterday? Tomorrow?'

'Is it?'

The screw nodded. 'It is now. And it looks like now is your lucky day. They're letting you go. No more weapons charge, no more murder investigation. Nothing.'

'Yeah,' Sticks said. 'I figured something like that would happen.'

'OK,' the screw said, 'then let's get a move on.'

Sticks moved slowly. When the memories came, it usually took a few minutes for the weight of them to leave him. In those first few moments, he always felt like an old, old man. Later in the day, and more so tomorrow, and the day after, he would begin to feel young again, and capable of anything, but for now, it felt like a lead weight was hung around his shoulders.

'Can I ask you something?' the screw said.

'Ask away.'

'Just who the fuck are you?'

Sticks eyed the pig. 'They call me Sticks. I'm nobody you wanna know.'

Butch Stone was one cruel dude.

Stone, just back from a six-month contracting gig in Iraq, was tall – six feet, three inches – lean, rippling muscle from head to toe. He was strong – as a kid, he had once thrown a fat guy out a wide second-storey window like the guy was a bag of rice. His government had taught him all sorts of tricks – how to jump from an airplane, how to fast-rope from a helicopter, how to survive a long walk across a hot desert with nothing but a Mars bar and an empty soda bottle.

Cruel, that's how he thought of himself. A cruel dude. But sometimes, like now, pleasantly high and half-drunk on mid-morning rum and pineapple juice in the dappled sunshine of a warm new day on Saint Mark's island, he would wonder: was he really all that cruel?

He gazed out at the turquoise water. From this vantage point on the dining patio at the island's biggest hotel — swank beyond measure to the locals, second rate like the rest of this island to any retired auto worker from Michigan with a pension — he could drink in a sweep of shoreline to the east. He thought of it as just that — shoreline. It wasn't really a beach. There was sand, but it didn't arrange itself into the kind of wide swath the typical island tourist was hoping to lounge upon. Ten yards wide in places, almost nonexistent in others, the sandy strip was lined with palm trees and small, brightly coloured wooden huts, built on stilts half a storey high. An almost-constant breeze blew in from the water. That was good, because whenever the breeze died, you noticed it right away. First, and almost instantly, it became very hot in the sun. Next, within a few minutes, the biting sand flies and the mosquitoes came out.

Some of the huts had docks that extended out from their beachfront porches and into the water — not only was there no beach to speak of, but there were sharp limestone and coral formations close to the shore, which made wading out into the water in bare feet something of a hazard. What you wanted was a dock that extended far enough out so that at high tide you could jump right into warm, calm, beautiful deep water. That's what Stone had — he could see his bright purple cabana from here — and that was more than plenty for him.

His hut was nestled at the edge of the mangrove forest right at the furthest visible curve of the shore — just past a fence maybe a quarter of a mile from here. That length of the shore was supposedly part of a private resort — off limits to the locals, but of course any guest could bring in any local they wanted. Their whore. Their drug dealer. Satan. Whoever. And of course, if they wanted, the locals could simply walk along the sandy strip to the fence, then wade out a few feet into the water to reach their destination inside the resort. At low tide, they didn't even need to wade.

Stone knew that if he stood and turned around, he could catch a glimpse of the depths of the shanty town that started about two blocks from the beach, and made up much of this town. Underhill, it was called, as far as Stone could tell, because it sat nestled at the bottom of a rise that went up maybe two hundred feet above sea level – the highest point on the island. Large whitewashed and pink shell-coloured homes clung to the lush green hillside, offering the island's few rich inhabitants what must have been fantastic views of the water.

The poor folks who lived down below in Underhill were eager to please the tourists, an admittedly low-rent bunch themselves. Saint Mark's was not on the glittering map of Caribbean fabulousness. Its visible poverty made most tourists give it a pass and head for more sparkling locales, and that suited Stone just fine.

Stone took a gulp of his drink and sighed. He was thirty-seven years old. He estimated that when he was twenty-three years old, he had killed at least fifty men, women and children during the course of one impossibly long day and night. In his dreams, and even in some waking moments, he went back there – an ancient, ruined city by the sea, a warren of alleys and footpaths, mobs of angry black people, surging, swarming, and Stone with the big M60, hosing them down. 'Skinnies', he and his Army Ranger buddies had called these people – non-people, really, unpeople – and to get home alive, Stone had mowed down steaming, heaping platefuls of them.

He used to say, 'At home, I kill somebody, they put me away. I go somewhere else, I kill fifty somebodies, and they hang a medal on me.' He didn't say that any more – he didn't say much of anything funny any more, not about killing. Was it cruel to kill people? Maybe it wasn't. Maybe it was a job like any other. Just another humdrum day at the meat-grinder.

In any case, maybe he wasn't as cruel as he thought – or as cruel as he used to be. There seemed to be ample evidence of this new tendency towards softness sitting right next to him at his table in the bright morning sunlight. Her name was Roxana, and she was a local whore from Underhill.

Ample, indeed. She was a sexy beast, no doubt, a big girl, but he wouldn't exactly call her fat. She was fleshy. She was womanly. She had a lot of dark body to manhandle. And she had a beautiful smile. She looked as good in the first light of dawn as she did in the dim candlelight of midnight, when Stone had half a bottle of rum in him.

She was a quiet girl – maybe shy – hardly ever said a word, actually. Even now, after she'd got to know him a bit, she only talked once in a while. Boy, but when they got it going, she would howl and moan and carry on like a porn star, like a wolf howling to the moon. She would talk then, all right, and the things she said sometimes surprised even a man of the world like Stone. Heck, he had grown up in a world where you didn't say anything during sex. Evidently, she hadn't, and it was a big turn-on.

Stone liked riding this girl so much that it took several days for him to realise something fundamental about their relationship – he was being nice to her. He bought her things – food, trinkets, jewellery – over and above the agreed-upon price for the night. He told her stories to make her laugh, and he liked it when she laughed. He often cooked her meals in the fading afternoons, on the grill outside his hut. They would swim naked after the sun had gone down. And he hadn't traded her in for a new model, even after more than a week together. Had it been that long? He thought it had – he had been on the island for close to two weeks, and she had been the third local woman for hire he had sampled.

This morning, or this afternoon, or any time, he could just tell Macho to give him someone else. 'Hey, Macho, you know, I like her, but let's try somebody different tonight. Yeah, maybe one of those skinny ones I see walking around in the poom-poom shorts and the big high-heeled sneakers. Sure, give me two of them. Variety is the spice of life, you know what I mean?'

And it was. And Butch Stone had a reputation to uphold. Maybe he would do it – today, tomorrow, he would swap her for another girl.

It would keep him sharp. And cruel. And after all, this shacking-up act was getting a little too domesticated for his tastes.

Stone smiled at the thought of Macho. The kid was dark brown, about eleven years old, four-and-a-half feet tall, skinny. He probably weighed ninety pounds soaking weight and with a brick in each pocket. He hung around near the shoreline and the hotels, dirty T-shirt, faded cut-off jeans, flip-flop sandals on his feet.

Sometimes, when Stone was sitting in the chair on the deck in front of his hut, the kid would come walking up the strip of sand. That was, in fact, how Stone met him.

'Hey, mister, what's your name?'

Stone glanced down at the kid, whose scrawny frame stood at the bottom of the stairs to Stone's deck. Stone had been on the island less than a day – he'd come in the night before from Miami. The night before that, he'd left out of Amman. And when he'd arrived in Amman, he'd come straight from Baghdad. Stone was tired.

'Who's asking?'

'They call me Macho.'

Stone raised his eyebrows. 'Macho?'

The kid smiled, enough wattage in that smile to light up a room. 'You got it.'

'Well there, Mister Macho, I'm Stone.'

'No need for the Mister. Just Macho will do.'

It'd been the start of a beautiful friendship. The kid brought Stone his first bag of the local weed. Stone had smoked better, but it was good stuff. The kid had also started bringing Stone girls – that was the kid's real job. Macho was the world's smallest pimp.

Stone shook away the thoughts. All this thinking was for chumps. Stone preferred actions. And today's preferred action was to hang out on this patio overlooking the ocean, soak up the warm rays of the sun, enjoy the high from the weed he'd smoked earlier, and suck back fruity rum drinks. Maybe he'd keep Roxana around for a couple more days before he cut her loose. The thought of ditching her worried him just a little – she wouldn't be pleased. Or maybe she would. It was hard to tell with her – she was a quiet girl, after all.

Maybe she was getting bored herself.

Roxana had dreamed of the animals again in the night.

For as long as she could remember, she had dreamed of the animals. The dream changed sometimes, but often it was very much the same. She was in a clearing in a black forest, and she was tied to a stake in the ground. It was night, and on the edge of the clearing, there were animals. She could see their bright eyes in the darkness. As time passed, they would creep closer and closer. Usually, even though they had entered the clearing, she could only see their eyes. Sometimes, they would resolve into lions or tigers, or other big cats.

They would come and take away pieces of her. The big cats wouldn't tear or bite at her, they would just come and casually, very businesslike, take pieces of her away. They were like workmen clearing away the left-over junk after a long job – efficiently, almost absently, taking it all away. A leg would go. A hand, or an arm. Her breasts, her womb, her torso. And her head would go. Then there would be nothing left but herself – her soul, whatever, the essence of her being. Then they would come and take that too. She would try to scream at the theft of her very soul, but she never could.

Even when she was a girl – and she was now twenty-one years old – she had dreamed of this. Her mother had taken her to see a seer – an *obeahman* – once. The obeahman turned out to be an old woman, so creased and lined with age that she had become neither woman nor man. Roxana had sat in a dimly lit room alone with the old woman, who smoked a cigar that she held clenched in her gnarled fingers.

When the woman splayed her fingers out on the table, they reminded Roxana of the branches of the silk cotton tree, what many called the Coomacka tree. There was one on the outskirts of Underhill that towered over the tiny homes of the poor. Five hundred years old, they said, and at its base, nearly twenty feet in diameter. The Spanish had buried a treasure there centuries ago, and had then killed the two African slaves that dug the hole. Now the angry spirits of the dead slaves inhabited the tree. The shadow the tree cast was enough to give Roxana nightmares.

'Your name means dawn,' the old woman said, her voice a rasp. 'But I see no light around you.'

The old woman went into a trance. Her eyes rolled back, showing the rheumy yellow of her whites. Roxana suppressed the urge to scream and run out of the room. The old woman had gone to a place where she could open the Akashic Records – the great spiritual book of existence from the beginning of time. Once there, she could open Roxana's own record – to see what her many past lives had been, and in so doing, gain a sense of what this new life might hold for her.

'You lived in Africa a great time ago,' the old woman said, her whites still showing. 'You were a young girl, and your village was destroyed by an enemy. A tribe from deeper in the forest came and burned your village. They killed the men and boys, and the elders. They stole the women and the girls, taking them away for their pleasure. The slaughter was terrible. But you hid in a hole in the ground where food was stored, and you lived. When the enemy retreated with their gains, you crawled out of your spider hole. Then you were alone, wandering among the dead, and you were too young to help yourself. You were only five. I see you there, a five-year-old girl, lying on the ground, holding your dead father's hand.

'At night, wild animals came from the forest. You could not defend yourself, so they ripped you apart and ate you.'

Roxana stared into the old woman's white eyes. Goose-flesh rose all over Roxana's body. A shiver went down her back.

The seer stopped speaking in the gloom of the candlelight. A sound came from deep in her throat. She closed her eyes for several moments, and then opened them again. When she did, her pupils had returned.

She fixed her stare on Roxana. The ancient compassion there was somehow worse than the terrible emptiness of the whites from moments before.

'I'm sorry, child. I see you being devoured again and again, pulled apart over and over throughout the centuries. I'm afraid it's your destiny.'

Now, Roxana watched her companion – the one who called himself Stone. He was sitting across from her, talking to her about something. She hadn't been listening in some time, but she saw by his face that it was something he thought of as humorous. She nodded her head and smiled.

In this life, the men were the animals from her dream. She was doomed to stay here, a poor girl from the shanties in Saint Mark's, and the men would come and take her away, a piece at a time. They would do this until she was no longer beautiful. Then what? Maybe she would marry a local man – a fisherman or a trinket salesman – who would get drunk in the night, and beat her and call her a whore. Maybe he would weight her down, and dump her in the ocean to use as bait. And tiny fish would come and take tiny nibbles at her, tearing her away one tiny bite at a time.

All the men. All the men.

But this one was different – maybe. She had never been with a man like him. He had killed many people. He had also seen many people die. It seemed he had been a soldier for America, in many parts of the world. He was just now back from the terrible war in Iraq – where he had been paid a lot of money. He had told her this one night, in the grip of a bottle of rum, and he had wept when he described the bodies of the children he had seen. She had hugged him and his powerful body had shaken with the force of the sobs. In the morning, he seemed not to remember any of it. He had awakened in the first light, stumbled out of the hut, and gone for a swim. When he came back, he was fine.

Dare she like him? Dare she invest some hope in him? This man, with whom she had a business arrangement? If she thought about it, she might find that she had already dared.

'What do you say, Roxana?' he said now. 'The day is young. You want to go back to the hut for a little while?'

She shrugged – best not to show too much. 'OK,' she said.

'The fucking boat is dead,' Smoke announced to the group assembled on the covered aft deck.

To Pamela, Smoke looked like a vampire – dark rings of exhaustion encircled his eyes. His hands were black with grease. Apparently, he had driven the boat all night to get them here – wherever here was – and had then gone right to work on it.

Pamela had awakened this morning to discover that the boat was anchored in shallow water between two green islands, maybe a mile from the bigger of the two, maybe four hundred yards from the smaller. The bigger one was lush and seemed vast, stretching away in the distance to the left. Even from here, she felt she could make out a handful of rustic dwellings near the water. The smaller island was tiny, and she could see it more clearly – it had a line of palm trees bordering a golden sand beach. It seemed only a spit of land, actually, and as close as it was, she saw no one moving on it. Here and there on the water, there were other boats like theirs – moored at some distance from the bigger island. No boat was all that close to them – people on the water seemed to value their privacy. Further out, what looked like part of a much bigger ship – a freighter – seemed to be sticking up out of the water.

It was a beautiful morning, the sky clear and bright. The lurching, chaotic sea of the night before was nothing but a memory. When Pamela had awakened, she had gone for a swim in the crystal water – it was colder than she had expected, and the cold was a welcome shock to her system. It wasn't more than fifteen feet deep where Smoke had dropped anchor, and not fifty yards away, there was a massive, healthy brain coral on the bottom. The water was pretty clear – but not clear enough to see the crazy convolutions on its tan- and cream-coloured surface. Pamela had some scuba gear on the boat – she had picked it up with the idea of resurrecting a long-dormant hobby from her teenage years. If they stayed here any length of time, she was going to dive down and check out that coral.

She had come back on board feeling wonderful, but then the trouble had started. First of all, while there were some lunch and dinner options in the pantry to last another day or two, there was almost nothing for breakfast. The last of the powdered eggs, the last of the coffee, the last two pieces of bread. No juice, no butter. They had meant to go grocery shopping yesterday evening, but circumstances had prevented it. OK, the island looked like a place they could get some food, if it was safe to go there. Which led directly to the problem at hand – it had better be safe to go to the island, because the boat wasn't going anywhere else.

Pamela and Lola were at the deck table, sharing the little bit of food. Cruz was at the railing, smoking a cigarette and staring out at the water. Pamela glanced at him, but he made no sign. All she saw was the sun reflecting off his dark sunglasses. Cruz didn't seem quite himself today – the after-effects from the drug. It would be good to get him off the boat for a while. There'd been tension all along, and she'd seen it explode before.

Just a few days ago, off the coast of northern Florida, Smoke had taken Cruz aside, and asked him, point blank, what his intentions were towards Pamela. 'Aside' was a relative term on a small boat in the middle of the ocean. Lola was on deck, and although they spoke in low voices, she could hear them. Pamela, downstairs in the cabin she shared with Cruz, could also hear them.

'I don't know,' Cruz said. 'I can't predict what the future will bring.'

'I think you can.'

'What's the matter, Dugan? You want both girls for yourself? You afraid I'm moving in on your territory?'

Smoke had pushed Cruz then, and they had fought briefly. With Smoke's bad leg, Cruz got the upper hand right away – he had Smoke down in seconds. But then Lola was there – she told Pamela she had acted without thinking, kicking Cruz in the face with a side kick that didn't break his nose, but brought a trickle of blood. The next day, his face was swollen where she'd struck him. Pamela didn't think Lola had hurt Cruz, actually – he'd simply fallen off Smoke and looked at her quizzically, as if waking from a dream. It was hard to hurt a man like Cruz – you might crush his bones, shoot him, run him over, but would he ever actually feel it? She thought maybe not.

But the bad thing was that when Pamela heard the commotion above her head, she had grabbed her gun and raced upstairs. She pulled the gun on Lola. When Lola looked up from the fight, Pamela was there, holding a gun on her. Lola, her room-mate of two years, and Pamela was holding a gun on her. She loved Lola, but there it was, the gun in Pamela's hand, Lola on the receiving end. Amazing what love, or maybe lust, could do.

'Pamela!'

'Don't you dare kick him again,' she said.

Cruz put his hand out. 'Pamela, put the gun away. It's not a toy.'

'She was attacking you.'

Cruz stood, brushed himself off. He extended a hand to Smoke, but Smoke ignored it. Cruz shrugged, then walked over to Pamela and gently took the gun from her hand. 'We were having a discussion. It got a little heated. But not every argument in this life means you whip out your piece and whack somebody. Guns, you're gonna come to find out, are all about nuance.'

Cruz turned to Lola. 'How's your foot, Lola? OK? My face didn't hurt it any, did it?'

Lola played along, a pained smile on her lips. 'My foot's fine. Better than ever – it likes a little contact now and then.'

Lola and Pamela had held each other and cried that night. They were still friends. All was forgiven. But the situation worried Pamela. It worried them both. If they stayed cooped up on this boat much longer, Cruz and Smoke were liable to kill each other. Or, rather, Cruz was liable to kill Smoke. Smoke had his skills, but Cruz . . . he was in another league.

'What's the matter with the boat?' Pamela said now.

'Well, the boat was all shot to shit in yesterday's mayhem,' Smoke said. 'We lost the coolant system – a couple of hoses need to be replaced and the water pump is toast. I gotta take a closer look at the manifold, too. The boat barely hung on last night – she had just enough left to get us here. We're lucky the pistons didn't seize. Now here we are, and we're stuck, at least for now.'

'Where is here?' Cruz said. He didn't turn around.

'Saint Mark's is that big island out there. Half Third World slum, half smuggler's den, and half cheap semi-Caribbean tourist destination. Saw its better days about thirty years ago. Had some kind of communist revolution back in eighty-five, a couple hundred American marines stormed the beach in inflatable speedboats, shot the place up for a few days, and set things to right. Wouldn't want another rinky-dink island to go the Cuba way, would we? But between the commies and the Marines, the tourists decided the Bahamas were a better deal. Or Key West. Or anywhere. The island never really came back from that.'

'How do you know all this?' Pamela said.

'It's in my *Cruising the Islands* guide,' Smoke said, a wry smile on his face. 'Anyway, I've been here before.'

'Is it safe?' Pamela said.

Smoke shrugged. 'Is any place? We put some distance between us and the mugs from yesterday, but that doesn't mean they won't be here tomorrow. Or the next day. Or later today, for that matter.'

'What do you suggest we do?' Cruz said, turning around. 'Stay here?'

'I suggest we don't have any more fuck-ups like yesterday.'

Cruz just stared. 'And the boat?'

'I can probably fix it,' Smoke said. 'But I'm going to need parts. And I'm going to need time. And before I do anything I'm going to need some sleep. I've been awake for twenty-four hours.'

'How long will all this take?'

'I'll go on to the island tomorrow, or maybe later this afternoon, and see if I can get what I need. If I can, it'll take me another day to fix it, maybe two. If I can't get the parts, then I don't know. But I know this – we're going to be here a couple of days at the very least. In the meantime, somebody has to go on the island right now and deal with customs. We came in during the night, so the office was closed. That means we haven't officially entered their country. You can bet they know we're out here, and depending on whether they're sticklers for procedure or not, at some point they might want to inspect the boat, see all our paperwork, and know where we just came from. With everything that went on yesterday, we can't let that happen.'

'I'll take care of it,' Cruz said. 'If things look clear, maybe Pamela and I will spend the night in a hotel. Give everybody a little breathing room.'

Smoke nodded. 'You know what to do?'

Cruz shrugged. 'I've been around the block a few times.'

On the street, Sticks had to walk for a while to find a payphone. The city loomed up ahead as he trudged towards it, away from the jail, through a low-slung, weed-choked wasteland. Empty warehouses with faded signs painted on the sides – everybody out of business, by the looks of things. Dilapidated houses slumped together, paint peeling, siding falling off, with dilapidated people to match, out front tinkering with cars that were just plain dead.

Sticks crossed some railroad tracks. It was fucking cold out. He'd worn this light leather jacket up here three weeks ago. Three weeks ago it was still early fall – this jacket didn't cut it any more.

A black sedan was idling in a parking lot. The windows were dark, and the men he'd talked to the night before might have been in the front seats. It might have been his imagination.

When he finally found a pay phone, he dialled a collect call to New York. Jonah, calling for Orion Management.

A woman's voice accepted the charges. 'Orion Management, how may I help you, Jonah?'

'I just got spit out of the whale.'

'Please hold. Mr Orion himself will take your call.'

Several minutes passed. Sticks jumped up and down to stay warm. He shoved his numb hands into the pockets of his jeans, and jammed the phone in the crook of his shoulder. Eventually Vito answered.

'Kid?'

'Vito, I'm out. Just like that.'

'Where are you?'

'I don't know. A parking lot. Not far from the jail. Near some kind of sandwich shop. There's a cheque-cashing place here, too. Payday loans, that sort of shit. A lot of chumps rolling in and out, selling their souls to make it to next week.'

'We'll send somebody. Wait there.'

Sticks went inside the sandwich shop, stood by the window, staring outside. He practically dared somebody to ask him what he wanted. He just wanted to stand there, stay warm. Now and then, he'd cast a stare at the counter staff. Two guys, stiffs, and a teenage girl. Nobody said shit. Sometime later, he didn't know how long, a light blue car pulled up. Modern Jap styling. Honda, Toyota, who the fuck knew? The driver powered down the window. Jarhead-looking guy was driving it, like a cop or an ex-boxer. That had to be him.

Sticks went outside.

'Sticks? Vito sent me. Get in.'

Sticks climbed in. The car was warm from the heater. It was bull-shit to send those two spooks last night, the way they did. It was them saying, 'We're watching you. After all these years, we're still watching you.' Time would pass – long periods of time – and all that shit would be gone. Then something would happen, Sticks would get popped for one reason or another, and they would appear again. Them or some-body like them. Start calling him Jimmy. He hated that fucking name.

Sticks knew their game – they were hovering like vultures. They thought Sticks was going to be a high up in Vito's organisation one day, and they also thought they owned Sticks. They thought they could pull his strings. He hoped the day would come when he got the chance to show them exactly how wrong they were.

Sticks looked at the flat-top driving the car. The first thing the guy did, he handed Sticks a pack of smokes. Camels, that was more like it.

'Name?' Sticks said.

'Knox.'

'Cop?'

'Used to be.' The cop looked at him as they drove through the heavier traffic into the downtown part of the city. Sticks leaned back into the seat. With the warmth and the smoke he was starting to feel better. He hadn't slept – he felt like he could go to sleep right here in the bucket seat.

'Vito said to get you a hotel room – something nice – and get some decent food in you. What do you like to eat?'

'Steak,' Sticks said. 'Whaddya think?'

On Saint Mark's, the Immigration and Customs office was in a small shack at the docks near the centre of the tourist district. It shared the place with the harbourmaster's headquarters. The immigration and customs official was a dark, heavyset black woman in an ill-fitting brown uniform who seemed to sigh and roll her eyes every time Cruz spoke. A name tag pinned to her lapel identified her as Ms Rush. She sat at a brown teakwood desk, in front of a wallboard pegged full of photocopied notices to sailors. The demolished remains of some kind of sweetcake or heavy bread sat on a plate by her left hand. To her left, out a window with blinds half pulled against the sunlight, was the turquoise bay.

Cruz was still woozy, lightheaded, unsure of his footing. He was glad Pamela was waiting right outside this office – he might need someone to hold him up before this was over. The good doctor must have given him one hell of a dose yesterday – he felt like he had spent half the night drinking, and had an epic hangover. What's more, his memories of yesterday's events were hazy at best. He remembered what had gone down, all right – shit, he'd seen Goodman for the first time in years – but everything that happened seemed to have a fog around it. Every now and then, a shard of memory would suddenly become very clear, and Cruz would cringe in embarrassment. Was drugged-up, cheerful Cruz actually going to take Goodie and his two goons straight to the boat? And with no plan in mind other than handing them the money, smiling at them and wishing them Godspeed? That seemed to be the case.

'You'll have to bring everyone from the boat in with their passports, Mr . . . uh, Figueroa,' Ms Rush said now. 'I'm afraid we can't just have visitors floating in and out of here without any controls.'

'It'll be impossible to bring everyone from the boat in right now,' Cruz said. 'We have engine trouble and a couple of us are out there working on it.'

'That's fine,' Ms Rush said. 'We can send a couple of agents out later today to conduct a boarding and inspection. In the meantime, we ask that you, and everyone in your party, wait aboard your boat.'

Cruz laid two small coins on Ms Rush's desk. The coins were identical, and on the face of each was etched a young woman in flowing robes, holding a trident in one hand, the other hand resting on a large shield with the British flag on it. The coins could have been anything – quarters, maybe, or half-dollars. Pocket change. Just something Cruz put there because he was looking for something else in his pocket, or even for no reason at all. Around its circumference, each coin read:

ONE . OUNCE . FINE . GOLD . BRITANNIA . 1988

Ms Rush's hand casually landed on top of the coins. Oh so casually, the hand slid back again to the edge of the desk, disappearing into her lap. The coins themselves had disappeared as well. See? Magic. Ms Rush was a magician, just as Cruz had suspected she might be.

'I'm sorry, sir,' Ms Rush said. She had opened a wide ledger book and was writing something in it. She didn't look up. 'Did you say something?'

Cruz shrugged. His eyes seemed to scan the multicoloured flyers tacked to the wallboard behind her desk. *Dangers of hurricane season. No dumping in local waters.* 'Yes. I was just saying that I don't follow the markets every day, but a couple of days ago, I think I read that an ounce of gold was selling for $781 in London trading.'

'That's very interesting. How long did you say you were planning to stay here on Saint Mark's?'

'A few days. Probably no more than that.'

She nodded. 'I think a few days is a nice amount of time. Many of our guests find that a few days is more than enough. We islanders like it here, of course, but some guests come to find that a week is much too long.'

'I understand perfectly,' Cruz said.

Now Ms Rush looked up from the book, the pen poised in the middle of a line. She stared directly into Cruz's eyes. She gestured with her head, only slightly, at a skinny black man in khaki shorts and a pressed khaki shirt who sat just through the doorway in the other office. 'That man in there? He's the Harbourmaster. He's an important man, and he keeps a careful eye on who comes in and out. I understand that he follows the markets very closely.'

Cruz looked through the doorway and smiled. 'I wonder if I should have a chat with him.'

'I think he'll find what you have to say quite interesting.'

She finished her writing with a flourish, then stamped a few papers, and pushed the whole mess across the desk to Cruz. 'OK, Mr Figueroa, your paperwork looks to be in order. Enjoy your stay with us.'

'Thank you very much,' Cruz said. 'I'm sure I will.' He scooped up the papers, and went in to talk precious metals with the gold-bug harbourmaster.

Stone thought a lot about killing.

Too much. It seemed like all he thought about sometimes. He found that if he kept active enough, or high enough, or drunk enough, he could put it out of his mind. But as soon as he stopped doing whatever it was he was doing, his thoughts started racing, and the images came crowding in again.

He didn't like laying all this heaviness on Roxana. It wasn't fair. She was a young girl. She should be thinking happy thoughts . . . thoughts about her future. He glanced down at her, dozing nude on his bed in the heat of the late morning. A hot breeze came in through the screen door. He went outside to the deck with his beer and sat back in the wooden lounge chair. The sun was reaching its height – the day was sultry, heavy, and he settled in deep, gazing out at the water.

Roxana, he reflected, was a twenty-one-year-old whore, on a tiny island in the middle of nowhere. The circumstances didn't offer her many prospects for advancement. Currently, she was having sex for money with a guy nearly twice her age, who had killed so many people, and seen so many people die, that he could no longer keep track of it all – a guy whose mind seemed to be coming apart, a little bit more each day.

Happy thoughts about what future?

Jesus.

Focus on something. Focus on anything. How about the first time? Yeah, that'll do. Stone was already twenty years old when he bagged his first kill. It happened by mistake. Well, almost by mistake.

It was Philadelphia. Stone was hired muscle for a local don. Mostly, he rode along when Louie's strippers went to entertain parties. The parties were almost always thrown by young guys, frat boy types, and fuelled by booze and coke and God knew what else. The guys could get out of hand sometimes. Berserk was how they could get.

Louie didn't like it. The strippers were a sideline business for him, barely made a blip on his bottom line. But it was one of the first things he'd gotten his meaty little fingers into, and it held some kind of nostalgia for him. Also, he liked having the girls around, for obvious reasons. He didn't mind if a girl cut a side deal and made some money raffling off fellatio to drunken geeks. What Louie didn't like was a lot of frat boys pawing at the girls, trying to force them to do things they didn't want to do. He always sent two big guys along to keep everybody on the straight and narrow.

Louie kept newspaper clippings tacked to the board in his office about frat parties that had gotten out of hand and turned into gang rapes. He must have had some kind of service cut them out for him, because they came from all over the country. He had at least two dozen of them. He made everybody involved read them. It was serious stuff to him. You'd think sixty-year-old, full-to-brimming, pasta-eating, diamond-ring-wearing Louie was the father to these girls.

'Stone,' he'd say, 'you watch out tonight. Somebody gets out of line, you make him a lesson for everybody else.'

'I got it, Louie.'

Louie'd point a stubby finger at Stone. 'Don't patronise me, you fuck. Something happens out there tonight, it's your neck.'

'I got it, Louie.'

It was a bad night. Stone knew it would be a bad night. All the omens were bad. For one, it was raining. Not just ordinary rain, but down-pouring sheets of freezing, blowing late-autumn rain. For another, on the drive down to South Street to pick up the girls – the girls liked to party, and they liked to live near the action – a pebble kicked up off a cement truck in front of him and put a crack in his windshield. In a day or two, if Stone didn't get on it, that crack would spread and cover his whole windshield.

'Ah, heavens to Betsy, man.'

The kid in the passenger seat gaped at him. Three for three: the kid was a newbie, and had never done one of these before. He looked like old photographs Stone had seen of Babe Ruth – heavyset, jowly, like an upright bulldog. He was young, but already he looked old. He was some-body's nephew – large enough to maybe intimidate someone, but also too overweight for some of these jocks to take seriously, and already goggle-eyed and nervous at the prospect of the three girls they were riding with. His big limbs kept making unnecessary motions – legs crossing and uncrossing, knuckles tapping the dashboard, then the window, then the ceiling. Even with all the pent-up energy, his movements seemed to come with exaggerated slowness, like the kid was moving under water.

'You're the guy who never curses,' Babe Ruth said. It wasn't a question.

'That's right.' Stone was still seething about the windshield.

'How come you never curse?'

'Because it sounds stupid when people curse. I don't like to sound stupid.'

'I wonder something about you,' said the Babe. 'Do you ever think about cursing? I mean, in your mind, when something goes wrong, do you think of a curse, like fuck, and then choose to say something else?'

Stone looked at the kid. 'No.'

Stone had worked with the girls before. Nice girls, he'd had flings with two of them already. Not yet old enough to drink legally, and he'd already learned one painful, and ultimately useful fact of life: strippers were craaazy. They were nobody to try to have a dating, romance-type relationship with. Not unless you wanted to show up at the apartment and interrupt them having sex with the sixteen-year-old kid who just dropped off the pizza, or the handyman who came by to fix the sink.

One of the girls that would dance tonight, Martina – older than Stone by several years, tiny, brunette, with a slim, incredible body – did him a favour and gave it to him straight: 'Stone, I like you. I might even love you. I love sleeping with you. But you have to realise – I'm not for you. I have such a powerful sex drive that some days I shouldn't even go outside. I've had it since I was nine years old. I can't control it. I go totally insane. It's like a beast, and I have to feed it. I'll fuck the gas station attendant, or anybody, any random guy, just to make it stop for a little while. You should enjoy your time with me, but if you hang around too long, I'm going to break your heart.'

When they arrived at the apartment, the girls were all high as kites. They piled into the back seat, and brought a bottle of wine into the car with them. They did a few lines of cocaine on the way over. They pawed at each other, flashed, pulled out nipples, pulled up skirts, screamed and laughed. Stone glanced over at Babe Ruth – eyes wide, the kid was already GONE.

They pulled up to the house, an old rambling, ramshackle place. The music was thumping. Lights were going on and off. The whole house seemed to pulsate with the sound and light. Crowds of young males streamed in from the rain. They were hopping all over each other. Sometimes there were girls at these things – Stone liked that better. It took the edge off somehow. The guys behaved themselves. This didn't look like one of those.

This looked bad.

'You gotta stay cold, man,' Stone said to the Babe before they went in. 'Cold?'

'Yeah. Look alive in there. Don't get distracted.'

The kid dismissed it with a wave of his hand. 'I'm good, bro. Don't worry about me. Just hold up your end.' The kid's eyes were the size of frogs'.

This was trouble.

Stone was not a big guy. He was tall, and he was strong – but he was built more like a quarterback or, God forbid, a wide receiver, than a linebacker. The thing was, he was fast. He'd played football in high school, and besides football, he had done boxing, kick-boxing, wrestling. He figured nobody, pound for pound, was as fast or as strong as he was. In fights, some big guy would start something, and Stone would put the guy on the floor before the big guy could ever throw a punch.

Strangest thing: when it all went down, everything around Stone seemed to go slower and slower, from 78 rpm, to 45, to 33, to 16 and a half, sometimes all the way to eight and a quarter, molasses pouring from the bottle, sap oozing from the tree. People moved in slooooowwwww mo, while Stone moved like a jungle cat.

Stone would have all the time in the world. He could see in some guy's eyes where the punch would come from, where it would go. It was almost like he could see the guy's thoughts. The guy's brain is like: right hand, big haymaker. The synapses are firing and this message is travelling along down to the guy's arm. Meanwhile, Stone is moving normally. Right, left, right, left. Snap, snap, bang, BANG. Knee to the groin, blade of the hand across the throat, pulling the shots now because the big guy was already done and there was no reason to kill him – just some big dumb lug who didn't know better.

But the party was bad – worse than Stone even imagined. It was a frat party, but a lot of sporty types were there. There was a table in the centre of this big, threadbare sitting room for the girls to climb up on. Guys milled around – guys with rugby T-shirts, guys with hockey T-shirts, and guys with football T-shirts. Some big guys here, bigger than Stone by a lot. Bigger than Babe Ruth. The guys were sauced up, bombed, pushing and shoving, good-natured team rivalries going sour right before Stone's eyes. No girls. Not a single girl in the whole place.

Jesus.

Call it off. That was what went through Stone's mind. *Call the thing off. Tell Louie it looked bad.*

No. You didn't call things off ahead of time. That just wasn't done. Stone had never heard of it being done.

The girls started their little act, and it went wrong right away. Two girls, Martina and Nicole, were up on the table, dancing together, taking each other's clothes off, doing the lesbian fantasy thing. Cheers went up. The guys pressed in around them.

Some jock sprayed his beer at the girls. Stone grabbed him and said something to him. He couldn't even hear himself over the music. The kid glared at Stone, not understanding who he was. Sure. It was already eleven o'clock – the kid was too wasted to understand.

Stone caught a couple of secretive looks pass from here to there – looks he didn't like. Looks that said, 'We have a plan.' Stone didn't like people who had a plan.

It all went down in seconds. Three guys had Candi – the girl who hadn't gone on yet – cornered in the back of the room. They were playfully trying to pull her through a doorway. Stone headed over there. Where was the Babe? He glanced back, and more guys were pressing in close to the table. Hands reached out and touched the girls' bodies – that was a no-no.

Here we go.

Stone got hit by a bottle.

It surprised him, somebody hitting him from behind. Instantly he knew the plan. *Disable Stone and do what we want.* The bottle smashed when it hit him. A river of beer poured down the side of his head. He saw red – there was blood flowing down his face. He turned and the kid who had hit him was coming with a punch, a left. It was a big fat kid – no sportsman, this guy. Just some chub, probably lived in the house. Stone blocked the punch, but then two big guys had him by the arms.

Holy cow! *This fast? This fast?*

Images flashed, as Stone's eyes went wild in horror. They were dragging Candi out of the room now, no longer playing. Lose sight of her and she was gone. They climbed on top of the table, three guys already trying to pin the girls down there. They were dragging Stone to the floor. One kid was trying to pull Stone's shirt up over his head, make him blind – a hockey fight move. Hockey players were here.

Desperate, Stone wriggled like a snake. Three guys had him. Four. Five. If he went down, that was it. All over. Stone fell to his knees, an arm jammed behind his back. The kid back there was trying to break it, or dislocate it. It hurt. Through the raging storm of adrenaline, he realised that it hurt. They swarmed around him now, pushing him down, down, down – in another few seconds, he would be face down against the dirty wooden floor.

A shadow moved above him. Stone wrenched his head up and saw what was coming. The kid. Babe Ruth, still on his feet, up as Stone was down. He had a wooden chair in both hands. Suddenly, he loomed gigantic, the chair tiny in his monster grip. He swung it like a baseball bat, and knocked some kid's head out of the park.

Stone had one free arm.

Here came the Babe's chair again. Another kid gone. Two free arms.

Was this a good kid? This was a good kid. He really was Babe Ruth with that chair of his. He hit another kid and the chair splintered apart in his hands. Now he held two wooden legs, one in each hand.

Stone jumped back to his feet. He wiped the blood out of his eyes. He was free. He took a breath. Oh, man. He watched as it all slowed down, everything but Stone's anger. He was mad. He had never been so mad in all his life. The rage surged through him. Babe Ruth made eye contact.

They communicated through telepathy.

Do it, Stone sent.

Fuck this shit up, the Babe's eyes said.

Stone saw the guys near them get that uh-oh look. It was a beautiful thing. Not everybody had the look yet, but not everybody knew the plan had gone wrong.

Stone started swinging. A kid went down. Another. He kicked a kid in the face, working his way towards the table in the centre of the room. From the corner of his eye, he saw Babe Ruth: a jagged leg of the chair in each hand, ambidextrous, swinging, clubbing, moving towards the other room, in pursuit of Candi, like a superhero, making ground beef out of everything in his path.

The guys on the table had got the bad news – they climbed off the girls and jumped into the fray. Stone threw fists and elbows before the guys had barely moved. It felt that way – forty guys, and Stone and Babe Ruth were gonna burn through them all. Stone was jazzed. Stone was on fire.

He was in a corner, two or three guys there, slugging it out with them. They couldn't land anything.

Bang. Stone got hit again. From behind again. He saw stars, felt that tell-tale liquid splash down. Saw flying glass. The liquid stung – hard stuff burning into his cuts. He turned and it was that same fat kid – the one who had hit him with a beer bottle earlier. The kid hit people with bottles – that was his whole modus operandi. Hit somebody from behind with a bottle, fade into the woodwork, then come back and hit him with another bottle.

The kid brandished the shattered remains of the bottle. Stone slapped it out of his hand, the razor-sharp bottleneck flying across the room. Stone grabbed the kid by the head – a frightened kid now. He was a fat, tow-headed kid who looked like he had exited childhood a few weeks before. Stone whipped the kid down and around, one hand gripping the kid's hair, one hand gripping the kid by the back of his belt. The kid was lighter than air somehow. Stone's mind had time to calculate – fat weighs about half what muscle weighs. Sure, the kid is light.

There was a window right there. It was wide open, probably to let the breeze into the overheated room. Stone whipped the kid out the window like he was a twenty-pound sack of rice. It went that easily.

The three kids Stone had just been fighting all stood there, hands at their sides. The fun was over. Stone had just thrown a man out the window. He peered outside into the dark. The rain beat down. Although they were on the first floor, the ground apparently sloped down and away behind the house. There was a rubble-strewn backyard out there – it looked like an old washing machine was on its side among a lot of cinderblocks and other stuff. The fat kid was down amongst the garbage, lying there, his body at a sort of odd angle. It was hard to say what the deal was out there. Stone couldn't hear if the kid was screaming or crying because the music was too loud.

Stone looked around. Twenty people were staring at him, including two strippers in thongs, including Martina, who hadn't wanted to break his heart. He walked over to them.

'Get your clothes on. We need to get out of here.'

He walked into the other room. Babe Ruth was in the corner, slugging it out with four guys at once. Candi saw Stone and ran past him into the other room. Stone walked up to the battle, which dissipated as soon as he showed up – if the four guys couldn't tackle one Babe Ruth, they might as well give up the ship when his partner arrives. Babe Ruth's face was bloodied, his shirt torn away from his upper body, his hands ripped raw. The big man smiled. The smile died when he heard what Stone had to say.

'We gotta go,' Stone said. 'I think I just killed a guy.'

On the way out, somebody threw a beer bottle at them. It hit the wall and shattered. Stone barely noticed it. In the car, he glanced at himself in the rearview mirror. His face was a mask of streaming blood. He looked like a head-hunter, a cannibal from some primitive tribe.

'You know what?' he said to everybody in the car, but mostly to himself. 'That guy deserved to die.'

Now, seventeen years and many corpses later, in the tropical warmth of Saint Mark's, he sipped his beer and stared out at the placid water, lovely young Roxana sleeping quietly in the room behind him.

Killing that fat kid had been enough, he decided. He probably should have stopped there.

4

Lola was fed up with him.

She watched as Smoke hunched inside a clapboard shack piled up with machinery and tools on every flat surface, more hanging from pegs protruding from the walls, all of it old and dirty with grease and oil, but with sharp teeth glinting and glimmering, looking ready to come to instant life and bite the hands of the unwary. He was in the shadows, dickering with a short black man about the price and availability of certain parts. The black man was very dark, shirtless and skinny, and leaning on a wide piece of scrap metal.

Lola stood outside the shack in the blistering light of late morning. It was so bright out that the shadows on the dirt road appeared etched with a knife. Here and there, a few chickens pecked desultorily at the ground. Right after Pamela and Cruz left for the island, Smoke suddenly decided that he didn't want to take a nap after all – exhausted as he was, he wanted to get the parts he needed and get right to work. So they had put the little zodiac in the water and come ashore.

Lola and Smoke had walked half a mile in from the sea to find this place, asking here, asking there, and finally being directed to this shack – this was the man, maybe the only man on the island, who had the parts Smoke needed. And yet Smoke felt compelled to haggle with the man, dragging their negotiations on endlessly. Smoke had plenty of money, and this was *the only man* who had the necessary parts. Hello? What if he got irritated and decided he didn't want to sell them at any price?

Lola wanted to get out of the heat, but she didn't want to go into the oily workshop. She wandered away from the shack. Thirty yards down, there was a bend in the road. Just on the other side of the bend was a house, another clapboard place, in bright red, green and yellow. Three dark men stood in the shadow by the front porch.

One of them peeled off from the group as she passed.

He was a young guy, tall and slim, but well-muscled. He looked like a guy who either did some kind of physical labour for work, or spent a lot of time lifting weights. Then again, maybe he just had a great body for no reason at all. He had long hair in twists. He wore only a pair of shorts tied with a piece of rope, and flip-flops on his feet.

'Fine young daughter of Zion,' he said as he approached. 'Wait one moment.'

'Hello,' Lola said.

'American?'

She nodded, already seeing that the guy had some gambit in mind. As he came closer, it became clear how tall he was – much taller than Lola.

He smiled. 'Nice piece of American pie.' He gestured up the road with his head, and flexed the muscles and sinews in his wiry arms. Health and vitality, and a madcap sort of energy, came off this guy in waves. That, and the smell of alcohol – it was still early, and the guy had been drinking. Lola guessed he probably wasn't yet twenty years old.

'We saw you go up the hill with the old white boy. He your man?'

'And if he is?' Her heart was beating now, and she became aware of it. She was getting better at this. It was like she had invisible antennae coming out of her head – she *knew* when the shit was about to come down.

The man shrugged. His eyes roamed her body now, hungry, devouring her in a few short seconds. 'Body like yours, they must call him Happy Dick.'

It was her turn to shrug. 'Maybe they do.' It was all she could think of to say.

His hand snaked out suddenly – fast, like a rattlesnake strike. He grabbed her wrist in his big hand. 'It makes me sick to see you with him. Did you know that? It makes me sick.'

'That hurts,' she said. She tried not to put any whining into it. She didn't want to give this big oaf the satisfaction. 'Let go of my hand.'

'I want you to feel something. I want you to feel what a real man feels like, to see what you're missing with him.'

He began to move her hand towards the crotch of his dark shorts. She resisted, but of course he was stronger.

'You're going to pet the alligator,' he said.

Enough was enough.

She let her hand – her left hand, her weak hand – be guided to its destination. It rested there for second.

'Yes,' the guy said. 'Amen to that, sister.'

Lola stomped hard on the top of his exposed foot, left foot in sneakers coming down hard on the fragile bone where his right foot, exposed in its flip-flop, met his ankle. In nearly one motion, she also brought the blade of her right hand around and struck him across the throat. If he were shorter, she would have gone for the nose, but he was tall, so she hit what she could reach. It happened so quickly, he didn't know what to grab first – his foot or his wounded Adam's apple.

He made a sort of guttural croak, his eyes wide in surprise as he forgot all about the alligator roaming around in his pants. Lola took a step back, assumed a striking pose, then delivered a front kick to his left knee. He bent to hold the knee, the newest conflagration of pain flaring up in the inadvertent game of Whack-a-Mole he was playing with her attacks. Bent over, he was down to her height – exactly the position she wanted him in. She spun, firing a roundhouse kick that caught him solidly across the head.

When she finished her spin, he was down in the dust of the road, face first, blood and drool dropping from his mouth into the dirt. She glanced at the other two men, twenty yards away, still in the shade, to see if they wanted any part of this. They laughed and waved.

'Ty Weathers,' one of them said. 'Young boy with a big mouth.'

She looked down at him. He wiped his mouth and pushed himself to a kneeling position. She put a hand on him, maybe to help him up, maybe just to show him there were no hard feelings. He shook her hand off violently, then stood, not looking at her. He moved towards the porch, then changed direction and walked off towards another house set back in a field.

Lola turned and Smoke was coming down the road, his arms hanging heavily at his sides, both hands gripping the handles of dirty plastic bags, triply and quadruply bagged. She could see that he was limping just slightly – of course, his old-fashioned, 1950s gentleman's chivalry wouldn't dream of letting her carry anything. Hell, it was only half a mile back to the dock where they'd left the dinghy.

'Hey, look what I got,' he said, his brow already dripping with sweat. She glanced down into the bags. Dark, oily machine parts, unidentifiable, only something Smoke could love, lay wrapped in newspaper in both bags.

Smoke gestured with his head towards the kid stalking off across the field. 'What's the story with that guy?'

'I don't know,' she said. 'He must have fallen down in the road. I think he was drunk. I was just trying to help him up.'

Ty Weathers was not from the island.

In fact, he was just about sick of island life. As he banged through the screen door to the front porch of the ramshackle old farmhouse where he lived, he realised he was at his breaking point. He had been drinking all morning, and the alcohol had clarified his thinking for him – he'd had enough. It was time to take action.

He paced across the wooden floorboards and into his tiny room. There, he reached under his narrow bed and pulled out a length of thick rope and his machete in its leather scabbard. The tourists – the beautiful young black woman and her rich white sugar daddy – were probably staying on a boat out in the bay. If they'd trekked all the way up here to see Shep the mechanic, then they were looking for spare parts. Ty could tell by the way that the old white boy was walking, weighed down with bags like that, that it would take them a good while to make it back to the docks. Ty could take the back way and beat them there. In fact, he could be out in his skiff like any random fisherman, waiting for them, before they even got on the water. He unsheathed his machete for a second and ran his thumb along the blade – still plenty sharp. He put on a grey T-shirt, a straw sunhat and his Oakley shades, and glanced in the hanging mirror. Sure, he could be anybody. They'd never recognise him.

He put the rope and the machete in his satchel and slung it over his shoulder. Then he hurried out the back door and across the fallow fields.

Ty had come down here to live with his grandmom eight months before. He had tried to make a go of it as an islander. It hadn't worked. He had tried to get used to country living, staying here in the old house in the hills. But the quiet and, at night, the buzz of insects in the tall grass, just about drove him insane. He had tried to become a fisherman, but long, hot days standing in a wooden skiff, throwing net after net, just didn't appeal to him. It was backbreaking labour for almost no money. He had thought of making time with the local girls – the easy ones, anyway – but the girls on this island learned from an early age to treat their pussies like parking meters. All they had eyes for were the tourists. Some of these girls had been with so many tourists that Ty wouldn't dream of putting it to them – a man must have a terrible grudge against himself to have sex with somebody as poisoned as that.

'Don't that bother you?' Ty had said to a few of the young guys he'd met. 'They come here, these white men, and steal your women.'

'Steal them?' they'd say with a laugh. 'It looks like they pay damn good money. The girls make more than we do.'

The islanders had this whole live and let live thing going on, and Ty just didn't get it. Things that would make him seethe with anger, even boil over with rage, seemed to have no impact on them at all. It exasperated him. He'd try to school them on the way things were, the way real men should be thinking and acting, and they'd shrug their shoulders and laugh.

The truth was, Ty was an outsider here. He was an American. Nineteen years old, he had grown up in Wilmington, Delaware. He had lived most of his life with his mom and his two young sisters on the corner of Eighth Street and Monroe. It was a tough part of Wilmington. Row houses were sandwiched together every which way, people packed and stacked inside of them. Crack vials crunched underfoot on the sidewalks.

Across the street from their house, in one direction, was a vacant lot – they held dog fights there every Thursday night in good weather. You could hardly call them 'fights'. They were warm-ups, training bouts for the pit bulls. Basically, the owners picked up strays during the week – mixed-breed cocker spaniels, collies, whatever happened to be roaming around the streets – and fed them to the real killer dogs for the entertainment of the neighbours. It got the bloodlust going, and not just for the dogs. Meanwhile, the cops would cruise by in their cars and wink at it.

Across the street from the house in the other direction was a liquor store. The owner was from Pakistan. The locals called him 'the boss man'. He was a hard little man who kept himself, his family, and his product, locked away behind bullet-proof glass. He made no effort to hide the fact that he didn't trust black people. When you went in there, you walked up to the glass, peered at the bottles on the shelves, then made your order into a speaker. You slid your money through a narrow slot. Then the boss man put the bottle on a carousel, and spun it around to you. The carousel was so small that if you bought a six-pack of beer, it wouldn't fit. The boss man had to take out each beer, and spin them around to you one at a time.

From his earliest teenage years, Ty had been in trouble in Wilmington. Assault, vandalism, breaking and entering, stalking – the shrinks said he had an anger problem. He'd been in and out of the juvie lock-up so many times they practically gave him his own key to the place. His mom worked long hours just to keep her family above water and she seemed, not necessarily happy, but relieved, when he was locked down.

'At least I know where you are,' she said to him during one Saturday visit.

Over time, he had graduated to bigger things – he became a hold-up man, and not just any kind of hold-ups. He and his little crew specialised in holding up the crack dealers. It seemed like poetic justice – the dealers were fucking up the neighbourhood with their shit. And it had gone real well, until it didn't. Then it all went very, very wrong.

Now he was here on the island, a refugee from his former life, living with his old grandmom, and making do on the skimpy cheques his mother sent down every month. He'd been choking back his pride for so long that he had almost forgotten what it meant to stand on his own two feet like a man. But now he was remembering.

There was no way he could go back to Wilmington. Life here was a dead end. He realised as he paced through the fields and then down the road towards town, that the only way forward was by taking drastic action.

In the hotel room, room 409 at the Flamingo Inn, Pamela took a long shower – God, it had been weeks since she'd actually had a shower with this kind of water pressure. Still, it wasn't quite what she'd been looking forward to. The water was lukewarm – there was some kind of electric light switch gizmo attached to the shower-head with wires. She was afraid to touch it, so suffered the water at room temperature. When she let the water flow into her mouth, she was surprised to find out it was salty – she was bathing in seawater. They must have diverted water from the ocean into these hotel-room shower stalls.

It was nothing like the place they stayed the last time she took a real shower. They had come down the coast from Maine in a stolen power cruiser, moving fast, rarely stopping except to gas up and get food. The power cruiser was everything the *Saucy Jack* was not – sleek, fast, aerodynamic and cramped. Smoke must have stayed awake at the helm for days in a row, Cruz standing with him, chain-smoking, keeping him awake. They drank cup after cup of coffee.

The two men rarely spoke, and when they did, it was just a few syllables, uttered in hushed tones. 'We gotta get rid of this fucking thing,' Pamela heard Smoke say once. 'So keep going,' Cruz responded. 'It's all we can do.'

Pamela and Lola stayed below mostly, sleeping, playing cards, swaying with the movements of the boat. It was cold upstairs, there was no one to talk to up there, and there was nothing to see but open gunmetal water and mist. Below deck, sometimes Pamela and Lola would just stare into each other's eyes, or hold hands across the table. Their lives had changed – had ended, in fact – without warning and with lightning speed. Pamela guessed that during those first few days, she and Lola were in shock.

One evening, they noticed the boat had slowed considerably, and Pamela went up top to find out what was going on. They were passing a tall, conical lighthouse, red on the bottom and white on top, which was sitting on an outcropping of rock. Land was in the near distance, with glass and steel buildings perched not far from the water.

'Where are we?' Pamela said.

'Coming into Stamford Harbour,' Smoke said, his mouth clenched around a cigar. Black rings hung below his eyes. He looked like a haunted man, almost like the man in that painting, *The Scream*, by Edvard Munch. Pamela could picture him wrapping his arms around his head and having a complete breakdown right in front of her eyes.

'Connecticut,' he said. 'There's a restaurant here where we can pull in and have dinner. We can park the boat there while we're inside. After that, you three are going to get a hotel room for the night, I'm going to take off in the boat again, and we'll all meet up in New York tomorrow morning.'

'Why? What's going on?'

'We gotta get rid of this boat, and tonight's the night. I have another boat on City Island in the Bronx. It belongs to me, and I'm going to get it. When you folks make it to New York, we'll all climb on board and keep moving.'

'Smoke, you look exhausted. I don't think you should go on by yourself.' Pamela turned to Cruz. Cruz didn't look much better than Smoke – maybe a little further from a breakdown, but that was all. 'Cruz?'

Cruz nodded, a cigarette dangling from his mouth. 'It's OK. It's going to work. He'll make it.'

The four of them had a nice dinner that Pamela barely remembered. The restaurant had a seafaring theme, with fishing nets and big wooden wheels and paintings of sailing ships on the walls. It was beyond surreal to sit at a table and calmly order dinner from a waitress. There was very little conversation, and Pamela couldn't recall what anyone ate, including herself.

After dinner, Smoke left on the boat. Lola wanted to go with him, but he wouldn't let her. She was crying in the taxicab to the hotel. They pulled up in the gleaming circle in front of the hotel, and as they climbed out of the car, Cruz handed Pamela a slip of paper.

She held it like it might have a disease. 'What's this?'

'It's the marina on City Island where we're meeting tomorrow. See

93

that train station over there?' He pointed across a wide boulevard, with an elevated stretch of highway running through the middle of it. Sure, she could see the train station.

'That's the train in to New York. You take the southbound local, and get off in the Bronx at Fordham. From there, you take a taxicab to City Island. Give the driver this address. It's easy.' Then he kissed her on the cheek – cold, that. He didn't even hug her goodbye.

'What are you going to do?' she said.

He had already turned his back and was walking away towards the boulevard. He glanced briefly over his shoulder. 'I have some things to take care of. Don't worry. I'll see you tomorrow.'

The hotel itself was a Marriott, a beautiful one. The ceiling in the lobby was three storeys high, with giant windows, ornate furnishings, and an old train station clock tower in the middle of it all. They booked into a deluxe suite, made a pot of coffee, and took their cups with them to the roof deck, where they leaned on the railing and gazed out together on the night-time skyline of Stamford. Later, Pamela would take a long, hot shower, the jets on full, pounding and strafing her skin until it was bright red, and the bathroom was filled with steam. It was the best shower she had ever taken.

And part of what made it great was the uncertainty. As she stood on the roof with Lola, exhausted from days on the boat, shell-shocked from witnessing wanton cruelty, death and destruction, it seemed like they had come to the end of the line, maybe the end of everything. A cold breeze blew their hair back.

'Do you think we'll ever see them again?' she said.

Lola looked at her, tears rolling down her cheeks again. 'You know? I don't have any idea what's going to happen next.'

Cruz was glad to be on solid ground.

They'd found a room at a small hotel on the island, and Cruz waited while Pamela showered. The room seemed OK – feeble air-conditioner mounted in the window and trying mightily to dispel the humidity in the room, funky bright orange walls, wicker furniture, a lumpy double bed, and a decent view of the bay from a tiny deck. Cruz mused as he stared out at the water.

Two weeks ago, they had been in New York. They had stopped there to ditch the first boat and pick up the *Saucy Jack* – Dugan had kept the *Saucy Jack* in dry storage at a boatyard on City Island. Get this – he had paid the place for *five years* of storage, in advance. Locked inside a drawer in the galley of the *Jack*, just off the main cabin, inside this big boat that sat on a shelf for three and a half years, Dugan had kept another identity waiting for him, a passport and birth certificate in the name of Ed Aldrin. Cruz had to hand it to him – Dugan was as slippery as moss on wet rocks.

Cruz had left the girls at the hotel in Stamford and taken the train into Manhattan. He went alone – he had some business to attend to himself.

Late that night, gun drawn, he entered his former apartment at 72nd and Central Park West, right near the Strawberry Fields memorial to John Lennon. His bachelor pad was a big place on the ninth floor, with wall-to-wall carpeting, high windows, and a view of the park. When he came in, he found the front door closed, but unlocked. His employers had been there ahead of him.

Of course. They knew where he lived. The place wasn't demolished, not obviously ransacked, but they'd gone through everything. The windows were open, and at some point it had rained all over the floor. The drawers were open, stuff moved around. Stuff was taken out of the closets, boxes open. A couple of thousand dollars in mad money was missing from the drawer in his bedroom. OK, they could have it.

In the kitchen, there was a drawer where he kept plastic bags, some candles, a box of wooden matches in case of power outage, takeout menus, some fortune cookies he'd never bothered to eat, and a bunch of other shit. In behind it all was a key ring. He slithered his hand to the back of the drawer – the keys were still there. Sure, what would the keys mean to anybody, even if someone found them? A skeleton key, an old ignition key to an Acura he'd got rid of eight years ago, a MasterLock key, and what else?

Oh yeah, this key to the apartment he kept on the sixth floor of this very building. He took the stairs down there, watching, waiting, being very careful. Entered the pad – a simple one-room studio, with a kitchen, dining area, and a view of an airshaft and fire escapes out the back window. The place was sealed up tight – it felt close and smelled musty in there. Nobody'd been here in a while. That was good. Real good. Inside a manila envelope, which itself was tucked at the bottom of a cardboard box, in the back of the closet, behind boxes and boxes of junk Cruz'd bought simply to have something to pile in there – a hair dryer, an old television set, tools and electric hardware of various kinds – was a man named Luis Figueroa. Luis had a New Jersey driver's licence, a passport, and safe deposit boxes at three Manhattan banks.

Cruz went to two of those banks – he saved one bank for later, in case he ever came back here to New York, and needed access to some fast cash – and emptied the contents. He took nearly $150,000 in tens, twenties and fifties, and twenty gold Britannia coins – each one weighing exactly one ounce.

He had stopped himself then, just before hailing a cab and taking the ride back to City Island. He didn't need to go back out there. He didn't need to get on a boat again with Smoke Dugan. Nobody knew about Luis Figueroa. Luis could simply disappear west from here, then turn up on the coast of Mexico, along the waterfront in the West End of Vancouver, or strolling through the Ginza in Tokyo. Luis had money, and could go anywhere. Cruz did have claim to more than a million dollars waiting in a boat on City Island – his half of Dugan's big score. But he didn't really need the money. If he went back, the money wasn't why.

It was Pamela. He'd never been with a woman like her before — it seemed that maybe he'd never been with a real woman, or even a real person before. Until Pamela, he had just hired women as the need arose. These women didn't talk, or if they did, it was background chatter, television, celebrity superstars, nothing. Empty air.

Pamela had ideas, and Cruz liked something about that. Granted, she talked some crazy shit sometimes. One day on the boat, maybe a day out from Maine, she had given Cruz a test — This after all that crazy bullshit in Portland — five people dead, car wrecks, explosions — she had literally come on deck with a couple of sheets of paper and a pencil. It was a dot test — you read the question then filled in the dot next to the answer that you thought fit best. The possible answers were 'yes' and 'no'. Cruz had never seen anything like it.

'What am I supposed to do with this?' he said.

'Take it.'

In the old days, Cruz might have killed somebody who stuck a test under his nose. That is, if somebody even had the *cojones* to give him a test. But Cruz hadn't killed anybody in weeks, and he was beginning to think he might never kill again. Certainly, he wasn't going to kill Pamela. So instead of killing someone, Cruz started answering the questions.

You like to be engaged in an active and fast-paced job.

'Jesus, what is this?'

'Cruz, just take the test.'

You are usually the first to react to a sudden event: the telephone ringing or an unexpected question.

He glanced at Dugan, who sat at the helm, staring at the sea and smirking.

'What the fuck are you smiling at?'

Dugan looked at him. 'Hey, Cruz, take the test.' He glanced at his watch. 'Time's almost up.'

Strict observance of the established rules is likely to prevent a good outcome.

Cruz answered the questions – seventy-five of them. It was a psychological test, designed to gauge his personality. When he finished, Pamela graded it like a schoolteacher.

'There're no right or wrong answers. It's all just about how you are, and how you like to respond to things. You get a designation based on your answers, and it helps explain why you do some of the things you do.'

'OK.'

'See, these answers show you're an introvert. You don't like to be around a lot of people. I'm an introvert, too. That's interesting, right? We're compatible there. But you're also very careful – you like to plan ahead, and you make decisions after gathering a lot of information. That's where we're most likely to clash and have trouble. I have a little of that in me, but I can also be spontaneous, almost impulsive. You're meticulous and ordered. You'd think I'd be that way, working in a library, but a lot of times I have a short attention span, and so I just get frustrated and throw my hands in the air. See what I mean?'

Cruz shook his head to clear his mind of it. This was exactly the kind of straight-world bullshit that he didn't like – but from Pamela, it was ... well, cute. For the first time in a long time, Cruz felt strongly about someone. He wasn't going to say it was love because he didn't know what it was. He could leave Pamela behind, sure he could. But he would worry about her. She would be on the run, on a boat with Dugan and Lola. Dugan and Lola had their weapons, but could Cruz trust them to keep Pamela safe?

Maybe not. *Probably not.* They just weren't that good at it.

So he took the taxi. When he got out to City Island, the first thing he did when he climbed on to the *Saucy Jack* was to go up the stairs on to the deck where Pamela, Lola and Dugan were sitting in the fall sunshine. Cruz put the briefcase with the money on the deck table.

'What's that?' Dugan said.

'About a hundred and seventy grand, including some gold. If we're really gonna be splitting up the money, then add this to the pot.'

The whole move, from getting back on the boat, to handing over a chunk of his life savings, was a decisive break with the past. Cruz had always been an independent operator. Now he was on a team.

Now, weeks later, in a strangely coloured hotel room on Saint Mark's island, he noticed that the shower was no longer running. He turned to look just as Pamela came out of the bathroom, a towel wrapped around her. He realised, for the first time today, that this woman and her friend Lola had saved his life yesterday. Shit, he really was in a fog. Pamela saw him staring, smiled and let the towel drop to the floor.

Cruz was on the team, all right. And he was glad he'd made the right decision.

Ty had excellent vision – the eyes of an eagle, his mom used to say. His eyes were like everything else about him: damn near perfect. He was a superior specimen of a superior race. Tall, strong and fast, practically from birth. Quick reflexes. A sharp mind. He could put on muscle so fast that sometimes, after a long workout on the weight bench behind his grandmom's house, his muscles got so swelled up they looked like over-packed sausages. All this, and good looking besides.

He smiled. Yeah, he had a lot going on.

He stood in the back of his skiff, on a raised platform, guiding the boat through the shallows near some mangrove trees with a long fibre-glass push pole, like a fisherman would do. This pole, twelve feet in length, was the longer of two poles he kept on the boat. The shorter one was only five feet – and made of hard wood – not much use for pushing the boat along, but a perfect weapon for stick fighting. Hey, you never knew where, or when, the shit might go down.

With his T-shirt and sunglasses on, and his hair tucked up under his straw hat, and in these new circumstances, Ty couldn't imagine how they would recognise him. They had no reason to even think he would be here. He was stationed around the far edge of a curve in the shore-line from the visitor docks, waiting for them to appear. They wouldn't notice him, but with his eyes he couldn't fail to notice them – young black woman, a beauty, in a boat with an old white man. Ty just hoped he was right, and that they came out to play like he thought they would. He'd been here a while already – they seemed to be taking for ever.

Speak of the devil – here they came now. Two hundred yards away, motoring out into the bay in a small zodiac. The white boy gave it the gas and the zodiac zoomed forward, then to the left, heading in Ty's direction. Ty dropped from the platform, stashed his push pole, went to the folded-up outboard motor, and released it down into the water. He yanked the cord and the engine roared into life, belching exhaust. Now the fun and games would begin.

The one thing about island life – maybe the only thing – that Ty really enjoyed was riding around in this boat. He loved to open up the throttle and let it rip. Low to the water, moving fast, the vast blue sky above him, the wind in his face. This was living. If nothing ever went right again, at least he had moments like these.

The zodiac was faster than his boat, but that was OK. He wasn't trying to catch them – he was only looking to see where they would go. The charade was that he was a local fisherman out on the water. He was moving away from them, and they were coming up behind him. After a few minutes he let them pass, then turned right and cut on a diagonal across their wake.

He kept moving, behind them now and to their right. He let them go, putting distance between them. He didn't need to stay too close. He could still see them clearly and there was nothing but wide-open views out here.

They were headed toward Deadman's Island – that much was obvious. Deadman's was little more than a wide strip of sand, some scrub grasses and palm trees, and whatever junk washed up on its shoreline. Nobody lived there, and with good reason – at high tide, the island barely existed.

To add to its charm, local legend had the place haunted. Back in the 1800s, two landed gentlemen from Saint Mark's had gone to the island for a pistol duel over a lady's honour. The loser died where he fell, his blood mingling with the sand. Now his ghost forever walked that tiny strip of beach.

Ty slowed his skiff. He watched as far away, the tiny zodiac pulled up to a medium-sized motor yacht maybe halfway between here and Deadman's. There were a few other boats out that way, but they had all given each other a little distance for the sake of privacy.

He turned his rudder and headed in that direction. With a little luck, and a pinch of bravado, he figured he could coast right up to them, board their boat, and have the situation well in hand before they even knew what was happening.

The girl had some moves – that much was true. But this morning he had gone easy on her. He wouldn't make that mistake twice.

They were bickering by the time they reached the docks. The sun was hot and the walk down from the hills was long. Smoke limped heavily the last half of the walk, sweat pouring from his face and soaking his T-shirt. They had barely said a word to each other as they left the island and rode out here in the inflatable.

Now, as they pulled up to the *Saucy Jack*, and Smoke tied the dinghy to the bigger boat, they weren't speaking at all. Lola could have tied up the dinghy, but didn't even bother to offer. Smoke would insist that he do it – he always had to do everything, because he did it better. He would never say, 'I do it better', but the meaning was understood. Paternalistic – that was a word that might fit. Smoke spent a lot of time acting like he was somebody's father.

As Lola climbed on to the *Jack* with the plastic bags full of greasy spare parts, she realised she was tired – tired of Smoke, tired of this whole set-up, tired of everything. She tried to give him the benefit of the doubt, tried to summon from her memory a time, not so long ago, when they were happy together, but right now she couldn't picture it.

They should have waited a day before going on to the island. That much was clear. Neither of them had really slept last night – Smoke not at all – and they had pushed it too far by going to get the parts today. The heat could take the vinegar out of anybody.

Lola looked at Smoke as he climbed on to the boat. He was totally exhausted, maybe on the verge of collapse – face drained of colour, eyes drained of energy, entire body wobbly and not navigating the gap between the dinghy and the boat very well. Lola felt the weight of the bags in her shoulders – these things were heavy. It was hard to believe he had dragged them as far as he had.

'Where do you want the bags?' she said.

He barely glanced at her. 'Just set them down anywhere, if you don't mind. I think I'm gonna take that nap now. What are you planning to do?'

She shrugged, looked around. Was there an invitation hidden in there to join him in the bed? If so, she wasn't interested. She felt the sun on her neck, and the heat of it decided her. 'I think I'm going to take a swim.'

That stopped him. 'Alone? I don't think you should swim alone. It's not safe.'

'OK, Dad.'

He looked up and finally made eye contact. He frowned, the lines and creases in his face suddenly as deep as slot canyons. 'I only say it because I care about you.'

She tried to hold her tongue, but it didn't quite work. There was a lot on her mind, and now some of it began to spill out. 'That, and you're the one who always knows what's best.' She raised her hands, like he was holding a gun on her. 'Listen, I'm sensing a whole gender thing going on with you these days. OK? A whole male, father knows best thing. And I don't like it.' Even that, when she said it, wasn't really what she wanted to say to him.

'Liar!' she wanted to say. 'You fucking liar. You got a whole bunch of people killed, and you nearly got me killed, and now I'm trapped on this fucking boat with you, all over some lousy money you stole. How can I ever trust you again?' That's what she wanted to say, but didn't.

'You're female,' Smoke said. 'I'm male. Those are indeed genders. I also have opinions. So I'm a male with opinions. Whether they're the best ones or not, I can't say.' He raised a hand and waved bye-bye. 'Nighty-night.'

'You should probably drink some water,' she said.

He was already going below deck. 'When I wake up,' he said, and she watched the back of his head go down the narrow stairs.

Well, terrific. Lola was tired, but not so tired that she wanted to lie down with Smoke Dugan. She cast about for more ideas, and only one thing came to mind. She could change into her bathing suit, jump into the water and take a quick swim. OK, she wasn't the greatest swimmer in the world, and maybe it wasn't smart to swim alone, especially in open water like this. But it was a hot day, the water looked unbelievably refreshing, and she wouldn't stray far from the boat. It didn't matter what Smoke said – a quick dip would probably do wonders for her.

She trooped down the stairs after him to get her bathing suit. Smoke wouldn't like it, but that was fine. He could wonder, he could worry, but Lola was a big girl, and she was going swimming.

Stone stared intently at the woman and the man sitting a few tables away.

He was back on the restaurant patio, alone this time, the last of an afternoon lunch in front of him. He had paid Roxana the fifty he owed her, then given her a hundred-dollar bill as a tip, and sent her home. He told her he wanted to be alone tonight – maybe he would have Macho send her over tomorrow. *Don't call us, we'll call you.* The truth was, when next he saw the pint-sized tycoon, Stone was going to order himself somebody new. He liked Roxana, he really did. But hey, life was short, and they weren't exactly married.

Stone realised now that he had been watching the couple for a while – much longer than his conscious mind had been aware. He hadn't turned towards them. No. Stone was too slick for that. He just watched him out of his peripheral vision. His eyes were hidden behind black reflector sunglasses, and since he didn't look directly their way, they couldn't know he was watching them.

The woman was a pretty white woman, probably in her mid-twenties. Light brown hair flowing down, big sunglasses, shorts and halter top – the standard tourist get-up. But it wasn't the woman that caught his eye, actually. It was the man.

He was a skinny guy, razor-sharp features, dark, Hispanic, Panama-hat shielding his face. He was also wearing sunglasses. Had about a day's growth of beard, but looked like the kind of guy who probably grew it in scraggly and less than uniform.

The guy was setting off alarm bells for Stone like crazy. It was the scar – the guy had a long scar running down the side of his face. It didn't tan well, so the discolouration made it stand out in sharp relief.

Stone could feel his brain scanning through the databanks. He stared and stared. Finally, he hit the jackpot – a morning in the Florida Keys years before. He was in his late-twenties, living in a gigantic, airy house on an island just below Marathon. The place was built with giants in mind – cathedral ceilings, wide hallways with double doors everywhere, eight-foot bay windows with sweeping views of lush greenery and water. It sat on an inlet, and Stone used to motor out from there and dive the reef and the wrecks just offshore. The house belonged to Stone's friend and mentor, Bunker, a grizzled forty-something veteran of the Navy SEAL Teams. Bunker had a small plane at a nearby airstrip, and they were making runs together – Mexico, Panama, Colombia – bringing packages back for some people in New York. They were doing a brisk business.

That particular morning, Stone was up early, in the huge kitchen of this fantastic house, making himself some eggs. He was hung over – maybe even still a little drunk – from the night before. He had taken a few tokes from a joint, so he was definitely a little high. He was lost in thought, just sort of looking down at these eggs while they sizzled in oil in a rounded iron skillet. When he looked up, a man was standing there – a small man, Hispanic, with a scar down the side of his face. He wore a windbreaker jacket and slacks. His eyes were on fire.

'Phone for you,' the man said.

The phone hanging on the wall started to ring.

Stone picked up the phone and learned that life had abruptly changed.

And when next he blinked, he realised a long time had passed and he was still staring at that couple at the other table. It was Saint Mark's, it was a bright and sunny day, the light dappling in the turquoise water of the bay, and he was sitting on the patio of his favourite restaurant.

Cruz. The name of the man at the table was Cruz, he was a murderer for hire and, a long time ago, he had accepted a contract on Stone's good friend Bunker. Stone didn't think about what to do with this new information. He just acted. He picked up his drink, got up from his table and walked over to theirs.

Cruz and Pamela sat at their table, relaxing in the sun and gazing out to sea. It was early afternoon, and they were out for lunch at a patio restaurant.

Things were better now that they were off the boat. In fact, things were quite lovely here on the island. They'd had the first relaxing morning since they left Portland. The bed was lumpy and creaky, but they had made it work. They'd made love and fallen asleep in each other's arms. Ahhh, that was nice. No boat. No Dugan. Afterwards, they had lounged in bed for a little while, chatting about flying to Belize together – Cruz thought of it as a good way to put some distance between them, Smoke Dugan, and any more pursuit. But then Pamela had jumped on the idea, telling Cruz about the fantastic Mayan ruins she had always wanted to see, both in Belize and in nearby Guatemala. So Belize was looking better and better as a destination.

Cruz was nearly desperate to get off the boat – he figured that he and Dugan were just about ready to claw each other to pieces. Actually, the way it would go down, if it did, was Cruz would chop Dugan in the neck, then throw the old man's body overboard. At least, that's how it would have gone in the old days. The whole thing was trouble. Cruz didn't want to kill Pamela's friends. Friends? Yes, of course. If he killed Dugan, he'd have to kill Lola too, wouldn't he? No way would karate-kicker Lola stand idly by for a dead Dugan.

Cruz decided to put it out of his mind.

In any case, it was OK to stay right here in low-rent Saint Mark's for a while, and let the whole thing blow right over. Cruz had some more money stashed in a bank in Grand Cayman, and they could take their time getting there. He and Pamela had a million and a quarter stake in the money that was on the boat, and if they did go to Belize, that money would last a long time. Meanwhile, if any problem did come along, he and Pamela were armed, and he had taught both Pamela and Lola how to shoot. Dugan hadn't shown the slightest interest.

A man moved towards them. Cruz took in the guy instantly. Tall guy, long hair tied back in a ponytail, aviator sunglasses, muscle shirt, tattoo on one well-muscled bicep. Cruz could read it – four letters: RLTW. He had seen that tattoo before, or one just like it. The letters stood for *Rangers Lead The Way*.

Carrying a red fruity drink, the guy was weaving the slightest bit. No doubt he was coming to their table – he was staring at Cruz with something like a grin. It was like the grin of a shark – the threat was implied in all those rows of teeth.

'Shit,' Cruz said, 'here comes something.'

Pamela looked up from her menu. 'What? Where?'

Cruz pointed with the slightest gesture of his head. 'Right there.'

Pamela turned and made a small startled sound, like the screech of a quiet church mouse when she saw big Butch Stone bearing down on them. Cruz remembered Stone now – of course he did. He was ten feet away, then five. Cruz glanced back at Pamela and was alarmed to see her hand in her bag.

'Babe?'

'Ready,' she said. 'I'm fucking ready for anything.'

Then Stone was there. 'Mind if I sit down?'

'Pamela, wait.'

Pamela yanked her gun out of the bag and levelled it at Stone. Cruz heard her put on her best Hollywood cowboy voice: 'One move and I blow your fucking head off.'

Stone heard a gasp, but he didn't turn around. Suddenly, that low-level restaurant chatter died away as people nearby noticed that a tall man was standing near a table where a young woman was holding a gun on him.

'Say, Cruz,' Stone said, 'who's the moll?'

'The one who's going to shoot you full of holes,' the woman said. Her hands were shaking a bit, just enough to tell Stone she was the kind who would do it – she would pull the trigger prematurely. By mistake.

Stone didn't feel much of anything about the gun. In his mind, he merely identified it. It was a Glock – the smaller version of their popular semi-auto, the ones the big-city cops often used. More concealable, maybe a little better for the girlfriend's small hand. Stone looked at Cruz. It was almost funny, the thought that some trigger-happy little girl might blow his insides all over somebody's meal. No, it was actually funny – considering how he'd just spent six months in Iraq, had taken fire on at least two dozen occasions, had wiped a good friend's brain matter off his own boots, and yet hadn't got a scratch.

Stone decided to make an appeal to common sense. 'Cruz, if I wanted to kill you, would I walk up to you in broad daylight? In a restaurant? With all these nice people around? Who, by the way, are all watching us right now as the most interesting thing that has happened today, and probably during their entire trip.'

Cruz's hand reached over and gently took the gun from the girl. 'OK, Babe. It's OK. No problem here. We're going for meticulous and ordered right now, OK?' The gun disappeared into a red designer bag lying on the floor by the girl's feet.

Cruz gestured to the chair opposite them. 'Why don't you sit down?'

Stone glanced around. A few people were staring. Most people were trying not to, but were watching from the corners of their eyes nonetheless.

'Show's over, folks,' Stone said conversationally to the four people at the table nearest them. 'We're police officers back in the real world. Just a little prank among friends. Will you please tell those other people there that the show's over? Thanks very much.'

Stone sat down and rested his elbows on the table. He leaned in to talk with his new friends. 'Occupational hazard, Cruz. You go away on a little vacation, especially in the sunnier climes, and somebody from the life is bound to turn up. If it's the wrong person, it could end up ruining your good time.'

'How long's it been?' Cruz said.

'Ten years,' Stone said. 'Ten years since you iced my friend Bunker and I couldn't do anything about it.'

Cruz nodded slowly. 'How are you?'

'Great until a minute ago. Just got back from a stint in the Raq. They paid me a quarter of a mil. I was feeling real good. Got my own little island here, then you and the Mrs arrived.'

'Occupational hazard,' Cruz said and shrugged.

'As I think I just mentioned.'

'Still nursing a beef over that Bunker thing, Stone?'

Stone leaned back, smiled, gave him the expansive look. 'Cruz, I was young then. I didn't really know how things worked. Somebody pops my friend, naturally I want to pop the guy back, right? But New York tells me it's a no-no. You can't touch Cruz. Cruz is made of gold.'

Stone glanced at the girl, who was drinking all this in with big doe eyes. 'Oh, I'm sorry. You do know what Mr Goodbar here does for a living, don't you?'

'*Did* for a living,' she said with a sickly smile.

'Truth be told,' Cruz said calmly, 'it sounds like it's right on top for you. That's not a good thing.'

Stone smiled again, shook his head. 'I tell you, it's not like that. I've seen a lot of men die since then. Business is business. We're all good Nazis, and we do what we're told. It was just the sudden shock of seeing you, that's all.'

'Well, we won't be here long,' Cruz said. 'So you won't have to look at me. We've been thinking of getting off this island and moving on. In fact, we're leaving pretty soon.'

'Don't go on my account.'

'Not until we've had our lunch, anyway,' Cruz said.

This was the shit, right here.

Ty cruised up slow, cut the engine, and then drifted in towards the big blue yacht. Here was the little zodiac, so he knew it was theirs. He could feel his heart beating, pounding in his chest, the way it used to do in the locker room right before a high school basketball game, with the crowd just upstairs in the gym, chanting and pounding their feet on the floorboards of the bleachers, waiting for big Ty Weathers and the boys to burst out and put on a show; the way it also used to do when a few years later, three of them would be crowded in a narrow hallway, guns drawn, right before they busted down an apartment door on a stick-up job. Ty had a word for how he felt at moments like these – the word was 'explosive'.

He scanned the boat: nobody was up top. Not a soul on any deck.

Good God, was he gonna catch 'em downstairs in the bedroom, doing the wild thing? He could only hope so. He grinned wide at the very thought of it.

He tied up his skiff in five seconds flat – a couple of quick loops. They weren't giving style points today. He glanced at the horizon one last time – another yacht out there, maybe a hundred yards away, nobody visible. It was a hot, sleepy day, a good day to stay inside, have a few drinks, and take a nap.

He picked up his satchel with the machete and the rope inside, and slung it across his shoulder. Then he grabbed his pole – the wooden five footer – and leapt lightly on to the big boat. His feet barely made a sound as he landed on the swim deck. The pole was rock solid in his hands – he could feel how smooth and hard it was.

Next: up a few stairs to the main deck, then down a few more to the cabins. Fast, he had to do it, and silent, scanning everywhere, find them in their room together.

Up the first set of stairs, taking them two at a time. He moved sideways to the stairwell leading below deck. He waited there a few seconds, listening for the smallest sound, sensing for the slightest movement. He felt like a cat on the hunt.

Give me something. Give me a little gift.

Holy shit, and here it came right now. The sweet girl was coming up the steps wearing a little white bikini, so bright against her brown skin, her sexy Nubian body packed in there nice and tight. Her eyes were cast downward, looking at her feet. She didn't even see Ty standing here, waiting for her. She looked tired, or maybe sad. Maybe even a little bit lonesome.

Beautiful. Come here, girl.

Ty moved back one pace. He gripped the pole with two hands in the centre, holding it horizontal.

She reached the top step and came across the threshold.

Ty stepped in with the stick, bringing the right side around hard.

Wham – he caught her on the side of the head. He brought the left side around. Wham – right across the face. She dropped, knocked out cold before she even hit the deck.

Pole-axed! The bitch was fucking pole-axed!

He stood over her, breathing heavy. He waited a full minute as his breathing gradually slowed. She was down there below him, sprawled out sideways. Damn, she looked good. Were we gonna have some fun today? Yessir, you betcha.

He went into his bag and pulled out the machete. He took it out of its sheath, and waited some more. After another moment, her eyes started to flutter. Then they opened. That was his cue.

He reached down and grabbed her by the hair. 'Come on, bitch. Let's go see your little friend.'

He yanked her to her feet and dragged her down the stairs behind him. She was uncoordinated, still stunned from the lumps he gave her. She didn't make a sound. He knew that drill. She'd come around, by and by. Probably wouldn't be feeling too well when she did.

He entered the first cabin he came to, and here was the old boy, on his back, eyes closed, mouth wide open. He was breathing deeply, but not, Ty noted, snoring. That was a good character trait – after spending years of his life in dormitories for juvenile delinquents, rows of beds, sometimes two dozen boys to a room, Ty didn't like people who snored.

He let the girl slide quietly to the floor and approached the side of the bed. He put the machete in his left hand, his weaker hand. Then he made a fist with his right and reared back. One . . . Two . . .

THREE.

He pounded that face, hitting the sleeping man hard. Three times, four times, five times. The man was awake now, eyes open, startled, moving, struggling. Ty took the machete in both hands and held the blade to the man's neck. He watched the man's eyes go WIDE. What an effect. Ty probably should have had a machete back in Wilmington. It was a shame he never thought of it.

'If you don't wanna die,' Ty said, 'you're gonna do exactly what I say.'

The man mumbled something.

'What's that? Speak up!'

'There's money on the boat,' the man said. 'A lot of it. If you kill either one of us, I promise you won't see a dime.'

Money on the boat? A lot of money? Well, well, well . . . A day that had started out sour just kept getting better and better.

'Brother, I'm not here to kill anyone. That was never my intention at all.'

Ty kept the machete to the man's neck with his right hand. With his left, he unslung the bag from his shoulder and pulled the rope out of it. It was time to get down to business.

It was craaazy, seeing Cruz here.

Stone paced down the dirt road that paralleled the shoreline, towards his little cabana. A lot of time had passed, a lot of things had gone on in the intervening years, and yet Bunker could have died earlier this morning – that's how fresh it was. Stone remembered how afraid of Cruz he was that day. Twenty-seven years old then, a combat veteran, a murderer, a drug smuggler, but when he looked into Cruz's eyes, he saw the fires of hell, and he was afraid.

It's just the way it was – Cruz conjured up strong emotions for Stone. Cruz was a part of his life he thought he'd put in the past, but as soon as he saw him, all the old rage, all the old frustration, was right there on the surface again. And a new feeling joined them this time – curiosity.

Did Cruz seem the slightest bit jumpy? Maybe he did. It was impossible to punch through that old boy's crust, if memory served. And the girl? Forget it. She was wired for sound – you don't pull a gun in front of the citizenry unless you think it's about to go down RIGHT NOW. You don't draw in a situation like that unless it's draw or die. She was inexperienced, and she had shown her cards. And what she had shown was she expected the dance to start at any time.

Interesting. Very interesting.

Suddenly Macho appeared from a sandy, overgrown alley between two cabanas, and began walking in step with Stone. Macho took huge, exaggerated strides to keep even. He smiled his gigantic smile – the kid was an irrepressible optimist.

And always on the make. He dove right in, his voice lilting and musical, putting a little extra island into it for Stone's benefit.

'Hey, Stone, you wanna girl tonight? Roxana, she got the boom-boom, ah?' Macho held his hands out and mimicked the curves of Roxana's big butt. 'Yah, mon, real nice. You want her tonight? You like her, right? What is it? You want some smoke? Tell me, general, what's up?'

'I don't know,' Stone said. 'I'm thinking about trading Roxana in for a newer model. Maybe one of those little skinny girls. Variety is the spice of life, and all that. You know what I'm saying?'

Macho's smile faltered, but for only a second. He looked vaguely uncertain, then the smile came back on full-tilt. 'Oh, yeah. We got a saying on the island. What sweeten the billy goat's mouth will bitter his behind. You know that one?'

Stone glanced out at the shimmering water. Looking at the kid gave him an idea. 'Nope. Never heard it before. Say Macho, let's worry about all that later. I want you to do a little job for me. It's a secret job, real cloak and dagger. Like a spy. Think you can handle it?'

Macho flashed that award-winning smile. 'I can handle anything. I thought you was down with that by now.'

Macho sauntered into a little gift shop near the marina. When he came in, a little bell attached to a string jingled. The two aisles of the shop were packed with crap – conch shells, We Be Jammin' T-shirts, flip-flops, postcards and cheap snorkel masks. The proprietor was an old man Macho knew well – years before, a long time ago it seemed, Macho had been business partners with the man. Macho could sell anything, and the old man took full advantage of that fact.

Nowadays, the old man frowned on Macho's new direction.

'Christmas,' Macho said as he came in. 'Fresh flowers today?'

'Every day,' the old man said.

Macho went over to the flower case and picked through the meagre selection. He took a bouquet that wasn't too wilted. Ten dollars for them. They were worth half that amount. 'I'll pay you in ten minutes.'

'You don't have credit here no more,' the old man said. 'Every day the bucket goes to the well. One day the bottom falls out.'

Macho put up five fingers. 'Five minutes. If I'm not back, I'll pay you double.'

The man waved Macho out of the store.

Macho walked up the dock with the bouquet in his hand. His mark was about twenty yards further up, but he couldn't look like he was in a hurry. The device Stone had given him weighed heavily in his pocket. It was a small black box with two strips of adhesive glue on the back. It would take Macho's best sleight of hand to get it out of the pocket and stuck to the back of the boat just above the waterline, where it needed to go. Macho had had a book of magic tricks some time ago, and had learned a few of them, but had gotten bored of it and given the book to a young boy who lived nearby. He half wished he had kept up with it.

A fat white man with thinning hair and a greying beard was hosing down the foredeck of a thirty-foot sailboat. Macho approached him, asked him if he wanted to buy some flowers. He did it in a good strong voice, so that anyone nearby might hear. The man waved him away with hardly more than a grunt — rare for Macho, he took no for an answer from that man.

He approached a smaller, thin, dark man who was untying the lines from a dinghy. The man had a scar on the side of his face, which stood out almost in white against his brown Hispanic skin. There was a pretty white woman already in the dinghy.

'Flowers for the lady?' Macho said.

The man looked at him.

'Very beautiful lady.' Macho gave the woman his biggest eyes. 'I only wish these flowers were as beautiful as her.'

'Now that's a man to die for,' the woman said.

'How much?' said the man.

Macho looked downcast. 'Only twenty-five dollars.'

'Twenty-five? How about ten?'

'Cruz,' the woman said, laughter in her voice, 'what are you gonna do, bargain down a kid?'

'Twenty?' Macho said.

The man shook his head. 'OK, you win, sport.' He reached into a back pocket and took out a wallet.

As he did so, Macho knelt down and reached into the boat with his right hand. His left hand slid along the back of the dinghy, just above the waterline. He handed the woman the flowers. 'Lovely lady,' he said.

The man gave him a twenty. 'You drive a hard bargain, kid.'

Macho shrugged. 'It's a wonderful thing to buy flowers for a beautiful lady. All along this dock, I had no luck, but then I saw you, and I said, "There's a man in love." Lucky.'

'OK, Don Juan, that's good enough.'

'You like to smoke?' Macho said. 'Get high, mon?'

The two people exchanged a glance, shook their heads and laughed. 'Next time.'

The man had untied the lines and now he jumped into the boat. The boat began to drift slowly away from the dock. The man pulled the cord on the motor, once, twice, three times, and it roared into life. Macho had a bad moment where he thought the motor wouldn't start, and the man would begin to inspect it closely, maybe looking too closely at the back of the boat as well. If that had happened, he would have dropped all pretence and he would have run – already the boat was too far away for the man to jump back on to the dock. But it didn't happen.

Macho raised a hand. 'Farewell, my friends. Good luck.'

Macho walked back down the dock, popped into the store, and gave the old man ten dollars. Macho hadn't run the flower-selling scam since he was what? Nine-and-a-half years old. It seemed like forever ago.

The sun was strong as he walked up the road towards Stone's hut. He felt a moment of deep joy and he began to whistle a Britney Spears song. He remembered how he'd had a crush on her in his old flower-selling days.

Stone sat on the little deck of his cabana, looking out to the sea.

He was sitting in his chair, rum, orange juice and crushed ice in the glass next to him. He had his Panasonic Toughbook laptop propped up on the little plastic table in front of him. He loved his Toughbook. He could drop the thing, step on it, kick it down the block, and its shock-mounted hard drive would still work. If the blowing sand and grit from the desert towns of Iraq couldn't penetrate its hard, rubber-sealed, magnesium alloy casing, a little beach sand was no match at all. Heck, he could probably toss the thing in the water, fish it out later and it would still work. Sure, it weighed seven pounds and it cost twice what a computer with the same specs would cost in a normal laptop, but to Stone, money was no object when it came to durability. The Toughbook was a beast.

For the past half-hour, he'd been sipping one fruity rum drink after another and watching his GPS unit meander slowly around town in Macho's pocket. GPS stood for Global Positioning System, and right now his little electronic chatter box was pinging off three commercial satellites up in space, which were triangulating its signal, finding its location on Planet Earth, to within twenty yards. It gave you latitude and longitude, but Stone also had a program that would plot the co-ordinates on fairly good street and topographical maps.

Stone would finish one drink, pour some more from the blender bottle, then sit down again. He smoked one of Macho's joints – Jamaican ganja on its way to the US regularly fell off the smuggler's boats and into the precocious lad's hands – and watched the little tike take his merry time traipsing about just a few feet above sea level.

The high from the joint was just kicking in – the stuff was harsh to smoke, but it got you high-de-high – when the GPS unit suddenly started moving fast. Stone's attention had wandered a bit, and the GPS was already racing out of the harbour and into open water before Stone noticed. Evidently, it was stuck to somebody's boat, one driven by a crazy murderous hitman whom Stone knew well, and who was probably in a bit of a hurry to get off the island.

'Macho, you slick willie. That calls for a nice tip.'

Stone sat for a while, watching the GPS blink, moving away from the island. After a while, maybe ten minutes out to sea, it stopped. Sure, Cruz had a boat somewhere. He was anchored out there, and he zipped on home in his dinghy. That, in all likelihood, was what he was doing. When Macho got here to the house, he could confirm it, but for now that was the assumption Stone would labour under. Whatever was going on that made his girl so jumpy, Cruz didn't risk staying here on the island.

Well, well, well. All of this made Stone very curious indeed. Wouldn't it be nice to learn that Cruz had a big, fat price on his head? Stone had plenty of money, but it never hurt to have some more. After what Cruz had done, Stone would consider icing him for free. Preferably from a distance – maybe he would snorkel out with a bomb, and blow up Cruz in his sleep. Payback was a . . . hmmm, where to get a bomb on an island like this? Oh, I know. Ask the grade school pimp.

Stone smiled. He was getting ahead of himself. First he needed to find out what, if anything, was going on.

How to clear this all up?

Stone took out his satellite phone. It was a black Motorola, with a big retractable antenna to access the low-earth orbit system some four to seven hundred miles above him. The phone reminded Stone of the old cell phones from the 1980s – clunky, cumbersome, expensive. Over the years, Stone had got used to playing with the latest toys. In any case, these cabanas didn't have phones or TVs. This was a place to unplug and unwind, and Stone could see their point. Up to a point.

He dialled a number in New York City from memory, not expecting it to work. It had been a long while since he had dialled this number, and they were always changing the numbers. You had to be in the know to even know where to call. He waited a moment as his phone transmitted the signal up through clear blue skies, and shook hands with a satellite. Then the ringing started.

A voice came on the line. It was a pleasant female voice.

'Power Industries. Can I help you?'

Stone had never heard of Power Industries. That certainly wasn't what they were saying the last time he called. It could be a wrong number, but there might, just might, be an actual company, providing some product or service, which called itself Power Industries. He might as well take a chance.

'This is Mr Ripper,' he said. 'I've been away too long.'

'Please hold.'

Five minutes passed with Stone listening to syrupy muzak. His mind drifted. Macho might turn up here soon. Just as likely, the kid would go about his own business for the rest of the day, and arrive after nightfall. Or he might even wait for Stone to come out, knowing Stone wanted another girl tonight, and they hadn't worked out the details yet. The kid wasn't easy to predict – but he seemed to turn up precisely at the moment he was most needed. For whatever it was worth, Macho was much on Stone's mind these days.

A voice came on the line. It was the voice of a machine gun, or millions of pieces of gravel being dumped into a driveway. Big Vito was the man's name – the same man who had put a contract out on Bunker a decade ago. Somewhere deep inside him, it pained Stone to call this man. In fact, some part of Stone cried out in agony and rebelled against it. Then again, business was business, personal was personal, and you had to compartmentalise. Wall off those feelings and keep them in one tidy box, do what you had to do and keep those actions in another tidy box. Talking to Vito right now could be the way to punch Cruz's ticket. Years from now, there could arise some way to punch Vito's ticket. When you were on a long walk, you took it one step at a time.

'Kid?' Vito said. 'Long time, no see. Looking for work, eh?'

'I'm wondering that myself. Maybe I'm looking for some, maybe I just found some by accident.'

'What's up?'

'I'm on a tropical island. Enjoying some time off after working hard for six months. Just ran into an old friend of mine, a guy who carries a scar. He's a guy I think you might know.'

The big man's voice lowered. 'I find that very interesting. Are you calling from your hotel room right now?'

'No, I'm calling from a satellite phone.'

'A satellite phone? Jesus fucking Christ.' Vito sounded like he was talking to someone in the room with him. 'He says he's on a satellite phone.' He came back on the line. 'Do me a favour, OK? Call me back on a fucking pay phone.'

The line went dead.

BINGO!

Hunting season was now open.

5

Sticks looked at the clock. It was early afternoon, and he was tired.

He had only got out of jail this morning, and he hadn't slept last night. Knox the copper had put him up in a suite at this upscale place – the Portland Harbor Hotel. Jewel-bedecked chandelier in the lobby, smoothly efficient geeks to bring your shit upstairs – except all Sticks had was the clothes on his back.

He and crew-cut Knox had breakfast and a couple of Bloody Marys at a decent restaurant on the main boulevard down near the water. Sticks had the steak and eggs. The two men talked shit, talked jobs. Knox had been out of the life since he got sliced up a few years ago in a hit gone wrong down in Massachusetts. Knox had pulled up his shirt and showed Sticks the scar – thick and mean, it wrapped around his torso like a python. You had to like that scar.

So they ate and Knox dropped him off back at the hotel. Sticks rode the elevator upstairs thinking . . . what? Boring day. Make a couple drinks from the mini-bar. Watch something on the TV. If he was lucky, maybe a movie. Cops and robbers. Shoot 'em up, bang-bang. Tomorrow, if he was in the mood, he'd take a cab to the airport, find a plane with an empty seat, and fly back to New York. Then again, maybe he'd stay here another day. Who knows?

It wasn't terrible here – hell, he'd spent three weeks in jail, cold cinderblock and cement everywhere, with dog food for breakfast, lunch and dinner. He'd got sprung, and later that day was in a luxury suite with wall-to-wall carpet, a massive flat-panel HDTV hanging on the wall, and a giant bay window with views of the boats in the harbour. Most cons probably went home to flea circuses. Not that any of it really mattered to Sticks – comfort, discomfort, luxury, jail, whatever. It was all the same to him.

He had just fixed his second drink when a knock came at the door. He opened it and a tall blonde stood there. She wore a full-length fur coat over a short red mini-dress pulled taut to a tight, tight body. Big hair. Transparent high heels. She looked great – could be Ms Fitness USA. With the hair piled on top, and the heels, she ran at least three inches taller than Sticks.

'Yeah?'

She smiled – lots of straight white teeth. Beautiful. 'Sticks, right? Somebody named Knox sent me. Can I come in?'

Now it was Sticks's turn to smile. 'Oh yeah. You can come in.'

'You mind if I make myself comfortable?' she said.

She started off with some kind of weird striptease dance, probably designed to get her motor going more than his. She had done high leg kicks, rolled around on the floor, crawled across the bed towards him, all of this as pieces of her clothing dangled and then fell off. Hey, whatever floats your boat. Far be it from Sticks to put the kibosh on artistic self-expression. Then Sticks had climbed on that big girl body, and they had romped.

Now, three hours later, he was alone. Ms Fitness had left ten minutes ago. After the workout she'd given him, Sticks was starting to see where he might come to like this town. Then the phone rang.

Of course. Half drunk, bleary-eyed, the bleak light of an overcast

New England day outside his window, and now more action. Just out of jail, couldn't he have one fucking day off?

'Kid?' came the voice.

'Yeah?'

'Didja have a good time?'

'Yeah. Very nice. Thanks.' All on the company dime, and don't you forget it.

'I got news. Some friends of yours turned up somewhere.'

Sticks perked up at that. 'Oh?'

'I want you to go see them. Give 'em my regards. When can you be ready?'

'I'm ready right now. Where am I going?'

'Down to the islands.'

Sticks released a long exhalation. No sleep, on the move again. He'd need to call in one of his boys. The Death Squad, that's how Sticks thought of himself and the guys in his little crew. The name made him smile – call in Sticks, and put the Death Squad on the case. That's the ticket.

'Sounds nice,' he told Vito. 'I could use some sun.'

Smoke wouldn't say where the money was. Lola wished he would. She couldn't stand watching Smoke take a beating.

'Say it, motherfucker,' the big kid said. Ty, the men he was with had called him, Ty Weathers. 'Say where the money is.' He punched Smoke in the face. Then again. And again. Smoke was on the bed, wrists bound together behind his back with a length of rope, legs bound at the ankles and the knees. Lola was bound the same way, except she was sitting slumped on the floor across from the bed.

'Can't you hit any harder than that?' Smoke said. 'A big kid like you?'

Lola had only returned to consciousness a moment before. Her head ached dully from when Ty had hit her with the pole. With each heartbeat, the ache sharpened and seemed to pierce her whole body. She felt like she might vomit. She hoped not – Ty had stuffed a T-shirt in her mouth and tied it into place with another length of rope wrapped around her head. Lola was starting to sense that Ty wasn't from the island. He had so much violence in him, he reminded her of America.

The kid grunted. 'Maybe there ain't any money,' he said.

Smoke managed to smile at him through a bloody and battered face. 'No, there's definitely money. There's a lot of money.'

'How much?'

'Find out for yourself.'

Ty hit him again. Ty's hand was slick with blood – his own or Smoke's, it was impossible to say. Maybe a little of both.

Lola would tell him where the money was just to get him to stop hitting Smoke – only she didn't know where it was herself. All this time, all this terror, and it just now occurred to her that she had never seen the money in question. Two and a half million dollars that had upended her life and nearly made her dead, and she hadn't even asked to look at it. She imagined now that it was quite a sight.

It came to Lola that she wasn't really afraid. She was helpless, and Smoke was helpless. They were totally under this man's power. At the same time, it didn't frighten her. A memory came: nineteen years old, and she had recently buried her only family, her grandmother. Her grandmother's entire estate – four thousand dollars, the sum of a life of struggle and work – had come to Lola. So did her grandmother's old Ford. Lola had climbed in that Ford and driven it east. One day, she reached the coast of Maine, and sat on some rocks watching the waves crash ashore. Further out, some dolphins passed, and one of them leapt and breached the water, putting on a private show for her – there was no one else on the beach. She decided to stay.

By then, she was already a student of the martial arts. Three years had passed since she'd been gang-raped by a group of laughing boys at the back of a weedy and garbage-choked vacant lot, and she'd gotten very good at karate. In Portland, she began studying under a man named Yun. He was Korean, shorter than Lola, and sixty years old. He was a stern taskmaster to all the students, and a hard man, but he took an almost fatherly interest in her.

One day, in the dojo, while she was practising some moves, he said, 'You move well, but that's only one part of our learning. It's easy to see you're afraid of something. Until you release that, you'll never be a fighter.'

'How do I release it?' she said.

Yun smiled – in three months of coming to his classes, she had never seen him smile. 'I'll show you.'

Lola resisted daydreaming about Yun. It was a good memory, but one for another time. In the here and now, Ty put the blade of the machete to Smoke's throat. 'Maybe I'll just slice your neck up and ask your sexy bitch about the money. Looks like she's coming round over there.'

Smoke shook his sadly, as if he was dealing with someone terribly slow on the uptake. 'That won't do you any good. She can't tell you where it is. I'm the only one who knows.' Good Lord. Had she known that Smoke was this tough? She didn't think so. Stubborn, sure. Mule-headed, of course. But so tough that he could take a beating like this, then smile and shake his head? She'd never seen that in him before. And she realised now, in their moment of extremity, that she had some very good memories of Smoke as well. It was real – even though he had lied about who he was, about everything – their time together was real. Their long walks on the beach, their nights together on the deck, their car trips together up the coast, and all the times when he had encouraged her and told her in a thousand small ways that she was special. All of that was real.

Ty left Smoke and came over to Lola. His face was inches away from hers – his eyes were aflame with a concoction of anger and mirth, and a splash of what? Disdain. Worse than disdain – disregard, indifference to her fate. She wished she had seen the bad craziness in him earlier – he had gone down so easily this morning, she had almost managed to forget about him. 'What do you say, bitch?' he said. 'You know where the money is?'

She shook her head, slowly. Even that little bit of movement made her feel faint. If she could loosen these binds . . . it wouldn't make much difference. She doubted she could stand up, never mind fight a big man like this.

He turned back to Smoke. 'OK, old man, this is what we do next. I go to town on your sweet little bitch here, put it in every hole she has, then I chop her head off. What do you say to that plan?'

'Her name is Lola.'

Ty smiled, put one strong hand under Lola's chin and tilted her face up towards his. 'Lola. That's a nice name. You ready to be my girl, Lola? Look at that nice body you got. You ready for the alligator? What do you say, white boy? Is Lola here ready for the alligator, after all that time with little ol' you?'

Smoke still sounded calm. 'I say what I said before. Put even one more finger on her, and you don't see any money. Ever. You wear rags the rest of your life on this shitty little island, and one day, I come back here with some friends of mine and find you, and you die slow and painful, over a period of several days.'

Ty's grin didn't falter. 'See, but I don't believe you any more. I don't think there is no money. So if there's no money, then there's nothing to stop me from doing what I want to Ms Thing here, is there?'

'Do this,' Smoke said. 'Tucked under a shelf out in the main cabin there is my toolbox. It's a big red toolbox. You're gonna have to kind of crawl in under the shelf there and get it. Pull it out. It has a false bottom. There's a little button that unlocks it – it blends in pretty good, so you have to look for it. Open the false bottom. There's nearly a hundred and fifty thousand dollars in cash in there, plus some gold coins. I don't know what the coins are worth. Probably a lot.'

Ty looked quizzically at Smoke, then turned and gave Lola the same look. The question lingered there in his eyes: *Is he for real?* Lola nodded.

Smoke's voice came with more authority now – he had got the kid's attention. 'Keep in mind that's less than ten per cent of the money we have on this boat. You want the big money, you can have it. But you're gonna have to work for it. And the first thing you need to do, once you see that I'm not lying, is let Lola go.'

'Uh . . . I'll be back in a minute, folks.'

Ty left the room, and Lola stared at Smoke. Smoke rolled his eyes and shrugged. Lola could almost read his mind: *What a hell of a situation to be in.*

After a moment, Ty strolled into the room. He held the machete in one hand, and a giant wad of cash in the other. He smiled, but his face had taken on a dazed, almost vacant look. He stroked his chin with the money. Then he laughed and threw the cash on the bed. He walked over to Lola again and towered over her. He filled her entire field of vision.

'You know what, white boy?' he called over his shoulder. 'Thanks for all that money. But I'm gonna fuck Lola anyway. Then I'm gonna tear this boat apart, for the next three days if I have to, and find the rest of the money. And when I get bored every now and then, or tired, I'm gonna come back in here and fuck Lola some more. And you know what you get to do? You get to watch.'

Ty put the machete on the floor and peeled his shirt off. He shook his long twists of hair free. His chest and stomach were lean and rippled with muscle. His shoulders, arms, neck – he had muscle everywhere. The kid was practically an anatomy lesson.

He got down on his knees in front of Lola, and began to tug at the drawstring on his shorts. 'You watching, friend? Maybe me and Lola best should climb up on the bed with you so you can get a better view of the action.' He reached down, put an arm behind Lola's back, and an arm under her legs. He wasn't joking – he meant to pick her up and put her on the bed.

'What you think, Lola? There room for all three of us on that big bed? I think we're about to find out.'

'You'll die before you get there,' a voice said.

Funny thing – it was a woman's voice. And because it was a woman's voice, Ty didn't register it at first. Oh, he heard it, all right. He heard it fine. Like everything else about his body, Ty's hearing was just about perfect. It was just that Lola's mouth was gagged, so she couldn't be talking. Also, Ty had so many things on his mind just then – the incredible amount of money these people were holding on this boat, Lola's wonderful body, the white boy tied up on the bed, all of it. It was like some kind of fantasy unfolding right before Ty's eyes – and he was in the middle of it.

He was aware, too, that the adrenaline from the attack had already burned off. All that booze he'd sucked down earlier today had also worn off. He was dragging a little bit, starting to feel tired, and he knew that was a dangerous time. He'd have to be careful here and make sure he kept them straight on who was in charge.

All that money. Good Lord, deliver me from my suffering.

'You! Asshole. You're about to die.'

Ty's head swivelled to the right and standing there in the doorway of the cabin, gun drawn and pointed their way, was a young white woman. She had long hair, sort of brown, and wore denim shorts and a T-shirt. Nice legs. She held the gun two-handed, in a sort of shooter's crouch Ty had seen a million times on TV. He'd never seen any of the cowboys he'd dealt with in real life hold a gun that way. He noticed that the woman's hands were trembling, just a tiny bit.

Ty looked at Lola. 'Friend of yours?'

Lola shrugged.

'Well, the more the merrier, I guess.'

Ty let Lola slump to the floor and slowly stood, picking up the machete again as he went. He reached his full height and then stretched his back. He felt in no hurry to do anything just yet. He actually felt calm. In fact he smiled.

'Drop that knife before I blow your fucking head off,' the woman said.

Ty put a hand out to her. He looked right into her pretty green eyes. 'Girl, give me that gun. You're liable to hurt yourself.'

'I mean it, motherfucker. Drop the knife.' Her hands were really shaking now.

Ty took one languid step towards her.

'Shoot him, Pam,' the old man said from the bed. 'Don't wait. Just shoot him.'

'Hush now, brother. We're negotiating here.' Ty took another step. Then another. He moved very slow. He could see it – he could picture a scenario where she just handed him the gun and joined the other prisoners. Maybe she'd even tie herself up. 'Pam, is it? You don't want to shoot me, now do you, Pam? It's a terrible thing, to shoot a person. Take it from one who knows.'

The woman inched a step backwards, then began screaming. 'Cruz! Cruz, we need you down here! Please! Right fucking now! Cruz!'

Ty took a deep breath. Yet another person was coming. That was a bitch – he hadn't even heard them pull up. OK, it was nothing to get down on himself for. He'd been distracted by other things. But capturing four people? That was going to be a neat trick. He glanced at the money on the bed. Maybe he should just grab what he could and bull his way out of here. He was gonna have to play this one flexible.

Let's wait and see what Cruz looks like.

Three seconds passed. Then five. Ty heard feet coming down the steps outside the room. Cruz appeared in the doorway. He was a small man, and slim. He wore a loose-fitting shirt and slacks. At first glance, there was nothing intimidating about him. He had a scar on his face, slicked back hair.

'What's going on?' he said to the woman. Then he noticed Ty. Then he looked around the room at Lola on the floor and the white boy on the bed. This Cruz person didn't seem alarmed or even surprised by Ty's presence, by the fact that his two friends were both tied up, or by the white boy's bloody face. In fact, he looked like a man who had just put together the final pieces of a puzzle.

'Well,' he said, almost to himself. 'I guess we found out who belongs to that skiff upstairs.'

'You Cruz?' Ty said. 'We probably gonna need to talk.'

Cruz just stared at him. Ty thought he saw something there, in the man's eyes. He did, but what was it?

'Should I shoot him?' the woman Pam said, her voice just this side of hysteria.

'Nah. Give me the gun. I'll shoot him.' She handed Cruz the gun and he stepped fully into the room. He raised the gun and pointed it at Ty's chest. 'OK, big man. Drop the machete and get on the floor, face down. I'll give you three seconds.'

Ty didn't move. He merely looked down at the blade in his hand, then looked back at Cruz. The eyes – the thing in those eyes was still there. Ty had seen it once before. On his last stick-up job – the one that had gone wrong. He'd stood in a blood-splattered room, across a card table from a guy a couple of years older than himself. Five people were dead in that apartment, two from Ty's crew, three from the drug crew that used the place as its headquarters. Heart beating, Ty held his shaking gun on the only other person still alive – the leader of the other crew.

The boy was smoking a cigarette. A pile of money sat in front of him on the table. He looked around at the wreckage, the bodies, and then he smiled. 'Popped your cherry tonight, huh? Never killed nobody before?'

Ty nodded. There was no sense trying to lie.

'You better kill me,' the boy said. 'Because I know who you are. Ty Weathers. I used to watch you play ball.' He took a deep drag on his cigarette. 'I killed eleven men before now. And if I walk out of here tonight, I promise I'm gonna kill your mama, and your whole family, right in front of you. Probably skin them alive.'

Ty gazed into those eyes. A demon stared back out at him. The boy wasn't lying – he would do it. Ty shot him six times.

Cruz had the same eyes – murderer's eyes.

Now Cruz sighed. 'Oh well, a tough guy. Fuck it. Guess there's no sense even bothering with the countdown.' He sounded disappointed, and a little bit bored.

Ty dropped the blade.

'Very good. Now on the floor.'

Ty hesitated, still watching, still thinking. Was there a way to run out of here?

'I've been patient with you so far,' Cruz said. 'Luckily for you, you're catching me while I go through some kind of mid-life thing. Otherwise, you'd already be dead.' Cruz gestured towards the floor with his free hand. 'So, if you please. I'm not gonna ask you again.'

Ty slowly sank to his knees, then all fours, then went face first to the floor. The nubs of the well-worn carpet were inches from his eyes. A worrisome thought came to mind: he had been bad, very bad, to those two people. Now he was caught and they were about to be set free.

'Guys, what the hell is going on here?' he heard Cruz say above him. 'Pamela and I have been gone a grand total of . . .' he paused. Cruz was probably checking his watch. 'Four and a half hours. You make new friends this easily?'

Hours had passed, and now day was slipping into evening.

They had eaten a meal together in near silence – some rice and canned fish Smoke and Lola had picked up on the island before going to buy the spare parts. Two empty bottles of wine sat among the remains of the dinner. Smoke, his face aching from the beating he had taken, lit up a cigar and let the smell waft out over the water. The wine had taken some of the edge off the pain.

Far across from them, the sun had turned an angry red and was slipping beneath the water. It seemed to happen fast – one minute it was there, the next minute it was gone. As it did, the sky went pink, and then purple, like a bruise. The sky slowly faded to black, and lights became apparent, nearby on the other boats, and further away, on the island itself.

Lola had already gone to lie down for a while. Smoke, Pamela and Cruz stretched out around the table. The kid, who, as it turned out, was the same kid who had accosted her on the island, was bound hand and foot, gagged, and locked in the utility closet. The conversation gently danced around the subject of the kid – he was an eight-hundred pound elephant that nobody wanted to talk about. He knew about the money, so they couldn't let him go. At the same time, they couldn't keep him prisoner for ever. The possibilities for him had narrowed almost to a vanishing point. There was basically only one option left.

Smoke felt OK. He was too tired to really focus on killing the kid. It was an unpleasant thing to think about. Anyway, he wasn't eager to do it – his ego was damaged more than his face, and long years in this business had taught him that ego wasn't anything to hold on to. The intervening hours had relaxed him about the kid somewhat, and now he was feeling . . . philosophical.

If Smoke was angry about anything, it was that the kid had hit Lola with a stick. But was that good enough reason to kill somebody? How about escaping from here with the money – was that good enough reason?

Eh, maybe.

Smoke remembered the first night he had ever seen the money, the two and a half million dollars that were causing such a problem. It was also the first time he had ever intentionally killed a man.

It took place in a darkened living room in another life — the kind of living room in the kind of house that middle-class housewives looked at and salivated over in glossy magazines. Black leather furniture converged in the centre of the room. At the far end, there was a fireplace that was as clean as a hospital floor — split logs were piled inside it, but it probably hadn't been lit in years. Floor-to-ceiling windows looked out across the patio and the sloping lawn to the Long Island Sound. To the left of the patio, blue and red lights beamed up from the floor of the in-ground swimming pool.

On one wall of the living room there was a huge canvas — a giant orange dot on a white background. Modern art. The fat man, Roselli, was a collector. Roselli himself lay sprawled on the white carpet, his terrycloth robe opened to reveal the vast expanse of his belly, and boxer shorts with *Home of the Whopper* stencilled across the front. His thick legs stuck out at a forty-five degree angle, one foot bare, the other still wearing a soft grey slipper. Roselli had done a bad thing, and now he was paying for it. Nominally Smoke's boss, he had lied to Smoke and told him he needed a bomb to take down a cinderblock wall in a bank. Bank jobs, that was what Smoke liked — ones that took place in the middle of the night, with no casualties. The banks were insured for that kind of loss, the insurance companies were probably reinsured, and the reinsurers spread the risk all over the place. In a real way, nobody got hurt when a bank job went down. The missing money disappeared into a line item on a financial spreadsheet, which was stored on a computer in a corporate office far away from the site of actual heist. A month after it happened, the whole thing was already reduced to an abstraction, something for an accountant to daydream about while eating lunch at his desk.

But Roselli didn't use this bomb for a bank job. Instead, he used it to take down a passenger plane that was carrying a Russian mobster. Ninety-seven people on board, all dead to kill just one guy — it was a disgrace and Smoke had no intention of letting it slide.

So far tonight, Smoke had given Roselli a few jolts from a Taser pistol, and it looked like riding the lightning might have been enough to stop Roselli's big fat heart. Smoke hoped not, because killing Roselli wasn't the only activity he had planned for the night.

Smoke went over and pulled the big painting down from the wall. *Voilà*, the safe. The wall was red brick, and the safe was recessed deeply into the brickwork. Smoke could blow it out of there, but he doubted that would open it. By the looks of it, he also doubted he could carry it out to the car to open it later – in any case, he had parked half a mile away from here. Maybe a hand truck of some kind? He glanced around the living room. Sure, find a hand truck, then trundle this big gleaming safe down the road, through this exclusive community, and away from this waterfront mansion in the middle of the night. That sounded like a plan that would end with a police cruiser rolling up alongside of him.

'Evening, officer. This safe? Oh, just moving it for a friend of mine.'

Smoke's eyes fell upon Roselli. The bastard was moving. An arm drifted off the floor, one meaty hand coming to rest on Roselli's sweaty forehead. He groaned.

Smoke walked over to him, knelt beside him.

'O'Malley?' Roselli said, his voice hardly more than a rasp. At that time, most people knew Smoke Dugan as Walter O'Malley. 'I need a doctor, O'Malley. I'm gonna die here.'

'What's the combination to the safe?' Smoke said.

Roselli's eyes rolled back. 'Fuck you.'

Smoke put the Taser to Roselli's hairy chest. The probes were spent, but he could give Roselli another whack of the juice with the Taser's touch-stun feature. 'Listen, you fat fuck. You did it to yourself. You killed innocent children. You killed women. And this is where you make up for it. You give me those numbers and maybe you make it through this night. You don't, and you're gonna meet God in the next five minutes. And you know what? He's not gonna be happy when He sees you. In fact, I think He's gonna be really fucking pissed off.'

Roselli whispered something.

Smoke leaned close. 'What's that, Roselli? What did you say?'

'Go to hell.'

'Roselli, I swear to God, you're going to hell right now.' Smoke meant it. He was ready to give him the final dose.

A series of numbers – a moment later, the fat man was whispering a series of numbers. Maybe the whole God thing had got to him after all.

'My kids' birthdays,' he said.

Smoke went to the safe and punched the numbers in on the keypad. The door opened of its own accord. Smoke stared. There was some paperwork on a small top shelf. He didn't even look at that. On the bottom shelf – that's where the jackpot was. Stacks and stacks of currency tied in rubber bands. It took Smoke's breath away. All that dirty money, a mad jumble of denominations – hundreds, mostly, but also fifties and twenties and tens. No pattern to it, just random, anonymous bills that had flowed into the fat man's hands during years of under-the-table activities.

Smoke went back to Roselli. He put the Taser to the man's heart.

'You done good,' Smoke said. 'Maybe God will forgive you after all.' He gave Roselli fifty thousand volts, twice more, three times more. Later, after Smoke had packed up the money in a canvas satchel he found in the kitchen, he blew the whole house. Roselli shot up to see God in a flaming fireball.

'Who is this guy Stone again?' Smoke said now, on the boat. 'The one you're worried about?'

Cruz shrugged. 'Just a guy I used to know. I did a job once. He wasn't happy about it. I don't know if he's in with them any more – he said he wasn't. Said he just got back from Iraq. But he has reason to be suspicious. Calamity Jane here pulled her gun when he came to our table.'

In the last of the fading light, Smoke saw Pamela's face turn crimson. 'He looked like trouble.'

'He is trouble. We just don't know if he's trouble for us.'

Smoke regarded the burning end of his cigar. 'Shouldn't we know that? I mean, we're going to be here at least another day, probably two. Maybe more. I think I have what I need to fix this thing, but I don't know how long it's gonna take. Shouldn't we know if this guy is a problem for us?'

'Maybe we should buy another boat,' Pamela said.

Smoke took a sip of wine. 'Could be. If we bought it under the table, no paperwork, no dealings with the powers that be. This boat has the benefit that it doesn't really exist. Another boat? I don't know.' He shrugged. 'This boat also has some sentimental value for its owner. It'd be a shame to ditch it for no reason.'

'No, you're right,' Cruz said. 'We need to know what this guy's up to, if anything. I'll take a little nap, then go back tonight and check him out. Could be we're worrying about nothing. I don't know – I just got carried away back there.'

'Maybe I should go with you,' Pamela said.

Cruz looked at her. 'Sweetheart, have you ever night-stalked someone before?'

'It's never too late to start.'

'Don't worry, Cruz,' Smoke said. 'We'll handcuff her to the deck if need be.'

'You don't want me to go, I won't go,' Pamela said. 'You don't have to be jerks about it.' With that, she stood up and went below.

Smoke and Cruz were silent for several minutes after she was gone.

'Life on a boat,' Cruz said finally.

Smoke took a puff on his cigar. 'Yep.'

Late at night. Cruz slipped like a shadow into Stone's tiny kitchen.

He felt better already. He had watched Stone tonight – watched him in the crowded bar, already drunk and getting drunker. Cruz hovered in the darkness near the back exit of the place, behind some people, sipping a bottle of seltzer and watching Stone go through his moves on the packed dance floor.

When Stone came out on to the beach, Cruz was there, watching him share the remains of a bottle of rum with his girl. Cruz watched from behind as the two of them sat on the sand and lit up a joint. From forty yards away, Cruz could practically taste the sweet smoke of the herb wafting to him on the breeze.

The girl was probably some version of a prostitute – black, a local girl, very sexy, very slim and pretty, better than what Stone could probably manage to acquire at home. She's your girlfriend for a night or a week or a month, then leave her a generous parting gift to pay for the leaking roof, or her sister's tuition at the only Catholic school on the island, or maybe her aunt's diabetes. Cruz knew that drill – in some ways, it was preferable to having a real woman in your life, with their moods and their opinions and their personality questionnaires.

Easier, for sure.

Now, standing silently inside Stone's kitchen, he was still watching. Stone's tropical kitchen – three feet wide by five feet long, an electric stove with two burners, a small sink, a couple of cupboards, a foot of wooden counter space weathered and scarred from long use as a cutting board, and a mini-refrigerator. A few blackened cast-iron pots hung down from pegs above his head. Gigantic, slow-moving cockroaches – if Cruz picked one up it would fill his entire palm – trundled here and there, going about their dirty business.

Cruz's gun was out, held lightly by his side. Through a narrow doorway, Stone and the woman were asleep. Until about ten minutes ago, they had been going through their paces. In the darkness, moving, pushing, pulling, murmuring words to each other that Cruz didn't care to hear. Abruptly, right after they finished, just moments after the woman had given a long mewling howl, they had both gone quiet and still.

Too much booze tonight. Too much dope.

It all made Cruz's outlook much improved. Stone hadn't come here because of the money – he didn't know about the money. He hadn't come here to kill Cruz. The fuck was *on vacation*, an island holiday. Just like he said – back from the war and having a nice time. Stone was a beach bum at heart. Cruz couldn't kill a man on vacation.

Hell, he couldn't kill anybody these days.

Cruz thought of a holiday he'd been on, just about ten years ago now. Himself, he'd always hated holidays – never saw much use for them. Especially group holidays, of which this was one. He only went on this trip because Big Vito had invited him along, and in fact had insisted that he come. The only concession Vito was willing to make was that Cruz – who liked to be alone – could fly down by himself and stay in a different hotel from everybody else. But Cruz had to *participate*, just like everybody else.

'What gives, Vito? I like you, you know? I like to work for you. I like the guys. But I don't feel I have to go on a trip with you to prove it.'

'It's not that,' the gravel-voiced wonder said. 'This is a *team-building* trip. I've been reading about the idea, and I like it. So I'm taking some of my best producers down to Florida for some rest, relaxation and some team-building. Trust me, it'll be good. You'll see.'

Miami Beach three-day weekend: Friday afternoon, the six of them sat in a small conference room while some Ring-Ding talked to them about the Meaning of Success. Later, they had drinks served to them at a rooftop bar overlooking the ocean. They went to a steakhouse, had some more drinks, and everybody got a whore served up to their room. In the morning, Saturday, a few of the guys went golfing. Cruz elected to get a massage instead – he had never played golf. In the afternoon, they all went on a deep-sea fishing boat.

The fishing boat was run by Cubans. They were on the water, in the Gulf Stream, thirty miles out to sea. The boat bobbed in the heavy swells. It was a bright and clear day, very sunny, but getting towards late afternoon. About twenty yards away, a Cuban was in a dinghy, throwing chum into the water to attract sharks. He'd leave the chum, and when the sharks came he'd high-tail it out of there. The guys were drinking beer and taking turns with an Uzi submachine gun, ripping the sharks into Swiss cheese. And laughing. The guys were laughing a lot.

Fucking sharks. You'd think they would have figured the game out after a while. But no – the guys kept shooting them, and the sharks kept coming. Cruz wasn't sure who was dumber – the sharks or the guys.

Vito put a meaty arm around him. 'Cruz, you having a good time?'

'Yeah, Vito. It's good.'

'Come over here a second. I wanna talk to you.'

They went around to the other side of the boat, away from the shooting gallery. The blat of automatic gunfire came to them every few seconds. That, and the laughter, shouting and cheers. Cruz expected Vito to tell him to try a little harder – participate more. For the good of the team.

'I need you to take care of something for me,' Vito said. 'This,' and here he gestured back at the fun and games, 'this ain't you. I know that. And it ain't really why you're here, though I hoped you'd have a nice time anyway.'

'I am. I'm having a nice time.'

'Good. I'm glad. So here's what I need. I got somebody down in the Keys, OK? No good. I went in on something with him, and he's got some problems.' Vito made a gesture like he was snorting cocaine. 'I feel like I can't trust him any more. You know what I mean?'

'Yeah. I know how that goes.'

'Maybe you can go down there for me, talk to the guy.'

'Sure. When were you thinking?'

'Tonight.'

'Tonight?'

'Yeah. The boat goes in, we all go to dinner and maybe out for a few drinks. After that, late, you go. There's an airfield not far. Got a plane gassed up and ready. You fly down, you're there in half an hour. The plane waits, you talk to the guy real quick, and that's it. You'll be back before breakfast. Tomorrow we're gonna go to the dog track.'

Cruz read the dossier on the quick flight down to Marathon. A guy named Bunker – late forties, former Special Ops military guy, they called him Bunker because he'd been in Beirut when the Arabs blew up the Marine headquarters in 1983. He was a rough-and-tumble guy, and had kicked around a lot. Partnered with Vito on some shipments out of South and Central America – Vito's guys providing the capital, Bunker doing the heavy lifting in and out of the country. Bunker had played it above board the first few times, but then the shipments seemed a bit light. They suspected a problem, and had the truth confirmed by planting a spy in Bunker's midst – his girlfriend. She worked for Vito, and went deep undercover to get the facts: Bunker was diverting product, stealing money, living large, and doing heavy cocaine.

The dossier also described a young guy staying in the house with Bunker. Another ex-military guy, had done a few jobs for Vito. Vito had made the introduction between Bunker and this guy. Bunker had taken the younger man under his wing. They were down there in the Keys, going fishing, going diving, going drinking, and making runs to South America together. Vito liked the kid, and thought he had potential – decided the kid didn't know what Bunker was up to. Spare the kid – that was the message. The kid's name was Butch Stone.

The house in the Keys was a palace. Marble floors, wide-open spaces, huge windows and doors. It had a magnificent southern exposure, looking out on a blue-green inlet and lush mangrove forests. Two power-boats were parked at the private dock. It seemed like every window and door was thrown wide – white curtains billowed on the ocean breezes.

The sun was coming up – the sky was a weak yellow. Cruz stood in the wide bedroom, looking at the bed. The girl – tousled red hair, fleshy, big intelligent eyes that watched Cruz the whole time – got up nude, grabbed a pair of shorts and a shirt off the floor, and hustled out of there. A moment later, a car started up in the driveway and drove off. The Porsche or the Mercedes convertible? Cruz guessed the convertible.

He moved to the foot of the bed and waited.

Checked his watch: Almost time.

The man – balding, heavier than in the photographs, starting to show his age – began to stir. He sighed heavily and pulled a white pillow over his face to block out the growing light.

'Bunker.' Cruz said it low – he didn't want to disturb anyone else in the house. He raised the gun – silencer protruding from the end.

The man stopped. He lifted the pillow. Saw Cruz there.

'You know why I'm here, right? Vito sent me.'

'Wait,' the man said.

Cruz shot him four times, all in the face. Then he went over to the body to make sure. A formality: the man's head was lunch. Nobody home.

Cruz walked downstairs. The kitchen was like in a restaurant – gleaming, stainless-steel surfaces. Three stoves. Burners. Square feet of counter space. Double doors on the refrigerator. The kid, Stone, was in here, frying up some eggs at a burner, and bopping along to some music that played only in his head. He was a tall kid, thin, well-muscled, very athletic. He wore a pair of camouflage shorts and flip-flops – no shirt. His blond hair stood up in tufts and spikes. He had a tattoo on the rounded shoulder muscle of his right arm: *RLTW*

Cruz knew what it meant from the dossier. Rangers Lead the Way – the motto of the United States Army Rangers. Big fucking whoop. Cruz had no love for the military or the Government – they were foreign entities to him. Maybe they trained good killers, maybe they didn't. Cruz had just put one of their guys under with barely a whimper.

The kid looked up as Cruz walked in. He didn't seem particularly surprised to see Cruz. He didn't seem particularly anything. Maybe people just dropped in here all the time as the sun was coming up. Maybe that's why Bunker was so easy to kill.

'Hey, man, can I help you?'

'Phone for you,' Cruz said.

On cue, the kitchen phone began ringing. It was blue and it hung on the wall a few feet from where Stone was standing. It was the type of phone that was attached to the wall unit by a cord. Stone looked at it like it was alive.

'Pretty neat trick,' he said.

'It's for you. Pick it up.'

Stone did. He listened, looking at Cruz the whole time. Cruz imagined he could hear Vito's gravel-voice coming through the phone. Something in Stone's face changed as he listened – it hardened and set, like quick-pour concrete. After a while, he hung up.

'He told you who I am?'

Stone nodded. 'Yeah. Cruz.'

Cruz hated that – there was no need for Vito to give the kid his name. Regardless, he pushed on with the message. 'Do you understand?'

'Yeah.'

'In case you don't, I'll give it to you again. Bunker's girl is gone. That was her driving off a few minutes ago. She's not coming back. You can probably stay here in the house a few days, but I wouldn't push it too far. The mess upstairs – that's your problem. Take care of it before you go.'

Stone said nothing.

'Your eggs are burning.'

Stone glanced at the eggs turning good and crispy in the frying pan – like leather. Black smoke began to rise towards the ceiling. Stone looked back at Cruz. He stared.

Cruz turned to leave. 'Hey, kid. Cheer up. He likes you. If he didn't, you'd be dead, too.'

Now, on Saint Mark's, Cruz stood smoking a cigarette at the end of Stone's dock. It was ten years later, in the near pitch-darkness of an island night, and Cruz was thinking about sunrise on a different island.

Behind him, footsteps approached on the wooden dock. He turned and here came Stone, walking along in a bathing suit, carrying a pair of flippers, a snorkel mask and some kind of flashlight device that looked like it would clamp to his head. He walked up to Cruz. He was six inches taller. He wore the blank expression of a man who had been asleep five minutes earlier.

'Doing a little night swimming, Stone?'

'Cruz?'

'I didn't kill you tonight. I could have. I hope you're going to return the favour one day.'

In his dreams, Stone was covered in dust and in the blood of his comrades. His pants caught fire and one leg burned away before he could put it out.

But he never once got hit.

Mogadishu – Mog, the Rangers called it – was a sprawling relic from the Middle Ages that had been shot up like Swiss cheese by warring militias since probably before Stone was born. The people were starving and madmen were running the show. If Stone closed his eyes he could still see Mogadishu in his mind – a filthy warren of alleyways and foot-paths winding through shanties made of scrounged-up tin and assorted garbage. A few Western-style buildings remained, leftovers from Italian colonialism. All of them were shot full of holes. The largest intact buildings left in the whole city were the mosques.

The zonked-out kids riding around in the Toyota pick-up trucks with the big 50-caliber gun mounted on back – they called the Mad Max reject vehicles 'technicals' – didn't mess with Allah. They probably didn't care much for him, Stone thought, but they didn't shoot up his house. The kids chewed the local upper – a plant called khat – all day long, and by late in the afternoon they were wired and raring to rip it up. The Rangers called the locals 'Skinnies'.

The Americans had gone in on a helicopter drop to snag some local baddies – some guys from Delta Force were there to do the grab, Stone's group was only supposed to enforce the perimeter around the building. The mission got all screwed up, and now Stone was stuck with it for life – whenever he closed his eyes.

Every morning on Saint Mark's, the birds knew the sun was coming. Stone would still be asleep in his hut – asleep but awake. He could hear the gulls calling. But what he saw were the Skinnies – Skinnies by the hundreds, by the thousands – crowding down an alley, and Stone was there, on one knee and wedged in a corner, ripping them up with his M-16. Dust and stone flew all around him as the rounds from the Skinnies demolished the doorway all around him.

'What the fuck?' McCallum screamed. 'What the fuck?'

McCallum was out in the middle of the alley, crouched behind a tiny car, tearing them up with his M-60. That thing was a monster. Suddenly his head was gone – shot from behind. There was a spray of blood and bone, and McCallum's head just crumpled. Stone looked to his left and here was a kid – a small kid, maybe ten years old, and he had just capped McCallum with an AK-47. Stone whipped the gun around and capped the kid. Cut him down. Cut him in half.

He dashed out through the swarm of bullets and picked up the 60. The Skinnies were almost on top of him again. He had to kill them all – he could never stop. As soon as he stopped, they would kill him. He stood and opened up the 60 down the alley. It was their fault. These people were maniacs, savages. That kid should be home this time of night, not out here running around with a gun. Stone sprayed rounds like water. It was like hosing them down, only they came apart. People, real people, screaming, ripping up like rag dolls.

He screamed and they screamed. And when they screamed, it sounded like . . .

Seagulls.

Stone opened his eyes. Out the window of his hut, the sky was dark. A breeze came in the open door – cooler than before. The skinny girl who had replaced Roxana was pushed up against him. He couldn't remember her name – he'd have to find out in the morning. Her smell was thick on him.

It had all happened because of the jail time.

In 1991, Stone caught the first Gulf War on TV in the joint. He got a year and one day for killing the frat boy – unintentional manslaughter – and served every minute of it. They gave the cons Desert Storm on the box bolted high to the wall in the day room. It was the only thing on, and it was the only thing anybody wanted to watch. The screws wanted it. The cons wanted it. Heck, the warden and the social workers and the psychiatrist probably wanted it.

The boys whooped it up with every building that blew up, every bridge that blew up, every smart bomb dropped into every window, down every hallway, into every toilet stall, catching every Muhammad Omar Sharif in the seated position, with his pants around his knees. The good guys were raining death from the skies, and the bad guys behind locked doors ate it up like candy.

Stone did his time standing on his head. Literally. Every now and then he had to knock somebody unconscious to keep them out of his behind, so he didn't get any time off for good behaviour. But he was a placid sort, or he could swing that way. So when the trustee brought him a book from the library on yoga, he got into it. It had pictures of all the poses, and he aped them as best he could. Before too long, he was passing time doing headstands and lotus postures in the narrow confines of his cell.

When Stone got out, he went to see Louie.

'Thanks for coming to visit me,' he said.

145

'I paid for your lawyer, you fuck,' Louie said. 'You could've done ten years in there instead of just one. And believe me, those nine years of freedom didn't come cheap.' Then his look softened. 'Hey, Stone, I've had my own problems, OK?'

Louie looked older, and had lost a lot of weight. This robust, rotund man, who packed away the lasagna, was starting to look frail. A year could knock the stuffing out of an old boy Louie's age.

'Anything I should know about?'

'Yeah, my wife died.'

Stone stared at Louie sitting, diminished, behind his old desk. 'Jeez, Louie. I, uh . . . didn't know that.'

'Whaddya want, Stone?'

'I want to join the Army,' Stone said simply.

Louie shrugged. 'So join. You wanna get your ass shot off, it's not my problem.' He gestured to his office, the dusty plants, the old photos of Louie posing, not with celebrities, but with restaurant owners. 'Things are winding down here anyway. I'm gonna retire, find my place in the sun somewhere. I don't have no work for you.'

The Cold War had just ended and the Ruskies had recently gone belly up – the army was shrinking, not growing. 'They're not gonna take me, Louie. You know that. I killed somebody. They're letting people go as it is.'

'What can I do about it?'

'Pull some strings. Get me in there.'

Louie smiled, the smile a ghost of its former self. It brought something, an old spark, to Louie's eyes. 'You think I got strings like that I can pull?'

Stone smiled. 'I think you do.'

In September of '91, Stone reported for Basic Training. Most of the guys he did Basic with were just out of high school. Stone was the grand old man at twenty-two. He came to Basic fit, ripped, and tore it up. He was the fittest dog out there. The Army asked him what he wanted to do.

He said, 'I want to be all I can be.'

Jesus.

Now, so many years later, on the island, he eased away from the girl, slipped on a pair of shorts, and went out on to the dock. The night air was cool on his skin. He padded towards the end of the dock, but a man was standing there, smoking a cigarette. Stone came closer. His heart pitter-patted, just a bit, when he saw who it was.

'Doing a little night swimming, Stone?' the man said.

'Cruz?'

'I didn't kill you tonight. I could have. I hope you're going to return the favour one day.'

Stone shrugged, made no commitment either way. 'I don't think you need to worry about that,' he said. It wasn't like Cruz could read his mind. Then Stone sat down, slid off the edge and into the ocean. The tide was low, so he waded until he could safely dive under, then he started swimming. His arms pumped and in the dark water his mind saw the Skinnies, arms flying off, blood jetting, bodies falling.

Four in the morning.

Sticks sprawled in the passenger seat of a roomy Chrysler 300 rental car, waiting for everybody to show up. He was now officially exhausted. The air-conditioning pumped full blast to dispel the heaviness of the steamy southern night – the cold air was about the only thing keeping him awake. He had his seat reclined almost all the way back – far enough that he was close to dozing off, but not so far that he still couldn't see out the front windshield. To pass the time, he cleaned his fingernails with the five-inch hunting knife he'd bought in a general store on the drive out here.

The car itself sat in the weeds at the edge of a gigantic concrete runway at an abandoned airport deep in the heart of the Everglades. About all that remained of the airport was this runway and an empty control tower that squatted in the darkness about half a mile away.

To hear Mikey the Dunce tell it, the runway and control tower were about all that had ever existed.

'Tell me again, Mikey. I'm not sure I heard you right. What is this fucking place?' Sticks was always careful to call the gorilla in the driver's seat Mikey. Mikey D'Amato, who wished everybody would call him Mikey Tomatoes – a wish he only fulfilled by introducing himself that way to anybody new. People he'd just met would humour him and call him Mikey Tomatoes. Everybody who knew him more than a month – *everybody* – called him the Dunce, or just plain Dunce. They seemed to pick the name up by osmosis. Sticks was the only one who didn't call him that.

Sticks wasn't afraid of the Dunce, not by a damn sight, and he wasn't being polite. It was just easier to play the Dunce if you called him by his given name. Sticks could play the Dunce like a fiddle, yessiree. And the Dunce had his uses.

Sticks's question seemed to have awakened the Dunce from a nap. He blinked his dull eyes at Sticks. The Dunce had a big head and thick brow. The flicker of intelligence in his eyes was like that of an ox, or some other beast of burden. 'This airport?'

'Yeah. The airport.'

The Dunce shrugged. 'They were gonna have the Concorde fly in here. Like twenty years ago. They thought the plane was too loud to come in and out of Miami, you know, the sonic boom and all that, so they built this place way out here in the swamp. I mean, the fucking runway is two miles long. Then they decided to cancel the plane. So now this place just sits here.'

'Far out,' Sticks said.

The ups and downs of modern flight were much on Sticks's mind at the moment. Sticks himself had flown commercial air in some needle-nose jet down from Portland to Washington DC that afternoon. Sticks gritted his teeth through the security check – cheek by jowl with middle-America geeks, shoes off, no liquids, no toothpaste, no KY Jelly, bags searched and re-searched for any hint of terrorist bug-bite cream. The plane turned out to be narrow, two across the aisle, and it was a bumpy flight the whole way. As a rule, Sticks liked wide-body jets, big mother-fuckers that sat four hundred people – the more the merrier. Those planes never seemed to get any turbulence at all. From DC, he'd caught another narrow-ass plane to West Palm Beach, where the Dunce was waiting for him with this car. That second flight was even more fucked up – there were no drinks on the plane because of some bullshit logistics oversight. Nothing but peanuts.

Now they were sitting out here in West Bumblefuck, waiting for Goodman to show up here, and for a treetop-flying drug smuggler to drop out of the sky in some relic from the dawn of aviation. Goodman was a fugitive now – he was a person of interest in the investigation of a shootout, an explosion, a carjacking, and three violent deaths in Fort Lauderdale a couple of days ago – and he needed to get out of the country. The smuggler's plane would take them all on the final leg of the journey – to a dirt airstrip on their fabulous island destination.

Once there, the Dunce would play the tourist – the mark, Cruz, didn't know the Dunce, which meant the Dunce could do surveillance and, if all went well, maybe get close enough to spring the trap. In the meantime, the Dunce would spend his time cruising around the island, dressed like some rich New York geek, looking for off-the-beaten path island adventure, and at the same time trying to blend in with the other tourists. Sticks didn't know what Goodman was supposed to do – get in the way, most likely.

Sticks sighed. The Dunce was OK – smarter, probably, than people gave him credit for. But Sticks wasn't exactly looking forward to the low-altitude, kidney-knocking, white-knuckle puddle jump that the next few hours promised, and he damn well wasn't looking forward to doing it with Goodman, the big-mouth chatterbox. Sticks hadn't seen Goodman in several years, and you know what? He hadn't missed him.

Fucking A. That was an understatement.

Mind wandering, halfway between asleep and awake, he thought of the job that had brought him to this place. Vito had sent him to Maine to finish off a job that Cruz and Moss had fucked up. He had known Moss because he had worked a couple of jobs with him. Cruz he had known only by reputation. These guys were supposed to be two of the best – stone killers.

Cruz was an old-timer, a razor-sharp spick who had been working steadily since the late 1970s. Sticks was still in short pants, sizzling bugs on the sidewalk with a magnifying glass while Cruz was hiring himself out, carving up hard-ass pimps and dealers in Times Square. The story went that Cruz had killed so many people in his time that he had long ago lost track of the number. The legend proclaimed that when the time came to put a contract out on Cruz's mentor, an old Kraut named Oskar, Cruz was so cold he took the contract himself.

Moss was a beast – a giant ape of a man a few years younger than Sticks. He had stringy hair that sometimes hung down into a face that looked like it was carved out of granite. He was tall and he had muscles stacked on muscles – Moss could've played pro football. Sticks liked to work with Moss because there was never any bullshit – the marks got one look at that guy and they went as limp as wilted lettuce. All the fight went out of them. What was the fucking use, after all?

That's what Sticks never understood about the job. They sent these two animals together – plus another hitter called Fingers – on what looked like a routine assignment: collect an old man named Dugan and the debt he owed. Granted, it was a big debt – over two million in cash he stole when he iced Roselli in Roselli's own home. But all the same, this guy Dugan, he was hardly what you'd call a threat. And yet by the time Sticks got there, Fingers was dead, Cruz had joined Dugan's team, and Moss was sitting alone in his hotel room, drinking Jack Daniel's and nursing a face that looked like it had been folded, spindled, and not quite mutilated.

The last Sticks had seen of Moss, he had crashed a new Mercedes on to the steps of the town hall while in fast pursuit of Cruz and Dugan. Two weeks ago, a yuppie lawyer had let his dog slip the leash while walking on a beach outside of Portland, and the pooch had unearthed Moss's stabbed and strangled body. The cops had leaned on Sticks hard for information about that one, but cops didn't mean shit to Sticks. They couldn't intimidate him and they couldn't make friends with him. They couldn't use empathy. They couldn't trade him coffee or cigarettes. They couldn't use any of their fucking little tricks. There were video cameras in the interrogation rooms nowadays, so they couldn't even beat on him.

Wouldn't matter. Cops could break Sticks's ribs, knock out all his teeth, break all his fingers and cut his eyes out, and he wouldn't talk. Sticks was immune to cops, and to their little punishments and rewards. Sticks, as near as he could tell about himself, was a monster.

On the bridge, they had had Cruz and Dugan cornered. Sticks and his boys had chased these two dickheads through the Portland city streets. It was an awesome chase, the best time Sticks had had in a while. The fucking town was so Mayberry that it still had a drawbridge, and Cruz smashed right into it. They had them trapped. Sticks was just sauntering up when the cops got there. And that's when Cruz jumped. He grabbed Dugan by the jacket, and the two of them went right over the railing – the cops told Sticks it was seven storeys to the water.

'No way they'll live through that,' Sheriff Mayberry said. 'We lose eight out of every ten that goes off this bridge.' Of course they never found the bodies.

When Moss turned up dead, Sheriff Mayberry wanted to know who Sticks thought did it. 'Why don't you ask the two dead guys that went off the bridge?' Sticks said. 'You know, the ones who would never live through the jump?'

Sticks opened his eyes. Shit, he had dropped off there for a minute. The Dunce was dozing next to him in the driver's seat. Sticks glanced at the Dunce, baseball cap pulled down over his eyes. Every now and then, he let out a snort, and every time he did, Sticks fought the urge to cut his throat.

'Mikey, wake up. Hey. Mikey!'

The Dunce sat bolt upright. 'Eh?'

Sticks knocked the hat off his head. 'Don't go to sleep again, Mikey. The plane's here.'

And it was true. Over the low hum of the air-conditioning, he could hear the engine of a plane approaching. In another moment, he saw the lights of the descending plane suddenly come on, very low. It came down, the pilot bringing it to a stop after taxiing a tiny fraction of the massive runway, then immediately killing all the lights.

An instant later, a pair of car headlights went on in a pool of darkness on the far side of the runway.

'Goodman,' Mikey the Dunce said. 'He's been here all this time.' The Dunce glanced at Sticks. 'Did Vito say anything... about Goodman?'

'Yeah,' Sticks said. 'He told me no loose ends.'

The plane was small and old. It was so weather-beaten it looked like it had been through a war. The pilot introduced himself as Ed. He was an aging hippie freak, with long white hair pulled into a ponytail, a beard, a big potbelly and a chain of love beads around his neck. He was missing one of his front teeth. But looks could be deceiving. Goodman was aware that this guy had been flying contraband for thirty-five years – ever since he'd come home from Vietnam – and was a millionaire probably ten times over.

'Here's the deal,' Ed said as the four men briefly stood on the vast darkened runway. 'You just hang out back in the cargo hold and everything's cool.'

Goodman had been hiding out in a safe house – no more than a shack, really – back here in the swamp for the past two nights. Cut off from his wife, his home and his businesses, he had spent the sweaty time in his boxer shorts, pacing the creaky old floorboards of the place, wondering about alligators and waiting for the cops to come tumbling through the windows. His girlfriend Rita had run out yesterday on a mission of mercy. Good girl, very sharp – she had changed cars three times to elude tails, and brought him extra contact lenses, a twelve-pack of beer, a bucket of Kentucky Fried Chicken, and her own beautiful, sexy body to comfort him in his time of crisis.

Hell, he hadn't been able to perform with her. The stress, the anxiety . . . who knew? The cops had tossed his office. They'd come to his house with a search warrant, and an arrest warrant. His wife Clara was in hysterics, wondering where he was. She had to stay in the dark for now. He'd even missed his hormone shot yesterday. He was off his programme, and while he knew it wasn't possible for his age to kick back in so soon, he was already feeling old. Shit. If he never saw this fucking swamp again, it would be too soon. He was beginning to realise that it might be a long time before he could come back to the States.

Ed the pilot was still talking: 'The flight's gonna take about an hour, hour and a half, and I've made this run about one million times. The plane don't look like much, but she'll hold up – she's a Beechcraft 18, a Twin Beech, the last of her breed, and there's not much they can throw at her that she hasn't seen. We're gonna head due north from here, running low over land for a while to beat the radar, so you're gonna feel some bumps – it's nothing to worry about. One important thing – I know who you guys are, and I tell you now that I'm fully armed up front and I don't tolerate any fucking around. I assume none of you know how to fly a plane. So let's do this: you guys let me be, you stay calm and behave yourselves, and I'll get you all there in one piece. Agreed?'

There was no response. Ed stood for a moment, staring at them.

'Agreed?' he said again. 'It's my fucking plane, fellas.'

'Agreed,' they said in a lackluster chorus, like reluctant schoolchildren.

The skinny guy, the one they called Sticks, actually raised his hand like he was in school. 'I been awake for, like, thirty-six hours straight. I been drinking coffee all day. If I need to take a piss, where do I go? It don't look like you got a bathroom in this heap.'

Goodman smiled at that. Oh, he had heard all the stories about Sticks the maniac, and had met him several times before. But even so, it was hard to believe this kid was a contract killer. Vito claimed that this short drink of water was one of the best they had. That begged the question: had things really got this bad? Who the fuck were they hiring these days?

Ed pointed to the cargo door. 'There's a couple of water jugs in the back there. Feel free to piss in those.'

Fucking Goodman never shut up. What was the matter with this guy?

They sat on heavy crates in the lurid darkness of the cargo hold – ten feet high, maybe twenty feet across. Piles of strapped-down boxes were everywhere in the shadows behind them, all of it looking strewn around haphazardly, all of it looking like junk. The plane itself bounced and bucked – Sticks was nearly bounced off his crate a couple of times. Wind was coming in from somewhere, and you practically had to shout to be heard over the engine noise.

Mikey the Dunce had brought out a quart of whiskey for the ride. They passed it back and forth between the three of them, steadily getting drunk. Sticks, having gone so long without sleep, wired on caffeine, and with barely any food in his stomach, found the whiskey going straight to his brain. His synapses crackled and fired – it felt good. He began to feel very fucking alive, very fucking alert, and very, very murderous. Meanwhile, big shot Goodman talked the whole time, his patter bouncing from one meaningless and stupid topic to the next. As Sticks watched, Goodman's bald head reflected dim light from somewhere – a beacon in the darkness, almost as if the chrome dome itself was a weak source of illumination.

'We're an invasive species,' Goodman shouted.

'What?' the Dunce said. 'What's that, Goodie?' Poor Dunce – always sincere, always eager, always ready and willing to swallow a line of bullshit.

'Humans. We're an invasive species. I've been reading about it the past couple of months. We came here from another planet. We're like the kudzu vines up in Georgia, or the tree frogs ... I forget where. The thing is, a species from someplace else gets artificially moved to a new place, and then can't adapt to the new environment. It out-competes everything, kills everything off, and multiplies out of control. That's what we do, and that's why everything we try to do to save this planet turns to shit. We don't belong here.'

He shrugged his heavy shoulders. 'We're an invasive species, you know? We're doomed to fuck everything up. We couldn't stop if we wanted to, so I say let it rip.'

'I thought you were Catholic,' said the Dunce.

'I am. My wife goes to Mass every Sunday. I sponsored a new class-room at the parish grade school. It has a plaque with our name on it over the door. Just because we came here from another planet don't mean I'm not Catholic.'

The bottle came around and Sticks took another swig. They hit some turbulence and the jolts passed from the wooden crate straight up Sticks's spine.

'Fucking Vito,' Goodman shouted now over the roar of the plane's engines. He took a swig of the whiskey.

'Yeah?' the Dunce said.

'Yeah. He fucked me up. I had things going straight. Suddenly, he calls me up out of the blue, gives me this bullshit job, and now look at me. I'm a hunted man.'

'Yeah, I heard about that,' the Dunce said. 'I heard you were in, like, retirement. Going legit. Now your whole world just came crashing down, right?'

'That's right. I own hotels. Golf courses. The fucking Maestro played my course one time. Why am I out doing Vito's dirty work? I mean, I've known Vito my whole life, but what's right is right. And this . . .' – here he gestured at the shuddering and rattling airplane, threatening to come apart around them – 'this ain't right.'

·'I gotta take a piss,' Sticks said. He slid off his crate, then bounced and bumped his way into the darkness behind them. He found one of the water jugs on the floor, and let a long stream flow into it. He braced himself with an arm against the wall.

Goodman's voice floated back to him. 'What's the matter with that guy? He a fan of Vito? Like, president of the Big Vito fan club?'

The Dunce's voice: 'Nah. He's just in a bad mood. Just got sprung from the joint, ain't slept, and he ended up coming on this job. I think he'd rather be in a hotel with a whore than bouncing around on this shitty plane.'

Sticks slid the hunting knife out of his jacket, and pulled it from its sheath. Its sharp edge gleamed in the dim light thrown off the top of Goodman's head.

'Well, he oughta cheer up. He thinks he has problems? Look at the fucking mess I'm in. Lack of sleep is the least of it.'

True enough, Sticks thought. *True enough*.

Goodman upended the bottle, taking a big long gulp, getting that pleasant burn in the back of his throat. As he leaned back, he felt a stinging sensation in his neck. Jesus, that hurt. Now it was in his back. Two, three, four places. He dropped the bottle and it shattered at his feet. He tried to turn, but felt the stabbing again in his side. He caught sight of Sticks, hovering behind him, knife in hand, the blade dark and glistening.

'What the fuck?'

He turned to Mikey the Dunce, but the Dunce was backing away. He grabbed for the Dunce's arm, but missed. His mind raced. Sticks was still there, arm moving fast, like a rotor, stabbing him in the face now.

156

In the face!

Goodman pushed to his feet, and bulled his way past Sticks. He ran into the curved wall of the plane, bumped his head, turned around. Sticks was still there, right with him like a swarm of bees, stabbing like a madman. Goodman punched Sticks in the face. Sticks took a step back, shook his head, then smiled.

'You're gonna like retirement,' Sticks said.

Goodman sank to his knees. He felt too weak now to lift his arms. Sticks stabbed him at will. Goodman looked up and Sticks's hand was red with blood. Sticks's eyes were demon eyes. Goodman slumped all the way to the floor.

He lay there, mind floating, vaguely aware that Sticks and the Dunce were standing above him. He daydreamed – the video arcade screeching and pinging below him, the sound of money pouring into his pockets, while out the window the sexy teenage girls swung and shook their asses as they sashayed down to the beach.

Then Sticks's face was close to his. Goodman looked, and Sticks's teeth were an inch away. They looked big, and razor sharp, like the teeth of a wolf. Or a monster. 'You got soft,' Sticks said, 'then you fucked up a job. Then you blamed Vito. It was YOU, not him. See what I mean?'

'Fuck you,' Goodman said.

'Yeah. Fuck me.'

Somewhere, Goodman heard a bolt thrown back. Suddenly an icy wind blew through the cargo hold.

'Mikey, help me with this guy. He weighs a ton.'

Goodman felt them take his arms and drag him towards the open door. He was totally limp – unable to do anything. The lightheadedness made him afraid. He could pass out like this. It was important that he didn't pass out.

'Jesus,' the Dunce said. 'Who's gonna clean up all this blood? Look at it. It's all over the floor. Ed's not gonna like that.'

'After I talk to him, Ed's gonna be happy to be alive,' Sticks said.

Goodman was near the edge. The wind was in his face. The floor was hard and cold. Below him, there was nothing but darkness. Above him, he could see stars and wisps of cloud. They were moving fast. The plane bucked and shuddered, and Goodman's head bounced.

'See?' Sticks said. 'We're already over the water. This flight isn't too bad.'

They were going to throw Goodman out of the plane. His mind recoiled at the thought of it.

'Kill me,' he said.

Sticks's face was near him again. Goodman saw a streak of wild delight in those eyes. 'What?' Sticks said.

'Kill me. Please kill me.' Goodman had heard pleading many times before, but never from his own voice. He hated the sound.

'That's what we're doing.'

'Yeah, but—'

'Don't worry,' Sticks said. He gave Goodman a playful smack on the cheek. Then he gripped Goodman's jaw in his hand, and squished his cheeks and mouth into a kissy-face. Sticks talked in a sing-song voice, like a person might speak to a newborn baby, or to a favourite pet cat. 'You're bleeding pretty bad, aren't you? Yes you are. If you live through the fall, the sharks will come and take care of you. Yes they will.'

Sticks shoved him hard and Goodman tumbled out of the plane. He fell through the air, darkness all around him. He plunged, faster and faster, going end over end. He screamed but could not hear. A face came to him – that of his wife Clara, alone and wondering where he had gone.

As Sticks stepped off the plane on to the dirt airstrip in the first early light of a Saint Mark's morning, the hot breeze hit him. It was going to be a scorcher. He glanced around at the thick green forest that surrounded the airstrip, and fancied he could almost taste the salt of the ocean in the air. They'd said this guy Ed could land an airplane on a postage stamp with his eyes closed, and now Sticks saw how true that was. The runway looked like it was just about long enough for a half-court game of basketball. After that was the tree-line.

No rest for the weary today – Sticks had to push through his exhaustion and meet with Stone this morning. That was OK. The ride over had got Sticks a little bit jazzed, the fear in the pilot's eyes when Sticks explained to him what had happened to Goodman had amped up the juice a bit, and all of it reminded him of something he had allowed himself to forget during his recent time in lock-up. He liked to work. He liked it so much that he often did it in his spare time as a hobby.

The Dunce was loading guns, ammo and their bags up by the taxi. The jigaboo driver was standing there, arms folded, watching the shit pile up with an aloof stare. Lazy, island-living, coconut-eating motherfucker. Jesus. Sticks hated jigs, and he hated lazy people. This driver was starting with two strikes against him – he'd better watch his mouth on the way to the hotel.

Sticks grunted, affirming his own feelings, and gazed up at the first light of dawn.

'You say something, Sticks?' the Dunce said.

'Nah. It's nothing. Just looking forward to getting back to business.'

6

As a child, Ty Weathers had studied the escape artist Houdini.

Ty stood inside the narrow closet where they'd put him. His ankles were tied together, about six inches apart — just enough room so he could walk when they let him out. His hands were clasped together and tied that way, but were also tied to the rope around his ankles, and then tied to yet another length of rope that went up and around his neck. If he jerked his hands around too much, that tightened the rope around his neck, cutting off his air.

'You know that's illegal, right?' he'd said to the man Cruz, who had tied him up this way. 'It's against the fucking law. You can't tie somebody so that they end up strangling themselves.'

Cruz had shrugged and given him a blank look. 'Call a cop.'

Ty had dozed in and out all night. It was impossible to sleep standing up like this, and there was no way to get down on the floor — the fucking closet was too small. Anyway, if he even tried, he'd probably choke himself to death.

With all those hours on his hands, he'd had a lot of time to think. And he'd spent much of that time thinking about Lola. She was a beautiful Nubian prize. Even the way she had taken him down yesterday morning – you had to give her credit. Put a man twice her size right down in the dust. With his eyes closed, Ty imagined the lines of her face, and her body in the bikini from yesterday, and he realised he'd like to get to know her better. Talk to her, find out where she was from, and how she ended up here. That'd be hard – but maybe not impossible – now that things had turned out like this. After all that drama, she had probably hardened her heart against him. It was a shame that he had hit her – he admitted that was a mistake. But you know? What was she doing with that old white boy? Even if the man had all the money in the world, she really should have more respect for herself.

At some point, in the middle of the night, Cruz had come and unlocked the door. He led Ty up the stairs and outside to take a piss off the side of the boat. It was late, the stars were out, and far away, the island was quiet. Looking around, Ty noticed that his skiff was gone.

'Where's my boat, man?'

'I sank it. Shot it full of holes, tossed a few extra bricks we had lying around in there, and after a little while, it went under. No sense calling attention to ourselves by having a dead man's boat tied up and visible here.'

'But I'm not dead, sucker.'

Cruz smiled at that. 'So you claim.'

When it was time to go back in the closet, Ty didn't struggle or complain. He wanted Cruz to think he was a model prisoner. He wanted Cruz to let his guard down, even the tiniest fraction.

'Good night, Ty,' Cruz said as he closed and locked the doors to the cramped closet, plunging Ty back into total darkness.

'Good night, Cruz.'

Now, as early morning light came through the crack between the closet doors, Ty thought about Harry Houdini. For a while – maybe he was nine years old at the time, maybe ten – Ty had gotten off on Houdini. He had all the books Houdini had written. He had all the books people had written about Houdini. He had tried all the card tricks, and the magic tricks. He had learned the simpler escapes – the rope escapes – Houdini had done early in his career. Ty hadn't moved on to underwater milk-jug escapes, or upside-down escapes while dangling from buildings, but he probably would have, if his mom had let him.

What was the thing about escaping when you were tied up with rope? The thing was slack – when people tied you, they always left some slack somewhere. Even people who worked with ropes all the time left a little slack. That was the nature of ropes. The trick was to find the slack, and move it around – through tiny jerks and wiggles of your body – to someplace you could use it. Tricky, what with the noose around his neck getting tighter every time he moved too much. But if he thought about it, he could sense a little bit of slack, the smallest possible amount, around his wrists. Maybe there was something he could do with that?

Very gently, as the light grew stronger in the closet, Ty began to test the slack in his ropes.

Stone met Sticks in the bar at Sticks's hotel. The bar was three steps down from the threadbare hotel lobby. It was semi-dark in there, with smoked windows along the back wall giving a view of the pool area and the ocean beyond. Stone passed through a small jungle of tall, potted plants – like rubber tree plants – as he entered. He touched one – plastic. They sat on stools at the bar – an unsmiling islander poured the drinks without speaking a word, and spent any downtime leaning on his elbows.

'I can't stand this fucking heat,' Sticks said, passing his napkin across his sweaty forehead. 'You know that? It's like fucking hell outside. It's a little better in here, but not by much.'

Stone drank in the sight of him. A skinny guy – too skinny. Bone thin, they used to call it when Stone was a kid. The guy reminded him of the half-starved dogs he'd seen wandering around in Iraq. You could count the ribs on them. You also didn't want to get near them – they were vicious from hunger. Sticks wasn't mangy like the dogs – his hair was slicked back and he seemed somewhat put together. But his look was out of place on an island like Saint Mark's. Pale white skin, almost translucent, like soap. Jeans, boots, and a black T-shirt with the Rolling Stones on it. *Tattoo You*. That was a long time ago – the guy must buy his shirts at a memorabilia store. His arms hung down from the short sleeves like wayward threads. All of this, and bloodshot eyes with dark rings around them – the guy could be a vampire.

This was the guy they'd sent down from New York? He was the one who was going to take care of Cruz? All right. So be it.

One thing Sticks had right – it wasn't much cooler here in the bar than it was outside. Being out of the sun provided some relief. But it seemed like the air-conditioner, which had been going full blast just two days ago, was out of order. So the place had taken on a heavy tone of humidity. The very air seemed to weigh you down. In fact, the floor of the bar was carpeted in dark red, and the carpet seemed to soak up the moisture like a sponge. Stone had felt his sandals sticking to the floor as he walked in.

Sticks was on his second fruity rum drink, and they'd only just started talking. Stone had barely given Sticks the set-up.

'So when I recognised it was Cruz, I sat down with them. Probably dumb, but hey, I was drunk, and I didn't know you guys were after him. That's when his girl pulled the piece, and I figured something was up.'

'What'd she look like?'

'The girl? Good looking. Nice bod. Brownish hair. Young, younger than Cruz.'

Sticks shrugged. 'Could be her. Probably don't matter who it is. Go on.'

'After a bit of chat with them, the fun wore off, so I cut out. But I paid a little kid to follow them.'

164

'A kid?'

'Yeah, some kid I bought a bag of grass off once. He's a good kid. I couldn't follow them because I stick out like a sore thumb around here. So I got some little black kid to do it. There's a million little black kids on this island. I'm sure they never noticed him. In any case, they left the restaurant like half an hour after I did, walked down to the marina, got in an outboard and took off. I haven't seen them since. Must have spooked them, because they took off into open water.'

'Just took off for open water, eh?'

'That's right.'

'There's been a lot of that going around,' Sticks said. 'People taking off for open water. Any idea where they were headed?'

'No idea. Could be anywhere. Like I said, they haven't been back. Care to tell me what the deal is?'

Sticks shrugged. 'Yeah. Here's the deal.' He reached into the pocket of his jeans and brought out a white envelope. It was rumpled and damp from sitting in his sweaty pocket. It looked like the kind of envelope you might send a business letter in, but it was swollen fatter than any business letter. Sticks tossed it on to the table in front of Stone.

'There's ten large in that envelope. That's your finder's fee for tipping us off. Cruz and a guy he's with, an old timer who calls himself Smoke Dugan, are running around down here with a couple of girls – one white, one black – and about two and a half million in cash. Dugan killed a boss named Roselli and stole the money. They sent Cruz to get it back, but now Cruz is in on it with him. That's the beginning of the story. The end of the story is I'm down here, I'm gonna find Cruz and Dugan, eat them both for lunch, and head on back to New York with the money they stole.'

'That's some story,' Stone said.

Sticks gestured at the bar around them, and the island it sat on. 'I'm gonna stick around here a while, soak up some sun, maybe get one of these jigaboos to fly me around in a seaplane, see if I can spot our boys.

In the meantime, if you happen to find them, you let me know. There'll be another ten in it for you, if you do.'

Stone nearly choked at the idea of this pale stick-figure soaking up the sun. Instead of choking, however, he picked up the envelope. It was meaty. He put it in the side pocket of his shorts and snapped the button closed. 'Sounds good, Sticks. I'll let you know if I see them. I'll keep a low profile next time.'

Sticks was getting up to leave. He drained the last of his drink. 'You do that. Vito said you're a good kid. Said you just got back from the war. How was it?'

'Not great.'

'Yeah, that's what they all say. Shoot any ragheads?'

'Some. Yeah.'

'Good man. I'll see you around.'

When Sticks was gone, Stone ordered another drink. He glanced around the bar. He spotted Roxana sitting at a table halfway across the restaurant. She was about a three-quarter turn away from him, but he could tell from the body and the hair that it was her. Great body, long black hair. Great hair – he loved to get his hands wrapped up in it, and smell it. She was sitting with a tourist, a well-muscled guy in a striped polo shirt, with slicked back hair. A greaseball. The guy was hairy – hairy arms, hairy hands, hairy knuckles. He glanced over and saw Stone looking at him. Stone played it nonchalant, kept looking for another second or so, then moved on.

His breathing changed. Stone was good at monitoring his own vital signs – his breathing had just become shallower. His heart was beating faster. OK. Roxana had a new client. Couldn't blame her. Life was life, and work was work. What'd he think? She would carry a torch for him? She was a hooker, and even though he liked her, he had asked for a different one to keep things interesting. *He* had dumped *her*. So now Roxana had a new john. Relax – that's how it worked with hookers.

Back to the matter in hand: two and a half million dollars in cash?

And he knew exactly where Cruz was, probably within twenty feet. Wow. The only word for that was . . . wow. Stone had just made a nice chunk of change in Iraq, but 2.5 mil was enough money to hang out down here just about for ever. Sure, he'd have to leave Saint Mark's, but there was always the Dominican Republic. Trinidad and Tobago. Cuba. Belize. Costa Rica. If he could pull this job off, he was in for a nice long vacation. All that good diving. All that good dope. All those lovely ladies in all those lovely places – they'd put Roxana right out of his mind.

He glanced back at that table – now Roxana was listening intently to what the new beau was saying to her. She didn't seem to like what he was saying. She must deal with a lot of jerks in her line of work. Jeez, couldn't she find some other kind of job?

Man, forget it.

There was the question of what to do about the people in New York – the people who sent nightmare monsters like Cruz into action in the first place – but that question had an easy answer. Don't tell them. Kill Cruz, kill this guy Dugan he was with, and take the money. New York never even had to know about it. If they did find out, there was a simple answer to that as well: keep moving. Stone was a trained commando – he knew how to avoid people, and if people came for him, he knew how to take them down. All the action he had seen in his life, and he'd never taken a bullet. Not once. Were they going to send a whacked-out city slicker like Sticks to some remote Peruvian jungle town to find Stone, when Stone thrived in just such a place? He really doubted it.

There was a lot to do. He needed to move fast. It wouldn't be easy to spot Cruz from a seaplane, especially if he was lying low, but you never knew. Sticks could get lucky up there. So tonight, Stone had to go out on the water and take a look at what Cruz was up to. Soon after that, he could figure out what his own move was going to be, and make it. Two and a half million dollars? Wow. Not bad.

He decided not to look at Roxana's table again, but then did it anyway. Physical longing went through him in a sickly wave – an urge to just be pressed up against her, body to body. Not even having sex – just touching. Tough break for her, stuck on this island when Stone was moving on to better things.

Stone's ship had come in, and it was something to behold – a great big custom-made mega-yacht from *Lifestyles of the Rich and Famous* was pulling into port, and he was about to sail off to a life of fabulous adventure. If he hadn't seen her with the hairy greaseball just now, Stone might have considered taking Roxana along with him.

Something was wrong with the air-conditioning.

Mikey Tomatoes – sometimes called Mikey the Dunce – sat in the lounge at the hotel with a nice fleshy local girl, watching the action unfold at the bar.

No fucking air-conditioning. Unbelievable. It was like a fucking sauna in here. What a trip. Mikey had found some kind of salamander or gecko in the bathroom of his room this morning – squashed it flat with his penny loafer, in fact. The salt-fish and fried dumplings he'd had for breakfast was spicing up his acid reflux. And now this – sitting in the lounge sweating because the air-conditioning was off.

But Mikey was an optimist – that's how he played life. So what was good about this trip so far? Plenty. For one, it was good to get away.

The job had appeared right out of the blue – Mikey had got word about it yesterday afternoon. He'd been coming out of the shower at his bachelor apartment in Brooklyn Heights. It was a nondescript place, one bedroom, one bath, a couple of grimy windows – a fallback position since his separation and divorce. His wife was a bloodsucker, bleeding him for alimony and child support, while all the while bad-mouthing him to the kids. She'd also walked off with the house and the Mercedes. She was a sharp one, all right. Shrewd. He'd come to believe she had a private eye following him around – she kept telling the judge he was hiding money from her. Less than a year ago, in fact, Mikey had spent a month in jail as a deadbeat dad.

The only reason he hadn't murdered her by now was that the cops would bust him the next day – nobody in the world had a better motive for killing that evil bitch. He was chewing on all this – a regular hobby of his these days – when the phone rang. Sticks, out of jail, and offering him work. Did he want to get out of town for a little while? Fly down to the islands on a job? Pretend he was a tourist? You bet he did.

Mikey'd flown down to Miami last night, and he and Sticks had come in on the hippie puddle jumper early this morning. Mikey frowned at the thought of that flight. It was really too bad the way Goodie died. Mikey had liked Goodie, but a job was a job. And it was good to be reminded how things went sometimes – if Mikey wasn't careful, one fine day he could be the guy getting stuck with knives and thrown off a plane.

In any case, they'd gotten in early enough that, after he and Sticks had split off from each other, Mikey'd had time to take a nice swim in the ocean. Best of all, when he'd come out of the water, some little black kid was hanging around, leaning on a palm tree, about ten feet from Mikey's towel. Mikey's first instinct was the kid would try to steal something. Wrong. The kid was not shy, and made an introduction immediately. Turned out the pint-sized entrepreneur was the local drug dealer, *and* the local pimp. Good kid. Mikey scored a bag of weed, and this nice piece of tail sitting across the table from him. Pressed for time by then, Mikey was faced with a decision – the whore or the pot before the meeting? Mikey had elected to take a bounce with the whore before sampling the contents of the bag. If the pot was half as tasty as the whore, then the kid had a customer for life.

The kid had said, 'I'm your man. You don't need to talk to anybody else.' And now Mikey believed him.

So Mikey had sat at the table with the whore, had a few drinks, and made small talk. The whore had got kind of surly since they'd come down here – maybe she was in a big hurry to get back to Mikey's bedroom, and that was fine with Mikey. But for now, Mikey's job was to watch the action at the bar — about fifteen yards away. Sticks was over there, meeting with a guy they called Stone. Sticks didn't acknowledge him and Mikey didn't acknowledge them. See, that was the game — he was acting like a dumb geek tourist.

He was supposed to watch the meeting with Stone, get a make on what the guy looked like, and then follow him around. Stone had no reason to suspect him — he was just some guy, down here for a little fun and sun. Apparently, Stone had claimed over the phone that he didn't know where Cruz was, but nobody really believed that. Sticks thought that if he dangled the $2.5 mil in front of Stone, Stone would suddenly remember where Cruz was — and forget to share the information around.

Stone was a tall, thin reed of a man. But built like a machine, no doubt. Ripped. Looked a little like the white kid that used to play wide receiver for the Giants. Wore his hair high and tight, like the military geek he was.

Yesterday, on the plane from New York, Mikey had read the book on this guy — worked for the organisation when he was a kid, bodyguard, bouncer, did a spell for manslaughter back in the day. Got out a year later, joined the flag wavers, got sent to Africa. The guy must enjoy asking for permission to take a shit — out of one government can, and right back into the next. Anyway, he was one of those kids that got stuck in some Third World shithole city overnight — Mikey had seen the movie — and lit the place up rather than get his body parts dragged through the streets by the angry hordes. Came back home with the screaming meemies — did a lengthy pop in the booby hatch. He was what you'd call an institutional man. Prison, the army, the lunatic asylum. Got out of the nuthouse, came back to work for us. Did a few jobs — smuggler, killer for hire. Pretty good at it, but not a go-getter — he'd rather spend his time living in a tent on a mountainside. Too much combat had loosened his screws a little. Dropped out of sight for a long while and people figured he was dead, probably by his own hand. Then, a phone call out of nowhere: 'Just got back from Iraq. Ran into Cruz on this island. Anybody mind if I pop him?'

Good kid, Stone – but he shouldn't forget who he worked for. Now that Mikey had a bead on him, Stone would probably lead them straight to Cruz.

Mikey looked at the whore. Her pretty face seemed sad. Mikey'd had a few drinks and was feeling good, but he didn't like the whore pouting like this. After all, he couldn't go straight upstairs with her – he was going to have to take a little stroll right now, see where Stone was going after he left here. He needed her to stay happy until that was over.

'What's the matter?' he said. 'Something bothering you? You want another drink?'

Variety is the spice of life.

That's what the bastard Stone had told Little Macho. It wasn't that he didn't like Roxana any more – it was just that he wanted to spice things up with somebody new. Well, wonderful, if that's what he wanted. But she'd seen him looking over here a few times now – jealous, probably. Good for him. Meanwhile, she was doing it today with Mikey the Tomato, a hairy brute in heavy aftershave. Yes, that really was his name. He introduced himself to her as Mikey Tomatoes.

Mikey the Tomato had a chest like a bear, and that was OK. But that thick pelt of fur went all the way around to his back, too. He had hair on his shoulders. She had noticed he had hair growing out of his ears – not out of the ear canal, but out of the tops of the very ears themselves. He was a strong man, squat and powerfully built like an ape. And he was a man who liked to pound a woman into submission – nothing sexy about it. She was already sore from this morning, and she had a hunch he was going to want some more in a little while. And he was a dumb man, talking nonsense mostly.

Maybe Macho could find another girl for him? Roxana was tired of all these men. She might like to take a few days off.

One thing did fascinate her about Mikey, however: he was obviously interested in the meeting Stone was having at the bar. Now that the meeting was over, and the pale, skinny stranger had gone, she could tell that Mikey was still watching Stone, just a bit, from the corner of his eye. Did he sense something about Stone? Did he notice how Stone had been glancing over here?

'What's the matter?' Mikey said now. 'Something bothering you? You want another drink?'

Roxana nodded, and Mikey gestured to the waitress for two more drinks.

'Tell me something,' Roxana said, 'if you don't mind?'

Mikey smiled. 'I don't mind. I'll tell you anything you want.'

Roxana moved her shoulder just a bit, gesturing ever so slightly at the bar. 'Who is that man there?'

'What man?'

'The tall man at the bar.'

Mikey didn't look where she had gestured. He shrugged, staring at Roxana's neck like he was thinking about biting it. 'I don't know him. Never seen him before. What are you talking about?'

'It seems like you're watching him. Maybe.'

She wasn't ready for his response. One strong hand slithered across the table and grabbed her arm. 'You know something?' he said. 'You're a big healthy girl, but you got bones like a bird.' Slowly, and without any apparent effort on his part, he began to squeeze her wrist. Within a few seconds, it began to hurt. She tried to pull away, but it did no good. He could snap her wrist easily, right here, with all these people around.

He raised a stubby finger, not quite to her face. He looked at her, the threat all in his eyes. To anyone else in the bar, she realised, they were just a tourist and a local girl, having an intense and intimate conversation.

'You're a very beautiful girl, OK? And you want to stay that way, so it don't pay for you to be nosey. I'm not looking at anybody, and even if I am, that's none of your business. We can have a very nice time, you can make some nice money, and if you think you see me looking at somebody, remind yourself that I'm not doing what you think, and anyway, what do you care? I'll be gone in a couple of days, right?'

He gave her one last, long squeeze. The bone went right to the breaking point. He could crush it to dust. 'Right?'

'Right. Right. Yes.'

He let her wrist go. She pulled it back, but could still feel his phantom hand there like a vice. He was a good man to stay away from. She would run out the door right now . . . only he hadn't paid her yet for this morning.

'OK?'

'Yes, I'm OK.'

'Good. Now let's go. I want to take a walk.'

The waitress was just coming with the fresh round of drinks.

'Now? We just ordered more drinks.'

'That's OK. They're paid for. Come on.'

Roxana stood, baffled, until she turned and saw that Stone had just walked out of the room. She caught a glimpse of the back of his T-shirt and shorts as he stepped through the lobby and into the glare of the sunlight.

'No time to waste,' Mikey said, pushing her ahead of him. 'Let's move it.'

You get weird dreams after a conk on the head.

Lola lay alone in bed in the cabin she shared with Smoke. A knocking sound came from somewhere, monotonous and repetitive. It annoyed her because without that sound, she'd probably still be asleep. It seemed like only moments before she had been with Yun, the karate teacher, nearly four decades older than her, whom she had taken as a lover when she had first moved to Portland. Yun, dead four years now, had been walking her through the bombed-out ruins of Seoul, where he had grown up as an orphan in the aftermath of the Korean War.

Yun didn't smile when he spoke. He was a kind man, but a hard one, and he never smiled. 'Your fears are because of your attachments,' he said. 'Only when you realise nothing has any substance can you be free. Let go of everything, including yourself. It's all illusion.'

Yun always used to say things like that. But soon he morphed into Smoke, who stood above her and gently put a rough hand on her cheek. There was concern in Smoke's eyes, even fear. Smoke hadn't let go of his attachments, she supposed. None of this was an illusion to him.

'Did I lose you?' he said. 'I was afraid I had lost you.'

She put her hand on his. 'You didn't lose me. You're never going to lose me.'

When she opened her eyes, it was to daylight coming through the skylight above her. Her head ached dully, and in an instant, the memories of the day before raced in. She counted herself lucky — considering the knocks she had taken, a dull ache was better than a sharp pain. And a thought came: had Smoke lost her? He hadn't lost her to death, no, but it was possible that he'd never really had her in the first place.

She remembered a time they had driven upstate in Maine to the town of Rangeley. It was November a year ago, and all the trees had lost their leaves. Still, the lovely little town was situated on a vast lake, and was ringed by purple mountains. They rented a cabin right on the lake, and built fires in the fireplace morning and night. In the early evenings, they would drive out of town into the surrounding forestland, looking for moose. With the trees bare, the big gangly creatures had lost their cover, and so they counted sixteen moose in two evenings of looking — Smoke called it 'a mother-lode of moose'. One night, a rainstorm knocked out the electricity, so they nestled together, drank wine and ate cheese sandwiches by the light of the crackling fire. It was one of her fondest memories and she had been madly in love with Smoke then. But that Smoke – the retired engineer – wasn't *this* Smoke, the gangster who took punch after punch in the face and still smiled and cracked jokes. She'd thought it before so she might as well think it again – their lives together had been a lie.

Now, on the boat, Lola stood on unsteady legs and went out to face the day. She was already dressed in shorts and a T-shirt – she must have changed into them before going to sleep, though she hardly remembered it. She stepped into the main cabin and discovered what the knocking sound was. From inside the utility closet, Ty Weathers was banging on the doors. It sounded like he was using his head.

'Can I help you?' she said.

'Lola?' came a muffled voice.

'Yes.'

'They ain't fed me all night, and I gotta pee. I gotta go pretty bad – I can't hold it much longer.'

Lola rolled her eyes. The very act made her dizzy, and reminded her of the exact amount of pity she felt for him: none. 'I'm sorry to hear that,' she said.

'Lola, please! They got a rope around my neck in here. They're trying to cut my air off.'

'I want to ask you a question,' she said. 'You're not from around here, are you?'

'Wilmington, Delaware. Grew up right in the ghetto.'

'That's what I thought – you're from America. Do you suppose that's why you hate women so much? Living in the ghetto did that to you?' She found that this was more than just a whimsical game she was playing – she really was curious about the answer. She'd been curious for a long time, but she'd never before had such a captive audience on whom to put the question.

There was a pause on the other side of the door. It lasted several seconds, as if she had struck Ty speechless. 'I don't hate women,' he said finally. 'I like women. I like you the most. You're a beautiful Nubian princess who got lost somewhere – separated from your people. I want to get you back where you belong, put you on a throne.'

'Uh, Ty? You were going to rape me yesterday, remember? You hit me on the head with a pole. Twice. Maybe you're not aware of this, but that's not what you do to people you like.'

Another pause came. 'Lola, I gotta pee. OK? Let's talk about all this later.'

Lola went upstairs into the sunlight. Smoke was there, half buried in the uncovered engine well, working to bring the boat back to life. His hands were black with grease, his face smeared with it where he had wiped the sweat off.

'Good morning,' she said.

'Good morning to you.' Smoke smiled, his bruised face a map of where Ty had beaten him. Did Smoke like getting hit? Was that the secret? He cocked a thumb back downstairs the way she had come. 'I wouldn't bother with that guy. If he pisses himself, we have disinfectant we can spray on him. Summer Breeze, I think it's called.'

She climbed the next short flight of steps to the deck, where Cruz and Pamela lounged. The remains of breakfast were in front of them. Pamela's hair was wet, and she was wrapped in a big plush towel – must have gone for a swim, like Lola had intended to do the day before. Also, a big gun, the paint job a dull matte black, sat by Cruz's right hand. A long silencer protruded from the barrel. That gun was an ugly piece of machinery.

'Hey, look what the tide washed in,' Pamela said. 'Looking good, hon. How are you feeling?'

'Better,' Lola allowed. 'I slept a long time.' She slid into a chair at the table. 'Our prisoner says he needs to relieve himself.'

Cruz and Pamela glanced at each other. 'I'll take care of it,' Pamela said.

'Are you sure?'

'Cruz! I'm your girl, remember? I can handle any man.'

* * *

Ty really did have to pee – he wasn't lying. And he really was hungry – these motherfuckers hadn't given him so much as a table scrap in all the time they'd held him here – he guessed it was close to eighteen hours by now. So that much was true.

What was also true was he had slipped the ropes. Just like Houdini, baby! The rope around his neck had gotten so tight while he was freeing his hands, he had damn near passed out from lack of oxygen. But once those hands were free, it was nothing to get that lynch-man's noose off his neck. Then all it took was a little bit of flexibility to reach down and get the ropes off his ankles.

All he needed now was somebody to open these doors. He could probably smash them down with his bare hands, but they'd hear him doing it, so that was no good. By the time he busted through, they'd all be standing there, worst of all Cruz, guns at the ready.

No, he needed to sound pitiful enough that they opened the doors without suspecting what would happen next.

A sound came on the other side of the doors – was it a key entering a lock?

'Ty?' came a female voice, the voice of the other woman on the boat here. What was her name? 'Are you ready to behave yourself in there?' she said. 'I'm gonna let you out for a minute.'

'I'll behave,' he heard himself say. He said it weak, pitiful, in the voice of a man who has given up all hope.

But inside, he felt that engine revving – it was time for the show again.

Outside the closet, Pamela slid the key into the lock.

She was still riding a high this morning. They'd only been here one full day so far, and already it had been eventful. But that wasn't what had gotten her high. Cruz had come to her in the night. She had meant to stay awake while he went to the island – he would be in danger and she was worried about him. But instead, she fell asleep, and when he came back, it all unfolded like a dream.

In the dream, she was asleep in a high bed, draped with white curtains. A dark stranger came to her window. He passed through the window, floating, feet not touching the floor. Was he a vampire? Then he was in her bed, biting her neck, riding her, as she rode waves of pleasure, up, up, up . . . to ecstasy. This morning, they had done it again. And afterwards, when she went in the water, she had to fight the urge to strip down and swim in the nude. She felt so alive, and natural, like a nymph or a mermaid. She decided she was living a life that many women would fantasise about – and to think, when she was in high school, she never even had a date to the prom.

During the night, she had lain awake with Cruz for a little while.

'How did it go?' she said. 'With Stone?'

Cruz made a non-committal gesture with his shoulders and his hands. 'It went OK. He's got some local girl with him. He went out. He got drunk and high. Danced a little – he's a pretty good dancer. Came back to his hut, they did their thing, and they both passed out. A little while later, he came out to go swimming in the dark. I was waiting there when he came outside. When he spotted me standing on his dock, he looked like he saw a ghost.'

'Did you . . . ?' Pamela's question trailed off. She and Cruz, even now, had never talked about what he used to do for a living. There hadn't really been time, but on a deeper level, Pamela didn't want to know the details.

'No. He's a guy on vacation. I'm like a bad memory to him – he just wants me to go away.'

'That's good. I mean, that you didn't . . . do anything. Right?'

Cruz shrugged. 'I don't know. I thought about it. But like I said, I don't think I do that sort of thing any more.' He stared at the ceiling. 'If I could have done it three weeks ago, then I'd probably be the only person on this boat still alive right now.'

She rolled over and put a hand on his chest. 'See? You wouldn't want me to be dead. So it is good.'

He smiled. 'Yeah. Real good.'

Now, she shook her head of the memories. She had to pay attention while letting Ty out of the closet – it would be no good if she lost control of him. She turned the key in the lock, and opened the door.

Ty stood there. He was tall. He wore only a pair of denim shorts, held up with a length of rope, and he was in awesome shape – he looked very, very strong. And he wasn't tied up any more – all the other ropes lay at his feet.

He smiled. 'Girl,' he said, his voice just above a whisper. 'I gotta go.'

He sprang out of the closet, rumbling over her with a burst of speed and strength. She felt herself knocked backwards and down, as if she'd been hit by a car. A gasp escaped her, and she reached out, grasping for anything.

As she hit the floor, her fingers locked on to the waistband of his shorts. She couldn't let go – her fingers were caught in there! She pulled, trying to stop him, or trying to get her fingers loose – she wasn't sure herself – as he dragged her along the floor. He grunted with the effort, then did a crazy, circling dance, the loose-fitting shorts falling down his legs. He spun away, naked now, and made a dash for the stairs.

Pamela watched Ty's muscular ass climb the stairs, pumping legs taking them two at a time, as he disappeared up into the sunlight.

Cruz and Lola never seemed to speak.

Cruz sat there now, and the moment Pamela went downstairs, it seemed like he and Lola lapsed into an uncomfortable silence. Maybe she would try to say something, maybe he would, but he suspected that whatever they said wouldn't get much traction, and soon they would be quiet again. It was a beautiful day in paradise, the sun glistening off the water, the trees of the island in the distance. And Cruz felt good – Stone looked like no problem, the kid in the closet downstairs was neutralised for the moment, and Dugan had said he was making good progress on the engine this morning. Good enough, in fact, that maybe they would motor out of here within another day or two – possibly even tomorrow. So if things were this good, why were he and Lola sitting here not even looking at each other?

He'd seen her glance at the gun when she sat down. The frown that passed over her face was like a cartoon frown, a clown-face frown. Cruz felt like picking it up and saying, 'This old thing?'

It was like a phobia Cruz had now – this fear of killing. Some people couldn't get on airplanes. Some people were terrified of spiders. Cruz couldn't bring himself to kill anybody – not a good character trait for somebody in his line of work. Maybe there was a therapist somewhere he could talk to about this, or even better, a hypnotist. Some guy could dangle his pocket watch in front of Cruz, put him to sleep, and convince him to start killing people again.

This thing last night with Stone: in the old days, Cruz would have killed Stone without hesitating. He wouldn't have been interested in whether Stone was on holiday. He would only be interested in cutting loose ends. With no orders to the contrary, he would have shot Stone while he was in bed, his gun no more than a few feet from Stone's head.

Or the kid yesterday, Ty. The kid had seen the money. He knew there was more. That was a loose end if ever there was one. If Cruz opened a dictionary right now and looked up 'loose end', there'd be a photo of Ty on the page. In two days, or two weeks, or a hundred years – whenever they moved on again from this island – what were they going to do with Ty? Just let him go home? Drop him off somewhere? That sounded like a very bad plan. Ty probably had friends – angry young men like himself, but with speedboats and maybe even guns. Nobody you'd want to meet on the high seas.

A shriek came from downstairs, yanking Cruz into the present. Pamela's voice. Lola's eyes went wide and alert. Cruz stood, grabbing the gun off the table.

Smoke's head and shoulders appeared in the engine well.

An instant later, a dark blur burst up the stairs from below decks.

It took Cruz a second to process – a naked black man appeared, moving fast, running to the side of the boat and diving over the railing and into the water. Cruz moved to the gunwale, already targeting. The water was clear as glass, and Cruz homed in on the dark shape taking huge, powerful strokes underwater.

Easy. Silencer on, pop him when he comes up for air. Put a couple in his torso to put the brakes on him, then take your time with the killshot.

Twenty yards away, the kid's head breached the surface. Silly kid, he stopped, turned, and looked up at the boat. Cruz sighted. He imagined popping the kid's head open like a ripe tomato. But he couldn't do it. Of course he couldn't.

A worrisome thing happened then – the kid smiled, turned away, and kept swimming. The smile was the disturbing part.

'Shit,' Cruz said.

Dugan was standing next to him. 'Wow, Cruz. We got trouble now.'

Cruz: 'Don't I know it. And I've got, like, a mental illness of some kind.' He offered the gun to Dugan. The kid was still in range. 'You wanna take a shot?'

Dugan waved a hand. 'You know I'm no good with those things. I'd probably shoot my own foot off.'

Cruz stared out at the dwindling figure of Ty Weathers. 'You know what? I'm getting too old for this shit.'

'Nah, you're still a young man.'

Cruz gave Dugan a baleful eye. 'For some things. But not this.'

Pamela appeared at the top of the stairs. She held the kid's blue denim shorts in one hand.

'Whaddya got there, Pamela?' Dugan called down to her.

She looked down at the shorts as if she'd forgotten they were there. She shrugged. 'I was trying to help him take a pee.'

Lola laughed. 'He won't get far without his pants,' she said. She had never even got up from the table.

* * *

'I'm telling you, something is happening.'

Roxana said it with enough force that Macho had to raise his hand up, palm outward, like STOP. Then he brought the hand down, palm facing the floor, like, 'OK, lower, lower.'

They were in the living room of Roxana's pale yellow shack in Underhill. The shack was half a storey high – on stilts for when the hurricanes came. 'Living room' meant it was the room where she did most of her living. It was neither the kitchen, nor the tiny cubby where she slept when she wasn't working. There were a few plastic chairs in the room, an old couch and a card table. It was not an exciting room.

The day was quiet – quiet enough that the lapping of the waves on the shoreline came to them on a warm breeze from a quarter mile away. If you were talking business, it was good to keep your voice low.

'Tell me again,' Macho whispered, thinking on it already, looking at all the possibilities. Yes, there might be something here. Something big, maybe – he didn't know. But certainly a little something. For both of them.

'So then he said he wanted to take a walk. But really we were following the man Stone. He was a hundred yards ahead of us. We followed him on to the sand, down to his hut, and then past it all the way to the end of the beach, hand in hand like lovers. But Mikey noticed where Stone lived – he looked, but he didn't look. You know?'

Macho nodded. He knew all about looking but not looking. 'Is he police?'

'I don't know. I don't think so.'

'Then what happened? After the walk?'

She shrugged. 'We went back to his room. He made me wait outside the room while he made a telephone call. And then more pounding. It's like having sex with a gorilla.'

'Then he sent you home?'

'He wanted to take a nap. He said he doesn't like people sleeping in his bed. Doesn't want to be bothered by somebody when he wakes up. He said come back later.'

'What did you make this morning?'

She frowned. 'Fifty. He's a cheapskate besides.'

Macho put out his hand. Roxana reached into her shorts, pulled out a ten-dollar bill, and gave it to him. Business was business, after all.

'I need you to go back.'

'Macho! I'm sore, I told you. He's an ape.'

'Hey, maybe you make some more money.' He put the smile on – he knew his smile charmed even the girls. 'Then you tell him I want to speak with him alone. Someplace private. Not near his hotel. It's very important. If he asks you, you tell him you don't know what I want, but the police have been cracking down. Maybe it's about that. Tell him to meet me at the West End, by the Split. Four o'clock.'

'What if he won't meet you?'

Macho looked Roxana's body up and down. He felt his smile going even broader. 'After all I've done for him? He'll meet me.'

After he left Roxana, Macho decided to go for a walk. He walked the alleys and the dirt paths between slapped-together tin- and panel-board shacks. He startled some stray dogs that were tearing at the flesh of something dead. They growled at him, and he made as if to kick them. They shied away, but not too far. He kept walking.

There were things Macho knew about himself. He was small for his age, and slim. He was charming, with a bright, winning smile – the tourists seemingly could not resist his advances. He was intelligent – smarter than any of the teachers in the school he no longer attended. He could do complicated math without a pencil and paper – he was constantly running expenses, percentages, profits through his head. He was in contact with no fewer than fifty providers and consumers of services at any time – girls, ship captains, dive masters, marijuana growers and smugglers, as well as myriad tourists, whose various tastes and desires were always on top of his mind. He dealt with many, many people, and he was not shy in any way, save one.

At twelve years old, he was doing a booming business. He spent his days and evenings haunting the hotel entrances, the marina and the beaches. He approached the tourists, especially the unaccompanied men, and discovered what they wanted. There were many things he could provide. Marijuana, sometimes locally grown, sometimes off the boats. It was very potent, so they told him – he didn't know because he had never smoked it himself. Women, young, beautiful, and dark brown – giving white men from America a taste of the exotic. Saint Mark's girls were sexual animals, so the men told him – he had never sampled them himself.

This was, he realised, the only way in which he was shy. He had been serving as the agent for these girls for two years now, and the opportunity to try it himself had been presented many times – practically on a daily basis. But he always declined. It worried him, to tell the truth. It gnawed at him. Was he man enough? Was he big enough? Would the girls laugh at him, then, if it turned out he wasn't? How did you even do it, exactly? So many questions. He thought maybe it was better to try it with a girl his own age – but he didn't get to spend much time with girls his own age.

What else could he provide the tourists? Boys? Yes, if that was to their taste, and sometimes it was. Usually, the first thing such men wanted was Macho himself – but he was off-limits. He had two boys he could call on – young men, really, nineteen and twenty, but both looked younger. He could hook tourists up with the best fishing, snorkelling or diving on the island. He could bring tourists to the best island cooking in Underhill – not restaurant or hotel food, but home cooking, the real thing. Anything a tourist wanted, Macho could pretty much provide.

The thing he provided most of all was discretion. Just last week, a man was here, staying with his wife in one of the hotels. They wanted marijuana. OK. But then the man, it turns out, wanted to do it on the beach with one of the girls he saw in the daytime. Could it be arranged? It could. And it happened in the sand, less than fifty yards from their hotel balcony, while hubby was out for a late-evening stroll alone.

And what did Macho provide his suppliers? That was plain – access. Macho had easy access to the tourists. A supplier didn't have to hang around, looking to provide a service. Macho could find out what service was wanted, and contact the right provider. Macho himself carried the marijuana to his customers – he'd never been searched yet.

Whatever agreement was entered, Macho took his twenty per cent commission. Sometimes customers paid more than the asking price. The pot smokers might tip Macho big – so taken were they with the island pot. The girlfuckers might also tip – so taken were they with the satisfaction they'd received. He tacked on an extra ten dollars to the cost of any joints he sold – as much as a fifty per cent mark-up. He took a finder's fee off the top of any fishing or diving expeditions he lined up. Macho often made one hundred dollars in a twelve-hour day.

He encouraged the tourists to keep the girls all night – and for days at a time, if possible. Often the tourists would give the girls an extra fifty dollars or so after a good night, and sometimes they fell in love with a girl they had kept for a few days or more. That's when the real money started coming in – money that might keep coming through the mail long after the tourist had gone home. Macho liked to see the girls make money, he liked to see himself make money, and he liked to see the tourists with smiles on their faces. Satisfied customers came back.

So where did the money go? For one, his family expenses were high – he had to pay for his mother's medicine. His mother was ill and could no longer work, and her medicine ate up a lot of Macho's income. Macho's sister was young and in school. He was the one who supported the family. Still, he was no martyr. He intended to build a business empire when he grew up. He imagined leaving the island, and going to Miami where he would one day own tall buildings. He was already working his way there. He managed the family's finances, and they had just over two thousand dollars in the bank – three hundred in checking, and more than seventeen hundred earning four per cent in a savings account. He also had over nine hundred dollars stashed under a loose floorboard in the shanty where they lived, and exactly fifteen hundred buried in a jar out behind the shack. Also, the ten bucks Roxana had just paid him and another thirty or so dollars he kept in his pocket in case of a shakedown.

Oh yes, the shakedowns. Macho was endlessly on the run from older boys who would beat him and take his money, if they could. The police sometimes stopped him and took whatever was on him – they never searched him for the drugs they knew he might be carrying, but they did take his money. It was a precarious existence. The truth was, he was going faster than was probably wise. He could go slow, keep a low profile, and slowly amass his fortune over a decade or more. He could do that, yes. But in a sense, the clock was ticking. He wanted to get off the island before his eight-year-old sister became a teenager. The best money for a girl on the island, by far, was in having sex with tourists.

Macho often thought of jackpots, and how to come across one. In all his time at work, he hadn't seen one yet. Oh, he'd a few nice windfalls – a couple of hundred dollars in one day, that sort of thing. But a real jackpot, a life-changing jackpot? Well, he had been beginning to think that such a thing didn't exist for the likes of him.

But now he was thinking about Stone. Everything about him interested Macho – the satellite tracker and the laptop computer, the American gorilla man doing surveillance on him, the deep sea dives and the spearfishing, and even the mysterious night-time crying about the things he had seen in war. Roxana had told him all about how Stone sometimes wept and even screamed, his wet face pressed against her breasts. Stone, who was almost always a little high or drunk, or both, but never sloppy. Stone, who after two quiet weeks on the island, was suddenly at the centre of something big. Macho reflected that he'd never had a client quite like Stone.

Stone might be the jackpot Macho had been looking for all this time.

* * *

Ty Weathers walked into his grandmom's house wearing a pair of bright red Speedos he had stolen off the deck of some tourist's multicoloured waterfront cabana. He had paused at the tourist's house just long enough to take the man's flip-flops, as well. Both the Speedos and the flip-flops were about a size too small. Ty Weathers had felt more comfortably dressed before now, that was for sure. It had been a long walk up into the hills.

His grandmom was on the couch, watching the TV. After sixty-four years, the old biddy's daily schedule was graven in stone. Church first thing in the morning, praise Jesus. Then an hour or two of 'fellowship', as she called it, which was a nice way of saying gossip and taletelling with the other church ladies. A stop in at the market for more gossip and to pick up the items she didn't pick up yesterday or the day before. Then back here to the old house for an afternoon of watching her shows. Dinner at five, then off to bed right after sunset, so she could get up and do it all at first light again tomorrow.

She glanced away from the TV as he came in. 'Boy, what in the hell are you wearing? Some kind of sex costume? You went out of the house dressed like that?'

'I slept at Marcus's house,' Ty said, choking on the lies as they spilled out of his mouth. Ridiculous to make up stories for this old woman – Ty was a grown man. 'My clothes got wet, so I had to borrow some of his.'

He went into his room, quietly slid the door shut, and glanced around for something decent to put on.

'I don't believe a word of it,' his grandmother called from the other side of the door. 'You want to whore around with those boom-boom girls on the beach, there's nothing I can do. But this ain't no flophouse. You can't just come and go as you please. You gonna stay out all night, at least have the decency to tell me beforehand.'

'Yes, Grandmom.'

'Your mother's back there, slaving away to support your ass. You know that? A real man would get a job, and keep it. A real man would be out making money, contribute something to the household. Then he could run around with whatever whores of Babylon he wanted.'

'Yes, Grandmom.'

Ty changed into a new pair of shorts and a T-shirt. His grandmother had shuffled away for the time being, praise Jesus. Sooner or later she'd be back, with some new thing to say. He sprawled face first on to his narrow bed and began to give this thing some thought.

The boat was dead – that had to be the case. Else they would have left by now. That was why Lola's white boy was down there working on the engine today. They were stuck here, and all that money on the boat. Ty had personally held at least a hundred thousand dollars in his hands yesterday – and the old boy said there was plenty more of that around.

Was there anybody on this whole rotten island Ty could trust with this kind of information? He didn't think so. Too many big talkers around. If he was going to get that money and manage to keep it quiet, he was going to have to do it himself. Take the money, and kill everybody on the boat, except, maybe, for Lola. Then what? Sink the boat? Probably not in shallow water like that, or that close to the island. Drive the boat out of here, take off for Nassau or Freeport? Could Ty even drive a boat that big?

Anyway, first things first. How to kill Cruz and them? The easy answer was his grandfather's guns. His grandfather had died ten years before, but he'd kept guns in the house. Ty had seen them – two old revolvers, six-shooters, looked to be in decent shape. Grandmom still kept them in shoeboxes on the top shelf in her closet. She had boxes of bullets for them, too – a box of .38 rounds, and a box of .22 long rifle rounds. Each gun had a speed loader in its shoebox along with it.

With the guns, and the ammo, and the speed loaders, Ty would be ready to throw down. And that made him think of Cruz, the man with the cold-blooded eyes. Cruz was up there on the deck of the boat today, gun ready. Ty couldn't miss the silencer on that thing. If Cruz had wanted, he could have punched Ty full of holes. But Cruz didn't take the shot. And that got Ty to thinking – maybe he wasn't such a stone killer after all. Ty smiled. Now how to get into her room, get those guns, and get out to that boat?

'Grandmom, can I borrow Poppy's guns?' he imagined himself calling through the door. Nope. That'd never work with this old bitch. It'd have to wait until the next morning, when she headed down to church. Grab those guns, borrow some unsuspecting fool's dinghy, and zip out there. Go in hard, guns blazing, and take no prisoners.

Well, one prisoner, if Lola surrendered. Then point that big boat towards open water, and leave this island behind. Head off to a bright future, a very rich man.

Yeah. Ty Weathers could feel his heart beating already.

7

Macho sat under a palm tree, watching the ape man Mikey Tomatoes come towards him. The man's wide, hairy chest was bare. His arms hung nearly to his knees, and he walked with a bow-legged swagger. Macho was meeting him all the way at the western end of town, down by where a hurricane had once ripped apart a seawall and cut the island in two. This had happened long before Macho was born.

From where Macho sat, he could see the lush green of the island's orphaned section – fifty yards across dark blue water. Islanders called the area the Split, and kids came down here to swim in the strong current that surged through the gap. Further inland, a rickety bridge connected the two parts of the island – but Macho had only been to the other side once. It was a swampy area of mangroves and a few clapboard dwellings. There was no electricity over there, and no pavement. There were also no beaches and no tourists. It was nowhere to go.

About thirty yards away, a handful of teenagers – boys and girls – were swimming and horse-playing in the water. As a general rule, tourists didn't come down this far. Macho noticed the Tomato eyeing the girls as he approached.

Macho stood up and tried on a smile. He extended his small hand for a shake, the way Americans liked to do. Mikey's big mitt swallowed his whole hand. The hairy man was covered in a fine sheen of sweat from walking all this way.

'So what's the problem, kid? The whore said you needed to talk privately, but this is a little ridiculous, don't you think?'

Inwardly, Macho winced at the word 'whore', but he made no sign. Why not just call her a girl? 'It's private here,' he said. 'Quiet. No one will overhear us. Would you like to sit down?' Macho gestured to the shade under the tree. 'I brought some water for us. I knew it would be hot.'

Mikey sat down and leaned against the tree. He took a swallow from Macho's canteen. 'OK,' he said. 'What gives? I'm a little bit busy while I'm here, and I don't like to get dragged away.'

Macho put on a look of honest concern. In order to best serve his clients, it was important that he know what their trip was about – and it was the type of thing he didn't easily forget. 'I'm sorry. I thought this was a pleasure trip?'

'Business, pleasure,' Mikey said. 'It's all the same fucking thing to me. I'm always working.'

Macho didn't sit down. In fact, he maintained a good distance between himself and the gorilla – maybe five yards. If he had to run, between the distance and the fact that the man was on the ground, he would get a good head start. He would run to the Split and dive into the water among the teenagers.

'I might know a little bit about your business,' Macho said. 'Maybe I can help you with it.'

Mikey squinted at him. He frowned. Already, he didn't seem to like what he was hearing. 'Yeah? How so?'

'You're following a man. A tall man. American.'

'Is that right?' Mikey's face turned red in the space of a few seconds. It was a little bit alarming to watch. It looked like the face of someone who had lost their breath. 'What makes you think that?'

Macho shrugged. 'You know what I do for a living. I have eyes and ears. Otherwise I can't survive.'

Mikey clapped his two powerful hands together. 'The whore told you.' It wasn't a question.

'No. Not her.'

'Bullshit. I know she told you. And I'll tell you something else – that whore is fucking crazy. I'm not following anybody. I should bust her lip for talking that crazy shit, and I should bust your lip for believing her.'

Mikey's face was almost purple now. Macho plunged on anyway. Behind him, the laughter and the splashing of the teenagers went on. A girl shrieked. 'Stop it!'

'I know the man. He's a client of mine. He trusts me. Like everybody does.' Macho put the smile on again, and found that it felt natural enough. So he turned up the wattage and let it beam. Then it felt even better. 'I do good things for people here on the island, and they trust me.'

'Yeah, you're the fucking welcome wagon. So?'

'So . . . we can agree to disagree. And if you're not interested in this man, then it can't hurt for me to talk to him, suggest to him that he move his location to another place – inside one of the hotels, maybe, or even to one of the outer islands where I know people. He likes to dive, this man, and he likes to swim. He might get a more – how would you put it – authentic experience, if he was on one of the smaller islands. Real island stew, like only the locals make. Tiger sharks in the water. You know.'

'You threatening me, kid? It feels like you're threatening me over some bullshit that don't exist, and I don't like it.'

Mikey didn't try to stand up. His body was coiled, like it would spring, but Macho could tell that Mikey would have trouble standing from his current position. It would take him a couple of extra seconds, and for that Macho was glad. It was a good idea to offer him a seat. Macho had the urge to take a step backwards, but he fought the urge.

'People who threaten me, bad shit happens to them. They get fucked up, you see what I'm saying? I'd hate to see something happen to you, kid, or to that precious whore of yours. I'd hate to see her face get all cut up, say.'

Macho took a deep breath. 'I have a second cousin,' he said. 'Much older than me. He's my uncle's cousin. When I was two, he had a fight with his wife. He cut her face with a kitchen knife – and he had a good reason. She was sleeping with another man. The police came and took him away to the big jail on Saint Joseph. He's been there ever since. I've never met him, but he's expected to come out soon. They say he went in as a young man, but he is coming out as a very old man – broken. All in ten years.'

Mikey smiled, shook his head. He spoke almost as if he were talking to himself. 'There you go, threatening me again. I've been to jail, kid. I did my time standing on my head, you know what I'm saying?'

'The jail here is not like the American jails, and when they put you in, they like to keep you for a long time. You lose weight – all the meat wastes off your bones. Your teeth start to fall out in less than a year – our teacher told us there are no vitamins in a bread-and-water diet.'

'Listen, kid, you're breaking my heart with this tale of woe. I'll tell you what – I gotta talk to somebody about this. That don't mean that I'm following anybody, or that I think anything you said was true. It just means I need to talk to somebody, and get back to you. Maybe we can come to some sort of arrangement.'

Macho nodded. 'You can tell that person I might also know something about who the man is following, if that means anything.'

It meant something – he saw the light change in Mikey's eyes.

'And how much are you looking to get paid for all this information you might have? For when I talk to the person?'

Macho had thought and thought about this. He'd added, subtracted, tried it eight different ways. Finally, he'd come to a number that he thought might be neither too high nor too low. It was a king's ransom to him, more money than he'd ever seen in one place – even more than everything he'd saved in his years of working. But he'd practised saying it nonchalantly, in the way that one of these men might say to another.

'I want five thousand dollars.'

If he got it, he had no idea what he would do with it. He couldn't put it in the local bank, he couldn't tell anyone he had it, and he'd be afraid to leave it under the floorboards at home. If he buried it behind the shack, he'd have to dig it up every night by moonlight to make sure it was still there. The money would constantly be on his mind – he might never sleep again. Well, that was a river he'd just have to swim when the time came.

The big man smiled. 'Kid,' he said, 'you drive a hard bargain.'

Stone enjoyed the late-afternoon sun from his deck, waiting for Macho to arrive. Stone was a little high, a little buzzed from the pitcher of margaritas he'd been serving himself all day, and he was feeling A-OK, thank you. No bad thoughts. No bad feelings. No need to have a gun here in the hut – no need to blow his own brains out today, or anybody else's for that matter. Just bad boy Butch Stone, all-American warrior, doing a little downtime in paradise, and feeling real good.

In a little while, he would go for a swim. Then he would wander over to one of the restaurants for a nice meal – crab legs, maybe. Maybe he'd run into Sticks and his buddy over there – ask 'em how the hunt was going. Good old reliable Stone, loyal soldier, here on a little rest and relaxation – couldn't care less about that $2.5 million in cash floating out there on the ocean, just outside Sticks's line of sight. It wasn't even on his mind, no sir.

After dinner, Stone would come back here, crash out for a couple of hours, and then, late tonight, head out and do a little night-time recon on what his friend Cruz was up to out there on the water. Just like the good old days, eh? Night-time operations – that's what we train for in the United States Army Rangers.

Night-time recon. Night-time air drops. Night-time amphibious assaults. Good stuff. We owned the night, and that's why the enemy was afraid of the dark.

He would do the recon tonight, that was, if Macho got his butt over here on time – Stone needed a boat, and the easiest way to get one was to have Macho acquire it. He realised, not for the first time, how lazy it could make you, when you had a guy like Macho to do everything – erase Macho from the equation, and suddenly everything could get squirrelly. If the kid didn't show up, Stone would have to go look for him. But he doubted that would happen – Macho kept the trains running right on time.

In fact, here came the little tyke now.

Amazing. Moving along the beach, narrow brown body in a pair of old jeans shorts – no shirt, no shoes, crazy head of unkempt hair. He looked dirty or sandy, like he'd been out playing somewhere. He banged a stick on the ground as he walked, his head cocked to one side – he looked like maybe he was talking to himself, telling himself a little story. *Mary had a little lamb.* It blew Stone's mind, come to think of it. Macho was a kid. That's all he really was. A little kid. It took a few tokes and a couple of drinks to make it clear, but there it was.

Do they even have schools on this island? Where're this kid's parents?

'Mr Macho,' Stone said.

The kid stayed on the sand, just below the wooden deck. The big smile. Light up a room with that smile. 'Mr Stone. The girl was good for you last night? And the smoke?'

'Everything excellent as always, young sir.'

'How can I help you today?'

'I'll be needing a boat tonight. Party of one.'

Stone watched the eyes – already making calculations. Who could he get? How much money? How much of a cut for Macho himself?

'A night dive? You'll need some equipment. I know just the man for you. A great captain. He'll bring you to where the hammerhead sharks gather, maybe an hour out from here.' Macho stroked his chin, apparently lost in thought. 'A little expensive, but maybe not so bad for a man of means . . .'

'It's not a dive,' Stone said. 'I need just a small motorboat, for myself. Could be a skiff with an outboard. No captain. I'll need it around eleven, let's say, and I'll have it back before dawn. I don't know – that's your business – but could be that the owner doesn't even have to know it's gone. If you see what I'm saying.'

Macho saw. Stone saw the look plain as day in his eyes. If the owner doesn't know, then we're talking pure profit for the pipsqueak entrepreneur. 'Can you have it back by four?' Macho said. 'Dawn might be late.'

'Four? Yeah, I can do that.'

'Then consider it done.' Macho turned and glanced back down the beach the way he had come. Nothing there – the nearest person was about fifty yards away, a heavy white woman in a sundress and floppy hat ambling around in the shallows, looking down through the pale blue water at her feet. 'Except for one problem. Maybe it's a small one. Maybe it's not that small.'

'Yes? What's that?'

Macho's face was serious now – Stone hadn't seen this face before. 'What would you say if I told you someone is watching you?'

Sticks.

'Right now? This moment?'

'No. Not now. Sort of always.'

'A man I had a meeting with?' Twenty questions with the kid.

'No, not really. More like a man who sat away from you and watched you have a meeting. A man who knows where you live – maybe knows something about who you've been watching.'

Jesus.

'I'd say tell me more.'

Macho looked at the ground, suddenly sheepish. The kid was like peeling back an onion – always more layers. 'It's hard for me to say this, but . . . would you pay somebody money to tell you more?'

Night had come in, and it had cast a pall over the boat.

Smoke sat in the engine well, out of sight of any prying eyes, rigging the strongboxes. You never knew who might be watching, and from where. Anybody – Ty Weathers, this character Stone from Cruz's past, anybody at all – could be out on the water, in any one of those boats, curious about what was going on over here.

The two bright silver boxes, which had been tucked away on the *Saucy Jack* for the past three years, were each about a foot long, eight inches wide and half a foot deep. They were manufactured from hard plastic resin – practically indestructible. They opened and closed easily, and yet when closed, they had a special O-ring seal that made them absolutely watertight. He knew, from the company literature, that they had been tested to a depth of one hundred feet off the coast of Alaska, without any leakage. They had to be watertight or the game lost its realism – nobody in their right mind would put money, or bombs, in a place where they were going to get wet.

Smoke hummed to himself as he worked. He had just a tiny bit of plastique left, his explosive of choice when he could get it. When he'd picked up the *Jack* on City Island, he'd found the explosive in the utensil drawer of the galley – a small chunk, like a nob of Silly Putty, just enough to make the pipe bomb Lola had blown up the two goons with in Fort Lauderdale, with a little bit left over for later. The leftover was only enough to rig one of these boxes to explode. The other box would be unprotected, but in the end, it didn't matter – it wasn't like Smoke was actually going to put any money in these boxes. Buried treasure was a cool idea. It was also a decoy.

Smoke was the only one who knew the boxes were fakes. He'd been overruled – everybody else on the boat felt that since Ty had escaped, the prudent thing was to bury the money. Smoke disagreed, but not too strenuously – instead, he agreed to carry out their demands, and then did what he wanted anyway.

As he worked, he thought of Roselli, his former boss. Dead – fried with a Taser and blown up in his opulent home. Smoke never thought of himself as a killer. And yet, he had done it. He had killed Roselli out of righteous anger. He could do it again. If Ty came back out here, Smoke would kill him if he had to.

Now, he looked over his handiwork. Two watertight boxes, one rigged to explode if the wrong person tried to open it, one not rigged to explode. Neither of them carried even one dollar of the stolen money. OK, these were ready to go. He lifted them out of the engine well, and slid them on to the deck.

As he climbed out, he saw his three boatmates staring at him. Their faces looked bleak. Cruz, the cold-blooded killer, who suddenly had a soft heart of gold; Pamela, the meek librarian turned bad-ass gun moll; Lola, the reluctant ninja. Man, he needed some time off from all this.

'What are you people looking at?' he said. 'The boxes are done.'

Stone crouched in a tiny outboard skiff tied to a seemingly random mooring two hundred yards from the GPS coordinates that the tracker on Cruz's dinghy was giving him. Stone wore a light neoprene summer wetsuit, a Farmer John to give his arms freedom of movement, and had some snorkelling gear right nearby – fins, mask and snorkel. He wore a utility belt with hunting knife, steel manacles, and a black nylon bag. Back in the old days, he'd have called the bag a 'snatch bag'. If the opportunity presented itself, he could use it for personnel extraction – slip it over the target's head, pull the drawstring tight cutting off airflow to the brain, and get moving.

It was a dark night, with no moon but many stars – an incredible glittering sweep of the Milky Way above him – and a few lights here and there out on the water. There were no lights where Stone was looking – Cruz's boat was anchored out there with lights off, hiding in the dark. Yes, Cruz was hiding all right. Two hundred yards was as close as Stone dared to get right now. As time went on, and he learned more, he would creep closer. Maybe tonight, if the opportunity presented itself.

Stone was deep into the kid now.

Maybe not the best position to be in, but that's where he was. The greaseball he'd seen with Roxana was shadowing him. Sure, it made sense now. He'd seen the two of them in the bar where he'd met with Sticks. Then, like an hour later, he'd seen them walking along the waterfront – passed right by his shack, as a matter of fact.

Admit it, he'd felt the sting of . . . something . . . when he saw Roxana with this meathead tourist. Jesus, the hookers of this world. But they weren't just a hooker and her john – he was actually coming down here to see where Stone was staying.

Well, that was no good. It was all right in the daytime, when people were around, maybe. But at night, when nobody was around? Did he really want a bunch of hitters from New York following him, and knowing where he lived? Maybe coming around his shack later at night, while he was sleeping, and . . .

But why would they do that?

No reason. Did they even need a reason? He knew these guys in his bones. They'd ice Stone if they found out he'd lied to them. They'd ice him because they'd had a few too many drinks in the bar and wanted to blow off steam. They'd ice him for no reason at all, for the heck of it, because one of them woke up in the middle of the night all sweaty and with an itch to scratch.

I haven't killed anybody in a month – might as well go cap Stone.

If they'd peeled off one of their guys and set him up to look like a tourist, just so they could watch Stone, then that was a bad sign. So Stone had moved indoors. Macho knew a guy who worked at one of the hotels, and who set him up with a room. Third floor, balcony above the pool. Ocean view.

Best part: Stone never had to check in. He paid cash to the kid – a week up front. He left most of his belongings at the shack, and moved his laptop, his toiletries, his kit bag and a few items of clothing to the hotel room. He wasn't even a registered guest – for all anybody knew, he was staying at the shack. When he got tired, was ready to sleep, he could go to the hotel. During the day, he could kick up his heels at the shack.

And in between, he could do the kind of thing he was doing now. Right now, now was the deal.

The kid had got him this boat. Exactly what he asked for – small fishing skiff, light outboard, with a couple of oars so he could cut the engine and row when he needed to be silent. It had a deep enough draft that he could lie down in it, like he was doing now, barely peeking his head above the gunwale.

Stone wore night-vision goggles attached with a band to his head – binoculars, actually. They were the real deal, Generation 3, converting the limited starlight available into electrical energy, then multiplying that energy to give Stone the impressive view he now enjoyed. It was a high-resolution unit to begin with, and additional optics magnification could put far away objects right into the palm of Stone's hand. Neat toy. He could see Cruz's boat, and he could see them moving around out there, all bathed in ghostly green. Very close – he could almost reach out and touch them.

Four people – two men and two women. Cruz was probably the skinny one. He could tell the women by the shapes of their bodies – good shapes. It made Stone think about looking for the kid again when he got back to shore – any girls still up, and available, this time of night? That made Stone wonder what Roxana was doing right now, and he put the thought away for good.

They were preparing for something over there on the boat. Three of them were on the aft-swimming deck, and there was a lot of focus around one person, one of the women – if Stone wasn't mistaken, it looked like they were going through a pre-dive check. They had given her something to carry, some kind of case. She was wearing something dark, like a wetsuit. She also had a pole or long gun, maybe a speargun. She was clearly wearing a compressed air cylinder. All of the variables gave Stone the assessment: she was about to go for a night dive. Furthermore, she was bringing that big case with her. As Stone watched, she did a giant stride entry off the swimming deck – she stepped out into space, her front leg extended out in front of her in an exaggerated fashion – then dropped vertically into the water.

The other two stood on the deck, milling around more than anything. When the woman resurfaced, she flicked on a bright headlamp – the only brief flash of light that Cruz and his crew would allow themselves. Then she raised her hand, made a gesture like saying, 'See you later', and dropped underwater with the box.

'Where you going with a box like that, honey?' Stone said. 'Bury some treasure?' Hey, hey, hey, pirates on the high seas.

It would've been nice to have a high-powered parabolic microphone out here with him, point it at them, and maybe get a sense of what they were talking about. But clear enough: they were burying the money, probably in the sandy surface where they were anchored. Stone watched and waited. There was always some drift when anchored like that, so it was natural that she would put it at the base of some kind of landmark.

Near the anchor? No, probably not. What if they had to hoist anchor and make a quick getaway? They'd never find it again. What else might be down there? Maybe an old wreck, or some kind of coral formation. Stone doubted it was a wreck. These people wanted privacy, so there's no way they'd anchor near a wreck – divers would be underfoot all day, every day. But a coral formation . . .

Maybe, maybe.

Could he swim under them and find the box without them knowing? Risky with ice-cold Cruz right upstairs. An image occurred to Stone. Him in this very same boat, maybe a hundred yards closer to them, maybe this time of night. Row very close – as close as he dared. Get hunkered down, night vision on, this time with a sniper's rifle. Tactical scope, bring them right to the palm of his hand. Heavy-duty sound and signature suppressor attached. Four people milling around out on that deck in total darkness. Four quiet shots – take Cruz first, then the next three in any order.

Row quietly over there, and board them. Dive and find their land-mark. Surface with two and a half million dollars in cash in a strongbox. Check the box for wires or any other obvious booby traps. Open it and confirm that he was a very rich man. Pull anchor and head for open sea in their boat. Dump the bodies at sea, and ditch the boat in sight of one of the outlying islands of the Bahamas. Frog-man to shore with the strongbox.

A lot of holes in that plan. Too many. What if he missed Cruz? What if he killed Cruz, missed the rest and they ran? What if he killed them all and couldn't find the box? What if he found the box, but it was rigged to explode and he couldn't open it safely?

Any other bright ideas?

After a time, the woman's head surfaced. She slowly climbed the boarding ladder on to the swimming deck and one of the men – Cruz? – gave her a hand getting in. She was only down there ten minutes – she must have put the damn thing right under them.

Five minutes after she had surfaced, Stone watched as two people boarded the dinghy, one of them carrying what looked like another strongbox, and raced away from the boat. He tracked them with the night-vision – they headed straight towards the small island a few hundred yards away. It looked like Cruz was one of them.

Splitting the money up – a little bit here, a little bit there.

After a few moments, they dwindled and disappeared. And for Stone, it was go time. He quickly donned the snorkelling gear, rolled over the gunwale and into the water.

* * *

Pamela, out of her wetsuit now, sat on the aft deck with Lola, slowly reliving the dive in her mind. She'd only got in about ten minutes of bottom time, but those were ten incredible minutes. She hadn't done a dive since she was a twenty-one – more than eight years ago now. Her parents had paid for her to have diving lessons when she was thirteen, and throughout her teen years, it had been one of her joys.

This had been a simple dive by the standards of those long-ago days – by today's standards it was an adventure. For one, there was that magical feeling of weightlessness – a feeling she had forgotten about, but which came rushing back to her as soon as she achieved neutral buoyancy. For another, she had broken the cardinal rule drilled into her head over and over during those long-ago lessons: never dive alone. Even more, it was a night dive – to Pamela, darkness always gave the underwater world an added sense of dreamlike beauty and mystery. Then there was the excitement of it – she went down in total darkness except for the headlamp, dropping twenty feet to the sandy bottom to bury a strongbox with over a million dollars in cash in it – buried treasure – at the base of a huge, multicoloured brain coral. The box was also a homemade bomb – if anybody but Smoke tried to open it, it would blow up. She could tell before she went that Cruz bristled at the idea of that, but thankfully he bit his tongue.

One last thing: the whole time she was below the surface, she was fighting that feeling of terror. She could barely keep her heart from racing, or her imagination in check. Outside the beam of the light, the entire underwater world was enveloped in spooky black darkness. Anything could come rushing out of those shadows – a shark, a monster, a human head. If anything did happen, there was no way the people on board the ship could help her – none of them had ever dived before. She was on her own down there.

She imagined eyes everywhere, watching her. She moved quickly, digging a hole in the sand with her hands at the base of the coral – she tried to make herself go slow, but it was no use. She found herself hurrying, and while she made a decent hole to put the strongbox into, she kicked up enough backscatter to temporarily blind herself – they called that a Braille dive when she was a kid. She scared herself badly enough, and so could have done a better job filling the sand in over the strongbox. Her heart thumped in her chest as she finished. She looked down at the spot – maybe two or three inches of sand covered the strongbox. As the silt around her face mask cleared, the area looked, for want of a better word, *disturbed*.

OK, it was time to go. Five more seconds, and hands would reach for her out of the darkness. Through an effort of will, she forced herself to stay there. She played with the hole a little more, pushing the sand this way and that. It was no use – the camouflage was as good as it was going to get. What difference would it make anyway? No one was going to come down here looking for the box. Nobody knew it was here. If anything, the disturbed sand would only help her locate it again when the time came to retrieve it.

'What do you think?' Lola said now. 'Do you think it's in a good spot?'

'I think it's in a great spot,' Pamela said, and found that she meant it. 'Nobody's ever going to find it down there.'

'This place is a disgrace,' Smoke said.

Cruz and Smoke trudged away from the dinghy, through the wet sand of the tiny island. Something about the ocean currents had turned the place into a garbage dump. Smoke played his flashlight here and there ahead of them as they walked. All along the water's edge, there was the detritus of a throwaway seafaring culture – empty plastic Clorox bottles, rusty beer cans, ripped plastic bags, broken plastic bait buckets, broken plastic of all kinds, copper wiring and rubber tubing of all kinds, a Michelin steel-belted radial tyre, various pieces of clothing and shoes, a metal weather-vane, the entire fibreglass bow of a sailboat violently sundered from the rest of itself, and countless other random bits of flotsam and jetsam.

The tiny strip of sand and grass was like a net, catching whatever happened to be floating by on the current. Walk ten yards and here was another ugly conglomeration of garbage — nets and ropes and bottles, cracked plastic toys, a bright orange traffic cone. As far as Smoke could tell from the evidence of this place, the ocean itself was a vast sea of human cast-off junk — normally invisible to the naked eye, but here rudely exposed for anybody who cared to see. But that was just it, wasn't it? Nobody cared.

A line of palm trees and scrub grasses bordered the beach. The forest, such as it was, seemed to be about fifty yards deep. There, it opened up to water again on the other side.

'Whaddya think?' he said to Cruz. 'Let's bury it in among the trees. We don't want to make it easy for the bastards, do we?'

'Whatever you say, Captain Crunch. I'm along for this ride, remember? Just here to do the heavy lifting.'

The two of them trudged off towards the tree line.

'Yes, Little Macho, I went back there this evening, like you said. Yes, he wanted to see me. Yes, he gave me another workout.'

It was a quiet night, and Macho met Roxana at her shack for the second time in less than twenty-four hours. Somewhere in one of the nearby houses, a radio played mellow hip-hop, and some drunk people laughed and talked. Roxana looked tired — more tired than he had ever seen her. She reclined in her chair, and looked at Macho through narrow eyes. She had a drink in her hand — a rum and coke — and she was smoking a cigarette. Macho didn't know her to smoke cigarettes that often. Mikey Tomato must have that effect on people — Macho himself had felt like smoking a cigarette, or taking a drink, or doing something adults did, after their meeting at the Split today.

Late this afternoon, a couple of hours after that meeting, he'd run into the Tomato again on the beach. The ape man had seemed normal, even relaxed. He was sitting in a canvas hotel recliner in his striped bathing suit, watching the girls down by the water. He had a drink by his elbow. He'd seen Macho standing nearby and waved him over. There were plenty of people around, so it didn't seem a problem.

'Hey kid, you holding any weed?'

'Just a few joints.'

'Let me have them.'

Macho was wary. 'I usually charge three dollars each for them. It seems a fair price. Very good stuff. Very powerful.'

'Tell you what – it is a fair price, and I'm happy to pay it. It's great stuff. But let's do this: I left my money up in the room. Give me the joints now, and send me up a girl this evening. That meaty chick who ratted me out to you – I like her. OK? When I send her home tonight, I'll send her with the money for the joints, all right? And I'll pay you five dollars apiece for them, for all the trouble you're going to.'

Macho stood there, but didn't say anything.

The Tomato put a smile on. He looked like a shark. He'd probably show that same smile as he sank his sharp teeth into your flesh. 'Hey, what? Earlier today? Come on, let's put that past us. Sometimes I get irritated. I didn't mean to threaten anybody. All right? I talked to my guy and he said he wants to meet – he just didn't say when. He's very interested in what you have to say. Maybe I'll know more later.'

Macho didn't know what to make of this man with the powerful arms and shoulders, the big hands, and the giant protruding stomach. He knew he was afraid of the man. He knew that he felt much better and safer around Stone. All the same, business was business. Stone had paid him only one hundred dollars for the information he'd given him – a lot of money, but not what Macho had been thinking.

'Stick with me, Mr Macho,' Stone had said. 'There's more where that came from.'

The hundred had gone under the floorboards. If he could stay alert, play the two off one another, there might be room for the jackpot. If it came down to choosing sides, he would probably choose Stone, but he had to stay flexible. A businessman stayed flexible. That's what Macho told himself.

'Come on, kid. Give me the fucking joints, whaddya say? You know I'm good for them. We'll let bygones be bygones.'

Despite his misgivings, Macho had given him the joints. What else could he do? His whole business, his whole success, was based on trust. And this man might be the one to get him the coveted five thousand dollars.

Now, Macho had come around to Roxana's house to pick up his cut. As they talked, she handed him thirty-five dollars from inside her shorts – his twenty-dollar cut from the hundred the Tomato had paid her, and the fifteen for the joints. So the Tomato was as good as his word.

'How was he?'

'He's an animal. I'm exhausted. I'm covered with bruises. I'll be sore for a week.' She shrugged. 'But he was more generous tonight. A hundred dollars. So with the money from this morning, I made one hundred and fifty for the day. Not bad.'

Macho noticed that about the girls – they always counted the high number, and never seemed to notice that they had just handed him twenty per cent of it. The costs of doing business, and they never counted them. The girls were hopeless optimists.

'We smoked the last of the joints you gave him. He said to come by his room tomorrow, and bring an eighth bag – he'll buy it from you.'

'Did he mention anything else?'

Her face seemed to go blank as she thought about it. Macho sometimes worried about Roxana – she wasn't the smartest girl on the island. Now she shrugged. 'He said maybe he'd pick a different girl tomorrow. Another variety lover, I guess. Which is fine by me. I don't need to see him again.'

'What about our meeting?'

'Oh, right. The meeting. All the secrets. He said when you come tomorrow with the bag, he'll show you to his friend. You can talk to him then.'

So it was settled. The big meeting would take place tomorrow. He would go to the Tomato's room with an eighth of an ounce, and they would talk about everything. That made Macho feel better. Mikey the Tomato had given Roxana a good tip – better than he'd given her before. And he'd remembered to pay for the joints. Things looked very promising.

'If I was you, I'd forget to go there,' Roxana said. She took a sip of her drink and looked at Macho over the top of the glass. 'Mikey Tomato is crazy. He scares me. And his friend can't be much better.'

Macho smiled – just like a woman to suggest he walk away from opportunity.

Stone surfaced from total darkness along the side of the cabin cruiser.

The two-hundred-yard swim had him a little winded, but he felt good. He had graduated from the Special Forces Underwater Operations Combat Diver Course at the naval air station in Key West, but that was fifteen years ago now. Two hundred yards wouldn't even be a warm-up at Key West, but years of lax training standards, lax eating standards, booze, and grass-smoking had taken their toll. There was no getting around it – Stone was out of shape.

Stone did a slow circuit around the boat, taking in its characteristics: forty-footer, maybe forty-five; old boat, twenty years old or more, boxy, with all the wind and water resistance that implied – he bet this thing wouldn't do better than twenty knots; covered bridge up top, with the aft deck a few steps down – two women were sitting at the table there right now, talking in low voices; down below, at a guess, two cabins, two heads and a galley. Stone came all the way around and reached the swimming deck and ladder. Tied to the deck with about ten feet of line was another dinghy – a small zodiac inflatable. As he watched, one of the women stood and came down the steps. After a brief pause, she went below decks.

The other woman lit a cigarette, stood and paced the deck.

Stone felt mischievous. He slipped off his fins and slid them on to the swimming deck. He took the manacles from his belt. There wasn't much time, so he had to move fast, and quiet. All at once, he heaved himself on to the swimming deck, then pounced to his feet an instant later. He padded up the stairs, yanking his snatch bag off his belt at the same time. He was as silent as the night itself.

The woman was in front of him, at the railing, smoking her cigarette and staring out to sea. He crept up behind her. It was the woman from the restaurant – the one with the happy trigger finger. At the last second, she turned, but he grabbed her wrists and slapped the cuffs on them. Then he slid the bag over her head and pulled the drawstring. He covered her mouth with one big hand. She barely had time to gasp.

'I don't want to kill you,' he whispered. 'So don't fight me.'

He pulled her down two flights of stairs to the swimming deck. He yanked the zodiac closer and pushed her into it. She fell, sprawling out across the benches. Did she hit her head when she landed? If so, good. It wouldn't really hurt her, but it might put her on Queer Street for a few minutes.

Someone was behind him.

He swivelled, throwing a punch as he did. Missed. The other person had ducked it. She – it was the other woman, a black woman, bouncy curly hair – punched low, once, twice, three times, very fast, to his groin. A wave of pain and nausea rolled upwards to his throat.

The woman sprang upwards her next punch catching him under the jaw. He fell backwards, expecting to hit water, less hurt than amazed. If he went in the drink, he was in trouble. Instead, he landed in the zodiac, on top of his prisoner.

He clambered to his feet and drew his knife, unsheathing it in one motion. He drew it back, the blade glinting in the darkness.

The black woman stood in a fighter's crouch, hands extended. She breathed heavily, but looked ready to jump into the zodiac with him.

'Don't do it,' he croaked. 'I'll stab her. I swear to God I'll stab her.'

For the moment, the woman held back. Stone sliced downwards, cutting the line that tethered the zodiac to the cabin cruiser. He pushed off hard with his foot. As the boats drifted apart, five feet, then ten feet, he moved to the outboard motor.

'Nice meeting you,' he called to the woman. 'If I spot you following me, I won't hesitate. I'll just kill her.'

He heard the outboard of a boat approaching – he wasn't sure, but it could be Cruz returning. OK. Time to leave. He yanked the starter cord, and the engine coughed and sputtered into life. Stone took a deep breath and got moving.

Sticks wasn't much of a sleeper.

He never had been, as long as he could remember. Too many bad things could happen, unannounced, to people who spent time sleeping. A couple hours here, a few hours there – that was about as much as he ever got. Sometimes, while sitting in a comfortable chair, a gun on the table at his elbow, he might suddenly drift off to sleep for a few minutes. It usually caught him unawares, and only after a long stretch with no sleep – his body and mind simply could not tolerate any more time awake. Then he'd be gone. When he woke up – alive so far – he'd find that he felt much better.

Something like that had just happened. After more than a day and a half with no sleep, he hadn't been able to keep his eyes open another second. Until a moment ago, he had been dreaming of something – of flying, but not just flying. Instead, he had gone barrel-rolling through the galaxy on the flight deck of an alien spaceship, a million miles an hour, the stars and planets zooming past in a buzzing, whirling, fantastic show of light. It had probably only lasted a few minutes, and now he was awake again.

Some people thought he was crazy for not sleeping, but Sticks knew better. A guy in his line of work? You had to stay alert and quick as a cat – that's how Sticks had thrived in this business for so long. You never knew when somebody was about to make a move on you. As he sprawled out on the bed, he remembered one of those times.

Years ago – Sticks was still a very young man then, maybe in his early twenties. It was night and he was in a hotel room in Miami Beach. The sliding glass door to the deck was open, and the sounds of waves lapping at the shore, and quiet, secret humping drifted up to him from somewhere below. In those days, a business relationship he'd been involved in had recently gone sour, and he had reason to believe someone wanted to punch his timecard for him.

He was awake, listening not to the sounds from outside, but to another, closer sound. He wasn't sitting in a chair, and he most definitely was not lying in bed. No. He was on the floor, rolled in a ball in the three feet of space between the cabinet and dresser combo that had the TV set bolted on to it, and the roll-top desk that held a green blotter, a telephone, and a room-service menu. Sticks was stuffed in there, sitting up and facing the door, a loaded, silenced semi-automatic on the ground by his hand. Next to that was a pocket knife, already open. He reached and picked up the gun, careful not to make a sound. His forefinger moved to the trigger.

As sometimes was the case, his bed had a dummy version of himself on it – a sleeping Sticks made from bundled-up clothes and extra pillows, covered with the threadbare blanket that came with the bed.

The sound Sticks was listening to was that of the door to his room sliding slowly open. The first door sound he'd been aware of in his brief sleep was of the lock being picked – quiet and fast, somebody who was decent at working the two-handed tumbler-pick method. Good for him – he was a pro, whoever he was. Now, as the door opened, a slight creak – almost no sound to it, not enough to wake a sleeping man – came and went.

The light from the hallway peaked in for a second, and two large shadows moved into the room. Then the room was back in darkness.

The shadows moved to either side of the bed. No one said a thing. Sticks's heart thumped in his chest, and a strange little tickle developed in his stomach. He was excited. He saw the first muzzle flashes as the shadows fired into the sleeping form. They were bright, nearly blinding, so he shut his eyes tight and listened instead. Silenced – quiet, flat clacking sounds – you could hear them where he was, but maybe not on the other side of the wall. Three shots each, four shots, five, maybe more.

They stopped, the smell of burnt gunpowder rising in the room.

Sticks opened his eyes, aimed the gun at the two forms. The closest was less than ten feet away. Should he shoot? Hard to say. That first muzzle flash was still imprinted on his eyes – what if he didn't get both of them? Hmmm. What if they just left, figuring they'd done their job? What if they turned the light on and saw him sitting here? Questions, questions.

They didn't leave. One of them pulled the sheet away.

'What the fuck, Tony? What is this shit? He's not even here.'

The sound had no fear in it – only anger at an inconvenience. Best to shoot now, Sticks decided, before they turned the light on. It would give him the element of surprise. They'd never expect shots fired from the floor.

He targeted. He squeezed.

Bang, bang, bang.

Very little sound, but bright flashes again. One went down. Hit? He thought so.

Bang, bang, bang. The other went down.

Sticks rolled out of his hiding place, gun in one hand, knife suddenly in the other. He was nearly blind from the flashes, but he moved fast, crawling forward on his belly like a snake. Like a worm. He found the first shooter on the floor. Still breathing, gasping for air. He groped up the man's body, found his throat, and slashed it with a deft thrust from the knife. The gasping stopped. The hot blood spilled out over his hands.

He waited and listened some more.

Someone was gasping on the other side of the bed. 'Tony?' a voice said, just barely above a whisper.

'Yeah,' Sticks said. 'I'm OK. You hit?'

'Yeah,' the voice said between gasps. 'Motherfucker got me. I'm hit bad. I think it got my lung. I'm all numb. I can't feel my hands. I lost my fucking gun. Did you see where those shots came from?'

Sticks stood up. He walked over to the lamp by the dresser. He fiddled around with the chain for a second. He never could seem to get the hang of these lights.

'Did you see where those fucking shots came from?' the voice said again.

Sticks turned the lamp on. It cast a dim yellow light into the room, mostly to the floor at his feet. He walked around the bed, gun pointed at the heavyset figure sprawled and bleeding all over his carpet. The guy was a fat meatball, hair slicked back, big meaty workman hands clutching at his chest. He'd come here wearing some kind of colour-splotched Hawaiian shirt – looked like it had a landscape painted on it, complete with pink flamingoes – a pair of slacks and leather shoes. Jesus, what an ensemble. The colour that was now dominating the Hawaiian shirt was red – it actually looked black in the low light, but Sticks knew better.

'Yeah, I saw where they came from,' Sticks said. 'They came from me.'

The guy's gun was about three feet away. The guy glanced at it, but Sticks shook his head. 'I wouldn't bother with that.'

Now, in a hotel room on Saint Mark's island, Sticks smiled. More than a decade had passed since then, but he had aged well. He was still fast. He was still sharp. He could kill anybody. Hell, he could do anything.

And all of it on just a few minutes of sleep.

Smoke was doing his man thing again. Didn't he realise she was feeling bad enough? Did he think she had *wanted* to lose Pamela?

'Jesus fucking Christ, Lola, we were gone for twenty minutes.'

The three of them stood in an uneven triangle on the swimming deck. She had just related to Smoke and Cruz the story of what had happened. Cruz seemed to take it OK, but Smoke was fuming. His eyes seemed to glitter red in the darkness.

'I mean, you couldn't have stayed together for just a few more minutes?'

'Smoke, I had to use the head. Pamela said she was fine. She had her gun with her – it was sitting right on the table. I was gone for three minutes, maybe less.'

'And you say it wasn't Ty?' Cruz said.

'No. It was a white guy. Tall. Thin. Blond hair.'

Cruz nodded. His face hardened. 'That's Stone. It's my fault. I could've killed him and I didn't. Even though I knew what he was capable of.' Cruz looked back and forth from Lola to Smoke. 'This sucks, but we have to split up again. I'm going on to the island. I'll leave you with two guns. Stay alert. If anybody comes who isn't me or Pamela, anybody at all, light them up. I mean kill them and wonder who they are later.'

Cruz moved towards the dinghy he had only just climbed out of.

'What are you going to do by yourself?' Lola said.

He shrugged. 'I'm gonna get Pamela back.'

8

It was easier than Stone had hoped, getting her back to his room. First, he went back to Macho's skiff and cut it loose from its mooring. He tied the skiff behind the zodiac.

Then, he zipped to the island in the zodiac, riding hard and fast through the darkness. He tied up the dinghy to the docks, amidst a mad jumble of other dinghies also tied up there. As he did so, Pamela sat upright in the boat, hands cuffed behind her back in the steel manacles – he had noticed she was starting to come around. He took the nylon bag off her head.

She looked at him, her damp hair wild and unruly from the bag. 'You're playing with fire, you know that? I mean, you could get yourself killed doing this.'

He slapped her, hard. Her head swivelled with the force of the blow, and she almost fell over backwards. He didn't do it to hurt her – he knew that in a few moments nothing would remain from the slap except a bit of a sting and the red mark of his hand on her face – he did it so she remembered who was in charge here. By the looks of her, the memory had just sunk in.

'Pamela, right?'

She shrugged.

'Well, for lack of a better name, I'll call you Pamela. Don't give me any trouble. OK? I wouldn't want to see *you* get killed.'

He hard-marched her through the dusty streets to the hotel, gun in her back, one hand firmly on her wrist, ready to apply power to the pressure point there. The few people in the streets all seemed to be drunk – he and Cruz's girlfriend probably looked like lovers, walking arm in arm.

Once inside the hotel, he hustled her up to his room, put the DO NOT DISTURB sign on the door for the maid service, then tied her legs together with duct tape, gagged her, and flopped her on to the bed.

She stared at him, eyes wide.

'Wait here a minute.'

He went out into the hall to the ice machine, got a bucket of ice, came back and found her already on the floor and inch-worming her way on her stomach towards the door. She moved with a rhythmic motion, bending up at the waist, then sliding herself forward with a push from her knees. Stone nearly laughed. He yanked her up by the arms and dropped her on to the bed again. He found he was breathing hard from the exertion and the little thrill of snatching her and getting her up here.

'Honey, I said don't give me any trouble. Remember?'

She nodded, big eyes giving him the contrite look.

He went to the refrigerator and made himself a rum and Coke, then began pacing the room, looking down at her form on the bed. Her eyes followed him. Boy, Cruz was going to have a heart attack when he realised she was missing – probably, he'd already realised. Stone had done it, all right – he had stolen Cruz's girlfriend right out from under him, much like Cruz had once stolen Bunker's life right out from under Stone.

Stone knocked down the first rum and Coke, then mixed another. It dawned on him that his response to events had been nearly flawless. He'd seen an opening, devised a plan on the fly, then executed it. He'd used initiative and improvisation, just like an elite soldier. He'd taken a risk and gained a powerful asset. Entire vistas of opportunity were open to him now – he need only decide how he wanted to pursue them.

He looked at his glass and saw the drink was gone. So he made another one.

He could ransom the girl back to Cruz. He could simply send Cruz a note that he had the girl, and just hold her a while, putting Cruz through an agony of fear. He could kill the girl. He could hand the girl over to Sticks in exchange for some more money, and let Sticks do the dirty work. He could even get the girl to explain where she put the strongbox he'd seen her dive with – then go get the strongbox himself.

A million, maybe two million underwater dollars. Get her to tell him where the money was – it probably wouldn't take much to get that information out of her.

She watched him, her eyes following along as he paced back and forth.

'I want you to know that I'm not going to hurt you – not unless you won't cooperate. If you cooperate with me, you'll probably be out of this room by tomorrow. OK? Now I want to ask you a couple of questions. I'm going to take the gag off your mouth. If you scream, I'm going to hurt you. Then I'll put the gag back on, so it won't do you any good.'

He loosened and pulled the gag off. She watched him, but didn't say anything. He pulled up a chair and sat near her.

'You're Cruz's girlfriend.'

'If you say so.'

'Do you know what he does for a living?'

'He's an investor.'

'Good. Very funny. No, he kills people for money. Yes, I see. Of course you already know that.'

'Isn't that what you do too?' she said.

'He killed a friend of mine once.'

'Have you ever killed someone's friend?'

Now Stone rolled his eyes, and took another slurp from his drink.

The buzz was starting to come on strong. She was a sassy chick, this Pamela. It was kind of sexy, to be that way. All the same, if she was going to be mouthy, maybe he'd have to put the gag back on her for a while. Let her stew in her own juices. Maybe after a few hours, she'd be willing to tell him a few things without so much chatter.

He could torture her, he supposed, but he really wasn't up for it. So he tried a different tack.

'I've watched you. Obviously, I know where your boat is. I've been trained to do surveillance, and I've been watching you almost the whole time, OK? I was watching you when you dove from the boat with a strongbox. I was watching when Cruz and his friend went to the small island with another box. Those boxes have the money in them, don't they?'

Her eyes went wide. Still, she said nothing.

'That's right, I know about the money. I called New York and found out all about it. They're sending some people down. They'll be here soon, maybe even today, and they're going to ask me where the boat is. See what I mean? I know there's something wrong with the boat. If it worked, you folks would've moved on by now, isn't that right? Well, when my friends get here, they'll go out there and kill anybody they find. They'll come here and I'll hand you over to them. They're paying me for this. Don't you see?'

'How much are they paying you?' she said quietly.

Stone lied easily. 'A hundred thousand dollars. I guess that means they want you pretty badly. But I'm willing to make a deal to save your skins.'

'We'll pay you more. We'll pay you twice what they're paying.'

Stone shook his head. 'See, it's not that simple. I work for these people. They're dangerous. If I'm going to double-cross them, it's got to be for a lot of money. It has to be enough to compensate for the fact that I'll need to go underground for a long time. Two hundred thousand won't cut it. Not by a long shot.'

'Listen,' she said, 'you can't do this. There're innocent people on that boat.'

'There are no innocent people anywhere near that boat,' Stone said. The drinks had gone to his head already – they'd gone past his head. He was enjoying this now, and clearly he had rattled her cage a bit.

Something like panic came to her eyes. 'Look, Cruz killed your friend, I understand that. It's hard. But these people are monsters.'

'That's right, they are. And I have a way you can avoid meeting them. You tell me exactly where you put that strongbox, I dive down tonight and get it. I check the contents, and if it's money, I bring it back here. I let you go, then you run and tell your friends the monsters are coming. When the monsters show up here on the island, I wait twenty-four hours before I tell them I know where you are. By then, you folks have exercised some ingenuity and got that boat started. Hopefully, you've already gotten far away.'

She was shaking her head. 'It won't work.'

He raised an eyebrow. 'Oh?'

'Smoke – he's the other man on the boat – rigged the strongboxes to explode. He's an expert with bombs. If you try to open one of those boxes, it'll blow up.'

Stone was afraid of that. That would change the plan some – he didn't feel quite up to defusing a bomb.

'Smoke, you call him, eh? Well, maybe there's some way he and Cruz can trade the money for you.'

She shrugged. 'If you can convince them to do that.'

'They want you back alive, right? I think I can convince them.'

'All right.'

'So tell me. First things first, where did you put that strongbox you dove with? Don't bother lying to me because I'm a diver, too, and I'm gonna go check it out. And secondly, what's a good way for me to communicate with Cruz without getting too close to him? He's got quite a temper, as you probably know.'

*   *   *

Cruz was in a rage.

True to form, it was a silent rage. Someone watching him would see nothing more than a pensive man smoking a cigarette.

He stood on Stone's dock as the first light of dawn appeared in the sky. The sun was rising for their third day on Saint Mark's. It seemed like they'd already been here a month. No one was home at Stone's cabin – not Stone, not the girl Cruz had seen Stone with the night before, not anybody. Hell, it didn't even look like the fucking bastard was living here any more. There were still a few things that probably belonged to him – some T-shirts and shorts, a pair of sandals, some food and some bathroom items – but it was cosmetic. Most of his stuff was gone. Of course it was. Stone, knowing what came next, had gone underground before he made the snatch.

Cruz walked to the end of the dock. The water was a pale blue all around him. A couple of black fisherman were out in skiffs. He gazed along the sweep of shoreline, past the funky, brightly painted cabanas – red, purple, yellow, orange – towards the centre of town, with its pink and shell-coloured low-rise hotels. He noticed the dip in the land where the shanties crowded together, lumped up against the lush green hillside. Pamela could be anywhere out there.

Images and memories flooded in. Eleven years old, let out of the youth home for a day to attend his mother's funeral. The service was in a run-down storefront church in Queens. When he arrived there in the car with the social worker, he noticed Shea Stadium looming across a highway and some wasteland from the street they were on. Inside the church, a few people prayed and wept. Not many. Cruz saw his aunt Yolanda with her three little ones – she was the only person he recognised. At the front, a wooden casket sat on a metal table, almost like a hospital gurney. Cruz floated up there. The casket was closed. He put his hand on the gleaming wood. The wood was cold.

Later, he stood outside in a small cemetery – it was fall and the trees were already dead. A busy street was nearby, with cars and trucks rumbling past. They had dug a big hole in the ground and the casket sat next to it on a bright green tarp. The preacher was saying something, but Cruz wasn't listening. He was trying to remember the last time he had seen his mother. He was trying to remember what his mother looked like.

Jesus.

'Here's where I would feel pain,' Cruz whispered to the calm blue water of Saint Mark's, 'if I was a guy in touch with his emotions.'

Cruz blinked his eyes and thought about what he was going to do to Stone. He found that if he focused on that, he didn't have to think about Pamela – whether she was alive, what Stone might have done to her. No – best to think about what was going to happen to Stone. Cruz remembered a time long ago. He was eighteen, and they had just let him out of the youth facility for good. They told him the next time he got busted, he was going to big-boy jail. It made no impression on Cruz. He wasn't afraid of prison.

He was living in a single room in Times Square – the bathroom was down a darkened hallway, and Cruz cooked his Ramen noodles and coffee on a hot plate on the bedside table. It was a hand-to-mouth existence, making collections for the local heavies, hustling for table scraps.

One night they sent him to collect from a heroin dealer who had fallen into his own supply – the dealer had become a junkie. It was OK to be a junkie, but not when you still owed money from the last load they had fronted you. It was not OK to owe.

They told Cruz, 'Make him pay.'

Cruz nodded when they told him this, but he went up to the apartment thinking, 'If the guy's on junk, how's he supposed to pay? He's not going to have the money.' He remembered the narrow stairs of the walk-up, the cabbagey smell of cooking on one of the floors, the soft piano music playing somewhere in the building. And his mind going round and round: 'How's he gonna pay me? How's he gonna pay me?'

He knocked on the door and they let him in. It smelled like shit in there. Four skinny, hollow-eyed addicts sat around on a ratty couch and throw pillows on the floor. The walls of the apartment were bare. In what must have been a fit of enthusiasm, someone had punched a couple of holes through the sheetrock. The junkies stared at Cruz without much interest.

'Monty?' Cruz said.

A junkie on the couch raised a limp hand, and Cruz soaked him in. He had sandy hair and sores around his mouth. He wore a Batman T-shirt and threadbare corduroy pants. He looked away, out a soot-stained window.

'What about the money, Monty? The two grand you owe?'

The guy shrugged. It was an awkward moment. They'd given Cruz a gun for this job, but he didn't even feel like pulling it. Monty didn't have any money – that much was clear. If Monty was going to get his fix today – and it was a safe bet that if the world kept spinning, Monty was going to get his fix – he was going to have to go outside and sell himself, or steal something, or hit an old lady over the head to get the money for it. Cruz was mulling this over when the junkie behind him and to his right reached under the throw pillow he was sitting on and came up with a gun.

They'd been waiting for him.

The junkie squeezed off a shot – the sound was deafening in the close confines of the apartment. The shot missed and the junkie took another one. Cruz's ears rung. Suddenly, the one called Monty had a kitchen knife in his hand, and he was less than three feet away. He darted forward, slashing at Cruz.

Cruz jumped back and pulled his own gun from his jacket. Saturday night special – he didn't even know if it worked. It was supposed to be for show. He was supposed to scare Monty into giving him the money.

Cruz shot Monty in the face, then turned and shot the junkie who had pulled the gun. The other two junkies had barely moved. Cruz shot them both.

In the aftermath, blood and gore painted the walls. Four dead junkies lay sprawled about in pools of thick blood. Their bodies seemed to have been bled white. The carnage in that room – the absolute, total carnage – was what impressed the young Cruz. It was almost a work of art – the nightmare vision of an artist gone mad.

All these years later, Cruz intended to make Stone his next masterpiece.

Stone slipped a note under Cruz's door.

That's how he started to put his plan in motion. Pamela told him that she and Cruz had a room rented – Room 409 at the Flamingo Inn, to be exact – and Stone figured Cruz would come back there sooner or later. In the first early light, Stone crept to the door. He spent a moment listening, and although he heard nothing inside the room, it gave him a little thrill, a mini-rush of excitement to be outside Cruz's door. Cruz could suddenly appear, walking down the hallway towards Stone. Or the door could swing open, and Cruz could be standing there, bleary-eyed and in a robe. Then, in an instant, all the intervening years would suddenly come to a climax and the two men would have it out to the death, right there in the hall.

Didn't happen.

Instead, Stone slid a single piece of lined paper under the door, almost like a hotel worker sliding a final bill for Cruz's approval. The note said: *Half the money (yes, I know how much there is), inside the back door of my shack. When the money's there, you get sweet Pamela back, safe and sound.*

Stone had decided the best way to do this was not to get greedy. If Cruz actually left more than a million dollars in cash inside the door of Stone's cabana, Stone would let Pamela go. He wasn't sure yet exactly how he would let her go – what the mechanism was – but he would do it. Maybe he would release her on that strip of sand where Cruz and the other guy evidently buried the rest of the money. That would also afford him the chance to take a quick look around, and see if he could spot where they might have buried the strongbox. Just leave her standing there on the beach at night, and cruise out into deep water in a skiff with a couple of extra gas cans aboard. Stone could easily make the run to Saint Joseph, buy a bigger boat for cash there, and be gone before anybody knew where to look.

Right now, Stone was putting the second part of his plan into action. He was sitting in the skiff he'd got from Macho, about three hundred yards out from his cabana. The skiff was anchored to the sandy bottom here, and covered with a tarp. Stone lay under that tarp, the top of his head poking up a few inches, watching the back door of his cabana with high-powered binoculars.

The sun was rising in the sky. It was going to be another hot day – it was already like an oven under the tarp. But Stone was a survivor – he was trained for exactly this kind of thing. Back when he was in Ranger School, they used to parachute deep into the Arizona desert, then hike for hours back to the base. Guys would drop left and right from exhaustion and dehydration, and the guys who could still go on had to carry the guys who couldn't make it. Stone never saw it, but from time to time, people would drop dead out there. It didn't surprise him. Eventually, they discontinued the exercise, probably for that reason – too many people dropping dead. But every time Stone did it, he was one of the strong ones. Every single time, he ended up carrying someone back to base.

What was a little heat? Sometime today, Cruz would find that note, and Stone suspected that Cruz wanted Pamela back. So sometime today, probably not Cruz, but somebody, some messenger type, would appear at that back doorway with a bag of some kind, and slip that bag inside the door.

Stone would have no trouble waiting for that moment to arrive.

Macho got a big surprise when he entered Stone's secret hotel room.

The room itself was nothing too exciting – there were hundreds of rooms on the island just like it. A big double-bed, a bedside table, a desk with a lamp, a large TV set bolted to the dresser, and a small balcony with two plastic chairs overlooking the pool and the sea. The room served Stone's purposes not because it was luxurious – it wasn't – but because no one other than Macho knew he had it.

Macho went there to look at Stone's laptop computer – the better to describe it to people who might be interested in buying it. He expected Stone might leave the computer in the room. What he didn't expect was the other thing Stone had left in the room – a woman gagged, shackled and tied to the bed.

Macho had let himself in with his own key. That was something he hoped Stone might understand – Stone could hardly hire Macho to secure him a hotel room away from his cabana, invisible to the dangerous men who had come to the island for reasons unexplained, immune to the prying eyes of hotel staff, and not expect Macho to keep a key to the room for himself. Macho needed to protect everyone's interests, especially his own, and to do that he had to know what was going on. So he gave Stone one key, and he kept one. He just didn't mention this fact to Stone. And since Stone had neglected to mention that he would be using the room to abduct people and hold them hostage, Macho figured that made them about even.

Holy cow, Macho had a lot on his mind this morning.

Five minutes before, he had watched Stone load up a bunch of gear on to the little motorboat that he, Macho, had obtained for him, then cast off and zoom out into the bay, heading for open water. As Macho watched, he was thinking how maybe Stone had left his laptop computer behind – the one with the information about where the boat Macho had put the tracking device on was located.

He was also thinking how when he went to see the Tomato and the Tomato's friend in a little while, maybe he could sell this computer to them – a little bit of added value for a little bit of added money. The knowledge that the computer even existed was probably worth some money, although Macho wasn't sure how someone might charge for that. Hint that Stone had an important device, then ask for money? Tell them that it was a laptop computer with a tracking program, hint that he knew where it was, then ask for even more money? That seemed like a lot of bargaining. Better to just get one big payment and leave before anyone became angry.

Macho was busy today – he had a few appointments before he went to see the Tomato and his friend. It was mostly busy work, but one deal that did look promising involved Roxana. Macho had met two Americans early this morning – preppy types from somewhere in the suburbs of New Jersey. Macho liked maps, spent a lot of time looking at them, and he had a rough idea where New Jersey was – basically, near New York City. Anyway, these two young men were out island hopping in a chartered yacht, they'd landed here in Saint Mark's two nights ago, and one of them had seen Roxana on the street. He told Macho he'd fallen in love at first sight.

Macho liked it when the tourists talked about love. Love, even if it lasted only a short time, was a win-win for everybody. The man wanted Roxana to come out to the yacht – which was moored about a mile out in the bay – for twenty-four hours, and to bring a friend for the other preppy. After twenty-four hours, the girls could decide to go home, or decide to stay, or they could all talk about it and figure out what was next. Macho also liked that kind of open-ended talk. It had the ring of expensive gifts and cash remembrances sent from faraway New Jersey. It had the ring of return visits and upgraded living arrangements. Not guaranteed, but the possibility was there.

Macho had negotiated a nice score – two hundred and fifty dollars per girl, plus tip, plus three full meals while they were on the boat. He'd got half the payment up front. Now all he had to do was track down Roxana, find another girl, maybe sexy young Marielda, give them their cuts of the advance money, and get them down to the docks to meet these rich preppies by twelve noon today. It was good that the Tomato didn't want Roxana again today – that saved Macho from having to explain why she was unavailable.

But back to the matter at hand – the items Stone had left in his room. The woman lay on the bed, following Macho with big eyes. She was the one whose boat he'd put the tracking device on. She wore shorts and a long-sleeved T-shirt. She didn't necessarily seem afraid – more curious than anything.

Macho stared down at the bed for a few moments, stroking his chin and wondering how he could benefit from this turn of events. She watched him as he watched her, but of course he was in the better position. He opened the bedside drawer and found the laptop in there. It was closed and the power was off. Macho didn't know much about computers, so getting the thing back on and finding the right screen would be a hurdle – hopefully, the Tomato would know how to do it himself. Right now, in any case, Macho was absorbed with this woman. He slid the drawer shut.

'How did you get here?' he said.

She shrugged, the gag clamped in her teeth.

'Did a man tie you up like this? A tall man with short hair?'

She nodded.

'Do you remember me?'

She nodded.

'Sure. You remember. I sold your husband some flowers for you on the dock one day. Does that make you suspicious of me now?'

She shrugged again.

'I understand. It would make me suspicious, too. But I promise I didn't do anything to you.' He gestured at her binds, then at the four walls of the room. 'You'd like to escape from all this, I'm guessing.'

This time the woman rolled her eyes and grunted. Could anything be more self-evident than her desire to leave?

Macho smiled. He liked the woman. She was pretty, and a little bit funny. It was nice that she could have a sense of humour about her predicament. 'Of course you would. Let me ask you a question. Do you have any money?'

She nodded, and he pulled her gag down away from her mouth. Stone had tied it tight, and Macho had to reach behind her head to loosen it.

She worked her jaw for a moment, then spoke. 'Thank you. That gag was starting to hurt. I have about thirty dollars in my pocket. If you can figure out how to get these manacles off and let me go, you can have the money.'

Macho hesitated. This was the part of the bargaining process he had long been adept at – feeling slightly offended at a potential client's first offer, helping the client to feel just how offensive that offer was, but also reassuring the client that Macho wasn't so offended that he wanted to break off the negotiations.

'Thirty dollars is a nice amount of money. I'm sure you don't mean anything bad by offering that much. But as a visitor, you probably don't understand how high the cost of living is here for the islanders. My mother's medicine, for example, is very expensive. It has to be brought here from the United States. And food prices, well you know, we hardly grow anything here any more.'

'Kid, what are you trying to say?'

Macho laughed just a little bit – an embarrassed giggle. He gestured at her bindings, then at the room around her. 'Well, thirty dollars, you know, that's hardly the pay somebody might expect for a rescue like this.'

'It's all I have right now.'

'I could just take it, couldn't I?'

She let out a long sigh. 'You see that I'm tied up here. You see that my life is in danger. Doesn't that mean anything to you?'

Macho stared at her, eyes soft and thoughtful. He had learned that sometimes the best thing to say was nothing.

'Yeah, I remember you,' she said. 'You were the one driving the hard bargain on the flowers. OK, Mr Capitalist. You let me go, I give you the thirty bucks, and we'll call it a down payment. Ten per cent. What do you say to that? I'll get you another two-seventy, and that'll make it an even three hundred. You'll have to wait until later to get it from me, but I promise I'm good for it. All right?'

Macho guessed from her eyes that she wasn't lying. In his line of work, trust was an important commodity, and the ability to trust was an important skill. He trusted, and that meant sometimes he got burned – but only rarely. People were usually as good as their word. He whistled at his good fortune. Three hundred dollars for a few minutes' work? Not bad. On any other day, it would be a windfall.

But today was not a normal day. Today he was going for a five-thousand-dollar payoff, and Stone played a big part in that. Macho needed Stone to feel comfortable that everything was going fine. If Stone came back and the girl was gone, he probably wouldn't feel that way. In other words, if Macho let the woman go now, he'd have to take the computer at the same time. Then he'd have to lug it around all day, or find a place to hide it. And either way, it would tip off Stone that something had gone wrong.

Macho couldn't afford to take that kind of risk.

'Three hundred dollars?' he said.

'Three hundred dollars,' she agreed.

He reached into the pocket of her shorts. It felt strangely exciting to have his hand against her leg, even through the fabric of her pocket – he almost never touched the girls he worked with. 'I'll take the thirty dollars now. Then I'll come back later today, let you go, and we can settle up for the rest later.'

'Kid! Hey, wait a minute, OK? Go to Room 409 at the Flamingo. There's a man there. His name is Cruz. He can give you the rest of the money right now. And let's make it five hundred. OK? Listen to me!'

With the thirty dollars safely tucked away in his pocket, he gently lifted the gag and put it back in her mouth. Then he reached behind her and tightened it, just enough to keep her quiet.

'Mmmph!' she said. 'Mmmmmmph!'

'I'm sorry,' Macho said. 'I apologise. I have another appointment right now. But I promise I'll be back later on to rescue you. If I can't do that, I'll stop by the Flamingo and tell the man where you are. No worries. You can ask anybody – I always keep my word. And I agree with you about the money – five hundred does sound better.'

It really sucked to be there.

When the kid left, Pamela struggled for several minutes, her arms tied to the headboard, her legs tied to the bedposts. She began to buck and thrash her body wildly, thinking what? Maybe she thought that it would loosen the ropes somehow, or that the sound of her crashing against the bed would alert somebody in one of the other rooms on this floor. Maybe it was neither – maybe it was just a way to work off some excess anger and frustration. Whatever it was, after a little while, she gave up on it and lay still.

She stared up at the ceiling, watching a large black spider slowly move from one side of the room to the other. It was fascinating, in its way, the spider living in a parallel world, going about its business, completely oblivious to her plight. She theorised that the spider must have something sticky on its feet because it was walking upside down, ten feet above the floor, in what appeared to be defiance of the law of gravity. She hoped that when the spider passed over her it wouldn't pick that moment to somehow fall and land on her stomach.

Time passed. The play of shadow and light changed, and it started to get hot in the room. Pamela daydreamed for a while, forgetting the spider. When she looked for it again, it was gone.

She began to think about herself, and how she had come to this place. It was an old habit, thinking about herself, and it usually ended up in an orgy of self-recrimination that she had nicknamed the Pity Party. The truth was she had always felt inadequate.

She was a librarian by trade – she had graduated with a Master's degree in Library Science. She had worked for years at the public library in Portland, but she had made few friends there. She remembered how, many times, she had gone around all day almost afraid to look anyone in the eye – especially the library patrons.

Before Cruz, she hadn't had a boyfriend in years, and Cruz had really only become her boyfriend after he burst into the apartment she shared with Lola and abducted them both. If it had been up to Pamela to approach Cruz, this little romance they were enjoying never would have happened.

What was the matter with her? Why was she so shy? Maybe it was her diet – she had read somewhere that meat-eaters were more assertive, and she tended to go with vegetables and carbohydrates. She'd also read that people who lifted weights tended to be aggressive – she tended to jog long distances. Could it be that simple? A change in diet and in the way she exercised? She didn't know. Maybe it was just her, an affliction she was born with. They should call it Pamela-ism, and give it a definition – 'the inability or unwillingness to have even the slightest positive impact on your environment'.

On this trip, she'd made a concerted effort to be more assertive, more commanding and more self-confident. She had even tried to be more mouthy and sarcastic, the way she imagined a gangster's girlfriend would be. And what was the result? She'd pulled a gun on Stone at breakfast, tipping him off that they were worried about running into people Cruz knew. She'd allowed Ty Weathers to escape. And now she'd been kidnapped and taken hostage, then had explained to Stone exactly where and how they were keeping the money. The only reason she hadn't been raped by Stone was because he either didn't feel like it yet, or he just wasn't that kind of guy. To top it all off, she'd been taken for thirty dollars by a kid who looked to be no more than twelve.

It all added up to a simple picture: the reason she'd felt inadequate her whole life was because she was inadequate – she just wasn't cut out for the challenges that life presented. Lola was born to do this sort of thing. Pamela was play acting. She could try as hard as she wanted, but she just didn't have the skills — she was like the world's shortest and slowest man trying to play professional basketball.

Pamela realised now that she was very tired, and she felt a little bit like crying. The worst thing about all this? She had to go to the bathroom. It wasn't bad yet, but if she stayed here long enough, it would be.

If she ended up wetting herself, then she really would cry.

Macho had made it too easy for them.

It was early afternoon by the time he got Roxana and Marielda squared away with their new lovers and got himself over to Mikey the Tomato's room. When finally he knocked on the hotel-room door, the Tomato himself opened it. He was unshaven, wearing a colourful shirt and khaki shorts. He was in bare feet and had a drink in his hand. He left the door open and headed back towards his balcony.

'Come on in, kid,' he said over his shoulder. 'We been waiting all day. Shut the door, will ya?'

Macho took three steps inside the room, and a gun appeared from his right. The barrel of it was an inch from his head. His heart skipped a beat, and his thoughts came in a flood. The door was still open — if he moved fast enough, screamed, ducked back, he might just make it. *Mama, please help me*. His muscles tensed for the sudden action.

Then the other hand belonging to the man with the gun reached out and grabbed his hair. And pulled. It burned — a sharp pain like he would pull out the roots.

'Shut the door, motherfucker,' the man said. 'Shut the fucking door before I blow your brains out.'

Macho reached back and gave the door a push. It slid shut and he heard the bolt catch in the lock.

'Good. Now get on the bed.'

The hand half shoved him, half threw him on to the bed. Macho looked for a way out, but the only way was out the door he had just come in. That door was blocked by the man with the gun – a short man, thin as a razor. He had slicked back hair and the narrow face of a rodent. His skin was bright white, like it never saw the sun. He wore a T-shirt, jeans and sneakers – not a man that would be comfortable on the island. Macho looked into his eyes and saw that they were very bright and aware, and very, very crazy. This was the boss, then, the man who wanted to meet him.

The Tomato stood in the doorway to the balcony and looked at Macho cowering on the bed. From the outside came the sound of gulls crying and waves lapping the beach. Those sounds seemed far away, and from another life.

'Macho, this is my friend Sticks,' the Tomato said. 'He's practically been dying to meet you.' The Tomato took a sip of his drink and grinned. 'Hey, I see you brought the bag. Excellent, excellent. Toss it here.'

Macho did as he was told – he tossed it high, hoping it would go over the Tomato's head and make it to the beach. The Tomato reached a hand and caught it as it went by. 'Nice toss, superstar.'

'So the kid's here,' the skinny man Sticks said. He stared at Macho the way a hungry man might stare at a sandwich. 'That's nice. And he brought the bag. That's even better. Mikey, why don't you roll us a fat one while I talk to the kid here and get acquainted.'

Sticks put the gun on the table. Macho glanced at it with longing – he'd never held a gun in his life, but today might be a good time to start. Meanwhile, Sticks pulled something from his pants pocket – a handle about five inches long. He touched a button and a blade slid out of it. Sticks held the knife in his hand and smiled at Macho.

'They call you Macho, eh? Well, like Mikey here already mentioned, they call me Sticks. You know why they call me that?'

Macho shook his head, said nothing.

'Because I stick sharp objects in your eyes. That's what I like to do.'

Sticks stared, held the knife up for Macho's inspection. Macho felt a lump rising in his throat. What he didn't want to do was show fear. He especially didn't want to cry in front of this man.

'Got any money on you, Macho?'

Macho shrugged.

'Well? Give it over.' Sticks put his palm out. Macho found himself reaching into his shorts and coming out with eighty-one dollars – the thirty he'd gotten from the woman in Stone's room, plus his twenty per cent cut from the advance the preppies had paid, minus four dollars for conch fritters and a Coke he'd had for lunch at a beachfront food stand. It was a nice stack of money – he should have taken it home and buried it before coming here.

Sticks took the money, counted it, and put it in his own pocket. He seemed calm, even cheerful. 'Relax kid, I'm just joking. I don't actually cut people's eyes out. That's my little joke. I tell it to loosen up the atmosphere. Listen, you want a drink? A beer, maybe something harder? Nah, you don't drink, is that right?'

Macho could not find his voice. The combination of Sticks's crazy, threatening eyes, his offhand manner with weapons and his friendly playfulness put Macho on a very bad footing.

'That's all right, you can talk. Do you drink?'

'N-no. No sir. I don't drink.'

'Well, you should start. Not for nothing, but life's too short. You could be dead tomorrow. Then you'd have missed out. I was drinking at your age, and I never regretted it. Smoking. Doing drugs. All of it. Say, you getting any pussy, a young kid like you?' All this jabbering, and the man never stopped staring. He looked at Macho like he would look at an interesting piece of furniture – like Macho was a curious object, not even alive.

Macho swallowed hard. 'P-plenty.'

'Oh, that's right. You're the p-p-pimp around here. Right? Good for you. At least you're getting some p-p-pussy. I bet the whores think you're cute – they like giving it to you, right?' Sticks raised his voice a notch, addressing no one in particular. 'It's a rinky-dink island, eh? I mean, where I come from, the pimps are big guys, tough guys. You wouldn't want to fuck with them. Well, I wouldn't mind, but we're talking about most people, you know what I'm saying? Anyway, here the pimp is some runty kid.' He looked right at Macho again. 'What's the matter with this place? They can't afford a real pimp?'

There was a pause while Sticks cocked his head and smiled. He was still grasping that knife, and still held it level with Macho's eyes. Macho realised how glad he was that Roxana was safe on a boat in the bay, and away from these men. She had been right about this meeting, and he had made a terrible mistake. It was good that he was the only one who had to pay for that mistake.

'Yeah, you. Macho. I'm talking to you.'

'Yes?'

Sticks talked slow, like to an imbecile, or to a small child, a toddler. 'Can't they afford a real pimp here?' Mikey the Tomato was laughing now, laughing at Macho. Macho still couldn't think of a thing to say.

With his free hand, Sticks slapped Macho across the face. The hand lashed out fast and hard, like a poisonous snake making a strike. A second later, Macho felt the sting and heard the ringing in his ear. A heat was rising on the left side of his face.

'Earth to Macho. Earth to Macho.'

'Houston, we have a problem,' Mikey Tomato said from the doorway.

'Heh-heh-heh,' said Sticks.

Sticks brandished the knife, pointing it at Macho's face, squinting down the blade like he was pointing a gun. 'So Macho the pimp wants to meet with me, play Let's Make a Deal. Wants to tell me what he knows about our friend Stone. Wants me to pay him a princely sum of money for the honour. Well, I say hell yes! I'll meet with the pimp. I'll talk to him. But you know what? I don't think I'll pay him anything. And I think he'll tell me what he knows anyway.'

* * *

'That's fucking great pot,' Sticks said sometime later.

Hours had passed in what seemed like minutes. Sticks felt like they were moving underwater. Everything they did went slow, while the hands on the wall clock raced around and around. Mikey the Dunce handed over the joint and Sticks took another toke. He sucked it deep, staring down at the human figure on the bed. It was good fucking pot. Give the islanders some credit – their shit got you high-de-high.

'Didn't I tell you?' the Dunce said. 'I mean, Jesus, I'm flying here.'

Outside, on the balcony, the sun was a glowering, angry presence – it was a hot fucking day out, and it was getting to be late afternoon already. The only relief all day had come from a strong breeze and the clouds that skidded fast across the sky, sometimes blotting out the sun. Sticks was stoned, he was drunk, and he was having fun taking his time with Mr Macho here. Meanwhile, the sky turned pink and purple and the light from outside played against the walls of this room. It was blowing Sticks's mind.

And that wasn't the only thing blowing his mind. They'd gotten a call from Big Vito about an hour ago – right here in the Dunce's room. The big man had called wondering why he hadn't heard from them. He'd heard about what happened on the plane from the pilot, and that was OK.

'But what about the other thing?' Vito said. Sticks was already pretty high by then, and he found it funny how Vito always talked around everything, calling two and a half million dollars 'the other thing'. Fucking Vito – he thought the cops had the whole world wired.

'We're on it, Vito,' Sticks said. 'I mean, we are right on top of it.'

'Yeah,' Vito's gravel-truck voice said. 'I've heard that kind of thing before. But what are you doing in the Dunce's room? I thought you guys were acting like you don't know each other.'

'Something came up and we need to work together right now. I'll tell you about it when I see you.'

'Sticks, don't fuck this up. That's all I'm saying.'

'Hey, Vito, do I ever fuck up a job?'

Vito didn't answer.

'All right, then. Consider this one in the bag.'

But after he hung up, Sticks realised something about this job. It wasn't going to play out the way anybody – least of all Vito – expected. It seemed goddamned silly to come down here and risk his neck to fetch more than two million bucks for Vito. And then what? Bring the money back to New York so Vito could peel him off maybe thirty grand and give him a pat on the head? Good boy, Sticks. What a good boy! Sticks didn't think so. What Sticks did think was that a chunk of change like that would buy him a nice long stretch away from Vito – hell, Vito could die of old age before Sticks ever had to turn up again.

That raised a question about Mikey the Dunce. Should Sticks let him in on it? And if he did, would the Dunce go along? Sticks reflected that the absolute worst part about cutting the Dunce in was the damage it would do to Sticks's share of the money. Two and a half mil split two ways was still good money, but not nearly as good as two and a half mil not split at all. Well, it was something to think about.

'Mikey,' Sticks said now, as he stared down at Macho's prone form. 'Do me a solid, eh? Mix me another drink, buddy. Rum and Coke, all right? Light on the Coke.'

'You got it, Sticks.'

The kid's wrists were tied to the bedposts – with his legs lying free, and his arms spread, the kid was shaped like a Y. He stared up at Sticks with wide, white eyes. The kid's face was puffy where Sticks and the Dunce had punched him up a bit, and he was dressed only in his cut-off jeans. His shirt was stuffed in his mouth. They hadn't even bothered to tie it on there. They'd just told him if he spit it out, they would cut his tongue off. They told him that if he screamed, they'd cut his eyes out. The kid had already pissed his pants. There was a dark stain on the front of his shorts. There was a dark stain all around him on Mikey's mattress.

Fear was a massive turn-on for Sticks. It was coming off the kid in waves. He could smell it coming out of the kid's pores. He could smell it in the kid's piss. He had to be careful here – he could get swept away by the kid's terror, do something heavy, and then they were stuck here with a dead child on their hands. Shit, who needed that?

Sticks smoked the joint down to the nub, swallowed what was left, and lit a cigarette. God, he felt good. He felt like his head wasn't even attached to his neck – like it was floating several inches, maybe even a foot, above his shoulders.

He walked over to where the kid lay. The Dunce came to the bed and handed Sticks his drink. Sticks took a slurp – the rum sent a shiver through his body. Sticks's tongue felt dry. It was like parched and cracked earth greedily sucking in moisture from a rainstorm.

'Get his legs,' Sticks said.

The Dunce obliged – he held the kid's scrawny legs down.

'So what I'm gonna do,' Sticks said, 'is ask one more time, just to make sure I have this right.' He reached with the burning cigarette towards the kid's right arm. There was a line of five burns on that arm – they matched the five on the other arm and the five on each leg. They were all companions to the ten across the kid's chest and stomach. One more burn would make a grand total of thirty-one on the kid's body.

Sticks reflected how cool it was to count numbers – he thought of the narrow strip of beach outside and how incredibly fucking cool it would be to count each and every grain of sand on that beach all the way down to the end of the island. Holy shit. Everything was just numbers, if you really thought about it. A million dead people in a war, ninety crazy-making days in solitary confinement, and thirty-one burn marks on some twelve-year-old kid – they were all just a bunch of numbers.

Sticks looked at Mikey the Dunce and considered mentioning it, the number thing. But the Dunce was bombed – he had that faraway look, like he had landed on a distant planet. Anyway, they didn't call him the Dunce for nothing. He probably wouldn't get it.

The kid was weeping now, tears running down his cheeks, snot running out of his nose. Sticks flicked a finger on to the kid's wet cheek, got some of his tears and brought the fingertip to his lips. He liked that salty taste – it reminded him of something, but he wasn't quite sure what.

'So Stone moved to the Oceana, on your suggestion,' Sticks said. 'Because you told him we were watching him. He hides out there in the daytime, and goes on the move at night. He's got a laptop computer in the hotel room with him – a toy he brought back from the war. Right now, it's folded up closed and stuffed in the drawer next to the bedside table. He has a satellite hookup, and he can watch where Cruz's boat goes with the computer because you put a monitor on Cruz's boat. He knows exactly where Cruz is at all times.' Sticks liked the sound of his voice repeating the information the kid had given him. He felt like a computer spitting out data.

The kid was nodding, frantically nodding. He looked like one of those bobblehead sports dolls. Sticks reached over and pulled the T-shirt out of the kid's mouth.

'And what was Stone's room number again?'

'Three-fifteen,' the kid said. 'Three-fifteen. Three-fifteen. Please.'

Sticks took another hit from the cigarette. 'And if we let you live, and let you keep all your parts, you promise you won't go anywhere near Stone again? You won't try to send him a message either? Because you know . . . what?'

'You'll find out. You'll find out and you'll kill me.'

'And your mom too, right? And your little sister?'

'Yes.' The kid was nodding like crazy. He was a nodding machine.

'Yeah boss, yeah boss, yeah boss,' the Dunce said, mocking the kid. Sticks got the sense the Dunce didn't really like the kid very much.

'OK, then that's what we'll do,' Sticks said. 'We'll let you go, and thank you for your patience with us. But I'm going to ask you to do one more thing before we do.' Sticks got very close to the kid's arm with the glowing red ember.

'I'm not going to put the shirt back in your mouth. But I'm gonna give you one more burn, just for old times' sake. Whaddya say? Cry if you have to, but don't scream. Don't say a fucking word. This is your life right here. Be tough right now and you walk out of here a new man.' He pressed the ember to the soft brown skin. The cigarette sizzled as it punched into the flesh. It was out of fucking sight, the way it just punched in there. A tiny stream of smoke rose.

The kid's eyes were pinched. His mouth was clamped shut.

He made a sound like, 'Ooooom. Ooooom.'

Sticks held the butt there. Smoke continued to rise. 'That's right, take it like a man,' he whispered. 'Show me what you got.'

The kid's whole body shook, like he was tied to the third rail and riding a jolt.

Sticks pulled the cigarette away and took another hit from it. He smiled, just to show the kid that all was forgiven. Unlike the Dunce, Sticks actually *liked* the kid. 'Good work, Macho. You can go back to your whores now. Just don't let me see your face again while I'm on this island. If I see you again, I'll kill you on general principles. You understand?'

The kid was silently weeping now, but he nodded his head.

'Sure, you understand everything. It's been a pleasure doing business with such a sharp young kid. You got potential. You really do.'

9

Cruz trudged up the stairs to room number 409 at the Flamingo. He had spent the day searching for Stone and finding nothing.

Well, almost nothing. He had found out the name of a young pimp – a twelve-year-old boy who called himself Macho – and who may or may not be the one providing girls to Stone. Cruz had even found the kid's house, a wooden shack on stilts, no more or less tumbledown than any of the others in the surrounding neighbourhood – the pimp was an anonymous kid from deep poverty, on the fast track from nowhere to nowhere.

The woman there invited Cruz in. They passed through a front room, into a sitting room in back. A two-room mansion. Grand. She offered him a wicker chair to sit in. Cruz glanced around at nothing. Nodded his head. 'Nice place.' Cruz thought it best to get the meaningless pleasantries out of the way early.

'Thank you,' the woman said.

At first, Cruz had thought she was an old woman – maybe Macho's grandmother. Now, as he got a look at her face, he saw she was actually a young woman, very pretty, maybe beautiful once, but lined and emaciated by care, and maybe by disease. In his travels, he'd seen them like this one before.

'Be careful who you touch,' they used to tell him back in Times Square. 'If you're gonna get killed, do it getting shot – not getting laid.'

The knowledge hit Cruz like a crowbar across the eyebrows – AIDS.

Well. That was tough. But it was a tough old world, and Cruz was here on business. How other people lived and died was none of his affair. 'I'm looking for your son,' he said.

The skinny woman lit a cigarette. She shrugged. 'Are you police from somewhere?' Cruz caught the musical lilt of her voice, made scratchy by cigarette smoke and hard times.

'I'm not anything,' he said. 'I'm actually looking for a friend of mine. Your son Macho might know where she is.'

She grunted. 'Macho. Why he calls himself that I'll never know. He's a skinny drink of Kool-Aid – the farthest thing from a Macho. His real name is Alexander. Anyway, one thing he doesn't seem to know is where his own house is. I ain't seen him here in three days.'

Cruz could see in her face that she was lying. He let his eyes roam the walls for a moment – across the small room were some shelves with photographs on them. He stood and walked over to them – a few family shots, a few of a cute little girl in pigtails, none of which interested Cruz. But one of them very much interested him. It was a shot of a handsome young kid with a big grin – the same handsome young kid who had sold Cruz some overpriced flowers on the docks just two days ago. A little younger, sure, but definitely the same kid. Shit. Stone was working with the kid, and had moved against Cruz right from the very start. Shrewd Stone, using a little kid like that.

In the photo, the kid's hair was cut tight to his scalp, and he wore a white-collared shirt and a blue tie. 'That his dress-up picture from school?' Cruz said.

'Yeah. The last one they took of him. He stopped going there, must be two years back by now.'

Cruz picked up the cheap plastic frame and slid the photo out. 'I'm gonna take this with me,' he said. It wasn't a request – it was a statement.

The woman sighed and waved her hand. 'Bring it back when you're done.'

Now, with a photograph of a smiling twelve-year-old as his prize after a full day of searching, Cruz opened the door to the hotel room, the room he shared with Pamela. He had kept himself under control all day by focusing on taking the next step, talking to the next person. Now, as he stepped into the funky tangerine-coloured confines of the room, he found that he was starting to shake – with rage, with loss, with exhaustion – he wasn't sure with what. All he knew was that he wanted Pamela back, he wanted Stone dead, and when the time came, he wanted to be the one who put Stone in the ground. He wanted to be able to kill again, if only for that reason.

He was so distracted as he came in that he nearly missed the small piece of paper on the floor by his feet. He picked it up, hardly even thinking about it – it was probably some kind of fucking bill.

Half the money (yes, I know how much there is), inside the back door of my shack, it said in neat block letters – exactly the careful sort of handwriting Cruz would imagine Stone used when on business. It was handwriting that was impossible to misread. *When the money's there, you get sweet Pamela back, safe and sound.*

Holy Christ. Cruz darted into the bathroom, splashed some cold water on his face, glanced at himself in the mirror – the eyes of a killer looking back, telling him what he needed to do. He took his gun from his waistband, checked it, put it back, and rushed out of the hotel room again, not quite sure where he was even going.

It was getting dark.

Macho stumbled home through the streets of Underhill. Two fat policemen that he paid off every week had seen him pass a little while ago, and laughed at him. One of them had spat on the ground at his feet.

'Looks like someone got what he deserved. Maybe you should go back to the fourth grade, little boy.'

Three teenage boys had come, turned out the pockets of his damp shorts, and when they found nothing inside, pushed him down in some prickly bushes.

'Macho pissed himself!' they said. 'Macho pissed himself.'

His face was swollen where the men had punched him. His arms and legs burned where the monster had stuck lighted cigarettes in him. He had given them Stone, and surely Stone would die now. They would surprise him in his sleep, kill him and take his computer. They would find the woman Stone had tied to the bed – the woman Macho had never told them about despite everything – and they would do things to that woman. Then they would find the boat with the other man on it – the man with the scar who was probably that woman's husband.

Macho realised these people would die now, but he couldn't help them. If he did anything, the monster Sticks would kill him and kill his family. What he was going to do now was go to his mother's house, and get under his threadbare cover, and not get out of bed for a week. When he woke up one week from now, perhaps they would be gone and he could treat it all like a bad dream.

As he approached the tiny shack where he had lived all his life – high up on stilts because of all the flooding in Underhill during the hurricanes – he turned around and glanced back the way he had come. The big one – Mikey the Tomato – was following about a hundred feet back, ambling along, taking his time, as if he were only out for a night-time stroll through the township. A few people stared at him, but he seemed not to notice or care. He just floated back there, making sure that Macho went home rather than anywhere else. Wonderful – now they would know where Macho lived. He had even told them about the money under the floorboards.

Macho was too tired to keep walking – he was too tired to pretend his home was just another makeshift shack in a sea of shacks. He climbed the wooden steps and lurched through the door. His mother was in the kitchen and she turned to look at him then – this proud woman who circumstances had forced to accept money from her young boy. She stared at her beaten, burned and humiliated son. He saw something in her eyes – the look of someone who had expected this moment all along. She held her arms out to him and he went to her.

'My baby,' she said. 'My poor, poor baby.'

She held him tight as he wept and in her embrace he recognised himself for what he was – a little boy in a hard world of men. He wanted to stay there for ever, and just be held by his mother. But after a little while, after the crying had subsided, he knew he couldn't let things stand as they were. He'd left that woman tied to Stone's bed, and he had to rescue her if he still could. He was – as he had told her – a man of his word.

'Mama,' he said. 'I have another appointment I need to keep.'

'Smoke, we gotta go in there!'

Lola felt like she was losing her mind. She'd been OK all afternoon. She'd made a late lunch – fish cakes, bread and a nice salad. The idea was that Cruz would turn up with Pamela in tow, and they'd both be hungry for something to eat. When they didn't show, Lola sat down with a glass of red wine to calm her nerves and waited for them to arrive – nothing. They never came. Meanwhile, Smoke just kept clanking away on that engine. Now and then, he'd try to turn it on – the engine would turn and turn, but not quite turn over. Sometimes greasy smoke would pour out of the engine compartment.

'Almost there,' he'd say, while slowly the pressure built in Lola's mind. By the time the sun started to set, she couldn't stand it any more.

'Where can they be?' she said.

'I don't know, hon. I can't worry about it right now.'

'Can't worry about it? Jesus, Smoke, we're sitting out here being useless while Pamela . . .' She didn't want to finish her thought.

'Lola, I'm not being useless. I'm getting the boat started. If and when Cruz and Pamela get back here, and even if they never get back here, we're going to need this boat to start. In fact, especially if they never get back here, we're going to need this boat. The most important thing I could possibly be doing right now is getting the boat ready to go. The most important thing you can do is relax, stay focused, and keep your eyes open in case that big kid comes back.'

Smoke was being so . . . logical. So removed, so calculating. It was driving Lola nuts. Didn't he care about Pamela?

'Cruz is a big boy,' he continued. 'He's been in and out of jams all through his life. I doubt there's much that could come up that he can't handle. If there's a man on earth who can find Pamela and get her back here, it's probably him. If there's anybody who can take care of this guy Stone, it's Cruz.'

She'd had enough. She realised now that she was pacing – more than pacing, she was *surging* back and forth across the deck, past the cold dinner, like a desperate animal in a cage. 'Smoke! You heard him say it yourself! Cruz doesn't . . . he doesn't do that any more. He can't. The two of them could be in there and defenceless.'

'Defenceless?' Smoke said. 'He's hardly defenceless.'

It was weeks, weeks of anxiety coming to the fore, weeks of waiting and running and feeling trapped on this goddamned boat, weeks of thinking that death was right around the next corner. It was the images of death – of killing people herself, with her own hands, and feeling that it was better them than her. Smoke had brought her to this place – she had killed for survival because she was with Smoke – and now he was standing around calmly, like he didn't care. Like it didn't much matter that her life lay in ruins and her best friend in the whole world could be dead or dying right this minute.

She couldn't take it any more. She had to act now! She had to do something.

'I don't give a shit,' she said. 'You can stay here. I'm going.'

'What are you going to do, swim? We don't have a dinghy and the engine's not fixed yet.'

She peeled off her sweater – it was all that covered her bikini. The water was warm, but not that warm – now that the sun had set, it would be chillier than before. She could put on Pamela's wetsuit, but she didn't want to waste the time going downstairs, getting the suit, and cramming her body into it. She gazed out at the island – she had never swum that far before. She figured she could make it to the island itself, but she'd be exhausted if she had to swim all the way to town. So make it to the island. Then what – hitchhike? There had to be a better idea.

She went down to the diving deck with Pamela's swim fins. She sat down, slid the first one on her foot, and clasped it shut. She started to slide the second one on. She noticed the lights of the nearest boat, maybe a hundred yards away. Smoke was rising from it – it looked like somebody was grilling something over there.

'Lola? Hon, what are you doing?' Plaintive now, Smoke, the voice of male reason, trying to reel her in. It was too late for that.

'I'm going to save my friends.'

She stood. Here he came, down from the deck, cane in hand.

She turned and dove smoothly into the water. The chill of it hit her as she plunged into the depths. She felt instant goosebumps rise. She broke the surface, her breath nearly catching in her throat.

'Lola! For Christ's sake!'

'I'll be back in a little while,' she called to him. Then she started to swim, making for the boat with the barbecue. She swam well – the diving fins made a big difference – all the while trying not to think of the monsters in the deep below her. Logically, she knew there were no monsters down there – but somewhere else, in some pre-modern part of her brain, or in some memory from her childhood, she knew there *were* monsters. Big ones. And they came as the dark gathered around her.

As she approached the boat, she began to notice things about it. It was a giant sailboat, bigger than their boat, and it had a dinghy trailing behind it – a small inflatable rubber zodiac with an outboard motor.

There was music playing on board – rap music. It was more than playing – it was blasting. She'd heard the song before, and it had a good, danceable beat. Trouble was, it had those nasty, women-hating lyrics that they all seemed to go for nowadays.

'Do you on the floor, baby! Do you some more, baby!'

A man on board was singing the words. Or, more accurately, he was shouting them. Drunk, in all likelihood. Well, she'd see, wouldn't she? She only wanted to borrow their dinghy.

She pulled the fins off and climbed up their swim ladder, the fins in one hand. The night air gave her a chill, and suddenly she stood in front of two men and two women. The men were young and white, with close-cropped hair, and were dressed in nearly identical khaki shorts and polo-type short-sleeved shirts. The women were young and black – at a guess, locals from the island. One was thin, in tight shorts, a bikini top and high-heeled sneakers – until a moment ago, she had been dancing in place to the bass line of the music. One was heavier, full-bodied, fleshy, with long flowing hair and the beautiful face of a magazine model. All four of them had a drink in hand. One of the men manned the barbecue, and one of the men stood nearby with a cigarette. The group turned as one, noticeably startled to see her there.

The man at the barbecue remained there, staring. He took a sip of his drink, then shook his head, as if to clear his vision.

The other man turned the radio way down. It was quiet on the boat now, almost silent. The guy flicked the last of his cigarette into the water. He held up his drink. It was a red drink – Lola figured it was fruity, probably quite tasty. In the glow from the red and green Christmas lights they had strung everywhere, she could see that his eyes were bloodshot. These guys had probably been drinking half the day.

'Well, well, well,' he said. 'What do we have here, a mermaid? I think I made that last batch of margaritas too strong, Pete. But I like the results.'

He came closer, eyes roaming her body. Lola was painfully aware that the chill night air made her nipples stand out firm against the tight fabric of her bathing suit.

'Can I use your dinghy?' she said.

He put his drink down. 'Can you use my thingy? Did you hear that, Pete? She wants to use my thingy. Sure. You can use my thingy. This young lady here, Marielda, just finished using it a little while ago, but I'm sure she won't mind if you use it, too. And you can use the rest of me with it.'

The guy got close – way too close. Three inches away, and starting to do some sort of bump and grind thing. Lola could smell the alcohol on him. She rolled her eyes. She had no time for this.

She rammed a knee into his groin. As he bent over, she gave him a hard flat palm across his face, driving him backward. He fell down, tripping over his own two feet more than anything. He landed on his back, his drink splashing all over his shirt. Then he sat up, hand to his face. Blood trickled from his nose. He stared at her, mouth gaping, eyes wide in pain and surprise.

Lola looked at Pete. He hadn't moved from his station at the barbecue. The young girls hadn't moved, either. One of them, the full-bodied one, met Lola's eyes and flashed a ghost of a smile. The smile was there for an instant, then replaced by a look of seriousness and concern.

'That little motorboat out there,' Lola said, not wanting to play the dinghy-thingy game any more. She gestured with her head. 'You mind if I borrow it? I'll bring it back later tonight. I had one, but something happened to it.'

He shrugged, looked down at the burgers he was broiling.

'Sure, go ahead. I don't mind.'

Roxana watched as the young American woman zoomed off towards the island on Pete's dinghy – the dinghy that had brought her and Marielda out to this gigantic sailboat. Roxana felt that she and the woman had shared a look for a moment – a look of understanding, or possibly sisterhood.

No doubt the woman was in wonderful shape – an athlete. She had muscles in her arms and legs, etched lines the way an artist might draw them, and a tight, flat stomach. And no doubt Roxana would some-times like to punch out these men – the tourists, even the men on the island – the way this woman just had. She would like to have that power over her own life and body.

She looked down at Rob, still sitting on the deck of the boat, hand to his bloody face. Rob was a jerk, the perfect ugly American, and Roxana was glad that he wasn't her partner on this little trip. Not that he hadn't already tried to make her his partner – early on, Roxana had learned that Rob was hoping to switch back and forth between girls. But Pete had put a stop to it.

Roxana glanced at Pete, still calmly cooking the hamburgers at the grill. Pete and Rob had identical, flat-top haircuts. Pete and Rob had almost the exact same taste in clothes. They'd been sailing on this boat together for three months. Yet Rob was loud and pushy and had no manners, and Pete was quiet and smart and even a little bit shy. Even so, Pete was the one in charge – the two were brothers, and Pete was the eldest by three years.

All these men. All these men and how they are.

Roxana'd had trouble sleeping last night, as tired as she was after her day with Mikey the big Tomato. It was more than the physical workout the ape had put her through that had exhausted her – the Tomato was a scary, dangerous man, with flat, dead eyes. Just being in his presence was tiring. It worried her that Macho was going to meet with him and a mystery man who was probably just like him. It worried her that the Tomato was following Stone, who, for all his faults, and his *need for variety*, was basically a good man. Early this morning, before first light, Roxana had left her home and walked to the great Coomacka tree on the outskirts of Underhill.

In the darkness, she could see the tree, and the shadow it cast, half a mile before she reached it. It towered ten storeys above the rusty tin roofs of nearby homes – by far, the tallest thing on this part of the island. The squawks of the cocks crowing all over the island at the first sign of light seemed to be the screeching voice of the tree itself. Its monstrous arms seemed to writhe in the breeze. She walked to the tree and touched the solid wood of its base. Through her fingertips she sensed how alive it was, and aware – even after five centuries of guarding this place. She sensed the angry spirits of the murdered slaves who inhabited the tree.

'Please,' she had said to the tree, her voice no more than a whisper. She wasn't quite sure what she was even asking it. She felt that it might know better than she. 'Please, please, please.'

Ty Weathers had seen Lola leave.

He sat in his little boat in almost total darkness, not fifty yards away from the yacht when Lola went in the water. He'd been listening to them argue on the deck, shouting at each other, and he'd been watching the white outlines of Lola's bikini move around up there with frantic energy. Man, she was something special. When he saw her hit the water and swim away, he figured she'd be back in a minute. Then, when he noticed she was still swimming, swimming, swimming away, he was sorry to see her go. When twenty minutes passed and she still hadn't returned, he breathed a heavy sigh. OK, no more Lola.

It seemed she had left the white boy alone on the boat. The other two people, Cruz and Pamela, were nowhere to be seen. If they were really gone, and it seemed like they were, that left Ty a nice opportunity to stroll on board, cap the white boy, and walk off with the boat and the money after a minimum of hassle.

OK, another two minutes of relaxation, another few deep breaths, and he would move. Dig it – he had fucking rowed out here. As darkness had descended on the docks, the only boat he could find unattended was a goddamned rowboat. So he had dropped in the bag with the things for his trip – his granddaddy's two ancient guns, a loaf of bread, six-pack of Energize! energy drink and a bunch of bananas, and a couple of changes of clothes – untied the boat from the dock, and put his shoulders to work. Even though it was work getting out here, and his arms and back were tired, the rowboat had the benefit of being absolutely quiet – the only sound that of the oars gently breaking the surface of the water. Ty had a smooth, powerful, controlled style with the oars – no slapping the water because of fatigue, no out-of-sync strokes.

As he sat there bobbing on the rising swells, an image of his grandmom popped briefly into his mind. He had waited until she retired for the evening before he left the house. He had been living in that ramshackle house with her for the better part of a year, suffering her constant henpecks and goadings – with a little luck, today was the last day he would ever see that old biddy.

He pulled the old guns out of the canvas bag – Jesus, look at these things. Dirty, crusty fucking things, but they'd do the trick all right. He glanced up at the yacht – all quiet now, except for the cranks and the knocks of the white boy fucking with that dead engine again.

Was it time for Ty Weathers to treat Mr White Man to a welcome? It certainly was – it was high time. He pictured himself walking up to the man and simply shooting him in the head. One shot, with no warning – the sound of it echoing back and forth across all the empty space out here. Nobody would know where it came from, and nobody would know what it meant. After that, a quick look around to see if the other two were home – if not, the boat and all its booty belonged to Mr Ty Weathers, late of shitty, dead end Saint Mark's island, current resident of the Big Time.

All righty, then. Let's do this shit.

Ty smiled up at the millions of stars beginning to fill in the dark sweep of sky above him. It was show time once again.

Cruz had barely gone twenty yards from the hotel when he spotted a child running towards him out of the darkness of a dusty side street.

'Mister! Wait!'

The kid ran up to him — sure enough, as the kid got closer, Cruz recognised the face from the photograph. The kid wasn't smiling this time — his face was puffy and swollen like a boxer who had taken a few too many punches in tonight's bout, and his eyes were tired and heavy with hard-won knowledge, like the eyes of a refugee.

'Macho,' Cruz said.

'Yes.'

'Do you have something to tell me?'

'Room 315 at the Oceana. Your wife is there.'

'Is anybody else there?'

The child shook his head. 'I don't know.'

'You wouldn't happen to have a key to the place, would you?'

Now the kid gazed at the ground. He would not meet Cruz's eyes. 'They took the key from me.'

Jesus. 'Who are they?'

'Bad men. From New York.'

Cruz felt something he'd almost never felt in his entire career — his heart skipped a beat. Cruz had never been much of a worrier. In fact, he'd come to believe he was one of those people who didn't have the capacity for worry, but right now he didn't like the sound of *bad men from New York*. He made a concerted effort to keep his mind clear of any images. If Pamela was locked in a room with bad men from New York, that could paint some very ugly pictures. Cruz sighed.

'OK, kid. I'll take care of it. Disappear, all right?'

Cruz started to walk away.

'Mister?' Macho called after him. Cruz stopped and turned around. The kid managed something like a smile. It looked a lot like how a corpse might smile, as worms crawled through its eye sockets.

'She told me you'd pay five hundred dollars for that information.'

'I'll tell you what,' Cruz said. 'For five hundred dollars, I won't shoot you. I guess that makes us even now.'

The Oceana was a ten-storey cinderblock high-rise, boxy and stern, like government buildings from the 1960s. As Cruz approached it, the only thing about it that suggested charm or fun was the neon *Oceana* sign halfway up its face, the name in orange with frisky blue waves underlining it. Cruz waltzed through the threadbare lobby, and paused in front of the sleepy desk clerk, who barely glanced up. She was a young heavyset woman, who was watching a tiny white television perched at her elbow on the desk.

Cruz took two hundred-dollar bills out of his pocket. 'I wonder if you can help me?' he said. 'I seem to have lost my key?'

'Room number?' the woman said.

'Three-fifteen.'

The woman glanced into a wide logbook. 'I don't have anyone booked in that room, sir. Are you sure—' She looked up at Cruz and saw the bills he held up.

Cruz looked deeply and directly into her eyes. She looked away, back at the TV. 'There's no reason to mention this to anyone. Do you understand?'

'Of course,' she said, handing him a room key.

Cruz climbed the stairs, taking them two at a time, at the same time sliding the gun from his waistband and fitting the silencer to the barrel.

At the door to 315, he paused. He listened for any sound inside the room – there was almost nothing, maybe a faint rustling. No one was in the hallway with him, though he could hear the chatter of television sets behind a few of the other doors. OK. Unlock the door, then plunge inside and kill anybody who wasn't Pamela.

Could he do that? Could he kill again?

At this point, he didn't have much choice. If he burst in there, he was going to have to kill somebody or get killed himself. He could do it, he decided. He could do it for Pamela, if for no other reason.

All right, so do it.

Cruz slipped the key in and very quietly turned it in the lock.

An instant later, he pushed the door open and slipped through, gun pointing everywhere at once, looking for targets.

There was nobody here – nobody, except Pamela bound hand and foot, gagged, and tied to the bed in the centre of the room.

Relief surged through his system. He ran to her and gently pulled her gag off.

'Cruz,' she said. 'Holy Moly, am I glad to see you.'

'Is anybody else here?' Cruz said.

'Like who? Stone tied me up and left me here this morning. The only person I've seen all day is the little kid who sold us flowers that time. He scammed me out of thirty bucks and left.'

Cruz had trouble asking the next question. 'Did Stone . . . do anything to you?'

Pamela rolled her eyes. 'Cruz, where have you been? Clearly he did something to me. He kidnapped me and left me here to rot. I haven't gone to the bathroom in over twelve hours.'

Nobody came – all day he had waited, and nobody came.

And as the hours passed with Stone hunkered down in the skiff, covered by tarp, waiting for somebody to appear at his cabin and leave the money, an uncomfortable thought began to form in his mind. It was probably there most of the day, but as the sun moved into the west it came on stronger and stronger, eventually becoming the only thing he seemed able to think about.

The thought was this: what if they had left? What if this girl Pamela wasn't important to them after all, and they had simply pulled up stakes, grabbed the money from the ocean floor and the small island, and sailed on out of here?

It was an ugly thought, all the uglier because he couldn't do anything about it until the sun went down. But as soon as the last of the light winked below the surface of the horizon, Stone made his move, and felt relieved to be back in action. This waiting around covered up in a boat wasn't doing his nerves any good – and this whole trip was no longer much of a vacation, was it? With Sticks and his sneaky friend on the island, Cruz out there in a rage somewhere, and Pamela a wasting asset in a hotel room provided him by a twelve-year-old pimp, hesitating was no longer an option.

Stone pulled the skiff to within a thousand yards of the boat. He tied it to an empty mooring, then he used the binoculars to verify the boat was still there. From there, he swam out to it. He swam without a tank – just fins, a snorkel and mask, and a diving headlamp. He swam to the boat in absolute darkness, moving through the water like a shark. He did it with his summer wetsuit on to give himself an extra layer of skin and add some buoyancy. He swam right up to their boat. He fought the urge to climb on board again.

He dove under and swam around beneath the hull for a minute or so. One idea was to attach a charge to the hull, and blow it out. It was a thought, but in water this shallow and placid, he might sink the boat and not actually kill anybody on board. Anyway, where would you get explosives on an island like this? He'd have to leave and come back.

He swam around the boat, doing circles in fifty-foot increments, looking for the brain coral Pamela had described. The water was maybe fifteen to twenty feet deep. At about a hundred feet from where the boat was now, he found the coral. He took a deep breath, dove to it, and when he was down there, put the light on it. On one edge of it, he found signs of a disturbance. The sand was different here. He dug down with his hands, and within two scoops, he hit the box.

He killed the light, surfaced, took another breath, and went down again. He didn't even need the light now. He felt the box with his hand – sure, metal strongbox with a suitcase handle. The same box he'd seen the girl go in with two nights ago.

He could take it. He could just take this one box and probably half the money. He could forget about the box he'd seen Cruz and the other guy take off with, and evidently hit the beach with that same night. Half the money would be over a million dollars. Jesus.

The reality of what he had hit him without warning. He'd just spent six months ducking shells and sniper fire, watched a good friend of his get killed, killed a bunch of people himself, all for less than a quarter of what he had right in front of him, right now. His for the taking – except he'd have to find some way to disable the explosives they'd wired to it. He ran his hands over the strongbox, caressed it. There was some kind of locking mechanism on the box – a combination lock. The explosives would be wired to that. Could he beat it? Not his thing – he'd have to get them to open it somehow.

Should he take the box?

No, leave the box here. Why carry around a box with a bomb in it? Especially since he already had Pamela captive? No good reason. Then another thought occurred – what if he somehow lost Pamela? It could happen. How about this one? *Move* the box. If anything went wrong, and Cruz and his people decided to leave, they'd come to get their box and find that it was no longer here.

That was the ideal plan.

Move this box. Try one more time to ransom Pamela back to them. If that didn't work, get ready to leave. If the opportunity presented itself, kill Cruz – the first chance he got. How? Stone had no weapon other than the diving knife he'd bought when he got here. So stab him – get him in the water somehow, where Stone had the clear advantage. If he managed to kill Cruz, then get the others to show him where the second strongbox was buried. Take all the money. If he didn't manage to kill Cruz, come back and grab this box from its new location, leave the island and figure out how to open the box later, on some other island.

Nobody was going to report the money stolen – if Sticks ever found these guys, all they could say was they don't know where half the money went. Sticks would probably figure it out – he didn't seem dumb

– but by then it would be too late. Stone would keep moving, stashing money here and there, staying ahead of them.

It would work.

Stone went to the surface one last time, and took another deep breath. Then he came back and pulled the strongbox out of the sand – it was heavy – and set about finding a better location for it.

Twenty minutes after borrowing the dinghy from the men on the sailboat, Lola padded up the stairs to the fourth floor of the Flamingo Inn.

She'd found a pair of flip-flops on the dinghy she'd taken, but they were too big. It was like trying to run in clown shoes. So she had kicked them off and come here in bare feet, careful not to pop her tyres on any loose gravel or protruding nails. It had slowed her down a bit. Hopefully, she wasn't too late.

Too late for what? That was the question. The truth was, Lola wasn't even sure if she would find them here. It just seemed like the natural first place to look.

She approached the door: 409.

So what should she do, knock? She felt weirdly exposed, standing there in the hallway on the aging floor tiles, wearing nothing but her bikini. She calmed her breathing and stared at the door. Listen. Anybody in there? She let herself go very quiet. Sounds floated up from downstairs – people in the lobby, talking and laughing. Sounds came in through the window at the end of the hallway – a breeze blowing, somebody shouting on the beach. Waves lapping at the shore. The backfiring blat of an old motorcycle, heading up into the hills.

She put her head very close to the door. There were sounds, all right. Somebody was in there. Rustling, movement, whispering.

Then came Pamela's voice, strained, but as clear as day: 'Oh my God!'

OK, Lola was going in there. She looked at the wooden door. Could she kick it in? She didn't know. She'd never done anything like that before. She knew the concept, though: in your mind's eye, don't picture yourself kicking the door. Instead, picture yourself kicking *through the door*. Lola raised her leg and smashed outward, leading with the ball of her foot.

The lock broke and the door swung inward.

Pamela was in the bed. A man was on top of her.

The man was Cruz. The two of them turned and looked at Lola standing in the doorway. Thankfully, they both had most of their clothes on.

Cruz shook his head. 'Weren't you supposed to stay with the boat?'

Pamela smiled and a violent shiver went through her entire body. She gestured at Cruz with her head. 'Honey, you got here just in time. Save me from this animal, will you, please?'

'Eureka! And praise fucking Jesus.'

Smoke stood on the main deck of the *Saucy Jack*, at the helm. The gun Cruz had left sat next to him on the console. After two days of tinkering, both engines had just turned over and barked into life. In neutral, he gave them full throttle and listened to the beautiful, roaring sound of freedom. Man, was that a load off his mind. Saint Mark's had got old, older than old, and it was past time to get out of here.

So what to do next?

He supposed he could hoist anchor and take this big girl into the marina. Then he could wander the streets of the island, looking for the rest of the team. For a brief moment after Lola dove into the water, he considered following her. But he had work to do getting this boat started, and that work had just now paid off handsomely. Also, he wasn't much of a swimmer, and if she wanted to run off like that, it was out of his hands. In any case, within a minute or two, it was clear she was swimming for that other boat nearby, and she would make it easily. Who she would meet on that boat and what kind of reception they would give her was another question. Smoke shook his head. He wasn't her father, but more and more it was beginning to seem that way.

Smoke took a cigar from his shirt pocket, unwrapped the cellophane, and lit up. The sweet smell of the stogie rose into his nostrils. Out on the water, the lights of the other boats bobbed here and there. From further away, the bright lights of the town shone outward into the night. Nearby, music played from one of the boats, probably the one where Lola had gone. Heavy bass – it sounded like rap music. Smoke didn't care much for rap music. He gazed out at that boat – it was strung up in red and green lights like a Christmas tree.

'Turkeys,' Smoke said.

He eased off the engines, letting them idle, turned around and saw Ty Weathers standing directly behind him, not five feet away.

'So long, sucker,' Ty said, and raised a gun to his face.

Smoke didn't have much time. He cringed – his eyes narrowing to slits, his face squinching up into a mass of wrinkles – and he barely had time to do that. The kid meant to kill him this time, no questions, no debate, no mercy. Smoke stared into the black abyss of the gun's muzzle, certain death awaiting him there. Instantly, his heart shifted into overdrive, pumping like crazy.

'Wait!'

Ty pulled the trigger and the gun blew up in his hand.

It was small, as explosions went – a bang, a puff of smoke, and chunks of metal flying in three directions. But it was big enough to take the index and middle fingers of Ty's right hand. Ty's mouth hung open as he stared at the ragged, bloody stumps where his fingers had just been.

Smoke had spent his life around professional criminals, and was struck dumb by the mistake of an amateur. *Holy shit, what kind of gun did this kid bring? Who was this fucking kid?* A long moment passed before Smoke found his tongue.

'Ty,' he said at last. 'Have you got some kind of problem with me? I mean, why don't you just do yourself a favour and stay the fuck home?'

But Ty Weathers wasn't done yet. He leapt at Smoke, launching a roundhouse punch with his left hand. It was a good, solid left, and caught Smoke on the side of the head. It rang his bell.

Ty came around with the right now, a crazy bitch-slap with half a blood-streaked hand. Then fired the left again, a hard jab this time, straight into Smoke's face. His head snapped back, and he fell against the console, Ty right on top of him.

Smoke tried to push him off, but the big kid was too strong. Smoke reached for the kid's face, but Ty slapped his hands away. Ty grabbed Smoke's head with both his hands and started banging it off the console.

'Motherfucker,' Ty grunted.

He said it over and over again, a kind of chant now, each syllable timed to when Smoke's head crashed into the console.

'Moth-er-fuck-er. Moth-er-fuck-er.'

Blood ran into Smoke's eyes. The kid had him bent down, just smashing his head over and over. Smoke understood now – Ty meant to smash the hard fibreglass steering console apart with Smoke's head. Could it be done? It'd be interesting to see.

Smoke glanced sideways and saw Cruz's gun sitting there, just a few feet away. It was Smoke's only hope, and it wouldn't be long now before Ty noticed it as well. If Ty picked it up, then Smoke was through. There was no chance – zero – that a gun belonging to Denny Cruz would ever misfire.

Smoke reached for the gun, brushed it with his fingers, and knocked it on to the floor. It made a loud thunk as it hit the deck.

The sound interrupted Ty's reverie. He stopped banging Smoke's head, and let Smoke slither to the floor. Smoke reached weakly for the gun. Ty looked down at it as though he had never seen one before.

'Motherfucker,' he said.

Some vocabulary this guy had.

Stone was tired as he opened the door to the hotel room.

He flipped the switch by the door, but nothing happened. Was the power out? No, there was light in the hall. Anyway, there was the Toughbook on the table with its LED lights on. Wait a minute – why was the computer on? What was it doing on the table? He glanced at the bed where he had left Pamela early today – nobody there.

That was a bad sign. OK, time to leave.

Something hard connected with his face. It rung his bell. He stumbled sideways, falling into somebody else. Behind him, the door slammed. Something hit him again, and again. He sank to his knees under the barrage – Jesus, was that a gun?

Sure. Pistol-whipped.

Cruz.

Stone lay face down on the carpet, his hand near his face. He was bleeding – he could feel the warm blood pouring all over his fingers. He didn't even have a weapon. Cruz had killed Bunker and was going to kill him, too. All day, Stone had waited for Cruz to show up with his money, and instead Cruz had waited for him here.

'Turn him over.'

Strong hands grabbed him and flipped him over. His head banged on to the floor as they let him go. A flashlight shone in his face. All he could see was the blinding white light in the darkness – it looked like a locomotive coming to run him down.

'Stone, you piece of shit, where you been? We've been waiting for you. You fucking lied to me.'

Not Cruz – Sticks. And another guy. Somebody clicked off the flashlight, and after the secondary image faded, he could see them, skinny Sticks and a hulking form on Sticks's right side.

'Sticks. What are you talking about?'

'You, you fuck. You lied. The kid told us all about it – he's working for us now. You got GPS on Cruz. You told me you had no idea where he went, but you been watching him the whole time. We're not dumb, you prick. We looked at your computer. We can see Cruz just as plain as day – his boat is parked right here at the marina.'

'The kid told you.' Stone said it just to hear how it sounded. He liked Macho. He wished he hadn't done that. Then again, business was business.

'That's right, the fucking kid. He ratted you out, dummy. Now you're gonna die. Wasn't that a stupid way to die? All for nothing?' Hands roamed over his body. They found his diving knife. For the moment, they missed the fat envelope with his $10,000 finder's fee in it.

'Whaddaya got here, Stone? A knife? That's nice. Mind if I have it? Well shit, you won't be needing it anyway.'

Stone blinked. In his mind, he ran through an inventory check. Head? Busted up, but OK. Awareness? Dizzy, but not in shock. Today was Wednesday. It was night-time. His name was Butch Stone.

Decision-making ability? Seemed OK. Body? Better than most. He could do something here, maybe take them by surprise if he got a little lucky.

He'd heard the door lock as he went down. Anyway, they'd expect him to go for the door. As he scrabbled to open the lock, they'd either shoot him, stab him, or pistol-whip him again. No good. What wouldn't they expect?

He rolled his eyes. In his peripheral vision, he spotted his only hope – the balcony. Three storeys down to the pool – and he'd have to dive out from the building to make the water. How deep? He didn't know. Hopefully, pretty deep. He let his eyelids flutter shut.

A hand slapped his face. 'Stone! Don't pass out on me. I'm talking to you right now. I want you awake for this.'

'Yeah, yeah. I'm awake.'

'Stand him up, Mikey. Let's put him in the chair over there.'

They yanked him up by his arms, practically tearing them out of their sockets. He went limp and they supported him as they walked him across the room. He was facing the balcony now – the door was open. They must have been hanging out on the balcony while they waited for him. That was fine – make yourselves at home, boys.

'Turn the chair around. Yeah, I got him, go ahead.'

The big goon reached to get the chair. For a second, only skinny Sticks had him, standing directly behind him, one hand under each of his arms. Stone slumped, but steadied his legs.

Only one chance at this – make it count.

He rammed his head back.

Crunch. He did it again.

Crunch.

He saw stars. The face fell away and the arms were gone.

Stone ran, two long strides taking him through the door and out to the balcony. He leapt, long-ago obstacle courses imprinted on his memory. He planted one foot on the railing, then another. The world spun. Something whistled past his head. Lights of the courtyard below him, lights from fishing boats out on dark water. Glistening water in the pool. Oh my God – people in the pool, even at this late hour.

Dive out! All the way out!

He dove.

He passed over the concrete lip of the pool, his shadow like Superman zipping by. Couldn't keep his form – his legs corkscrewed above and behind him. A woman screamed. Here came the water.

He broke the surface. *Hallelujah, the deep end.*

He went down, his hands breaking his momentum as he hit the concrete bottom. He swam towards the shallow end, and three sets of legs tangled down there. He popped up, just a few feet from a man and two women – a fat white tourist and two lovely locals, getting in some after-hours extra-curriculars.

'That was some dive,' one of the girls said. 'You scared the shit out of me.'

Stone looked up at the balcony, wondering when the bullets would start flying. Sticks was there with the goon. They stared down at him. No way would they shoot with civilians around. That would be too much public action for a job that was supposed to be low-key.

Stone waved.

'The Romanian judge gave it a 7.9,' Sticks said, his voice sounding calm in the still night. 'You fucking prick.'

Stone climbed out of the pool, and darted into the bushes at the edge of the property. He'd escaped, and the dive was exhilarating. The water in the pool had even revived him somewhat. But now what? He couldn't go back to his bungalow, and worse still, Sticks had his laptop with Cruz's coordinates on it.

As he passed through the bushes, a hand darted out.

He turned, ready to kill. His own hand lashed out like a blade. He stopped the lethal chop at the side of a boy's neck – the edge of his palm just touching his skin. He looked at the face – Macho, but a shell-shocked Macho.

'Stone,' the kid said.

10

Stone followed Macho through the alleys and warrens of Underhill. He moved quickly and silently, Stone just a few steps behind him. They passed between tiny darkened homes just four feet apart, the lights and sounds of television sets coming through the windows to them.

Macho seemed to be taking a path that would run into the fewest people. Here and there, Stone might spot a man out smoking a cigarette in the night air, or an old woman rocking on a rickety porch. The homes were battered, dilapidated, high up on stilts, a few of them leaning crazily. Many had small white satellite dishes mounted on the outside.

The poor people of the world, inside at night, staring at the hot babes and macho hunks of *Baywatch*.

They came to a home, no more or less tumbledown than any of the others. Macho stepped into the light coming down from one of the windows. Stone was taken aback – he was seeing Macho clearly for the first time tonight. One eye was half-closed, and his head had swollen like a rotten gourd. He had burns marks up and down his arms.

'Hey Mr Macho,' Stone said. 'They got you pretty good, eh?'

Macho's voice was just above a whisper. 'Yes.'

The kid had moved so quickly through the town that Stone hadn't had a moment to talk to him. All he knew was that Sticks and his two buddies had been waiting for him in his secret hotel room when he got home, and that from the evidence, they had planned to kill him. No, wait a minute: he also knew that Sticks now had his Toughbook with Cruz's exact location blinking away on a document sitting right on the desktop. And he also knew that he was getting tired – nearly in the drone zone now from lack of sleep, sitting surveillance, and taking an unannounced beating. It was night, and things were happening fast – by the morning, he could be out two million dollars.

'I betrayed you,' Macho said, casting his eyes at Stone's feet. 'They know what you're doing.'

'It's a little too late to tell me this, buddy. In case you didn't notice, I just came from seeing them.'

'They tortured me to get the information,' Macho said. A tear streamed down his swollen cheek. Then another, then a whole stream of them. His closed his good eye and his body began to shake.

'I see that,' Stone said. 'I really see that. They like to torture people. It's one of their things.' He crouched down in front of Macho. He raised the kid's chin with one hand. 'Hey, it's OK. I'm alive. We can still get back at them, but I'm going to need some weapons. And I'm going to need them right now.'

Macho perked up the slightest bit, but didn't smile. 'I think I know just the man.'

They rode an ancient, rusty moped out of town, up the dirt road and into the surrounding hills. Stone drove – the thing had a top speed of about twenty miles per hour, it smelled of oil, and greasy blue-black exhaust came in a steady stream from the rear of the thing. Macho had unearthed the beast from a locked shed next to a water pump in back of his house.

'I've never seen you riding this thing,' Stone said when Macho pulled the blue tarpaulin off it.

'It's my pride and joy. I keep it under lock and key because of theft. I own it simply to own it – not to ride it. I come in here and look at it from time to time. I take it out only once in a while, if I need to make a trip somewhere I can't walk. Usually I wait until late at night – I hope that most people have forgotten I have it.'

'Kid, you're old before your time. You're supposed to enjoy things when you're young.'

'I don't know if I have that option,' Macho said as he wheeled it out of the shed. He gestured for Stone to climb on to the front of the saddle. 'Let's go.'

Now, they climbed higher and higher into the hills, and the weather grew damp and chilly. They passed through some fog. Here and there, Stone caught glimpses of whitewashed homes set back from the road, usually hanging from the edge of the cliff. In the daytime, they must have staggering views of the water and the town below – not everybody was poor in Saint Mark's.

'How far is it?' Stone shouted, half thinking they'd pull over at one of these houses, and some rich white man in a smoking jacket would come to the door and welcome them into his armoury. Maybe he'd invite them to look through his telescope at the quarter moon in the black sky. Odd as it sounded, he believed Macho could have those kinds of connections. Wherever they were going, Stone found himself wondering where Sticks was, and if all of this was going to be too late.

'All the way,' Macho said. 'When the road ends, we're there.'

'How far is that?'

'Not far.'

They arrived at the road's end just a few minutes later. Macho hid the bike in some dense underbrush, taking care to make the bike invisible to any passers-by. Stone glanced around – it didn't look like the

Patrick Quinlan

area saw too many passers-by. A path led into the bushes, away from the gravel turnaround.

They came to a shack in a clearing. A pen had two fat hogs in it. An old broken-down pony stood nearby, grazing on some grass.

A thin black man in a pair of shorts and flip-flops stood in the yard. He was bald, with a ring of salt-and-pepper hair beneath his crown. His body was wiry, with well-defined muscles. He smoked a long, thick home-rolled. He watched the small boy and the tall white man approach with no expression on his face – not even curiosity.

'Macho,' he said. 'I heard your motorcycle. Looks like the sky fell on you.'

Macho gestured at Stone. 'I have a customer that wants to meet you.'

The man waved them over. They followed him to a rusty metal equipment shed. He turned to Stone as he fiddled with a lock on the door. 'I was in the war,' he said. 'Fighting the invasion. I still keep some goodies here.'

Stone looked around. 'There was a war?'

'You're American,' the man said. It wasn't a question.

'Yeah.'

'It's like an American to not remember. 1985. United States Marines. They came because we elected the wrong government. Three hundred and eleven islanders killed. Eight Americans.'

'I was fifteen in 1985.'

'Yes. And I was seventeen.'

The man threw open the doors to the shed. In the light of morning, Stone looked upon a small arsenal. Several handguns. A few hunting rifles. Two AK-47s. Boxes of ammunition, piled up. A long wooden box stood upright near the back. Stone reached to it, looked at the markings on it.

Well, well, well. Stone recognised the letters right away. РПГ, the Russian abbreviation of *Reaktivnyy/Ruchnoy Protivotankovyy Granatomyot*, or hand-held anti-tank grenade launcher in English – what most people would think of as an RPG. Stone's hands caressed the box, as he imagined holding what was inside. Stone was intimately familiar with shoulder-fired missiles like this one – the Skinnies in Mogadishu were bristling with these things, and more recently, he'd taken a couple of them off the hands of dead Iraqis. Heck, Stone had trained to use them when he was a kid in Ranger school, should the need ever arise. Low-rent rebel armies the world over made these a weapon of choice – they weren't much use against tanks, but they sure would blow a slow-moving troop transport or a jeep to pieces. In the right hands, they'd even take down a helicopter.

'Rocket launcher with grenade,' the man announced with a hint of pride. 'Russian-made. I can give you a very good price.'

Stone looked at the man. 'You think it still works? I mean, the climate here – the moisture, the heat?'

The man smiled. 'When you fire it, I guess you'll find out.'

'Holy shit,' Sticks said. 'What is taking this dickhead so long?'

Sticks and the Dunce sat in a rented speedboat, waiting for Cruz to get moving. Sticks didn't know shit about boats, but he knew this crazy bastard looked fast. It was a four-seater, with two huge outboard engines in back. The Dunce assured Sticks he knew how to drive one of these things, and he had certainly gotten it going and cruised out from the island with a lot of confidence.

All the same, Sticks felt like shit. The high and the drunk from earlier today had worn off, leaving Sticks with a throbbing headache. And Stone's little swan dive into the swimming pool an hour ago had put Sticks in a bummer of a mood.

Now, they sat in the boat with the engines off, lights off, and the boat bobbing around in the waves about half a mile out from the island. Sticks sat in the passenger seat, glancing every now and then at the open laptop in front of him, but mostly gazing out at the lights of the town and trying to control his nausea. He wasn't a boat person, and he wasn't an ocean person. The choppy, up-and-down motion of the water made him dizzy. It made him want to puke. Furthermore, he was wearing a bright yellow life vest – he wasn't much of a swimmer, and if this thing went down, he planned on surviving. He didn't feel the least bit ashamed to wear the life vest – a little self-conscious, maybe, but not at all ashamed.

He'd caught the fucking Dunce smirking at him as he put the vest on before they left dry land. 'What the fuck are you looking at?' he said.

The Dunce put his hands up as if Sticks had pulled a gun on him. He broke into a big, shit-eating grin as he did so. He was lucky Sticks didn't pull a gun on him. 'Hey, Sticks, do what you gotta do. If you're scared of the water, that's OK with me.'

'I ain't scared, you hump. I'm just careful. If you'd been a little more careful, we wouldn't have lost Stone up in the hotel room, and we wouldn't have to worry about him running around out here now.'

The fucking half-bright Dunce. Come to think of it, Sticks was getting tired of the Dunce. The guy was a glorified gofer, really. Sticks was the brains of this operation, and the Dunce was just along for the ride. It didn't make sense to split the proceeds of this job with him. Give the Dunce over a million dollars? For doing what, letting Stone jump off the fucking balcony? When you did the math, the Dunce's part in this thing just didn't add up. What did add up was Sticks acquiring two and a half million dollars for himself, and cutting the Dunce loose somewhere along the way.

'When Cruz does come out, we got no problem,' the Dunce was saying now. He sat with one meaty hand on the wheel, his body pimped back as far as the seat would recline. 'Boat like this? We can hang back as long as we want, then be right up his ass in no time. Shit. I've been driving boats since I was fourteen years old. Cruz don't have a chance of getting away.'

Sticks glanced at the smug look on the Dunce's Cro-Magnon face. It was all Sticks could do not to pull his gun and shoot the fucker right here. 'Hey, Mikey?' he said. 'Keep in mind we're not in a race with Cruz. It ain't about being up his ass. It's about tailing him to where he's got the money. And it's about not letting him see us.'

'I know that, Sticks. I'm not stupid, you know? I was just saying, just for the sake of conversation, that this is a fast boat.'

Sticks glanced at the computer screen and saw the lighted dot that represented Cruz start to move against the satellite image of the island and the surrounding water. The sudden movement of it gave Sticks a sick feeling of excitement deep in his belly. It was going to be a crazy night.

'OK, speed demon,' Sticks said. 'Get ready to show me what you can do with this thing. Cruz is on his way.'

The engines were running on Dugan's boat.

Cruz was at the helm in the rear of the dinghy, manning the tiller. Pamela and Lola were in the front, Pamela's arms wrapped around Lola to keep her warm – it had taken a bit of arguing at the docks to convince Lola to leave behind the other dinghy, the one she had stolen from a nearby yacht. That's how honest Lola was – she wanted to return the fucking thing. But Cruz prevailed on her. If all was safe and sound at the *Saucy Jack*, they could go back and get the other dinghy in the morning.

As they pulled up to the *Jack*, all seemed more than safe and sound. There was no sign of Dugan, but damned if the engines weren't running. He had fixed the boat, and just in time, too. The hell with Lola's dinghy – it was time to pick up the strongboxes and put this island in the past. With Stone out there, and unnamed *bad men from New York* – Cruz, a hardened killer for three decades, felt a tingle go down his spine at the thought – and crazy Ty Weathers probably bent on some kind of misguided revenge, it had got a little too crowded for Cruz's comfort. There was no sense hanging around here one minute longer than necessary.

The girls jumped from the dinghy as Cruz tied up to the boat. Cruz wasn't much with ropes, and it took him a couple of tries to get anything like a secure knot in place. By then, the girls had already bounded up to the main deck.

Cruz clambered across from the dinghy – *mind the fucking gap*, he thought, as the dinghy floated out to the end of its tether and he nearly went into the drink. Just then, he heard a gasp in the darkness, followed by Pamela's voice, nearly a shriek:

'Cruz!'

When Cruz reached the main deck, he confronted a scene right out of his past – the deck was wet with blood in some places and tacky with it in others, and two men lay sprawled out. The young black man lying face up, eyes half-open and staring, skin already going slack, blood all over his chest and missing a good chunk of his right hand, was clearly dead. The white man lying face down a few feet away might or might not be dead. Lola was kneeling nearby, but seemed unwilling to touch him. Pamela stood at the furthest edge of the deck, staring down at the scene with eyes wide in horror.

Well, might as well get it over with – Cruz took three steps to Dugan's body, kneeled, and turned it over.

Smoke Dugan blinked, then his eyes focused on Cruz. 'What the fuck are you looking at?' Dugan's face was a mess of blood and there was an ugly gash at his hairline. Cruz glanced at Dugan's hand – it was still holding the gun Cruz had left with them last night.

'Oh my God, Smoke,' Lola said and gingerly put her hands to his scalp. 'Look at your head.'

'You should see the other guy,' Dugan said, and his eyes rolled back.

Cruz put a finger to Dugan's neck – his pulse was steady and strong. Cruz looked at Lola. 'He's fine. Looks like he took a beating, that's all.' Then he addressed Smoke in a loud voice. 'Dugan, don't go to sleep just yet. I have a question. The boat – the engines are on. Is it ready?'

Dugan's eyes fluttered open again. 'The boat? Oh yeah. She's all ready to go. I fixed everything.' He grinned, and then slowly closed his eyes. This time he was passed out for sure.

Cruz looked up at the girls. 'Help me get him downstairs. We'll put him in bed for now, so he can get some rest. I want to get out of here inside of an hour, two at the most, and he's the one who has to drive this thing. Once we get him settled, I'll go to the island and pick up the strongbox buried there. Pamela, you'll dive and grab the other strongbox. And Lola, you'll hold down the fort. If anybody comes – and I mean anybody – who isn't me or Pamela, you shoot them. Just shoot them. OK?'

Cruz grabbed Dugan under the arms and got ready to lift him. Dugan's head hung sideways. Lola and Pamela just watched. 'Uh, ladies? Help me, please. Unless you want to see me drag Smoke Dugan down the stairs by his legs.'

'What about Ty Weathers?' Pamela said.

Cruz glanced at the corpse. He'd seen a lot of corpses in his time, and he found that this one didn't impress him very much. He shrugged. 'What about him? He shouldn't have come back. When we get far out to sea, we'll dump him overboard.'

Stone watched the dinghy zip away from the larger boat, headed for the small island, where presumably the other strongbox was buried. He focused in on the dinghy with his night-vision binoculars.

He pulled the dinghy closer, closer. Sure, it was a green and ghostly Cruz, running fast towards the small island where they had taken the strongbox. Stone had seen enough of the action on the boat to know that Cruz had somehow got Pamela back before Sticks and his buddy had reached her. That was OK – Stone wouldn't want those guys to get their hooks into a nice girl like that. But that near miss must mean Cruz planned on leaving as soon as possible – maybe even tonight – and of course he planned on taking Stone's money with him. It was

Stone's money now — at least, the strongbox he had moved was his money. He found that he didn't even care that much about the other box; it fell into the category of something nice, but not essential, to have.

Stone watched Cruz go, debating the outcome with himself. Cruz was the stuff of legends, and of nightmares. If there was one person in this whole silly drama that Stone was afraid of, it was Cruz. Cruz was a stone killer. Had Cruz been one of the men in his room earlier that night, Stone was sure that he never would have made it off that balcony. Cruz would have killed him immediately, in a no-nonsense fashion, then went and gotten a sandwich. Stone had an AK-47, he had two semi-automatic pistols, and he had the grenade and launcher. He'd bought the RPG to handle Sticks, but now that he thought about it, if anyone present was a candidate for the RPG treatment, it was Cruz. It would be both satisfying and practical – make Cruz pay the long-awaited debt of killing Bunker, and get the one man most likely to stand in Stone's way out of the picture right now.

Stone flipped up his binoculars and picked up the RPG. He felt the weight of it in his hands – light, about fifteen pounds. The launcher itself was a hollow tube about three feet long, the middle made of wood to protect the operator from the heat generated, with a flared end that would blow out a back blast about twenty yards long. The warhead itself was a simple high explosive warhead, weighed about five pounds, was long and green, with fins to stabilise it in flight. The launcher was reusable, but Macho's friend only had the one warhead, so one shot was all Stone would get. The whole rig was simple, sturdy, and used by peasant armies and ragtag militias the world over – Stone's model looked like it had held up well against the tropical climate.

Stone had spent his entire ten-thousand-dollar finder's fee tonight. The weapons dealer had pulled a highway robbery on him for the RPG and the guns – two thousand for the whole mess. Stone was hardly in a position to bargain him down on price. He wanted the weapons, he wanted them now, and he had the money. He didn't even blink. When they got back to town, he gave the rest of the money to Macho. Eight thousand dollars.

'I want you to share that money with Roxana,' he said. 'OK? Get yourselves something nice. Take care of your families.'

'Will you be coming back tonight?'

Stone shook his head. 'Probably not tonight. No matter what happens out there, I'm probably going to be in a big hurry afterwards.'

'You've been my favourite client,' Macho said. Stone looked for a hint of something in Macho's face – the conman's sincere lie – but didn't find it.

'Thank you, Macho. I appreciate that.'

Stone put the RPG on his shoulder and hefted the bag with the other guns. Then he turned to go. It was just another quiet night in the shanty-town.

'Stone,' Macho said. He held the meaty envelope with Stone's finder's fee in his hands. 'Do you think it's fair if I take five thousand, and Roxana takes three thousand? My mother is very sick, and anyway, I was the one who got tortured.'

'Macho, that sounds fine. Just don't let me hear that you lied to her about it, or didn't give her the three thousand. Because then I will come back, and believe me, you won't be happy about it when I do.'

Macho smiled then, and it seemed like a real smile. Crazy kid. Five thousand, three thousand, whatever. Stone didn't even feel like thinking about it.

Now, in the midst of the dark night on the boat, Stone put Macho out of his mind and slipped on his night-vision goggles again. A moment passed as he adjusted to the night-vision world. Then there was Cruz. He was just about to land the dinghy on the sandy beach of the island.

Stone put the RPG on his shoulder. He looked through the sight mechanism and focused. His hands roamed the weapon. Trigger mechanism, like so, and so. It took him a moment to get acclimatised. This thing had a reputation for inaccuracy, but if Stone knew one thing about himself, it was this: he had wonderful aim.

He took a deep breath. This thing would give off a whale of a signature, especially in the dark, so right after he fired it he was going to have to run.

OK. Be ready to move.

He found Cruz again, now moving slow as he came to land. If this Russian leftover still worked, then there was a good chance Cruz would be dead in just another few seconds.

'Dassvadanya, Cruz,' Stone said, and fired the rocket.

The fucking boat was stuck on something.

Cruz looked down – he was in shallow water. The outboard motor, maybe, stuck on a rock or in the sand? He didn't know. After all, he'd only learned how to drive this thing since they'd gone to sea. Boating had never been a pursuit of his until the last few weeks – he was looking forward to the day, coming soon, when he would have nothing more to do with boating. He was conscious of the fact that he was in a hurry, and that this snag was slowing him down. He was also conscious of the fact that he was tired – he'd been awake round the clock, probably close to thirty-six hours by now. He remembered standing on Stone's dock at dawn this morning. He'd been tired then, that was more than twelve hours ago, and he'd been going nonstop ever since.

He sighed heavily. Well, there was nothing for it, but to climb out of the boat, and drag it up on to the beach. He put one foot over the edge and into the shallow water – he noticed that the water, up to his calf, was kind of chilly. The sand was loose, and he sank up to his ankle in it, like before. Gross – it made him think of slugs and vicious centipedes and those bait worms with the rows of jagged teeth. Cruz was a city boy – to the extent that he wanted to be in nature or on a beach, he wanted it to be a resort of some kind. He didn't mind sitting on a patio somewhere, eating buttered crab legs, looking out at the glistening water – what he didn't want to do was slog through the muck just below the beautiful blue surface.

From the corner of his eye, he saw a huge flash. It came from the deep dark, maybe a couple hundred yards away. He looked over there – could have been a shooting star, except it was on the surface of the water. He kept staring at it, one foot on the boat, one foot in the muck. It could have been some fireworks, like from a Fourth of July exhibition.

There was still something there, low above the water. Flickering light, a trail of flame. By a trick of perspective, it didn't appear to be moving. Cruz searched back through the databanks – a projectile of some kind, which didn't appear to move. What did that mean?

A rushing sound came. Loud at first, then suddenly very loud.

Fuck – it was coming straight at him.

He put all his weight on one foot – the one in the boat – and launched himself backwards. An instant later, fire filled the night – an explosion in red and yellow. The heat washed over him and he felt himself lifted into the air. He went head over heels and the world spun. He hit the wet sand like a rag doll.

All went black and Cruz knew no more.

'Holy fucking shit,' Sticks said. 'Did you see that?'

He stood in their motorboat, watching with binoculars an explosion on the beach three hundred yards away. The sound carried back to him over the water, a long rolling boooom. Now there was a fire over there, against the dark sky. If he didn't know any better, he'd say he was looking at some hippie kids having themselves a little bonfire.

'Looks like Cruz just bit the dust,' the Dunce said from the seat next to him. The Dunce was sitting there with Stone's laptop computer, watching the display. 'The GPS went dead, just like that. The second that explosion came, it just blinked off.'

'Direct fucking hit,' Sticks said. 'That's out of sight.' He turned and trained his binoculars in the direction he thought the missile had come from. Nothing out there but inky darkness. 'That must be our friend Stone, right? Who else would have that kind of firepower? He had that little problem with Cruz way back when. Well, it looks like he just resolved it.'

'He must be armed to the teeth,' the Dunce said, with something too much like trepidation for Sticks's tastes. The fucking Dunce, man. You know what? A couple of days with the Dunce was a couple of days too many.

'Sure he is,' Sticks said. 'But it don't matter. I happen to know that Stone is something of a pussy.' He put down the binoculars – they were no use to him any more. 'I also happen to know that he just eliminated our biggest problem for us. Without Cruz, these folks are like lost little lambs. Lambs to the slaughter, to be exact.'

He looked at the Dunce.

'Mikey, whaddya say? I think it's about time we got reacquainted with Smoke Dugan, and with two and a half million in cash.'

Smoke Dugan stared at the fire on the horizon.

He'd come awake as they carried him down the stairs, but found himself unable to say anything to them. Then he'd lain in bed for a little while, just a blessed few minutes adrift with his eyes closed, while his mind reviewed and processed everything that had happened.

It all came back to him – that feeling of elation as the boat finally roared into life, then turning, and Ty Weathers coming at him, pulling the trigger. From victory to defeat in two seconds flat. Then the battle, and the pain, and afterwards, Ty's corpse lying nearby. Smoke remembered looking across at it, and speaking to it, but he didn't remember what he had said. For a period of time after Smoke shot him, it seemed like Ty was alive, and maybe he really was.

Then Cruz was there, with Lola right nearby. And Cruz was

talking, saying something that Smoke didn't like, something that made him uncomfortable. What was it? 'I'll go to the island and pick up the strongbox buried there,' Cruz said. 'Pamela, you'll dive and grab the other strongbox. And Lola, you'll hold down the fort.'

Smoke opened his eyes. Holy shit, they were going to pick up the strongboxes – the strongboxes with no money in them.

Smoke rolled out of bed, fighting the dizziness and waves of nausea that came over him. His cane was still upstairs somewhere, so he picked his way out of the cabin, lurching from wall to wall, and then dragged himself up the stairs. He reached the aft deck just in time to watch a missile arc low across the night sky and make a direct hit on something in the distance.

Lola came down from the main deck and stood next to Smoke. She held a semi-automatic in her hand, probably the one that had killed Ty Weathers a little while ago. 'That's in the direction Cruz just went,' she said. Her eyes were wide. She spoke in an absent way, like someone in a dream.

Far away, the flames jumped and danced where, hidden in the darkness, Smoke knew the small island to be. He felt a tinge of real embarrassment and regret looking at it. He'd thought about getting rid of Cruz, and now, just like that, Cruz was gone. He could imagine the flaming remains of the dinghy, gently bobbing in the tiny surf a few feet out from the beach, chunks of fibreglass burning on the sand. Maybe ten seconds ago, a small secondary explosion had gone up – in all likelihood, the gas tank and the outboard motor going.

If Cruz was anywhere near that boat when the missile hit, then he was in pieces – some on the beach, some in the water.

It was a nasty business, and it raised a lot of issues for Smoke. One – they had to get out of here, and fast. Two – the bad guys were on their trail, very close, and packing military-style hardware. Three – if Smoke tried to take off in the boat now, what was to stop them from firing another missile? Where the fuck did they even get a missile on an island like this – did they bring it with them? Four – somebody had to break it to Pamela that Cruz was dead, and to convince her to leave without him.

'That's Cruz,' Smoke said.

'How do you know? You can't know that. It could be anything out there.'

'Lola, I just know. OK?' Smoke looked into her big doe eyes. He didn't want to have an argument about it right now. He was dizzy, his head was still ringing where Ty had hit him, and they needed to get out of here. 'We have to talk. Listen, where's Pamela?'

'Smoke, you didn't. Oh my God. Say you didn't put a bomb on that boat and blow up Cruz.'

'No, hon, I didn't. Of course not. Where's Pamela?'

'She'll be back in a few minutes. She's just put her wetsuit and dive gear on and went down to get the other strongbox.'

Jesus. *She dove down to get the other pointless strongbox.* Smoke should have let them in on his little secret all along – had he done that, Cruz would be alive right now. How to break that one to Pamela – that he had killed Cruz with a decoy manoeuvre?

OK, they'd have to wait for her. That would give Smoke a few minutes to explain the situation to Lola. As soon as Pamela came up again, and was on board, Smoke would give it the gas, and run out to sea, lights off. Everybody would have to wear their life jackets – they'd just have to hope and pray that the bad guys didn't take it upon themselves to blow the boat out of the water.

'What about Cruz?' Lola said.

'A missile streaked across the sky and blew up the boat,' Smoke said. 'That's what you just saw. If it hit the dinghy, and I think it did, then Cruz is probably dead. That means real trouble. They can do the same to us anytime.'

'Why haven't they?'

'Because they want the money.'

'What's the plan?'

'No plan, really. As soon as Pamela gets back up here with that box, we pull up stakes and haul out of here. We hope they don't blow us up.'

'And leave Cruz behind?'

'What's left of him.'

'But you don't even know he's dead.'

'I have a pretty strong hunch. If I'm wrong, and he's still alive, then he's a big boy and can take care of himself. When it comes to survival, he's the best of us, Lola. None of us even come close.'

Lola seemed to think about it. 'And the money buried out there?'

'There's nothing buried out there.'

She stared at him, her eyes widening with sudden understanding. 'Oh, Smoke,' she said. Then her face hardened against him. It was something to watch – like the setting of quick-dry cement. 'You lied about that, too?'

'Yeah,' he said.

Stone moved fast.

He zipped across the waves, night-vision goggles in place. Speed was of the essence now, and he had been moving almost from the moment he fired the missile. In truth, he had lost a few moments. For one thing, he'd been shocked that the rocket still worked. For another, he'd been stunned at how accurately it fired – he hadn't actually believed he would score a direct hit. Then he had taken a moment to savour the loss of Cruz – the final settling of accounts. Then he'd sat down for about thirty seconds and come apart at the seams a little bit – for a second there, he thought he might start to cry.

But now he was moving, wind across his scalp, and it felt good. He pulled the boat right up to theirs, barely slowing down, throwing it into reverse just before he slammed into them. He didn't bother to tie up, and in an instant he was leaping across to their lower deck, brandishing the AK-47.

The two people on board hardly moved. Here was the old man and sexy young black girl, standing on the deck, staring at him. The girl half-heartedly raised a gun she held in her hand, looked at it like she'd never seen anything like it before, and dropped it like it was a hot skillet that burned her. The gun clattered to the deck.

'Don't move. I swear to God I'll kill you.'

'Do you see us moving?' the girl said.

'Where's the other one? Pamela?'

'She went down below to get something.'

'She's not going to find it.'

'Find what?' the old man said.

'The money you people stole,' Stone said. 'I moved it earlier tonight.'

'Pamela told you about it?'

Stone shrugged. 'I have ways of making people talk.' He looked around at the dark night. There wasn't much time — Sticks and his friend had the computer and might have followed Cruz here. They could be anywhere. Stone would have to dive and get the box and the girl himself. Then what? Set sail with these folks and put some distance between himself and Sticks. No sense in going back to that tiny island and sharing it with killers who wanted to put Stone under. He could drop these nice people off anywhere, on any deserted strip of sand. Somebody would come along and find them in a few days or weeks. Or years.

He whipped two sets of handcuffs out from behind his back — half of the four sets hanging there. He tossed them to the two people standing on the deck before him. Odd — they were being overtaken on the high seas by a man with an automatic weapon, and they didn't seem even the least perturbed. 'Put those on,' he said. 'No funny stuff or I'll shoot you right here.'

The box was gone.

Pamela had been afraid of that — she passed the light from her headlamp again and again over the place where she had buried it. She didn't like being down here underwater in the dark any longer than necessary, and yet she felt compelled to go over the spot again and again. Right at the foot of that brain coral, right where she had buried the box, the sand was disturbed, and a gaping hole had been ripped open.

The more she stared at that hole, the tighter she gripped her speargun.

So Stone had come here and taken it after all – even after she had told him it would explode if he tried to open it. Well, good for him – if he accidentally blew his head off, that was his own fault. But what was she going to tell the others? She hadn't even mentioned that she'd given away the hiding space to Stone. Hell. She hadn't given it away – she had told him about it in the hope of saving herself.

Suddenly the dark seemed to close in on her. Her headlamp cast a tiny circle of light in the endless blackness – the depths around her seemed alive with malevolent intent. She pictured what that light must look like to a creature with rows of sharp, jagged teeth just thirty yards away. The creature would be invisible to her, and yet her light would be a beacon, a dinner invitation, to the creature.

What if Stone was still down here somewhere? What if he had blown himself up and his corpse was down here, somehow snagged on the bottom? That wasn't anything she wanted to see, not after looking at Ty Weathers's very dead body just a few minutes ago. And what about Ty Weathers? He was a vengeful bastard in life, and if he had a ghost, you could bet it was nearby and watching.

OK, that's nothing to think about. Calm down, and change the subject.

Her mind raced through a menu of options, looking for something else to focus on. What about sharks? Big, aggressive tiger sharks frequented these waters – she knew that much. She felt her breathing starting to accelerate.

She gripped the speargun even tighter.

A shadow moved in the inky depths behind her. She turned and a beast surged out of the darkness. Its claw was on her, gripping her wrist. She recoiled in terror, but its grip was too strong. She could not escape.

Oh my God. Oh my God.

She fired the speargun, not aiming, not thinking. A spray of blood gushed into the water, the thing lost its grip, and she swam for all she was worth.

11

'I think we need to talk,' Lola said.

Smoke sat on the aft deck, back to back with Lola, hands cuffed, legs bound with lengths of rope. It seemed like a foolish and impossible position to be in — how many times could two people be attacked and tied up in just a couple of days? When Stone had jumped on board the boat, neither Smoke nor Lola had attempted to put up any kind of fight — Smoke figured after everything that had happened, they'd both been drained of all resistance. Speaking only for himself, Smoke realised he was just about exhausted — the fight with Ty Weathers was probably the most strenuous thing he had done in the past twenty years. Not only had it left Smoke physically spent, it had made him hungry, even famished. If he didn't pass out again, he was going to have to eat something soon, or he'd be in a damned bitchy mood.

Smoke was waiting to hear the muffled sound of his bomb detonating underwater. When it came, he hoped it meant that Stone went with it, and Pamela didn't. But it was all out of his hands now. He sighed. Everything was out of his hands.

'OK,' he said. 'I think that's a good idea. Let's talk.' He figured he could multi-task, listening to Lola while at the same time waiting for the bomb to go off.

'I've loved you more than any man I've ever met,' Lola said. 'I still love you. But I find more and more it's the memory of you that I love. And that's not really you, is it? That's the fake you.'

From Smoke's position, he could see out on to the water behind the *Saucy Jack*. A small motorboat, like a speedboat, was approaching, moving slow. There were two guys in it, a beefy guy at the wheel, and a skinny guy in the passenger seat. They were about thirty yards out – by the looks of them, they were city slickers and strangers to these parts. More bad news, in all likelihood.

'Lola . . .'

She was facing away from the water, so she couldn't see the new guests. 'It's the lying, Smoke. I can't stand it. I mean, how can I believe you any more? Almost everything you say turns out to be a lie.'

'Lola, we have more visitors.'

'Smoke, I can't worry about that any more. We're always going to have more visitors. We're never going to escape. Every time we turn around there's somebody after us, and it's always going to be that way. I'm tired of it.'

'Listen hon . . .' Smoke found that he wanted to interrupt her, stop her from saying what he knew she was going to say, the thing she must say after everything he'd put her through.

'No, Smoke, don't you see? By now, don't you finally understand? I'm not your hon any more. I've given this a lot of thought, and I could never decide which way to go. But when it turned out you lied about the strongboxes, that did it. I can't go out with you any more, Smoke. I think we should just try to be friends.'

'Well, well, well,' shouted the skinny guy from the motorboat. He had a strange, reedy voice. 'What do we have here? A boatload of people who can't find their ass with both hands, it seems. All tied up and nowhere to go.' He stepped off the smaller boat and on to the swimming deck of the *Saucy Jack*. The fuck was wearing a yellow life preserver. That clinched it for Smoke – oh yeah, the bad guys were here.

Smoke sighed again, realising there was a good chance they weren't actually going to get out of this one. For the umpteenth time, he cursed himself. He had done it – he had brought Lola and Pamela to this pass. Cruz? Cruz would have ended up dead sooner or later, regardless of whether they'd ever crossed paths. But Lola and Pamela were innocents – he, Smoke, had brought them to the brink of early, and what looked like watery, graves.

'Hey Dugan,' the guy said, the wild light in his eyes visible even from here. 'Remember me? Sticks, the guy who likes to stick sharp objects in your eyes? We met up in Portland a while back. That was some dive you fellas took off that bridge. One of the most amazing tricks I've ever seen, and I've seen a lot in my time.'

Smoke nodded. 'I remember. The last thing I saw, the cops had you surrounded and on your knees. How was the joint?'

'It was nice. Good food. Good people.'

'Make any new friends?'

The smile died on Sticks's face. 'I didn't stay long enough to make friends.'

'Guy like you? I figure you'd start meeting admirers your first night in.'

Sticks shook his head and grunted. He looked down at the deck beneath his feet and slowly the smile returned to his face. When he looked up again, he was beaming like a Jack O'Lantern.

'You guys thought you gave me the slip, but now I'm back in your life. Cruz got cooked, and so will you. Whaddya got on the boat here, a sexy chick and two and a half million in cash? Well, it's all mine now, Dugan. All of it.'

Smoke stared at the emaciated goon in the life vest. If Smoke had to die tonight, at least he'd seen everything. 'What's the matter, Sticks? You afraid of the water? Your mother never taught you how to swim?'

Patrick Quinlan

Sticks raised his hand. A hunting knife appeared there, as if conjured by a magician. Behind him and to his left, the speedboat had drifted about ten yards out. Still in the speedboat, the big goon drew a gun.

'I tell you what,' Sticks said. 'I'm not going to fuck around. The first one to tell me where the money is dies fast and easy. The hold-out gets it slow and hard. That sucks, but the law of the jungle prevails, as usual.'

To the right of Sticks, and just behind him, a hand appeared on the dive ladder. After a few seconds, the rest of an arm appeared, then a shoulder. Then came a head. Stone slowly dragged himself up from the deep, trailing the strongbox in his other hand. Even from here, even in the dark, Smoke could see a metal rod had punched through, and was now protruding from either side of, Stone's thick forearm.

Stone's jaw hung slack. His eyes were blank. His skin had been drained of colour – he had gone so pale his face almost seemed to glow in the dark.

'Uh Sticks,' the guy in the boat said. 'You better take a look at this.'

Sticks turned and soaked in the spectacle of Stone – a man thoroughly pierced by a blood-streaked spear. 'I guess it's a party now,' Sticks said.

For Stone, the searing pain was over.

When the spear had first gone through his forearm, there had been a long moment when he was confused. He hovered in the water, watching the girl Pamela swim away, dimly aware that something bad had happened. He had come up behind her, only intending to show her that he had the strongbox and to motion for her to go back up to the boat. But he had startled her, he could tell by the sudden fear in her eyes, and an instant later, he felt a jolt – the force of it rocketed through his whole body.

When he looked down, he saw the metal spear there – the pointed end had punched all the way through the back of his arm, about four

292

inches below the elbow, and the other end protruded from the angry red meat of his forearm. Stone saw blood, his blood, already clouding the water. He thought something odd then, something so foreign and unfamiliar that he'd never had occasion to think it in all the firefights and killing zones he had been through in his life:

I'm hit.

No one had ever shot him before. It seemed impossible to believe that someone, especially this someone, had shot him now. He wasted several seconds running the tape backwards, thinking how only a moment ago he hadn't been shot, and now he was. If he'd only gone straight back to the boat with the strongbox this wouldn't have happened.

Then the pain was incredible. It became everything to him. It was like the pain was the centre, and everything else about him – his past, his personality, and his desires – were only aspects of the pain. Stone was like a tiny insect riding on the back of the pain.

He reached down and touched the spear. It was real. It couldn't be real, but it was. He played with it for a few seconds, trying to move it, to pull it out or push it all the way through, but the pain became so bad he nearly passed out. A new thought came:

If I stay down here, I'll die.

He had no idea how much time passed. It seemed that he lost himself as he moved through the murk. The pain faded. Stone himself faded. The next thing he knew he was halfway up the ladder to the boat. Each step was a chore. The strongbox seemed to weigh a ton. He clambered on to the deck, only half-aware of who was around. He needed to go to a hospital. He needed to get out of here. He kicked his swim fins off – it seemed to take for ever.

'Medic,' he said. His voice was a rasp. 'I need a medic.'

'Jesus, Stone,' a voice said. Stone looked up and saw it was Sticks. Sticks was in jeans and a T-shirt, with a yellow life vest over the shirt. Oh yeah, that's right. How'd Stone forget that? There were no medics here. They were on an island somewhere – there probably wasn't much of a hospital here, either. The doctors probably shook rattles and implored the sky for rain.

'You're a tough motherfucker,' Sticks went on. He seemed to be in good spirits – his voice was laced with mocking good humour. 'I should kill you now just to be done with you. What do you have there, the money?'

Stone nodded.

'Well hand it over, big guy.' Stone felt the box disappear from his hand. Things seemed to spin before him. He closed his eyes and when he opened them again, he was looking up at the dark sky. He had fallen to the deck. Sticks stood over him, holding the strongbox with both hands, eyeing it warily.

'Dugan, you didn't rig some kind of booby trap on this thing, did you? I'll bet you did. It's kind of hard to believe that the famous bombmaker would have a box full of money, and no bomb to blow up somebody who tries to open it.'

Stone remembered something then – payback. He owed Sticks for what they'd done to the kid. He spoke before Dugan had a chance. 'He did rig it,' Stone said. His voice sounded far away. Could they even hear him? 'I disabled it earlier tonight when I moved it. I did bomb disposal in the military. Dugan's bomb was a piece of cake – he's an amateur. All you gotta do is bust that lock off. The bomb is dead.'

Sticks was very close now. Stone looked up and saw his teeth – the nasty biters filled Stone's entire field of vision. They were like big yellow grave markers. 'You're very cooperative all of a sudden,' Sticks said. 'I wonder why?'

'I'm hoping,' Stone said through gritted teeth, 'you'll take me to the hospital. Otherwise I might die here on this boat.' He gestured with his left hand at his impaled and bloody right arm. 'It ain't like in the movies. This thing hurts really bad. I think it might kill me.'

Sticks shrugged. 'Well, I hope you're right about this bomb. For your sake.' He backed away and raised his voice. 'Mikey, do me a favour, will you? Bust this lock off and open this box, eh?'

Smoke watched skinny Sticks pass the strongbox down to the man on the speedboat. The big guy was a thug – he looked like an ape hunched in the gloom. Smoke opened his mouth as if to say something, then slowly let it drift shut again. It was like watching the whole thing from under a strip of gauze – the action seemed far away and indistinct. As Sticks backed away, the thug ripped the padlock off the box with his bare hand.

'Jesus,' Smoke said.

'He's a strong boy,' Sticks said. 'OK, Mikey, let's see what it's got.'

'I don't know, Sticks,' the thug holding the box said. 'What if the bomb still works?'

'Nah, go ahead, Mikey,' Sticks said. 'I trust Stone.'

The guy looked up at Sticks. 'You trust Stone? He's been lying to you the whole time. He lied . . . about everything.'

'Yeah, but he needs us now.'

The goon named Mikey hesitated, appearing to think it over. Smoke could almost smell the bacon burning as the dumb brute's wires sizzled and misfired. 'Hey, Sticks. You know what? Get one of the prisoners to do it.'

Suddenly Sticks had a gun in his hand. He pointed it at his friend's head. All the while, Sticks continued to back away. Now he was backing up the stairs. 'Mikey, I'll tell you what. If you don't open that fucking box, I'll put a bullet in your brain. Test me to see if I'm lying. And you know me – I never miss.'

'Sticks . . .' the guy said.

'Go ahead, Mikey. We ain't got all night.'

Mikey didn't look convinced. Still, his hand touched the snap, caressed it, as if it were trying to decide, as if his hand would be the one to make the decision.

'Mikey, you got three seconds before I blow your fucking head off. Trust me. The box ain't gonna explode.'

Smoke stared, as if hypnotised. He was glad Lola was facing away from this. A flash came, and the top half of the one called Mikey went up in a shower of flame and blood. He was still alive, but probably wished he wasn't. His arms were gone below the elbow. His entire upper body was on fire. He beat frantically at himself, screaming and grunting. He pitched over backwards and lay in the bottom of the speedboat howling and moaning. He jittered and jived for several more seconds, then lay still. His body, and now the boat, burned on.

'No loose ends,' Sticks said.

Smoke closed his eyes. Too late. The sight of it was indelibly printed there – the afterglow of the fire burned on in his darkness like a fireworks display. Too much – watching the effects of his own handiwork was too damned much.

He opened his eyes again. The scene was OK now – just a boat, burning on dark water. If he looked at it just right, he could see that it was actually kind of pretty now. The sound of flames licking at the night reminded him of Christmas somehow.

'Smoke?' Lola said in a shaky voice behind him.

'It's OK, hon. I promise you it's going to be OK.'

Sticks lit a cigarette. He stepped over to Stone and twisted the spear in Stone's arm. Stone's face spasmed in agony, but he didn't scream. In fact, he must have passed out because Sticks slapped him a couple of times to bring him round.

'Nice trick,' Sticks said. 'Just in case you got the wrong idea, I let you do that. Helped me get rid of an item I no longer needed. But make no mistake: just because you helped me, doesn't mean I'm not gonna kill you. I'm gonna take my time with you, Stone. We're gonna get to know each other.'

He turned to Lola and Smoke. He pointed his gun at Smoke.

'OK, team. Obviously, there was no money in that box. So where is the money? You didn't spend it already, did you? I don't think so. Tell me, or I kill your sexy little friend there right now.'

Smoke didn't hesitate. 'The real strongbox is buried on that island over there,' he said. 'The one Cruz was going to. He and I buried it. With him dead, I'm the only one who knows where it is. You hurt this girl, and you'll never see a dime of it. I promise you that.'

'Is that so? It's a small island.'

'That's so. The island is small, but the way I hid the money, it'll take you a month to find it. I'm gonna go out on a limb here and guess that you don't have a month to hang around. So whaddya say? You let Lola go, and I'll take you to the money.'

Sticks smiled. 'All right, kid. I'm feeling generous today. I'll let her go. But after you show me the money.'

They took Stone's boat, Smoke at the helm. It was a small outboard, about fourteen feet long – Smoke sat on the swivel seat at the back, hand on the throttle, which also served as the tiller. Sticks sat on the swivel seat at the front, half-turned so he could face both front and back. He held a gun lightly in his right hand, and a flashlight in his left. He looked more than a little ridiculous with his life vest on. He smoked his cigarette and grinned with high good humour.

He called back to the boat just before they left. 'Run along now, Lola. Put old Smoke Dugan out of your mind. You're never going to see him again. But I promise you this: if you see me again, you're going to die. So run along. You're probably getting a half-hour head start.'

Lola lay on the deck, hands still cuffed behind her back, legs still bound. Sticks, for all his supposed confidence, wouldn't let Smoke untie her. The breakdown was like this: he'd leave her alive and on the boat, but she had to figure out a way to get free. The most obvious choice was to wake up Stone, and get him to do it. Or if Pamela ever showed up again – Sticks didn't seem to know that Pamela even existed, and thank God for that – maybe she could do it. Then somebody was going to have to drive the boat. The only one Smoke could picture doing it at this point was Stone – who, with his military training, could probably drive almost anything – but his face had gone slack with shock just after Sticks twisted the spear in his arm. No, Smoke didn't think Stone would drive the boat tonight.

The *Saucy Jack* was big, and neither of the girls had spent much time at the helm. That fact was at least partially the result of Smoke's own design. He'd actively discouraged anyone but himself from taking the helm. He'd figured Cruz would never kill the girls, but he might kill Smoke. Needing Smoke's skills would make Cruz think twice before doing anything rash.

All the same, Smoke thought, all the same. If they ran, anywhere at all, they'd probably be OK. It was clear to Smoke that Sticks was on his own now – he'd just killed his own man. Nobody was coming down from New York to back up Sticks – if anybody came, they'd come to kill him.

Lord knew, if the girls actually ran, eventually they'd figure out where the money was, and they'd be rich. But they weren't going to run, were they? He thought on that for a second. Nope, not a chance. Shit.

He turned back towards the boat. Lola stared at him from the deck – Lola, who had just broken up with him, but still wanted to be friends. If she was going to live, Smoke had to find some way to kill Sticks. So there it was – he had already killed one man tonight, it had damn near wasted him, but somehow he was going to have to kill another.

Smoke turned away from Lola, gave the outboard full throttle, and he and Sticks took off into the night. He set a bearing straight for the remains of the dinghy, burning on the beach half a mile or more away. The boat skimmed the swells, and for a moment, with the breeze blowing past and the sensation of dark speed, Smoke caught himself feeling good. If he had to die tonight, he could think of worse places to die.

It took about five minutes to reach the island. Smoke glanced back and saw that the boat had faded from view – its lights were indistinct from the lights of any other boat spread out across the water. He slowed as they approached the beach. Here, the dinghy was clearer – its remains drifted in a few feet of water, sloshed around by the tiny waves, flames guttering now, almost out. It had been a dead-solid hit. The burning piece of the dinghy was only about half the boat – the rest of it was just gone.

Smoke pulled the skiff up on to the beach. He realised that he had no plan in mind – absolutely none at all. He intended to simply walk up the beach, dig up the strongbox, show Sticks what was inside, and hope for the best.

'Looks like that hump Cruz finally bit the dust,' Sticks said. He shrugged off his life vest, and dropped it in the boat.

'Sure looks like it.'

'He was one evil bastard.'

'He wasn't that bad,' Smoke said.

Sticks tossed Smoke the flashlight. 'Let's go, Dugan. It's been a long fucking day, so let's try to keep the chatter to a minimum.'

They set off across the beach, Smoke in the lead lighting the way, Sticks following several paces behind, the gun pointed at Smoke's back. 'Dugan, make even one funny move, and I'll shoot you in the balls. Then I'll spend the next three hours cutting off pieces of your body and throwing them to the fish while you watch.'

'Right. I think you mentioned something like that before.'

Sticks was taken aback by the sheer amount of stuff that had floated up on to the beach. 'What is this – garbage beach?'

'You should see some of the crap out at sea. Miles of junk. It makes dead zones out there – you've never seen anything like it.'

'I don't want to.'

It didn't take long to reach the tree where the box was buried. Smoke took a sturdy length of driftwood from among the flotsam in the sand, and began scraping a hole in the ground. In a few minutes, the stick made a thunking noise – he'd hit the box. In another few minutes, he had it uncovered. A fine sheen of sweat covered his skin and dampened his clothes, despite the cool night air. He found himself breathing heavily. His heart beat merrily along – the time of reckoning was at hand.

What the hell was he going to do?

He reached down and pulled the box up. Sticks held the light on it.

'All right, Dugan. This is the moment of truth. Let me back up a bit here and you can open it.'

'This one won't explode,' Smoke said.

'Yep, I've heard that one before.'

'No, for real. I ran out of explosives. Anyway, why would I blow up the money?'

Sticks stepped back about ten yards. 'So open it.'

Smoke fiddled with the lock. His hand was shaking the tiniest bit. He got the combination, and opened the lock. Sticks stared at him, flashlight in one hand, trained on the box, gun in the other hand, trained on Smoke. Smoke opened the box, and held it up for Sticks's inspection.

The box had two red bricks in it.

'You motherfucker,' Sticks said. 'Now you die.'

Cruz was alive.

He opened his eyes and at first, saw nothing but darkness. Gradually, he became aware of flames burning nearby and the acrid smell of smoke in the air.

He didn't know what had happened – he couldn't remember. All he knew was that he was lying in the sand, his clothes mostly burned off, patches of his skin burned, and the rest soaked with water. The sand was damp and stuck to his back. His skin was in searing pain. He didn't know where he was or what he was supposed to be doing here. All he knew was that he heard voices – maybe he was having an out-of-body experience. He began to think of himself in the third person. Was Cruz dead? Were they the voices of angels speaking to Cruz?

'Looks like that hump Cruz finally bit the dust,' a voice said.

'Sure looks like it.'

'He was one evil bastard.'

'He wasn't that bad.'

No, not angels. Cruz lifted his head and stared across the sand at the two figures about thirty yards away. They had just pulled up in a boat. Sure, the sound of an engine was what had awakened him. They were two men, and their backs were to Cruz. They began to move off down the beach, one walking first with a flashlight, one trailing behind. Cruz let them get a good distance away, then stood slowly and on unsteady legs, and followed.

He remembered this beach – the one with all the garbage washed up on it. He and Dugan had buried a treasure here sometime before. He glanced ahead again. Sure, one of those men had the funny, shoulder-hunched shape of Dugan. The other was speaking.

'Dugan, make even one funny move, and I'll shoot you in the balls. Then I'll spend the next three hours cutting off pieces of your body and throwing them to the fish . . .' Sure enough, it was Dugan, and this other one was threatening him.

Cruz was having trouble walking. His head didn't seem to be screwed on right. Everything – the sand, the sky, the ocean – seemed to slide sideways. He sat down for a minute, and his hands moved along the sand next to him. His right hand found a long length of wire. He held it up to his eyes – about three feet long, copper wire, very sturdy. He found himself wrapping either end of the wire around his hands, almost so his hands were tied together, but with about a foot and a half of play between them. The wire dug into his palms and the backs of his hands. It was a good feeling, a familiar feeling – all the same, he wished he was wearing gloves, the thick leather gloves of a workman.

With a sigh, he got heavily to his feet again, following the path the two men had taken. In a few minutes, he found them again. The skinny man's back was to him. He was shining the flashlight across an open space at Dugan. He was also pointing a gun at Dugan.

'You motherfucker,' the man said. 'Now you die.'

He fired a shot that whined off into the night.

'Hey, Sticks, let's reconsider this,' Smoke said.

Sticks, that's right. That was a name that rang a bell with Cruz. Not a good name. No, not a good name at all.

'Where's the money, asshole?' Sticks said.

'I don't know. Somebody must have got here first.'

'I'm through fucking around. Three seconds and you die, money or not. One . . . Two . . .'

'Sticks, wait a second.'

Cruz stood less than five feet from Sticks now. He glanced down at his hands – of course, there was a reason why he had wrapped the wire around his hands. And there was a reason why it felt so good.

Suddenly, his body remembered everything. He sprang into action – no thought, no questions, just pure movement like a big jungle cat. He took two quick steps, stood directly behind Sticks, and slipped the garrotte around his neck. There was a moment, a brief instant, when Sticks sensed something behind him, but he moved too slow. Cruz made fists with his hands and criss-crossed them with savage speed, pulling the wire taut.

The effect on Sticks was electric. His body thrummed, then began flopping like a fish. The flashlight flew away like a bird. Sticks fired the gun in his hand, straight into the air, then seemed to forget it was even there. After another moment, he couldn't pull the trigger again if he wanted to.

The wire bit deep into Cruz's hands – he could feel it drawing blood from his palms, much as it drew blood from Sticks's neck. He redoubled his effort, then again. The gun sank from Sticks's hand, landing with a soft thump in the sand.

Cruz let go and Sticks's lifeless body oozed to the ground. Cruz gingerly unwrapped the wire from his hands — deep slashes, red and bleeding, marked either side of each hand. He stared down at them.

Dugan walked up to him. 'Cruz, you're alive.'

'Sure looks that way.'

'I thought you couldn't kill anybody any more.'

Cruz glanced up from his bloody hands. He took a deep breath, enjoying the sting of the lacerations on his skin and the salt air filling his lungs.

'I think I feel better now.'

Stone, awake from his latest fainting spell, couldn't get the spear out.

He touched it a few times, moving his hands along its length, both front and back. It stuck out a good foot in front — maybe six inches behind. It hurt to move it any amount. It hurt to even move his body — as he stood and then busied himself around the boat, now and then he jarred it or bumped it on something and pain would shoot up his arm and through his entire body — through his entire being. Pain so intense that he would seem to pass out for moments at a time.

It was a wonder he was functioning at all — a hit like this often made people go into total shutdown. He'd seen it — the pain would crowd everything else out, and all you could get from them were screams of pain, or passive compliance, or blank stares. But Stone seemed like he was going to continue functioning — he was still bleeding, but he was beginning to think he could keep going and maybe even go the distance.

He had ignored the black girl Lola's pleas to untie her. He had ignored her presence almost entirely. Somewhere deep in his mind, he realised she was a saucy and sexy chick, and that in other circumstances she'd be a major focus of his attention right now. But under the new realities, she just didn't hold much interest for him. He could hardly expect to mate with anyone, what with being impaled by a spear and all. *Impaled* — boy, he didn't like that word.

Instead, he had gone downstairs to the head, found a bottle of Advil, and downed a dozen of the pills all at once. He doubted they'd have much effect, but it was worth a try. He had also grabbed the AK-47, the sound suppressor and the night-vision binoculars he had stashed earlier tonight. Just before diving, he had stuffed them all under seat cushions in the main cabin, and he was glad he had – no doubt Sticks would have taken them if he'd known they were there.

Now, armed with the assault rifle and the night-vision, the idea was simple: whoever came back, whenever they came back, let them get fairly close – thirty yards, say – then rip them up with the AK. Easy.

He set up along the edge of the boat facing the beach – ever mindful of the new appendage sticking out from his arm. He slid the binoculars down into place and waited. Not long – somebody was already coming back, two figures in his longboat just pushing off from the beach even now.

'Stone?' a voice came from behind him. 'Stone, what are you doing?' She was a talky chick, and Stone didn't feel much like talking.

'I'm ending this. When Sticks gets back, don't think for a minute he's gonna go light on us. He's a lunatic.'

'What if it's not Sticks?'

'Don't get your hopes up. It will be.'

'What if it isn't?'

'Doesn't matter. I'm finishing everything right here, tonight. I pledge no allegiance to Smoke Dugan, or you, or anybody. I've killed a lot of people. The only reason you aren't dead is you're a woman – I don't kill women if I can help it.'

A small voice replied, 'Smoke is my fiancé.'

Stone didn't even bother to turn around – everything hurt too much right now to make unnecessary moves. 'I'm sorry to hear that. Looks like you'll need a new one.'

Stone started at the boat – maybe halfway across now. Two men – one sitting in the upfront seat, one back at the tiller, just the way they had left. In a few more minutes they'd be in perfect range. Sticks would be holding his gun facing backwards, pointing at Dugan. They wouldn't even know what hit them — the first burst from the AK should take care of them both. The boat's forward momentum should be enough to bring it most of the way here to the yacht — then Stone would grab the boat and the second strongbox, dump the bodies overboard and head back into town. Maybe Macho could find him a doctor who could take care of this spear — Stone could lay up hidden for a day or two, then tear out of here. Not much of a plan, but something.

Here they came now.

Stone sighted on the boat. *Take the front man out first.*

He took a deep breath. Ten more seconds . . .

'Best thing you can do is look away,' he said to Lola, who was breathing heavily somewhere behind him.

Pamela surfaced from the black water along the edge of the *Saucy Jack*.

She had swum away in a blind panic, no idea where she was heading. In the first few seconds, she had lost the speargun and her headlamp had been knocked askew, the light shining sideways. She didn't care — she kicked like mad, her legs churning, plunging her into the darkness ahead. At first, she didn't even realise who or what it was that had attacked her. Only after several moments, when her legs began to ache from her ferocious kicking, and it was clear that she had escaped, did she stop and have the presence of mind to play the incident back.

Sure, it was a man and not a monster who had come at her, and she had shot him. She could still see the burst of dark blood in the light from the headlamp as the spear penetrated his arm. And she could see the look of pain and surprise in the eyes of that man — Stone. He was hurt, she realised, and he probably wouldn't be much of a threat to her with that spear sticking out of him. If the spear hit a big enough blood vessel, and he didn't get immediate medical attention, he might even die. With that thought in mind, she turned around and started back to the boat.

Now, lurking in the darkness along its edge, she took off her head-lamp, her face mask and her mouthpiece. She shrugged off her other gear – her oxygen bottle, her buoyancy compensator – all of it went, and she let it go. She reached down and pulled off her flippers. She let them go, too. All of this neat stuff – it could be replaced.

She had no idea what was going on up top, but if Stone had come here, then there was probably trouble. When she climbed on to the boat, she had to be ready for action, and a bunch of diving gear would only slow her down.

Stripped down to only her wetsuit, she took a deep breath to calm her mind, and moved around towards the diving ladder.

Lola chewed at her leg binds.

Her ankles were bound tightly together, but it was only rope. And not just rope, but rope that had been at sea, rope that had been exposed to sun and salty air and probably water and time. So she bent at the waist, as far over as she possibly could – years of martial arts training not going to waste – and began gnawing on the strands. Each bite was a ferocious tug of war, and she was not sure which would give out first – her teeth or the rope. But the rope started to fray the tiniest bit, and she kept right on chewing.

She got herself down there with her manacled hands behind her. Despite everything, it gave her a very nice stretch to her lower back and her hamstrings. Boy, she missed the regular exercise she used to get before they'd moved on to the boat. She hoped that one day she would be able to return to it – she pictured herself in some distant, exotic land, on a bright blue mat with breathtaking mountains in the background and the sea in front of her, running through a series of yoga Sun Salutations. Mmmm, nice.

Focus, dammit!

She gnawed and gnawed, like a beaver cutting sticks for a dam. She stopped, took a breath, and looked at her work – she'd hardly made any progress at all. The ropes were still wound good and tight, a little torn, a little frayed, but still strong. She took a deep breath and looked up at the night sky, hoping for what? Deliverance, maybe. And what she saw when she looked up was Pamela.

Pamela stood there in her wetsuit, hair hanging down her shoulders. Ever the librarian, she put her index finger to her lips, 'Shhhhhh.'

Lola glanced at Stone's muscular back. Beyond him, she could see the running light of the approaching skiff. She turned back to Pamela. How could Pamela take out someone as strong as Stone, even as injured as he was? Then it came to her – the solid bone at the crown of Pamela's head ramming into Stone's delicate facial bones. Lola began making frantic head-butting gestures at Pamela.

Pamela didn't understand. 'What?' she mouthed silently. 'What?'

'Best thing you can do is look away,' Stone said.

He raised his rifle to fire.

'Head-butt him!' Lola shouted. 'Head-butt him!'

Pamela, finally getting it, dashed towards Stone.

Lola kicked her legs madly, but it was no use – the ropes didn't budge. 'Stone!' she screamed. 'Don't shoot!'

At the last second he turned around. Pamela was right behind him, and Lola saw he was wearing crazy goggles over his eyes. He looked like a madman, like the killer at the end of *The Silence of the Lambs*. Pamela head-butted him, her forehead connecting with his face and his goggles. His gun clattered to the deck and he stumble-stepped backwards into the railing. His legs slipped out from under him and he flipped right over the railing and disappeared.

Pamela sank to her knees. At that instant, Lola heard the heavy splash as Stone hit the water. Pamela's hands strayed to her forehead, then came down again – bleeding. She had cut herself – on Stone's face or on his goggles, Lola didn't know.

She looked back at Lola. 'Jesus, girl. That really hurt.'

Lola glanced to her left. The skiff was pulling up to the back of their boat. As she looked, Cruz stepped on to the lower deck. Cruz was alive. He carried a gun lightly at his side.

Smoke hurriedly tied up and climbed on after Cruz.

'Where's Sticks?' Lola said with a tongue that seemed as thick as a sausage.

'Good news,' Smoke said, beaming nearly ear-to-ear. 'Cruz can kill people again. He took care of Sticks for us.'

'Wonderful,' Lola said. All the more reason to get off this boat as soon as possible, and start a new life alone.

'Where's Stone?' Smoke said. 'Let's take care of him too, while Cruz is still feeling in the pink.'

'Yes, let's,' Cruz said. 'Considering how he let me have it with that missile and everything. I wouldn't mind returning the favour.'

Lola and Pamela passed a look between them. Unlike the crazy head-butt pantomime from before, they understood each other perfectly this time.

'Stone's dead,' Pamela said from the deck. 'He got up before, all delirious, talking all sorts of nonsense, you know, with the spear sticking out of his arm. It must have nicked a major blood vessel, because he started bleeding like crazy, like it was coming out of a pump. He walked around the deck a bit, then he just kind of died on his feet, and fell overboard.'

Lola turned to her old room-mate in astonishment. She had never, to her own knowledge, heard Pamela tell such a bald-faced and creative lie before. Something about the criminal lifestyle definitely agreed with Pam. It brought out the artist in her. Lola sensed this little foursome was going to break up soon, and that Pamela was going to zoom off into the wild blue yonder with Cruz. In the very recent past, that would have worried Lola, but now it didn't. Pamela, the formerly shy and retiring librarian, was going to do just fine as Cruz's sidekick.

'Are you sure he's dead?' Cruz said.

'Positive,' Pamela lied again. 'I saw the light go out in his eyes. He's shark bait.'

'Well, score one for you, then.' Cruz nodded in approval, then gazed down at Pamela. 'Hey, what happened to your head? You're bleeding.' He knelt on the deck and put a hand to her forehead.

'I tripped and fell climbing out of the water. Banged my head. Silly me.'

Closer to Lola, Smoke had burst into a huge grin. 'Ready, kids?' he said, clapping his big workman hands together. He kneeled and began gently, even tenderly, untying Lola's binds. 'About time we got out of here.'

Lola glanced at Smoke. She had said her piece to him earlier, and she wondered now if she had really meant it. He seemed cheerful, like he was ready to forget what she said and have everything go back to normal. And, damn him, a cheerful Smoke was a charming Smoke. She felt the ice in her heart melt just the tiniest bit.

'Smoke, what about the money?'

He shrugged. 'It's in the engine compartment. I figured that would be safer than stashing it in a couple of lousy strongboxes. Since I was in there working, it was easier to keep an eye on it, too.'

'What do you guys think about divvying up the spoils when we reach the Bahamas?' Cruz said. 'I have to tell you, this boating life is wearing me out. Pamela and I were talking the past couple of days about chartering ourselves a plane to Belize. We thought we might disappear into the rainforest for a while, maybe check out the Mayan ruins.' He hesitated. 'Uh, just the two of us. No offence, you understand.'

'I think that's a fine idea,' Smoke said. He looked meaningfully at Lola. 'As long as everybody else is agreed.'

In her mind's eye, Lola watched that bright blue yoga mat on that stunning hillside become even brighter, and clearer in her mind. The funny thing was that as she watched, the camera pulled back a little bit, revealing more of the scene. Now, she was doing her Sun Salutations, and ten feet away, Smoke was sitting in an upright beach chair, reading a newspaper, with a glass of red wine at his elbow and a sweet-smelling cigar in his mouth.

'I'll miss Pamela like crazy,' Lola said. 'And I'll miss you, too, Cruz. But I guess we can always talk on the telephone.'

Stone was dreaming.

All around him, Mogadishu skinnies swam, looping and diving underwater. Fifty, one hundred skinnies, dressed in Third World modern-style, crazy cast-off Western clothing. The water was bright blue, and the skinnies moved with impossible grace, circling around him in a beautiful ballet. The water was thick with them. Gradually they changed, and became giant sting rays, moving in the same wonderful patterns, but the water became darker as well, darker and darker, until it was lit only by night-time luminescence.

He opened his eyes.

He was in terrible pain. Above him there were stars. He was in water, staring up at the night. He became aware that his hands and legs were churning the slightest bit, helping the buoyancy of his wetsuit to keep him afloat. He had been paddling nearly unconsciously.

The sound of a boat engine came to him from nearby. He reached to his head and put his goggles in place. He remembered now, they had been knocked askew by a head-butt from Pamela – brother, that woman was going to be the death of him.

Everything seemed like a dream right now, or a nightmare. This whole island holiday had been one long hallucination.

The boat, the big cabin cruiser, receded from him, picking up speed, gaining distance. Sticks must have got the money, and was wasting no time getting out of here. All right. Stone had no urge to see Sticks again. Or any of them. Getting mixed up in this whole thing had been a terrible mistake.

Where did that leave him now?

Well, he could just float here, and get eaten alive by sharks – a very real possibility. He was trailing blood in the water, after all. Or he could start swimming for shore, and in all likelihood, pass out from loss of blood and drown.

Any other possibilities?

He glanced around. A few hundred yards away there was another boat. This one was a sailboat and it had red and green lights strung all over the main mast like it was Christmas – Stone supposed that it wouldn't be long before Christmas. Might as well get an early start. There seemed to be music coming from that direction as well.

He could make for that boat – it might be his only chance to live.

He got started, swimming through the darkness for what seemed like a long time. It hurt to move and he had very little range of motion – he couldn't do the crawl without hitting the spear against his body. He could only do the breaststroke and that just barely. The boat, even after several minutes of swimming, still seemed impossibly far away. Dugan's boat was long gone.

After what seemed like hours, Stone looked up and the boat was right there. Sure, they had a stereo system on there, and they were blasting it. The place looked like a party was going on. The music was rap music – not Stone's favourite kind of music.

He reached the ladder to the deck. Slowly, laboriously, he climbed on board. He heaved himself on to the deck. The spear caught on the lip of the deck and Stone nearly passed out from the pain.

He glanced up. Two young guys stood there, preppies, each with a drink in their hand. With them were two local girls – one of them was Roxana. She looked great, wearing a dark dress, her hair loose and flowing, her brown skin glowing. Then the full significance of her presence on this boat hit Stone and he frowned. Jesus, couldn't she stop for even one night? She was right back in the soup again?

The four of them stared down at Stone.

'Do you mind,' Stone said, 'if I borrow your dinghy?'

Acknowledgements

The book in your hands got there through the efforts of many people. I'd like to mention some of them.

Literary agent extraordinaire Noah Lukeman has worked harder on my behalf than anyone I've ever known. I doubt this or any of my books would have appeared had I not met him several years ago.

Thanks to Brian Dunleavy for once again reading an early version of the manuscript, and giving me helpful comments and suggestions. Thanks to Jason Norman for his perceptions about living on the water, and about Caribbean islands and culture. Thanks to Peter Eagleton for schooling me about the finer points of fixing a boat engine, especially one raked with gunfire.

Thanks to Joy for making it through yet another book with me.

Very deep thanks to the entire team at Headline Publishing. It remains my special privilege and pleasure to publish books with them.

Patrick Quinlan

It's no exaggeration to say that Marion Donaldson, my editor at Headline, basically taught me how to write a sequel as we went along. I'm continually thankful for her insights and her patience. Her feedback improved this book immensely. In fact, I probably never would have finished it without her.

Sarah Douglas at Headline has been a wizard at communicating what's expected of me and by when, and at getting me the information and materials I need to do my job. I'm a little embarrassed by how much I've come to rely on her.

I'm sure you'll agree that artist Craig Fraser delivered an awesome knockout punch with the design of THE DROP-OFF book jacket.

Special thanks to publicity manager Becky Fincham for the astonishing amout of ink I've seen these past couple of years – you know, I actually never tire of reading about myself.

Thanks to copy editor Marian Reid for numerous improvements to the original manuscript, and to eagle-eyed proofreader Kate Truman for her attention to detail. Thanks to Sarah Kellard for keeping production of the book on track.

Thanks to Jo Liddiard, and the Headline marketing team. Thanks to the sales force who got the book into the bookstores, and to the booksellers who put the book into the hands of the readers. Thanks to Vicki Mellor, specialist crime editor at Headline, for the title THE DROP-OFF and for welcoming me into Headline's crime family.